**Praise for these other novels by *New York Times*
bestselling author Allison Brennan**

"If you haven't been reading Brennan's truly exceptional
Lucy Kincaid/Sean Rogan series, then you have been
missing out . . . In this mind-blowing installment, Brennan also gives readers a fascinating look into the mindset
of her epic villains. A chilling thrill-fest from beginning
to end."   —*RT Book Reviews* (4½ stars, Top Pick!)
on *No Good Deed*

"Allison Brennan reaches new heights in *Poisonous*, and
this smart, sophisticated entry in the Maxine Revere series
raises her to the level of Lisa Gardner and Harlan Coben."
        —*Providence Journal*

"A fast-paced, suspenseful read with interesting characters and sinister twists that keep you turning the pages for
more."   —Karin Slaughter

"Allison Brennan's *Poisonous* has it all . . . A twisty and
compelling read."   —Lisa Unger

ALSO BY ALLISON BRENNAN

Cut and Run

The Third to Die

Nothing to Hide

Too Far Gone

Abandoned

Breaking Point

Shattered

Make Them Pay

The Lost Girls

Poisonous

No Good Deed

Best Laid Plans

Compulsion

Dead Heat

Notorious

Cold Snap

Stolen

Stalked

Silenced

If I Should Die

Kiss Me, Kill Me

Love Me to Death

Carnal Sin

Original Sin

Cutting Edge

Fatal Secrets

Sudden Death

Playing Dead

Tempting Evil

Killing Fear

Fear No Evil

See No Evil

Speak No Evil

The Kill

The Hunt

The Prey

Cold As Ice

ALLISON BRENNAN

St. Martin's Paperbacks

This is a work of fiction. All of the characters, organizations, and events portrayed in this novel are either products of the author's imagination or are used fictitiously.

First published in the United States by St. Martin's Paperbacks, an imprint of St. Martin's Publishing Group.

COLD AS ICE

For information, address St. Martin's Publishing Group, 120 Broadway, New York, NY 10271.

www.stmartins.com

ISBN: 978-1-250-76786-8

Our books may be purchased in bulk for promotional, educational, or business use. Please contact your local bookseller or the Macmillan Corporate and Premium Sales Department at 1-800-221-7945, ext. 5442, or by email at MacmillanSpecialMarkets@macmillan.com.

Printed in the United States of America

St. Martin's Paperbacks edition 2020

10 9 8 7 6 5 4 3 2 1

Prologue

ONE YEAR AGO
Michael Thompson sat in the jail cell after his arraignment. He hadn't spoken a word since his arrest, except to his lawyer. Even with his lawyer, he was brief and to the point. His plea was not guilty, even though he had killed the man.

He had expected this day for years. Not because he felt remorse for his crimes —those he killed had committed far worse crimes—but because he still, deep down, believed in the system. That someone would see him, a camera would catch him, an alert cop would arrest him.

It was none of the above. It was a mistake on his part, a stray fingerprint that led back to him.

He was normally careful. *Unlucky thirteen,* he mused.

Spending the rest of his life in prison didn't worry him. If he was given the death penalty, he would accept it. Dying did not scare him.

He'd been dead inside for seven years. Seven years, two months, four days. The day his daughter's broken body had been found.

A crime that could have—should have—been prevented.

A crime that killed his daughter, gutted his marriage, destroyed him.

"You have a visitor."

Mike looked at the guard, then rose from his cot.

"Walk to the bars and turn around, please."

He complied. He had no beef with the guards here. They were just doing their job. They'd shown him respect and he would return the same.

He was handcuffed through the bars, then the guard motioned to the control room to unlock the gate.

Beep.

Click.

Slide.

The guard escorted him down three halls and through two locked doors.

Buzz.

Click.

To the row of rooms that were reserved for prisoners and their lawyers.

It wasn't his lawyer sitting in the small room.

It was a friend, a colleague of sorts. Mike doubted he knew the man's real name, and it didn't matter. What mattered was that they worked for the same man, a true visionary.

The guard unlocked his handcuffs, then reattached the cuffs to the ring on the table. He left the room without comment. Did he know the truth?

He might. His friend was not a lawyer; he shouldn't be here.

"I am sorry," Mike said.

"There is no reason to be sorry. We talked to your lawyer and cultivated a source in the police department. The evidence is fairly solid, and they have also connected you to the situation in San Antonio."

Mike nodded. He'd feared at the time that the girl had seen him; she had at least seen the rental car. He also suspected his image had been captured at the rental car pick-up, even though he did everything reasonable to trick any surveillance. Though he hadn't used his own identity—he never used his real identity when working a job—it would only be a matter of time before they were able to trace that burned identity to him.

He hadn't expected it to take two years, but that was two more years of righting wrongs. He couldn't complain.

"*He* wants you to know that he appreciates your loyalty and that he loves you as a son. Getting you out of this situation might be difficult—"

Mike shook his head. *He*—his mentor, his savior—had given him hope when he had none. "I don't expect to get out of it. I'm okay with that. I'm at peace."

"You shouldn't be here."

"But I am. And I have a second mission here, inside, that I can fulfill. Please, thank him for the new life he gave me. Thank him for his faith and support. The police will push, will want to know who hired me, but I will never betray him."

"He knows. You have remained silent—which is exactly what you should continue to do. Your imprisonment will ultimately help us in the long term. Our boss finally sees a way to punish Sean Rogan. But it's a difficult and complex plan which will take time to implement. A year, maybe longer."

"I have time."

"You won't see me again; it might be too risky. If it works, you'll know during the trial. I may be able to find a liaison so you have all the information you need. It won't get you freedom, but we will fight against the death penalty."

Mike said, "I'm not afraid to die."

His friend reached out and shook his cuffed hand. "I'm really going to miss you, Mike. When this is all over, I'll visit as often as I can."

When Mike was back in his cell, he mulled over what the plan might be, and how Sean Rogan would be punished. He didn't know the man, but he had heard plenty of stories. He'd offered to add Rogan to his list, but his boss said no.

"There are other ways to right wrongs, and death is too good for Rogan."

Chapter One

Siobhan Walsh Rogan watched as her new husband and his team helped the six terrified girls into the old Hummer.

Even before he took her hand to help her into the vehicle, she could read his mind.

"No," she said. She jumped back down and stared into Kane's brilliant blue eyes and knew her instincts were right. "*No*," she said, more emphatic. "Do *not* go after him."

She ignored the gnats flying around her head, the distant sound of a lone rifle, the curses of the man restrained in the doorway of the house Kane and his men had raided.

He didn't say anything. He stared at her, face blank. *Almost* blank. Was he actually smiling?

"See, you can't even argue with me!"

"I'm not going to argue with you, Red. Get in the truck."

"No."

His gaze narrowed just a fraction, but it added three levels of mean to his expression.

"It's an order."

"Don't even."

He pulled her away from the truck, away from his team and the girls, all of whom were watching them far too closely.

"I will find him; I will stop him."

"It's not worth it."

"Was it worth it to rescue Hestia nine years ago?"

"This is *not* the same thing. We have the girls! We're getting them to safety. Just like we did with Hestia."

"Blair escapes, more girls are at risk. You know it, I know it. Dyson and Lucky will take you to the convent. Ranger's with me. I know what I'm doing, Siobhan."

He looked like the cold, hardened mercenary he'd been when she first met him. The mercenary she had loved and hated. The hero she wanted and feared for.

She couldn't stop him. She knew that. She wanted to—because she had never loved like this before. But she loved Kane Rogan because of who he was, and *this* was who he was. He hadn't wanted her to come because the rescue was dangerous, but he also recognized that her unique skill set working with young victims would be instrumental in making the extraction easier than it might have been with only four armed men. He trusted her when she knew it was difficult for him to put her in danger.

She had to trust him.

This was who Kane was. She didn't want to change him. She couldn't if she tried.

She didn't want to lose him.

Yet another reason why she loved him so much.

"Don't get killed, Kane Rogan. I will never forgive you."

He kissed her. So hard it almost hurt, then he touched her face, and she saw the love in his expression, the love he had a hard time showing. "I love you. Go."

She went to the truck. Dyson handed her a gun, nodded to Lucky that they were ready. "Eyes open, Red," he said.

Ranger had already made sure the girls were both secured and unarmed. He squeezed Siobhan's hand and said, "I'll protect him."

She nodded, even though she wanted to scream that this was too dangerous, foolhardy. Human traffickers were a dime a dozen, and even though Peter Blair was one of the worst out there—an ex-patriot who would do anything for money—they could find him another way.

They didn't have to follow Blair into territory he knew better than they did, when he was surrounded by people loyal to him, willing to kill for him.

It's too dangerous, Kane. Change your mind.

Lucky turned the ignition and drove away, down the mountain. The last thing she saw was Ranger following Kane back to the house that had once held these victims. Four dead men littered the ground; the fifth was injured and trussed up by the door. Kane dragged him inside the house; Ranger followed and closed the door.

Peter Blair had gotten away, an evil man Siobhan had been tracking for even longer than Kane. Yet, though she'd seen the brutal handiwork of Blair and his men time and time again, she didn't want to know how Kane and Ranger would find out where he went.

Lucky sped off toward the setting sun and Siobhan prayed for Kane's safety.

I love you, too.

Chapter Two

Three years ago if Sean Rogan had seen two police cars and an unmarked sedan in front of his house, he would have driven by until he knew exactly what was going on. But now, his first thought was fear.

Lucy.

He immediately dismissed the thought that Lucy had been injured in the line of duty. Someone from the FBI would have called him. And while his son now lived with them, he'd dropped Jesse off at school not ten minutes ago, so these cops weren't here because of something related to Jesse or the school.

Still, that twitch in his gut had him seriously wanting to pass by without a glance at his house, and he usually trusted his instincts.

He wished he'd trusted them now, but he clicked the garage door opener and pulled his Jeep Wrangler into his parking slot on the right. Lucy's spot on the left was empty; she had left for work more than an hour ago. A quick glance over his shoulder confirmed that the cops were here to talk to him. The uniformed officers were getting out of their cars, and two detectives emerged from the sedan.

He didn't recognize any of them.

If it was one car, he wouldn't be concerned. RCK—the security consulting firm his brothers had co-founded, and for which he served as a principal—worked closely with law enforcement on a variety of projects. At the end of last year, Sean had assisted in an SAPD case. Between him and Lucy, they knew several cops on the force.

But this was three cars and he knew none of the cops.

That worried him.

He walked around to the back of the Jeep, looked straight in the eye of the cop closest to him. Plainclothes. Detective. Six feet tall, blond hair, blue eyes. The other detective was female, younger, Hispanic, not a good poker face. She clearly didn't like him, but Sean had never met her before.

"Can I help you?" he said, his voice sounding calm and chatty when that was the last thing he felt.

"Sean Rogan?"

"That's me."

The detective smiled, trying to put Sean at ease, but that only made Sean more uncomfortable, especially since the female detective stood there as if she was ready to draw and fire on him.

"Detective John Banner," he said. He didn't offer to shake his hand. He was keeping his distance, about twelve feet. "This is my partner, Kris Mendez. We were hoping you could come down to the station and answer some questions."

"About what?"

"Mona Odette Hill."

Mona?

Shit.

"Why don't you come inside?" he said, motioning toward his house. "I'll make coffee."

"Ms. Hill was murdered Monday night and we'd like

to talk to you about that. It would be better if you come with us."

What the hell was going on? Mona was *dead*?

Monday.

Sean had gone to Houston on Monday and met with Mona. So these cops might have a witness who saw him near her condo. Fine. But that didn't mean he would go down to the fucking station and *talk*. "No, thank you, I'm happy to talk with you here." It took all his control not to tell them to screw off and call a lawyer. Something was going on, and Sean had the distinct impression that they thought *he* was involved.

Banner had said Mona was murdered.

They wanted him to come to the station.

Nothing good would come from him going to the station.

What did you get yourself into, Mona?

Banner glanced at his partner. They communicated silently for about two seconds, then Banner said, "Mr. Rogan, you're under arrest for the murder of Mona Hill."

Banner nodded to one of the officers, who cautiously approached Sean.

"What the hell?" he said, though he knew he shouldn't say a word. "First you want to talk, now you're arresting me?"

"Turn around," the officer said. "Kneel, and put your hands on the top of your head."

Sean didn't move. He was being arrested for murder? He took everything in. The two detectives. Four uniformed officers. Coming to his house—after Lucy was gone, after he returned from dropping Jesse off at school. Did they know his routine? Did they plan it this way? How long had they been watching him?

"Mr. Rogan, please comply," Banner said. "I know your wife is a federal agent, and you have friends in the department. I don't want this to become a sticky situation."

He had no choice.

"I'd like to call my wife." He actually wanted to call JT Caruso, the head of RCK. JT would know exactly what to do and would get him the best lawyer.

You know what to do, Sean. Don't say anything. Not one more word. You're innocent, but that doesn't mean squat. Keep your mouth shut and don't piss off the cops.

"You'll be able to make your calls as soon as you've been booked in Houston."

"Houston? You're taking me to Houston?" So much for keeping his mouth shut.

Mona Hill lives in Houston.

"Yes, Mr. Rogan," Banner said. "We're with Houston PD. The San Antonio officers are assisting us this morning."

So they'd planned to arrest him from the beginning. They wouldn't have brought the officers if this wasn't the endgame.

"I'm armed," Sean said. "I have a concealed carry permit in my wallet."

"Thank you for that," Banner said. "Are you carrying anything besides a handgun?"

"A knife in my right front pocket."

He hated this. *Everything* about this. It was bullshit. He considered resisting, but that wouldn't do him any good, and could get him shot.

You should have driven by when you saw the cop cars. You've turned soft, Rogan.

The SAPD officer repeated, "Turn around and kneel, put your hands on the top of your head."

Sean didn't like that his partner had his hand on his holstered gun. Did they think he was going to run? Fight? Shoot?

He said to Banner, "If you just tell me what's going on, I can come down on my own with my lawyer."

"That won't be possible."

"Why the hell not?" Sean snapped, hating that he was letting his fear take over. "You know my wife is a federal agent. My sister-in-law is a fed. You must know I have government contracts, security clearance. You can ask me to come in and talk and I'll be there."

"I did."

"I mean on my own, with my lawyer."

"Too late."

"You didn't give me the fucking choice!"

"Are you going to make this difficult, Mr. Rogan? Do I need to add resisting arrest?"

"I'm not resisting, I'm talking."

"You're a flight risk, Mr. Rogan," Banner said. "I'm sorry it came to this, but I have no choice. I'm only going to ask you one more time. Turn around, put your hands on your head, and kneel."

He could bolt into his garage, the house. Lock the door. It was steel-reinforced. His security was the best. He could go to the panic room he'd recently put in and wait this out until he figured out what was going on.

But that would make him look guilty.

So he complied, resisting an overwhelming urge to run. His entire body tensed; he would not do well behind bars. He already felt like a caged animal and the cuffs weren't even on his wrists.

Then two of the SAPD officers approached him. One searched him and removed his gun, handed it to his partner, who unloaded it and handed it to Mendez. She put it in an evidence bag. The officer found his knife that he kept in his pocket and also handed that to his partner.

"Do you always arm yourself to take your kid to school?" the cop said.

Sean couldn't let him bait him. This cop was nobody, and Sean wasn't going to say a word until he knew exactly what was going on and why these cops thought he killed Mona Hill. He'd already said too much, arguing with Banner.

His left wrist was cuffed, pulled behind his back, and then his right arm was brought down.

"Relax, Mr. Rogan," the officer said.

He tried. He couldn't. He valued his freedom more than anything. He'd spent a few days in jail before, he could not—would not—spend the weekend behind bars.

"Come on now," the officer said, pulling his arm tighter than necessary.

"Mr. Rogan," Banner said, "you're drawing attention from your neighbors."

Sean's face heated. He didn't look around. He wasn't resisting, but he couldn't force his body to relax. He winced as the cop jerked his arm up and back and clicked on the handcuffs.

Murder. They're arresting you for murder.

You didn't kill Mona Hill

Why do they think you *killed her?*

They wouldn't arrest him solely on the word of an eyewitness—there had to be evidence. Question him, sure—but they wouldn't arrest him. What did they have? Why did they believe *he* killed her? Anything they had would be circumstantial. He was in her condo. He couldn't tell anyone, especially the cops, why he was there. Not until he talked to a lawyer.

Unfortunately, he hadn't told Lucy. There were two reasons he hadn't told her, not the least of which was because Lucy didn't like Mona. Neither did Sean, but they had an understanding, and in this particular situation they had a common enemy.

You should have told Lucy.

He had a very, very bad feeling that this was all a setup.

You are screwed, Rogan.

Banner said, "Can we take a look in your car?"

He glanced over his shoulder and looked Banner in the eye. "Do you have a warrant?"

He took their silence as a *no*.

"We'll get a warrant; you can just make this easier."

"I do not consent," he said clearly.

The officer who had cuffed him took hold of Sean's elbow and pulled him to standing, then escorted him to the squad car. "Watch your head," he said and helped Sean into the back.

The cop closed the door and Sean was alone. His eyes burned. Rage and embarrassment tore him up inside.

And fear. Fear that this setup was going to get him killed. He had enemies in prison. So did his brother. So did Lucy.

Maybe that's why he was bring framed for Mona Hill's murder. It wouldn't matter when the cops realized he was innocent, by then he might already be dead.

Chapter Three

When Lucy Kincaid walked into the FBI office that morning, her boss Rachel Vaughn called out to her before she sat down. "Lucy, the ASAC needs to see you."

There was something about her tone that caught Lucy's attention, and when she put her briefcase down and turned to her, Rachel's expression was blank. Yet . . . something in her posture said *concern*. Her tension told Lucy that something was definitely up, even though her face was emotionless.

Lucy mentally reviewed all her cases and couldn't imagine what was wrong. Was she in trouble? Did she screw something up? She would have heard or sensed something, wouldn't she?

"Is there anything I need to know?" she asked Rachel. She wished her boss would give her some sort of clue.

"She's waiting for you."

Then Rachel turned, walked into her own office, and closed the door.

Not good.

Lucy put her purse in her desk drawer, then walked slowly from the Violent Crimes squad to the opposite side of the building where the administrative offices were housed. She hoped someone would approach her and give her a clue as to what was going on. Everyone seemed to be going about their business and didn't give her a second glance. A few people said good morning. If something was going on, only Rachel knew about it.

She braced herself for a reprimand, though she couldn't imagine about what. Or maybe one of her cases was falling apart and she needed to go over evidence with the US Attorney's Office. Or she was being transferred.

Last year she'd seriously considered requesting a transfer because she felt that there were some serious problems for her in the office, but over the last few months, everything had been great. She and Rachel now worked well together after an initial rough patch. The Violent Crimes Squad was fully staffed, Lucy got along with everyone, and she was no longer a rookie.

Maybe it's nothing bad.

Except Rachel hadn't looked her in the eye.

It's bad.

She walked into the administrative wing and ASAC Abigail Durant was standing outside her door talking to her admin. She saw Lucy and a cloud crossed her face, then she covered it up.

"Agent Kincaid, thank you, you can come in."

Had someone died? Been injured? Was she being written up? Something more serious?

Stop. Listen.

She walked in and was surprised to see SAPD Detective Tia Mancini sitting at the small table. "Hello, Tia."

"Lucy."

Tia also looked serious.

Abigail told her admin no interruptions, then she closed the door and sat down at the table.

Lucy had a million questions, but didn't say a word. She looked from Tia to Abigail.

Abigail spoke first. "Detective Mancini has some information for you. She told me first and asked how to handle it. I said be up-front and to tell you everything she can."

Lucy hadn't worked with Tia on a case in more than a year, but they'd become friends. Tia was a sex crimes detective and had been helpful in several of Lucy's investigations.

When Tia didn't immediately say anything, Lucy said, "Tia—just tell me. Straight-out."

"Fuck," Tia muttered. "There's no easy way to say this, Lucy. I was asked to come down here because my boss knows we're friends. And because we're friends, I can't be involved in the investigation at all." She hesitated, then said, "Sean has been arrested. I just received confirmation that he's in custody."

It took Lucy a second to process *arrested*. "Sean?"

"Houston PD arrested him for murder."

"Murder." She was repeating the words but they weren't registering.

"I don't have all the details, because like I said, this isn't my case. It's a Houston case and we loaned out four SAPD officers to transport him. He's on his way to Houston right now for booking. I'm sure he'll call a lawyer, but of course if you want to start the process, go right ahead. This is a courtesy conversation, but dammit, I know you'll pull out all the stops. And you should."

"Wait wait wait," Lucy said, putting her hand up. "Sean. What the hell, Tia? *Murder*?" She couldn't imagine . . . Sean . . . cold-blooded *murder*? Never.

Was this related to what happened in Mexico, when he'd rescued Jesse from the cartels? People had died and Sean had likely killed one or more people. Lucy didn't ask questions, didn't want to know the details. But why would Houston cops arrest him? Then there was the situation when she'd been held captive as bait for Kane, and Kane and Sean had gone down to Guadalajara and taken care of the situation. But that was all south of the border. Certainly they would have heard something about that before SAPD. Before Houston PD. And if it was an international situation, they'd have the FBI or another federal agency take him into custody.

There was the situation down in Hidalgo with Kane, but they'd been told no charges would be filed. Everything Sean did had been out of self-defense. He'd been *kidnapped*, dammit!

Why *Houston*? What the hell was going on?

Lucy couldn't think of anything that would place Sean under suspicion of murder.

Not suspicion. They arrested him. They have evidence. Something solid . . .

"This is wrong," Lucy said.

"I'll tell you what I know, which isn't a lot. Mona Hill was shot and killed Monday night in her apartment. Sean's fingerprints were found at the scene and there was a witness who heard Sean and Mona arguing. No murder weapon but they are in the process of getting a search warrant for your house, his vehicle, and his plane. They have evidence he flew in his private plane from San Antonio to Houston on Monday and flew back the same night."

"Mona Hill?" She sounded like a damn parrot.

"I know that you've used her as a CI. I helped facilitate that, and she's always been straight with me. I don't know if that's all going to come out, but you need to be aware that it might, in case there's a pending investigation."

"I didn't use her as a CI, not officially. I talked to her once last year when we were looking for the trafficked girls in San Antonio. The other time you and I interviewed her together as part of our investigation into Harper Worthington's murder. That's it." But Lucy knew that Sean had tapped Mona for information several times. She just never asked the details because she didn't want to know.

Lucy turned to Abigail, worried that this might come down on one of her cases. "I put Mona's name in the report, I talked to her last February when we were looking for Bella Caruso and the girls who were trafficked from Phoenix—"

Abigail nodded. "I remember the case, you're not in trouble here, Lucy."

She was. Because if Sean was arrested for murder, she was in deep trouble.

"Sean's prints, his plane," Lucy said to Tia. "What else?"

"He was on camera going into the building and leaving more than an hour later. I don't know the time, just that it was evening. Again, this isn't my case, this is only what I was told by the detective in charge. John Banner. He seems like a good cop, Lucy."

"Not if he arrested Sean," she snapped, and wished she hadn't. She itched to call Rick Stockton and find out what the hell was going on.

Why had Sean gone to see Mona Hill?

Lucy despised the woman, but she'd helped when Lucy needed it.

Why hadn't Sean told her he went to Houston?

Monday . . . she had worked late. She and Nate had been called in to provide security for a member of Congress who was hosting a series of town halls in his district. It had been an uneventful day that went long into the evening. She and Nate then grabbed a late dinner and she got home just after eleven. Sean was there. He didn't say anything about going to Houston. It was about an hour flight, then twenty minutes from the small airport he used to their house. So he would have had to have left Houston no later than nine thirty P.M. to be home before her.

She didn't tell any of that to Tia. She might be a friend, but she was also a cop, and Lucy had to figure out what was going on before she knew who she could trust with the information she had.

Sean wasn't going to do well in jail. There were many concerns—the fact that she was in law enforcement. The fact that his brother was an enemy of the drug cartels.

That this might be a setup to assassinate him.

Her stomach twisted, but she kept her cool.

She had to, for Sean.

"Abigail—" Lucy began.

Abigail put up her hand. "We can't interfere in this investigation, Lucy. You know that. But I can give you a leave of absence."

"I appreciate that, but Sean is in danger in jail. I need someone with authority to explain that to the Houston police. They're not going to listen to me."

"He's not a cop," Abigail said.

"No, but considering his involvement in several high-profile investigations and his work with RCK, the fact that Sean and his brother Kane both had bounties on their head by the drug cartels, one bounty because of work Sean was doing for the FBI—I shouldn't have to explain this, you know what RCK does."

"You're right. I'm sorry, I should have considered that. I'll see what I can do."

"Thank you." But Lucy couldn't trust that Abigail would protect him. She trusted her—to a point. She liked and respected her and she was one of the most diligent and smartest agents Lucy knew. Still . . . this was a prickly situation and Abigail didn't know just how much trouble the Rogan family had caused certain criminal organizations. If any of those groups knew that Sean was behind bars it would just take one call to put the bounty back on his head, in a place where he was defenseless.

Lucy had to talk to Rick Stockton. He was an assistant director of the FBI and had more clout than anyone else. Plus, he would do anything in his power to protect Sean. He couldn't get him out of legitimate charges, but he could make sure that he was safe while in custody.

"While you're on leave, Lucy, I need to remind you that you can't insert yourself in this investigation. Let the police do their job. You're Sean's wife, but you're also a sworn agent and I expect you to conduct yourself as such."

"May I go?"

She nodded. "Please, tread carefully. I hope this is just a misunderstanding, but Sean needs to be honest with the investigators."

Lucy had to leave before she said something she would regret. No way would Sean tell them anything, even though he was innocent. Sean didn't trust most cops, though over the years he'd learned to trust a few of them. He'd had problems in the past with overzealous FBI agents.

He also had a record. Sean's crimes were nonviolent, and the one he was caught for was before he was eighteen. It should have been expunged. But Lucy didn't know what was in his FBI file or what Houston PD might have access to.

She rose and said to Tia, "Thank you for telling me in person."

"I'm sorry about all this."

"I'll find the truth."

"Houston PD will find the truth," Abigail said. "Lucy—"

"Sean is innocent," she said. "Sean would never kill anyone in cold blood."

Why were you at Mona Hill's apartment, Sean?

"I need to go," she said, and walked out before Abigail or Tia said anything else.

She ran back to her desk and grabbed her things, then looked around for Nate. He wasn't in the office. She wasn't going to talk to anyone else about this, not until she had more information. On her way out of the office, she called Nate on his cell phone. He didn't answer. As she slid behind the wheel of her car, he texted her.

In court for the Diaz case.

She couldn't tell him about Sean over text. She responded: *Call me when you have a break.*

She tried Sean's number, on the off chance this was all a screw up and he'd already been released.

It went to voice mail after four rings.

She pulled out of the parking lot and called the one person she trusted more than anyone, other than Sean.

"Hey, sis," Jack answered.

"Sean's been arrested for murder. They're transporting him to Houston, I don't know any details, other than the victim is Mona Hill and she was killed Monday evening. I'm going home. They'll be getting a warrant I'm sure, I need to be there."

"Who is Hill?"

"She ran a prostitution ring in San Antonio, skipped town, and Tobias Hunt and his organization put a bounty on her head at one point. Sean kept in touch with her and she's the one I reached out to when we were looking for Bella last year, and—"

"Now I remember. Have you talked to Sean?"

"No. They just told me when I got to work, and his phone went to voice mail. He's already in custody. I have no messages or texts from him, and I . . . I don't know what to do. He needs a lawyer, he needs help, Jack, he can't be in jail. He can't . . ." Her voice cracked and she forced herself to calm down. Deep breath. She couldn't lose it. Sean needed her to be strong, he needed her to take care of business.

And he needed her to find out what was going on. If she acted hysterical, she'd get nothing.

"Lucy? You there?"

"I don't know what to do, Jack," she admitted. "I have to help him. I don't know how. He didn't kill Mona. I don't believe it."

"I'll call JT and we'll get the best fucking lawyer on the planet."

"What if—"

"Shh, don't talk, don't say anything about Sean or this case or Mona Hill, *nothing*. Understand? Not over the phone. Run a complete security check on the house before talking, then use Sean's landline."

He was right.

"What did they tell you?" Jack asked. "Just what they said, no opinions."

She told him exactly what Tia told her, no embellishments. She ended, "They're in the process of getting search warrants."

"You need a lawyer present when they serve the warrants. But if they get there before a lawyer, read it with a fine-toothed comb. Don't let them take anything that isn't explicitly listed. It needs to be reasonable. But they might take electronics if they can make a case that they need them, and the RCK lawyer is going to fight that because Sean works for us. We have sensitive information. They'll likely seize any firearms, but if they have ballistics they should only take guns that fire that caliber."

He was telling her everything she already knew, but hadn't thought about.

"I need to call Kane," she said.

Silence.

"What? I know he and Siobhan are out of the country, but he'll come back for this."

"Kane's missing. I found out last night and took the

last flight to Hidalgo. I talked to Sean this morning—he wanted to join me, but I said no. I didn't think I would need him, I have Ranger and Dyson waiting for me at a safe house."

"Kane's missing?"

"Kane has been on the heels of a major human trafficking organization for years, and one of the leaders was identified with a confirmation on his location. Siobhan went with him because there were six victims involved. They rescued the girls—they are at the Sisters of Mercy convent—but Kane didn't make it back. I'm hoping by the time I get there, Ranger will have a line on him and it'll just be a matter of extraction. Where's Nate?"

"In court, he doesn't know yet."

"I'll tell him and ask him to stay with you until I get there. I'm hoping this situation with Kane will be resolved in twenty-four hours, and then both of us will be there. Don't go anywhere alone."

"This isn't about me, it's about Sean! What if someone is setting him up to kill him? He's helpless in jail."

"Sean has never been helpless, and we don't know *what* this is about. Do what I say, Lucia," he said firmly. "I need to talk to JT and Rick. Expect the unexpected. We're in this together, understand?"

"You're right, Jack. Thank you."

"Be smart, Lucy. Go back to your training. *All* your training. I need you to be stronger than you've ever been, keep a cool head. We will get through this. Also, don't use your cell phone to discuss this with anyone—just in case. The phone on Sean's desk is secure, plus he has a secure cell in the safe. Get that phone, keep it with you, I have the number."

He ended the call and Lucy took a deep breath. Jack was right. Falling apart wouldn't help Sean.

She had many friends, but most of them were cops.

Asking any of them for help would put them between a rock and a hard place.

Except for one. Sean and Kane had saved DEA Agent Brad Donnelly's life two years ago, and while they told Brad he owed them nothing, she knew that Brad felt indebted to the Rogan family.

Lucy needed help and she trusted Brad. She called his cell phone.

"Donnelly."

"It's Lucy. I would never ask if it wasn't important, but something . . . it's extremely . . . hell, it's a mess, Brad, and I don't have many people I trust. I trust you."

"Anything."

"Sean's been arrested for murder and I need information. I don't want to talk on the phone. Can you meet me at my house?"

"I'll be there in twenty minutes."

Chapter Four

Lucy must know by now that he'd been arrested.

Sean hated that he couldn't be the one to tell her. What had they done? Sent a couple cops to FBI headquarters? Called her down to the station? Were they questioning her? They would—just to get his alibi. She would have to answer, she was a sworn agent, right? Did they have spousal immunity? He didn't know the rules on that, just vague information.

You're innocent! Why are you thinking this way?

Because he'd been in the back of a police car for the last hour driving across Texas to be booked and charged with a crime he didn't commit.

He was going to lose it before they arrived, and he had to keep it under control.

And this arrest was going to stop him from finding his brother.

Jack told him to stay put, that he'd call if he needed him, but Sean planned to be ready to leave on a moment's notice. Kane was missing—Sean didn't want to lose another brother. He'd planned to fly down to Hidalgo to be closer to Mexico if Jack needed his help.

Now, they were on their own. Of course, Jack, Kane, and their team were more than capable of handling the situation south of the border—they'd been mercenaries half of Sean's life. But Kane wasn't the young man he used to be, and Siobhan was also down there. The least he could do was help protect the convent and his sister-in-law.

Was Kane's disappearance and his arrest connected? That seemed extraordinary, but Sean couldn't rule anything out.

He closed his eyes, tried to slow his heart rate. He needed to think. Figure out what was going on and how to get out of this mess.

Lucy probably had a hundred questions, not the least of which was why he'd gone to Houston to see Mona Hill in the first place. He should have told her, because it affected her—it affected both of their families. But on Monday night, he was still figuring out what to do about the information Mona gave him. He'd told her what to do, she told him to go to hell, they'd argued, she'd seen the light, then he left.

He certainly hadn't killed her over their disagreement. He needed her—as much as she needed him—and her death was more than an inconvenience.

But he couldn't tell the cops any of this. If he omitted some things—not lying, because they'd catch him in a lie, but simply not giving them the background—they would be suspicious. His meeting with Mona Hill made no sense out of context.

He needed information, but the cops that were driving him wouldn't talk—and if they did, they didn't know anything important. This was a Houston case, and these were SAPD cops.

Dammit, Mona? What happened to you after I left Monday night?

Sean hadn't wanted to talk to Mona Hill, and he certainly didn't want to fly to Houston to talk to her in person. But she'd given him no real choice.

She'd called him Saturday morning. He ignored her. Jesse had a soccer game, then he and Lucy had a rare night alone because Jesse had spent the night with a friend. He ignored Mona on Sunday the multiple times she called. Then Monday morning she called again and Sean answered. Irritated.

"What do you want, Mona? Odette? Or whatever you're calling yourself these days."

"Don't you dare turn your back on me, Sean Rogan. You are no saint, and if you don't think I don't have a few tricks up my sleeve, don't test me."

"Do not threaten me," he said.

"I don't want to. I don't want anything to do with you. But you made this mess and I need you to fix it."

"Explain."

"I have to see you as soon as possible."

There was fear in her voice, and her fear won his curiosity because Mona Hill wasn't a woman who feared much.

"I need more."

"Tobias."

"He's dead."

"Someone from his operation is fucking with me, and I know exactly who it is . . . dammit, Rogan! Do you think I wanted to call you? Do you think I want to be in your debt? You're a blue-eyed devil, but only a devil can stop these demons."

He hadn't wanted Mona to come to San Antonio, but she sounded scared and angry enough that she might try to. She told him that she would if he didn't meet with her. Lucy was working late Monday, so he'd texted Jesse that he'd be late and to eat leftovers for dinner. Sean then flew his Cessna to Houston late Monday afternoon. When he landed, traffic from the small airstrip to her condo was miserable, but it was still light when he arrived.

Mona lived on the top floor of an upscale complex in a trendy downtown area. Prostitution clearly paid well.

Sean had kept tabs on Mona over the last two years. She was a survivor—and so was Sean. In San Antonio, Mona had run call girls and specialized in blackmail. She had several important people on her go-to list if she or her girls ever got into trouble. Mona wasn't violent, she didn't work underage girls or deal drugs, but she was certainly no saint. And when she made an alliance with a ruthless criminal, she ended up on the FBI's radar.

She found herself on Sean's radar when she threatened Lucy.

They had a truce: because Sean had looked the other way so Mona could disappear—and the FBI could apprehend a fugitive—she agreed never to return to San Antonio. He told her no more blackmail. Prostitution was illegal, but if she ran a clean operation, he'd keep his mouth shut.

She had some dirt on him. Nothing that would be easy to prove, but he didn't need rumors circulating about what he may have done. And Lucy knew what happened. He'd told her without details, only the outcome.

Some things were better left unsaid.

So he and Mona had a truce, a quid pro quo relationship that was mutually beneficial, though they didn't communicate much because they didn't like each other.

Sean knocked on Mona's door at six fifty Monday night.

She opened the door and stared at him. "Took you long enough."

"You're lucky I came at all."

He walked in, she slammed the door behind him. He looked around. Nice place, new construction—not more than five years—clean and sparsely decorated. Mona looked good, too—wore jeans and a thin, shimmery short-sleeved dark tan sweater that matched her skin. Minimal makeup, hair expertly braided. She looked much better than she had when she'd run girls in San Antonio.

Maybe not dealing with the scum of the earth helped.

"You're lucky I called you at all after you ignored me all weekend," she snapped back.

"Tell me what's going on, Mona. No games."

"I saw that little bitch."

He sighed. "Are we going to play twenty questions?"

"Elise! Elise Hansen! Or Hunt . . . or whatever the fuck name she goes by. First time was Friday night, I was making arrangements for a special party, walked back to my car and wham! *she was right there, in my face. Looked right in my eyes, turned, and walked away. I was so stunned I didn't say a word, thought I was wrong, then I went after her but she just vanished. It shook me, Sean. She is a piece of work—you don't know the half of it. I thought she was just this little skank, but she's a psycho. I called you on Saturday morning, but then thought okay, it was nothing, I didn't give a fuck you didn't call me back. But Saturday night, there she was again. I was coming in late—took care of a girl who'd been roughed up, then took care of the bastard who bruised her—"*

"I don't want to hear."

"I didn't kill him. I cut him off, made sure everyone knew not to do business with him—he wants to get his jollies by hurting girls, he can fucking do it somewhere else. And she was here. In the lobby. Just sitting there as if she were waiting for someone. She saw me, smiled, and walked out. I couldn't sleep, couldn't eat, and then I called you a hundred times on Sunday and you ignored me!"

"You're sure it was her?"

"Yes."

"And she didn't say anything?"

"No."

He narrowed his eyes. "No? You're holding back, Mona. If you want me to help you, you need to tell me everything."

"I wasn't going to call you again, I was so angry that you fucking wouldn't pick up your phone, then this morning I found a note."

He was really getting ticked off by Mona making him ask for everything. "What note?"

"See for yourself. My desk."

Mona walked into the kitchen. He watched her, made sure he could see her at all times, before crossing the room to her desk.

The desk was bare, except for a laptop computer. "What game are you playing?" he asked.

"Top drawer." She poured herself a Scotch and downed it.

Sean opened the drawer. Paper, pens, pencils, bills, a couple of flash drives. He saw an envelope with a child-ish scrawl that might have said "Mona."

He held up the envelope. "This?"

She nodded.

He took out a single piece of folded paper. In block letters, a short threat:

Mona:
You abandoned me two years ago. I don't forget
or forgive. You will be the first to die. Today?
Tomorrow? Next month? You won't know when,
you won't know where, and I'll have so much fun
making you squirm. You can't hide here—you
can't hide anywhere.

Love,
Your Worst Nightmare

It sounded like Elise Hunt. Sean could almost hear the singsong laughter of her voice. Her brother Tobias was a vicious gun and drug runner who was killed nearly two years ago, thanks to Kane. Nicole Rollins was Tobias's cousin, a corrupt cop taken out by SWAT at the same time. Elise was their psychopathic half sister. She'd landed in juvie for only two years, walked away three weeks ago when she turned eighteen, slate wiped clean.

At that time, Lucy had been informed of her release and told that Elise was relocating to Los Angeles, where she'd inherited property.

"You're positive you saw Elise?"

"It was her."

"Where did you find this?"

"On my desk. She got in here. In my fucking apartment, Rogan!"

Sean shouldn't have touched the envelope, but he'd only touched the letter by the corners. He found another envelope in the back of the drawer and put Elise's threat inside it. "You need to take this to the police—"

"Bull fucking shit. I'm not going to the police. You think they'll protect me?"

"Don't shout at me, we're on the same side here."

Shit. RCK should have been on top of this . . . they should have been monitoring Elise from the minute she was released. Clearly her trip to Los Angeles was short-lived. But she had a purpose. That little bitch did nothing without a purpose, as twisted as it might be.

Los Angeles . . . her father Jimmy Hunt had been extradited from Mexico to the U.S. and was in prison in Los Angeles, so that was the likely connection.

Had Elise and her father concocted a scheme for payback?

"She's going to kill me," Mona said. "You have to stop her."

"You need to file a police report."

"And say what? That I ran girls in San Antonio and was supposed to take her out of town when this asshole PI who'd already broke into my apartment and trashed my computer told me to leave or he'd hurt my sister and nephew?"

With every word her volume increased and he finally said, "Shut up!" He forced himself to calm down. He couldn't lose his temper with her. "I never threatened anyone," he said through clenched teeth.

She rolled her eyes. "Right."

"I told you I would tell your sister where her trust came from, and it wasn't from your fucking death. Don't go and twist things around when you asked me to come here and help you. I have plenty on you that the cops would be interested in knowing, Ramona Jefferson." He spat out her real name—a name that had a death certificate attached to it.

"I'm sorry. I'm sorry! I'm just so freaked out. She scares the living hell out of me."

That he believed. "First, you need protection."

"That's why I called you."

"I can't stay here and protect you." If Elise was in Texas, he needed to protect his family, first and foremost. "Call the police. They will follow up on this threat. Elise is dangerous—"

"Then why the fuck did they let her out of prison?"

"You have money. Last time I saw you, you had a bunch of bodyguards."

"I have a couple guys I hire, they don't live with me! But—Elise isn't like normal people, you know? She has a screw loose."

That Sean knew.

"I'll track her. Find out where she is and what she's doing and maybe I can get someone to put the fear of

God into her." He couldn't do it, not knowing where she might show up next, but he could hire a PI to follow her, make sure she wasn't doing something illegal. Encourage her to get out of Texas, he hoped.

First he had to locate her.

But Elise Hunt . . . shit. She was as unpredictable as she was insane.

Not insane. Sociopathic, violent, remorseless, but not legally crazy.

"You think she'll listen? That girl is a fucking mess. You don't know the half of it, Rogan."

Elise Hunt was planning something. Once she took out Mona, she probably had a list of people to go after, not the least of which was Sean and Lucy. Lucy had testified against her, Sean had stolen her family's drug money and turned it over to the feds. Elise might not even be planning on killing Mona. She might just be playing with her, scaring her, which she'd clearly already done.

Sean looked at his watch. He had to get going, Lucy would be home by eleven, and he needed more information before he told her what was going on.

"I'm going to give you a list of things to do. This is important, Mona."

She opened the refrigerator and took out a bottle of American beer, put it on the counter.

"I don't want a drink."

"Fine, be that way. Just tell me what to do." She took out her phone and opened up the note app.

Sean rubbed his eyes. Okay, she was scared. He got that. Hell, Elise was only eighteen but she scared the shit out of Sean because she was unpredictable. And Mona had helped him and Lucy when they needed it. She was a criminal, but she wasn't all bad. No one was all bad.

Except anyone with the last name of Hunt.

He picked up the beer and twisted off the cap. Took a

long swallow. "I'm going to find out where Elise is and what she's doing, but you need to protect yourself. I still think you need to take that note to the police, but I get it. You don't want to go to the police. So, first thing, get a full-time bodyguard . . ."

If Mona was killed Monday night, chances were the police found his prints at her place. On the desk, the door, the kitchen, the beer bottle. But they should also have her phone, and would know that she had called him once Saturday, four times on Sunday, which he'd ignored, then Monday late morning, which he had answered and spoke to her for about three minutes.

He could say that she had hired him, except that she hadn't. She hadn't given him money or signed a contract. She'd essentially blackmailed him. Well—that was harsh. They had an understanding, and mutually assured destruction usually worked well. But he had more to lose than she did, because he was married to a cop.

You should have told Lucy about Elise from the beginning.

Should haves weren't going to do him any good now. Lucy would be angry because he was trying to protect her, but he hadn't wanted her to worry about Elise until he had more information. His home security was solid, he knew Lucy was covered at work, and he went over advanced security with Jesse.

Sean had begun tracking Elise Hunt. She had no digital footprint, but he'd found the property she'd inherited in Los Angeles and hired a PI to sit on it. Most of the Hunt property had been seized under asset forfeiture laws but her lawyer had managed to get her a chunk that had been owned by her mother prior to her birth. That alone was worth more than a million for the land only.

Elise had flown to Los Angeles after being released

from juvenile detention. She was out, free and clear, no probation. She likely had numerous fake IDs, she could have a car, but there was no record of her—under her name—returning to Texas.

Nico, his PI, had eyes on her Tuesday afternoon, but that was only a few hours after Sean put Nico onto the case. No change in her status since, and Sean didn't know what good it would do sitting on her property, though he'd asked Nico to keep tabs on her for a week.

That's where he was in his investigation when he was arrested this morning. Today he had a scheduled meeting with the warden of the facility Elise had been housed in, a longtime decorated corrections officer named Kathy Pine, but that wouldn't happen now.

Dammit!

You should have told Lucy.

He told himself to shut up. Of course he should have. If Elise Hunt was behind this, Lucy had to be doubly careful.

He wished he could get a message to Lucy to keep the meeting with the warden. She might have information they needed, and now he'd be a no-show.

He remembered the last thing he'd said to Mona Hill before he left Monday night.

She walked him to the door, unhappy, hugging herself. "Mona," he said. "Look at me."

"You don't care about me."

"You're wrong. You called your bodyguard—that's the first step. Do exactly what I told you, okay? And if you see her, call the police—then call me. There must be a cop you trust."

She snorted. "Trust?"

"You know what I mean."

"There's a guy. Likes one of my girls, treats her well, he might help."

"*See? You have someone. Talk to him. Seriously, if you see her again or if she leaves another note, let me know. And like I said, change your locks first thing in the morning. Bolt this door when I leave.*"

"*Fine. Right. Okay. Thanks.*"

"*She's eighteen, Mona. She might be a nut job, but she's still a kid.*"

And then he left.

Mona had been alive. Even though he hadn't heard from her again, he wasn't worried—and he'd been focused on tracking Elise.

Now he knew he hadn't heard from Mona because she was dead.

Chapter Five

When Lucy arrived home, the garage door was up and an SAPD patrol car was out front. Sean's Wrangler was in the garage, and for one moment she was elated—that Sean was home and everything she'd been told was wrong. She ignored the officer, parked next to Sean's Jeep, and closed the door. She went in, checked the alarm—it was on—so she coded that she was home and to secure the property, which would alert her if anyone stepped onto the grounds. She wanted a heads-up if any agency was about to serve a warrant.

For now, all was quiet.

She opened the laundry room—Bandit, their three-year-old golden retriever—was relegated to the laundry room and sunroom when they weren't home. He was well-trained, but the run of the house might be too tempting. He still acted like a puppy at times and got lonely when no one was home. Sean had lost one sneaker in three different pairs because Bandit was bored while unsupervised.

Lucy knelt and hugged him tightly, his tail wagging frantically, hitting both sides of the door jamb. "I know, I'm never home at this time," she said. She would *not* cry. She took a deep breath, got up, and walked down the hall to Sean's office. Bandit followed her and immediately walked behind the desk, where he curled up on the dog bed and thumped his tail while watching her. If Sean was working, Bandit was here with him.

Lucy called Jack from the landline, but he didn't answer. She opened the safe and retrieved the secure cell phone. No messages. It was fully charged and she put it in her pocket.

She didn't know who to call, but then the landline rang.

It was JT Caruso, one of the principals of RCK.

"Are you alone?" he asked.

"Yes. Jack said he was going to call Nate, but Nate's in court. I called Brad Donnelly, and he's coming over. I don't know how he can help, but—"

"That's good. Until we know what's going on, you shouldn't be alone."

"Sean's the one in danger."

"The RCK lawyer is already working, and we're bringing in a top criminal defense law firm based in Houston."

The words *criminal defense* made Lucy's stomach turn. This should not be happening.

JT continued, "It looks like Banner asked for a narrow warrant for the time being—to search Sean's plane, car, and home for a .45 caliber gun. I have a list of the .45s that Sean owns—he has two."

"He keeps the Colt in the bedroom, and the other is probably in the gun safe. He usually carries his 9mm when he goes out."

"You'll have to open the gun safe if they come with the warrant, but even if they only have a warrant to search for the murder weapon, they could still search your entire property. If they see something suspicious they could ask for an expanded warrant."

"Is something wrong?"

"Not necessarily. Have you learned anything else?"

Was JT being cautious or did he have a reason for concern that he wasn't telling her? She let it go for now.

"No, nothing," she said. "I was going to tell you Sean doesn't have an alibi on Monday. I didn't get home until late, it was after eleven. Sean was home when I arrived, but he could have been out."

"Jesse?"

"I haven't asked him, he's still at school. According to Tia, they have Sean on security cameras at about the time of the murder."

"We'll have an outside expert verify the time stamps, but let's assume that he was there. Why would he meet with Mona Hill?"

She didn't know what to say.

"Lucy, you there?"

"I don't know."

"Mona was the prostitute who helped us last year, right? With my sister?"

"Yes."

"Okay, and have you or Sean used her information since?"

"I haven't, I don't trust her. Didn't trust her. But Sean has tapped her for information a couple of times, including a missing persons case he was working."

"He knows you have issues with her."

"Yeah."

"Assume he had a legitimate reason to talk to Mona Hill, okay?"

She would, though he should have told her. Just because she didn't trust Mona didn't mean she didn't understand that the woman could have valuable information for a private investigator or law enforcement.

"Is he working on anything for RCK?" she asked.

"Yes, it's computer security related, and he does that from his desk. He's scheduled to go to Miami to work on site at a government defense contractor to debug a new program, but that's not for a couple weeks."

"This arrest is going to hurt your business, isn't it?"

"That's not important right now," JT said. "I'll take care of RCK—Duke and I are already running through every conceivable scenario where someone might want to take Sean temporarily off the board. But I suspect he's working a side project. Duke's going through the system logs to see what he was doing. Do you know if he had something going outside of RCK?"

"Nothing he's mentioned to me." She paused. "He's been a bit preoccupied this week, and he was talking to someone in Los Angeles named . . . hold on, it'll come to me . . ."

"Nico Villanueva?"

"Yes—that's it. Who is he?"

"A contractor for RCK, private investigator we use in the L.A. area. I'll call him, but this is good. Nico served with me in the Navy, I've known him for years."

A warning beep echoed.

"What was that?" JT asked.

She checked the security pad and watched as Brad walked up the front pathway. "Brad's here. DEA—you met him, right?"

"I know him. Good."

"Should I search the house?"

"For what?"

"I don't know—bugs?" That sounded stupid. "I need to do something."

"You have plenty to do. And I'm certain Sean does regular sweeps for listening devices."

Of course he did, she thought.

JT continued, "As soon as I wrap up the situation with the lawyers, I'll call you. Before Sean even arrives in Houston, he'll have a lawyer on site."

"I'm worried about him, JT. If he goes to jail tonight—they may not even arraign him until Monday."

"We're doing everything we can to make sure he's released on bond before the end of the day. Hold tight, okay?"

The door chimed.

"Okay." She hung up and went to let Brad inside. He closed the door and said, "Prick out front actually tried to stop me."

"He's just doing his job."

"He wanted to know my business. I flashed my ID, kept walking." He put his hands on her shoulders and squeezed. "You okay?"

"I don't have time not to be okay."

She led Brad into the kitchen and filled him in on what she knew, which wasn't much.

"I called a buddy of mine in Houston—a vice detective I know well. He'll sniff around, knows that it's sensitive. You can trust him like you do me."

Lucy made a pot of coffee because she had to do something while she waited for JT to call her about the lawyer. She itched to head to Houston herself, but feared she'd just be sitting around and not be allowed to talk to Sean anyway.

"What?" Brad asked as he watched her pace.

"I've grown complacent. Everything has been great for months—honestly, the last few cases I've had were interesting but uneventful. It's been calm. I've been able to enjoy my evenings with Sean and Jesse and for the first time I felt normal. Totally, completely normal. And now . . . oh, shit. Jesse."

"Where is he?"

"School. I have to tell him."

"I can go get him for you."

"That won't work—there's a restricted list of who can

pick him up during the school day. Nate's in court and Kane's out of the country." She hesitated, then realized she needed someone to confide in. "Kane's missing. Jack went down to a small village outside Saltillo to find him."

"Saltillo *is* a small village. What was he doing? I thought he'd retired."

"Semi-retired," Lucy said. "A human trafficker he's been keeping tabs on was moving young girls. Siobhan is down there with them, they rescued six minors, but now Kane is missing."

"Can I do anything?"

"Help me with Sean. Nate's in court and I've been sent home, so I'm just waiting for information and it's driving me bonkers."

"I'm glad you called. I'll do anything I can. I wish I could help Kane and Jack, but I don't have a lot of resources in human trafficking."

"Jack's on top of it, but I'm worried about him, too. First Kane goes missing, now Sean is arrested."

Brad frowned.

"What?" Lucy asked.

"Is there any connection between these two events?"

She thought, shook her head. "I can't see how. Mona Hill was a prostitute. She didn't have any connection to human trafficking, and Sean made sure she didn't use underage girls. She helped us last year, remember?"

"I do. I just don't buy that whole prostitute with a heart of gold bullshit."

Lucy laughed. She shouldn't, but she needed to. "Trust me, she has no heart of gold. It's all about self-preservation, and Sean made it clear to her that if she crossed that line he would take her down." She bit her lip. "I shouldn't have said that."

"Don't censor yourself around me. If you want to go get Jesse, I can stay here."

She did . . . but what would she tell him? "It's early. I have no information for him, and he's going to have questions. I'll get him when I know something."

The house phone rang, which was a rarity, and she practically ran to Sean's office to grab it. "Yes?"

"Sean asked Nico to track Elise Hunt. Why?"

It was JT and he sounded angry.

"She was released from juvie three weeks ago, but she's in Los Angeles." And Nico was a PI in L.A. "I don't know why Sean would keep tabs on her."

"Has she threatened you?"

"No. I was told about her release. She turned eighteen and they cut her loose. I made my statement when she was arraigned two years ago."

"Which was?"

"That she's a danger to society and needs to be tried as an adult, not given a minimum security plea deal. They opted to give her juvie until her eighteenth birthday. You should know all that."

"I do, but you testified against her, right?"

"Yes. So did Sean, Detective Mancini, Brad, others. You can't possibly think that Elise Hunt is behind this."

"I know what Nico told me. Sean called him Monday night and asked him to find out where Elise Hunt is living, what she's doing, her associates, the exact terms of her release, the whole nine yards. He's been following her. Staked out her house starting early Tuesday—didn't lay eyes on her until late that afternoon. He's been sending reports to Sean, he's sending them to me now. Sean didn't tell you any of this?"

"No," she said, her chest tight. Mona Hill had betrayed Elise Hunt. Was that why Sean went to see her? Because he wanted to warn her about Elise's release? He could have called her. He didn't have to go there in person.

"I told Nico to keep close tabs on her for the time being, but we need to know what was going through Sean's head. There are no restrictions on Elise—no parole, no probation. She was given a plane ticket to Los Angeles because that's where she has property that she inherited from her family—what wasn't seized under asset forfeiture laws."

"Someone had to be taking care of the property," Lucy said. "They owned it free and clear, but there would be property taxes and other expenses."

"Nico said that three people live there other than Elise. All he has are names and basic descriptions; he gave that to Sean, who was running a background check on them, but now we're doing it from here. He's sending us photos as well."

JT continued. "RCK has retained a law firm for Sean. Garrett Lee is an investigator with the law firm, a former cop who we've worked with in the past. He'll be working with you on any warrant issues. He's based in San Antonio and he has a good relationship with SAPD. Felicity Duncan is a criminal defense lawyer in Houston, with the same firm, and she'll be representing Sean during this process. She is hands down one of the best criminal defense lawyers in Texas. Hell, the country. Sean is in good hands."

Lucy closed her eyes, tears burning, but she controlled them. She would not break down.

"Lucy, you okay?"

"I need to do something." Every word was difficult to get out.

"Garrett will contact you directly. Until we know exactly what's going on, you play everything by the book. Get badge numbers, IDs, confirm everything—including Garrett's identity. He's a six-foot-two-inch, half-black, half-Chinese health nut. He would be difficult to miss, but assume nothing. Do not talk to the police without Garrett with you, understand?"

"I can't just sit here."

"For now you can. They're not going to let you see Sean until after he's booked. We need Nate to stay with Jesse—if this is at all connected to Elise Hunt, until either Jack or Kane get there, Nate is the only one I trust. Understand?"

"I haven't told Nate. I didn't want to tell him over text."

"Jack did. Nate needed to know what's going on."

"I understand," she said quietly, rubbing her temples.

"We're going to get Sean out of this," JT said. "But there's a process, and because he's in the system right now, we have to use the system."

What did that mean? If they had known this was going to happen, would Sean have run? Arranged to turn himself in? Her law-and-order personality told her that running was a sign of guilt . . . yet Sean had had bad experiences with law enforcement in the past, and he didn't trust the system, not like she did. Jack and Kane had spent most of their lives in the system . . . while also working outside the system. They saw things more as they were then as they wanted them to be. The good and the bad.

"Lucy?"

"How are they going to protect Sean in jail?"

"Felicity understands the danger to Sean. She'll be at the police station before he arrives. She has a team of lawyers and investigators at her disposal. Trust me, Lucy. I will do everything in my power to keep Sean safe."

Chapter Six

Lucy inspected Garrett Lee's identification before letting him inside the house. He was even more imposing than JT described, and older than she expected—in his early fifties, with gray dotting his temples and crow's-feet framing his dark eyes.

She introduced him to Brad.

"Can we sit somewhere?" Garrett said. "We have a lot to go over, and not much time."

Lucy motioned to the formal dining room. They rarely ate in there—but the kitchen didn't seem appropriate to the solemn moment.

"First, JT gave me a short list of people who, for lack of a better word, we'll call Sean's defense team, which includes you, Agent Donnelly, as well as Agent Dunning, who will be joining us when he's done in court. As Sean's spouse, you do not need to speak to the police, but I recognize that you may have a conflict because you're a federal agent. Don't let them manipulate you into saying anything—and do not talk to the police or anyone about Sean's case without me.

"As for the warrant, I've already spoken to SAPD and the liaison who is working the case with Houston. They're searching Sean's plane now. One of our associates is with them. They are sending a second team here; they'll arrive shortly. The warrant is limited. They are looking for the murder weapon and the clothing that Sean wore that night—they have a color image from a security camera in the building. They'll be taking all his jeans, for example, because he wore a pair of jeans. He wore dark sneakers, the video is unclear on the brand so they'll be taking all dark sneakers—basically everything but white. They'll be testing the clothing for blood or other physical evidence that might tie Sean to the crime scene. They have a warrant to search his vehicle as well for any of the items on the warrant, plus to test the carpet and upholstery for blood and fibers. The murder weapon shoots a .45 caliber bullet, so they can technically only take guns capable of shooting a .45. Your service weapon is a .40 caliber and because all FBI weapons have ballistics on record, you won't need to turn yours over. However, every other weapon—whether registered to you or Sean, as long as Sean would reasonably have access to it—that fits the specifics on the warrant, they can take. Not just .45s, but any gun that is capable of shooting a .45, which may be more than the two JT mentioned to me."

He paused, seemed to consider what he was going to say. "I have an acute understanding of Rogan-Caruso-Kincaid Protective Services, and I know that there are some operations conducted in and outside of the U.S. that may not be perfectly . . . legal. JT assures me that any weapons used in any RCK operations are handled differently and will not be present in your house, but I need to warn you that if they test a firearm and it was used in the commission of a felony, that can be another charge brought against Sean. So even if we clear him of this accusation, he may be facing other charges."

"When we clear him," Lucy said. "He didn't kill Mona Hill."

Garrett looked at her, didn't say anything.

"You need to believe it," Lucy said. "Or I'll tell JT I'll find an attorney who has faith in Sean."

"This isn't about faith or trust, Mrs. Rogan. This is about evidence."

"Sean is innocent of these charges; I will prove it."

"You need to tread carefully here," Garrett warned.

As far as Lucy was concerned, this wasn't a topic open to discussion, but she didn't see the point in belaboring the matter. "When can I see my husband?"

"First things first. JT informs me that there is a safe on the premises. They'll need access to the safe. You know how warrants work. They can look for what's on the warrant, but if they see anything else during the search, such as drugs, if they are in a place that is reasonable for them to search, they can add those charges or get an expanded warrant."

Lucy wasn't worried about drugs.

"JT also tells me that you have a top notch security system that can record everything."

"Everything in the house and on the grounds, except in the master bedroom and Jesse's room."

"We're going to record the search but I'm not telling them. By law we don't have to tell them that we're recording because this is your private property. But you can't lie if asked, understand? You can choose not to volunteer information, but if they ask you if they are being recorded, you have to tell them that they are."

She doubted they would ask. "Of course. I'm not going to lie about anything."

"And they'll likely send a cop to chat you up. Don't engage. Even if you know them—even if it's a friend, like Tia Mancini."

Brad spoke up. "Do you know what they have on Sean?"

"Not much more than you know, I'm sure. Mona Hill was killed between seven thirty and eight thirty P.M. on Monday."

"That precise?" Lucy asked. "Based on the autopsy?"

"She made a call to a pizza delivery place at seven thirty P.M. At eight thirty he entered the building to deliver the pizza but she didn't answer the door. He called the apartment and there was no answer. He left and ran into a man identified as Christian Porter in the lobby. Porter was in Ms. Hill's employ as a bodyguard and general . . . handyman, shall we say. According to his statement, she called him shortly before seven thirty and asked him to come over because there was a threat to her life. Porter heard a male voice in the background and they were arguing about something, but he couldn't hear what was said. He asked who was there, and she told him Rogan, but he was leaving."

"The police told you that?" Lucy was surprised.

Garrett smiled for the first time—a slight smile, almost sly, but he didn't answer her question.

"Porter paid for the pizza, went upstairs, and found Ms. Hill's body. She'd been shot twice, in the back."

Lucy involuntarily shivered.

"You are aware of Ms. Hill's business?"

"Yes."

"The police will use that against Sean. That he was meeting with a known prostitute. That he had a relationship with her or one of her girls, that perhaps she was blackmailing him. They know Mona Hill's reputation, and that she had been in San Antonio and was associated with Tobias Hunt's operation before she disappeared and showed up in Houston."

"That's . . . no. No."

"You have to be prepared. They will bait you. They'll

say things that will make you want to defend Sean. You might think you're helping, but anything you say could be used against him."

"You have to believe that Sean was not in a relationship with Mona Hill or anyone else."

"You're a cop, Lucy," he said. "Often, a spouse has a secret life, or things they keep from their significant other."

Like Sean not telling her he was going to Houston.

"I'm not blind, Mr. Lee. I'm specifically saying that Sean wasn't having an affair, nor was he paying for a prostitute. The police must have something more than Porter's statement."

"They know that Sean flew into Houston Monday evening and arrived back at the small airfield at eight thirty-five P.M. He used an Uber, based on security footage. It takes about thirty minutes to get from Mona's apartment to the airstrip. They have Sean entering her building at six fifty and leaving just after eight that evening. And thus Porter's statement that he heard them arguing over the phone becomes more compelling. Houston PD is putting together facts and evidence, and his statement is part of that. The murder weapon is key—they need to find it or everything else is circumstantial."

Lucy's stomach fell.

Brad said, "If they don't have the murder weapon, why did they arrest him?"

"They feel they have enough evidence to go to a judge. I don't know their exact reasoning—I have sources, but not in Houston. My guess is they felt that Sean is a flight risk." He paused, looked from Brad to Lucy. "I'm aware of Sean's background. His juvenile record isn't going to be an issue—they can't use it, or even see it. It's been expunged, as part of his plea agreement when he was seventeen."

Brad glanced at Lucy, surprised.

"I'll tell you later," she said. "I sense a 'but.'"

"Sean's FBI file is sealed, but they could ask to open it. I don't know if they will, I don't know what's in it, but Jack doesn't want it unsealed. If it goes that far, it would be up to a federal judge."

Lucy didn't know what was in his file, but he'd had an FBI agent gunning for him up until a couple of years ago, and once something was put into the record it was impossible to get out. But Sean had high-level security clearance to work on computer security for various government agencies and contractors, so whatever was in the file couldn't be *that* bad.

"Felicity is going to do everything in her power to ensure that he's arraigned today, and then we can post bail. But—and I'm being perfectly honest with you here—I think they're going to keep him all weekend and hold off arraignment until Monday. That tells me they need more information—more evidence—in order to ask for a higher bail, or no bail. You know how these things work. The earliest he'll be in Houston and booked is noon. Then he'll be questioned. They'll drag it out as long as they can to prevent him from getting out this weekend."

"That's bullshit," Lucy said.

Though she would do the same thing in their position. If she believed that her suspect was guilty and could commit another crime or was a flight risk, she would arrest him on a Friday and hold him over until Monday to make sure they had all their ducks in a row before they had to go in front of a judge.

Garrett didn't comment. He looked at his phone.

"What?" Lucy asked, leaning forward.

"They found a .45 in Sean's plane, in a locked box under the pilot's seat. Revolver, two bullets missing. They also found a bit of clothing or a towel that it was wrapped in. My assistant couldn't see exactly what it was."

"Do you honestly think that if Sean committed cold-blooded murder, he would leave the murder weapon in his own plane?" Lucy said.

Her chest hurt. She could not believe that this was happening.

"You have a lot of friends in San Antonio. Ashley Dominguez, the head of the lab, recused himself."

"He was likely asked to," Lucy said. "Ash is a friend. The prosecution could claim he tainted evidence." But she would much rather have someone she trusted processing the evidence, and there was no one better than Ash. "Garrett, I need to see the evidence."

"That's not possible right now."

"Sean is innocent, and this whole thing stinks. I need to talk to him and find out what's going on. If he went to see Mona in Houston there was a damn good reason. And if it's connected to Elise Hunt—I need to know what's going through his head."

She shouldn't have said anything about Elise, but judging from Garrett's expression, JT had already filled him in.

"You need to stay far away from Elise Hunt," he said solemnly. "She served her time and you can't approach her."

"She's dangerous and sociopathic," Lucy said. "She is capable of anything, literally. I do not say that lightly. She killed a man in cold blood by injecting him with poison, then set the stage to make it appear as if she'd given him oral sex. She then immediately went to another man and had sex with him for money, while setting him up to be blackmailed. She had a family held hostage while she took the father at gunpoint to embezzle money from his accounts. I can go on."

Garrett put up his hand. "Elise Hunt was not convicted of any of those crimes, and therefore in the eyes of the law she is innocent. You need to stay away from her."

"I understand her better than anyone," Lucy said.

"Be that as it may, let me do my job—and that is to protect you and Jesse from legal harm. My colleague Felicity will protect Sean's rights. I can't have you investigating this case—possibly obstructing justice—because you have a vendetta against an eighteen-year-old."

"It's not a vendetta!" Lucy said, hating that she sounded shrill.

Brad interjected, "Garrett, you need to get up to speed on the Nicole Rollins and Tobias Hunt investigation, because that is the only connection between Mona Hill and the Rogans."

"I am fully aware of the Hunt family criminal enterprise, but we don't know that it is the only connection."

Brad said, "Then you know I had a traitor on my team for years. Rollins killed a half dozen federal agents, including my boss. The only reason Lucy even talked to Mona Hill during that investigation was because of Elise Hunt. *That* is the connection. Elise Hunt *is* the connection."

As Brad said it, Lucy believed it. Nothing else fit.

"I am up-to-date, Agent Donnelly. My firm has been on RCK retainer since Lucy was assigned to the San Antonio office."

That was news to Lucy, and her surprise must have shown on her face, because Garrett explained. "As a precaution. Any RCK cases that Sean works, for example, I know about, in case he needs legal representation."

When they first moved to San Antonio, Sean hadn't been working for RCK, so that didn't ring completely true to Lucy. She wondered what else was going on, but she didn't ask. She'd ask JT when she talked to him.

"You need me," Garrett continued. "And you need to listen to me."

Lucy would—to a point. "You need to trust me when I tell you that Elise Hunt cannot be underestimated. Do not let her youth deceive you. She is cold, methodical, and vicious. Worse, she's unpredictable."

"We have no evidence—none—that Elise Hunt is involved, so you need to tread carefully," Garrett said.

"I know that girl better than anyone, and I'm telling you that this thread is all we have right now. Sean contacted a PI in L.A. late Monday evening about Elise—that would be after Mona was killed, right? According to the time line? That would make sense if Mona asked him about Elise, maybe Mona found out that Elise was released and called Sean because Sean is the only one who would understand the danger."

Except no scenario Lucy could think of would tell her why Sean hadn't told *her*. Why he hadn't clued her in on whatever he was doing.

Except one, and it was as clear as day now that she thought of it.

He was trying to protect you.

From what? Why? They'd gone around and around about this for years, practically since they first met, and they'd both agreed that good and bad, they needed to know the truth. Too often one or both of them had kept information from the other in an effort to protect them or spare their feelings, when knowledge was the only thing that could truly protect anyone.

It was clear that Garrett didn't like what she was saying. He was trying to protect her from legal harm. She trusted the system a lot more than Sean did. Yet . . . there had been times the system had failed.

"I'm not going to talk to the police without representation," Lucy said. "I'm not going to tamper with evidence, or do anything that might get me or Sean in trouble. But I can't promise not to look into Mona's murder. If the police believe that Sean is guilty, they're not going to look any further."

And if that gun they found in his plane matched the murder weapon, they would absolutely believe he was guilty.

"We'll table the discussion for now."

Lucy didn't comment. "When can I see Sean?"

"I'll talk to Felicity, but it won't be until late this afternoon at the soonest, and probably not until tomorrow morning. It's a three-hour drive."

She wanted to see Sean tonight, but if she went to Houston and couldn't see him, she would be stuck in a hotel. She'd wait to confirm with his lawyer.

The security panel beeped and Garrett glanced over at the tablet Lucy had at her side.

She didn't even have to look. "They're here."

"Let them in, let them do their job, and keep quiet."

Chapter Seven

Nate sent Lucy a text message that he was leaving the courthouse. He was done testifying and he wasn't needed back in court.

This was his least favorite part of the job. First sitting around doing nothing while waiting to testify, then listening to bullshit coming out of the defense. All that time wasted for less than fifteen minutes of questions. In this case, nine minutes for the prosecution, three minutes for the defense, then a two-minute follow-up for the prosecution.

Ridiculous waste of time and money.

Nate went down to the courthouse guard office to retrieve his service weapon, then called Jack on his cell phone as he exited the building and headed toward the parking garage.

"I'm at the safe house," Jack answered. "No word on Kane, but Ranger has some intel we need to verify."

"I'm leaving court now to pick up Jesse. He doesn't know yet, right?"

"No. Tell him the truth, no sugarcoating it, but tell him we're on top of it. Lucy's on edge, but she'll pull it together. She'll want to go to Houston, and I need you to stick to Jesse like glue until we know that this isn't a trap or setup. Did Sean talk to you about Elise Hunt?"

"No," Nate said. That bothered him. Sean usually confided in him about anything security related. Sometimes for help, sometimes just for a sounding board.

"Anything else odd or out of the ordinary?"

"Actually, yes. On Tuesday he texted me for Ryan's cell phone number. I didn't think much of it, but now I wonder why he didn't just ask Lucy."

"Ryan Quiroz?"

"He's the SSA up in Austin, but he partnered with Lucy the first year she was here."

"Sean didn't say why?"

"No."

"Can you think of a reason?"

"Ryan used to be a cop in Houston, before he joined the FBI. He was born and raised there. But I don't know why he'd call Ryan for help and not just ask me."

Nate walked up the stairs to the third floor where he'd parked.

"Sean has a reason for everything, so don't take it personally," Jack said. "I'm going dark in a few; call Ryan, follow up, find out what Sean was thinking. Ryan might not know, but it'll give us one more piece to the puzzle. If you need anything, call JT."

Nate stopped at the top of the stairs. Three SAPD squad cars were parked around his truck, including a K-9 unit.

"Dunning, you there?"

"Something's wrong."

"Talk to me."

"Six cops and a K-9 unit are searching my truck. I have to go."

He ended the call and walked over to the group of cops

and showed his badge. "FBI Special Agent Nate Dunning. What's going on?"

Nate only recognized one of the cops by sight, but couldn't remember his name.

"That's my truck. Where's your warrant?"

"I'm Sergeant Warren," the officer in charge said as he approached. "This is city property, and our K-9 unit hit on your truck during rounds this morning. We ran the plates, tried to reach you, but there was no answer."

Bullshit, Nate thought. He didn't have any missed calls from a number he didn't recognize. "Out of my truck. Now."

This was all wrong. Nate didn't believe in coincidences, and the fact that his car was being searched the same day that his best friend had been arrested for murder told him that this was somehow related.

"Sadie, our German shepherd here, responded to your truck. You have a joint or something, I honestly don't give a shit, you take that up with your office. But this isn't a joint."

"And how the hell do you know that?"

He knew something—Nate could see it in his eyes—but he didn't respond.

"Got something, Sarge," one of the officers said. Warren started back toward Nate's truck, and Nate followed, then Warren turned and said, "Stay there, Agent Dunning."

Warren motioned for two officers to stand with him. One was the familiar cop—a glance at his name plate reminded Nate who he was. Williams. Jeff Williams. He'd been friends with Ryan, they'd gone for drinks a couple times when Nate was a rookie, but Nate hadn't seen him since Ryan transferred to Austin. Williams looked sheepish, but didn't say anything.

"I'm calling my office," Nate said and hit one of his speed dial numbers. Neither cop stopped him.

He called Zach Charles, the squad analyst. "Zach, I need Rachel now."

"On it."

A few seconds later, Rachel answered. "Nate?"

"SAPD is searching my truck at the courthouse. They claim a drug dog reacted to it."

"Who's in charge?"

"Sergeant Warren."

"Stay there. I'll find out what's going on."

The officer standing next to Williams smirked. Nate stared him down as he ended the call. The smirk disappeared.

"Holy shit," one of the cops said.

Nate made a move toward his truck to see what they'd found, but the formerly smirking cop put his hand up.

The cop searching Nate's truck held up a package that appeared to be a kilo of something. The plastic wasn't see-through, but the shape and form—Nate knew exactly what it was.

Someone was setting him up.

Just like someone set Sean up.

"There's sixteen of these bad boys under the lining," the officer said.

Sergeant Warren came over. "Your truck, Agent Dunning."

"Not my drugs."

"You have a baggie of coke on you, I might buy that a criminal planted it on you. But sixteen kilos?" He looked over. "What is it, Parker?"

Parker held up a test tube that was now blue. "Cocaine. Fuck, at twenty a pop? You're looking at over a quarter mil on the street."

Warren looked at Nate. "A quarter million in product."

"My boss is on her way."

"We need to take your weapons."

"No."

"There's sixteen kilos of cocaine in your vehicle. Don't make this more difficult for yourself."

"I will stand here and not move until my supervisor gets here."

"You will not remain armed and put my officers at risk."

"What is your fucking problem, Sergeant?"

"What's yours, Agent Dunning? I'm doing my job, and you're not cooperating. Williams, take his sidearm. Don't fight me on this, Dunning. What else are you carrying?"

"Nothing else on me, sir," he said through clenched teeth.

"Sorry." Williams mumbled so low Nate almost didn't hear him as the cop pulled Nate's Glock from his shoulder holster, then patted him down.

Warren said quietly, "You feds think you're all squeaky-clean, then come into *my* house and put *my* men and women under a microscope. Don't think I don't know what's going on."

Information began to click into place. The FBI had taken down several corrupt cops, including one who had seduced an FBI agent in order to access confidential information which he then shared with a known drug dealer and cop killer. Nate thought that the air had been cleared between the agencies, but there was still tension among the rank and file. And clearly, they all knew that Nate had helped take down the bad cop.

Nate didn't respond to Warren baiting him, though he ached to punch this prick in his arrogant face. He stood there, at ease, falling back into his military training to not respond in the face of an adversary. His drill sergeant had put him through far worse than this jerk.

"Let's see what else you have in that tricked-out Ford

you have there, shall we?" Warren said. He turned to his men and women. "Finish it."

They hadn't taken his phone. He texted Lucy.

Someone planted sixteen kilos of coke in my truck. I'm being detained by SAPD and can't get Jesse. This is no coincidence.

Chapter Eight

Lucy stared at her phone. Nate was in trouble.

Sean *and* Nate were in trouble.

Sean was looking into Elise Hunt. He talked to Mona Hill. Nate had arrested Elise, he'd been part of the SWAT team that came in and killed Elise's sister. Was that the reason? Revenge?

Dammit, Sean!

She wanted to put her frustration aside, but something big had been going on this week and he'd kept her out of the loop, which meant that he was trying to protect her. She'd believed they'd gotten over this hurdle! He'd promised no secrets.

Maybe he didn't take the threat seriously. Maybe he was looking into it . . . trying to confirm . . . but why keep her in the dark?

He had his reasons. She'd find the truth, but first things first.

Keep Jesse safe.

Get Sean out of jail.

Find out who killed Mona Hill.

Clear Nate's name.

The person who killed Mona was likely the same person—or same group—who had planted drugs on Nate.

One of the female SAPD officers was watching her closely, and that's when Lucy realized that she'd likely been assigned to keep tabs on Lucy while her house was being searched.

That irritated her. Sure, she knew they were just doing their job, but it grated on her that she was being watched in her own home.

She was standing in the kitchen alone, except for the watchful cop. Brad was outside with the pair of cops searching the pool house, and Garrett was monitoring the search inside.

She walked outside to talk to Brad. The cop followed. She turned and said, "You can wait here, Officer."

"I need to keep you in sight at all times, Mrs. Rogan."

"Agent Kincaid," she snapped, and wished she hadn't. Now the cop knew that she'd gotten under her skin. That this whole damn search had gotten under her skin. "Keep me in sight, but stand back," she said.

She walked outside. Bandit ran up to her. He looked concerned—if a large, happy golden retriever could look concerned—and stayed at her side as she walked over to where Brad stood outside the pool house. She motioned to her friend, who came over, his face set. "They found two guns in the pool house. A rifle—which they claim they can take, though I think that's bullshit—and a handgun. Small pistol, looked like a .22, but I couldn't be sure because they didn't let me in."

"I'll leave that all to Garrett," she said. She kept her voice low. "Nate texted me. Someone planted sixteen kilos of coke in his truck, he's being detained by SAPD."

"Nate? Are you shitting me?" Brad shook his head. "I'll find out what the fuck is going on, this is ridiculous."

"Shh," she said, looking at the officer, who was too close for comfort. She moved farther away and Brad followed. "I don't know any of these cops."

"Jane Travis is in the pool house. She's okay, I've worked with her a couple of times over the years. But I don't know anyone else."

"Sean was arrested, Kane is missing, and now Nate is being detained. This is no coincidence. You need to be careful. If this"—she waved her hands to indicate the search—"is all related to the Hunt family, you're in as much danger as any of us. Strength in numbers and all that."

"Does RCK have proof? Other than Sean hiring a PI to look for Elise Hunt?"

"No. But Nate's in trouble, and he's our best friend. He was involved in the Rollins investigation. I have to assume that anything Nicole or Tobias knew, Elise knows. Hell, I don't know, Brad!" She forced herself to remain calm. "Nicole had an SAPD officer on her payroll. He's now in federal prison. He may not be the only one."

"Eric Butcher," Brad spat out. "I trusted him. We worked together on three different active warrant searches and he was one of them all along."

Butcher had pled guilty and provided information on how Nicole Rollins recruited cops in San Antonio. He didn't turn in any of his colleagues, but gave enough information that they found two more on her payroll. But that didn't mean there weren't more.

Money wasn't the only thing that motivated cops to turn.

"If you want me to stay and watch your back, I will."

"I'm safe here. As safe as I can be. Do you really think you can find out what's going on with Nate?"

He nodded. "I'm in a unique position to help considering I'm DEA. If drugs are involved—especially in that quantity—they're going to call us in, even just to consult."

"I have a huge favor. I'm sure Nate will be fine—he'll

probably be here soon—but if something happens and he has to deal with this drug situation, can you stay here with Jesse when I go to Houston?"

"Absolutely."

That relieved her. She didn't know who else she could call in to watch her stepson. Jesse was thirteen—almost fourteen—and a smart kid who had been training with both Kane and Sean. But he was still a kid, and she needed him safe.

"Thank you. As soon as the police are done here, I'm going to get Jesse. Please keep me informed every step of the way about Nate, and I'll let you know if I learn anything about Sean or Kane."

He squeezed her shoulder. "We're going to find out what's going on, Lucy."

They walked back into the house, but after Brad left Lucy felt suddenly very alone. She went to the kitchen to make fresh coffee. She needed something to do.

Garrett came in behind her. "Where's Donnelly going?"

She hesitated, and Garrett frowned. "I can't help you if you're not honest with me, Lucy."

She looked around. The officer following her was on the far side of the kitchen, pretending to look at her phone. She motioned for Garrett to come over to the kitchen sink. In a quiet voice she told him what she knew about Nate. "Brad's going to find out what's going on."

"Does JT know?"

"I don't know. Nate texted me." She pulled out her phone and forwarded Nate's message to JT.

Garrett spoke quietly. "The warrant is specific, but they are taking every firearm they have found except for the shotgun and the rifles and your service weapon. They can do so. I think it's just them flexing their muscles, because it's clear that they believe that the gun they found in the plane is the murder weapon, they've already sent that to ballistics and put a rush on it, but they won't have results before next week. They've also taken a lot of Sean's shoes and clothes; again I think just to flex. They're almost done."

"Good." She needed just five minutes to decompress and figure out what was going on. "When they're gone, I'll get Jesse. Either Nate or Brad will stay with him while I'm in Houston. He shouldn't be alone, but I'm not going to take him—it would destroy Sean if Jesse saw him in jail."

Her head began to ache.

"Agent Kincaid?"

A tall cop walked in. Plainclothes, forties, blond with blue eyes.

"Yes."

"I'm Detective John Banner, with the Houston Police Department."

She stared at his outstretched hand and didn't shake it.

"Aren't you supposed to be interviewing my husband about now?"

"I wanted to supervise the search. We're leaving now, and I apologize for the disturbance—"

"Just cut the crap, Detective," she said. "You can go."

He looked at her, unfazed by her comment. "We have what we need. As your lawyer can tell you, you'll be asked to come down for questioning. We can do it here, in San Antonio, for your convenience."

"I'll be in Houston this afternoon to pick up my husband."

"That won't happen."

"I'll have his bail ready. I'm already working on it." She wasn't, but knew that RCK would be. They had resources that she didn't have and probably knew more about Sean's finances than she did.

"We're keeping him in custody over the weekend."

"You can't do that."

"We are."

"I need to see my husband."

"I can arrange that this weekend. He'll be at the main jail."

"There is no reason to keep him over the weekend."

"I have seventy-two hours to arraign him, and I'm going to take every minute. He's a flight risk."

"He has family here. A son. A wife. A business."

"And he's a cybersecurity expert who would know exactly how to disappear if he wanted to."

"He's not going to run. He's going to fight back because he's innocent and I don't—"

Garrett cleared his throat and said, "My client would like to see her husband tonight. As a courtesy, I hope you can make that happen."

Banner looked from Lucy to Garrett, and then back to Lucy.

"I have your contact information. We'll see."

He looked at his watch. "I need to go, but one word of advice, Agent Kincaid: I've done my research. I know who you are, I know who your friends are. Stay out of my case. I would not have arrested your husband if I didn't have solid evidence of his guilt, and if I find out that you're interfering, I'll arrest you for obstruction of justice."

"Threats are unnecessary, Detective," Garrett said.

Lucy fumed.

"Sean is innocent, and your evidence is shit," she snapped.

"I don't arrest the innocent," he said without blinking, then turned and walked away.

Lucy stepped forward and Garrett grabbed her arm, holding her back.

"Going after him isn't going to help," Garrett said.

"He's a fucking asshole," she said, not caring if Banner heard her. Took a deep breath. She didn't sound like herself. "I need to get Jesse." She looked at her watch. "It's almost his lunch hour. I want to be the one to tell him. I have to . . . Garrett, Sean is not guilty. He's not."

She couldn't very well say what she was thinking out loud. That *if* Sean had killed someone, he wouldn't be caught so easily. He wouldn't keep the murder weapon. He would have a solid alibi. He wouldn't be caught on a security camera. But that certainly wouldn't help Sean's defense. The only way Sean would be getting out of this was for the Houston police to be able to prove that he didn't kill Mona Hill . . . and right now, if they really had found the murder weapon in Sean's plane, that meant finding out who really killed Mona and planted the gun there.

The police wouldn't believe that he was being framed. That was up to her to prove.

Chapter Nine

Brad Donnelly took precautions to make sure that he wasn't followed. He wasn't quite as paranoid as the Rogan clan, but after the last two years, he'd become more security conscious. It was certainly suspicious that Sean, Kane, and Nate were all out of the picture.

Sean and Lucy, along with Kane Rogan, had literally saved his life when he'd been tortured by a drug cartel. Lucy repeatedly told him he owed them nothing, but he ignored her. It was more than his life they saved. It was his confidence, his future; they rekindled his faith in humanity. He'd been destroyed after his division was torn apart once they learned Nicole Rollins—an agent he'd trusted for years—had led a major drug operation under his nose and used the DEA to make her family rich, leaving behind a trail of blood so long and thick they were still uncovering some of her crimes two years later.

So yes, he owed them, and he would for the rest of his life. He was okay with that. He loved his job, he was good at it, but in the end, the job only mattered because there were good people in the world who deserved good cops protecting them.

He sent Nate a text message to call him—he needed more information than Lucy had. Then, when he was certain he wasn't being followed, he called Detective Jerry Fielding, his liaison with the San Antonio Police Department. They had worked numerous cases together, and he was a straight shooter.

"Jerry, it's Brad. I'm calling about the cocaine your people found in an FBI agent's car. Can you tell me what's going on?"

"I can't."

That surprised him. "Can't?"

"Look, you and I have a good relationship, but things have been strained between all of us since Butcher was arrested. He's denied everything, said he was forced to make a plea, and the fact that he got ten to fifteen, it has caused a lot more problems."

"The guy is guilty, Jerry. He was working for Rollins. He should have got life and is lucky the AUSA agreed to a plea. Rollins killed a half dozen agents, including my boss."

"I'm not justifying anything, but you didn't testify against him. Three FBI agents did."

"Are you saying this is all a fucking setup?"

"No. The K-9 officer was doing his job. I know Officer Smith—hell, you know him. Ramon Smith. He's worked on several joint operations."

Brad did know Smith. He was a solid cop, former MP in the Army, all-around good guy.

Jerry continued. "When the dog hit on the truck, they ran the plates and found out the truck belonged to an FBI agent." He paused. "Look, Smith called his boss because he recognized it was a sensitive situation. It was his boss who decided to take the opportunity to search it. It's legal, and he wants to make a stand on it. It's going to get ugly."

"Nate Dunning is not a drug runner."

"I don't know Nate, but I trust you, Brad. We've been

in this field a long time. This isn't between me and the FBI—I have friends there. I'm just saying, you need to back off and let this play out. They want a full investigation, just like the FBI demanded of Butcher. Otherwise, they'll cry foul, and none of us will want to work in a city where no one trusts anyone else."

"Don't think I don't know what your people are going through. But this is fucking *bullshit*."

"I'm sorry, Brad. This case is way over my head, and I think you should sit this one out, too."

Brad ended the call. No way in hell was he sitting this out. He called Aggie Jensen, a smart young rookie who'd started with him eighteen months ago. She was a bit quirky and sometimes too casual in an office format, but he never called her on it—he liked her ability to think of every possible contingency as easily as she breathed. Not to mention she was a young, tech-savvy recruit who'd graduated top of her class at the DEA training facility at Quantico. Brad had run a secondary background check on her and she was exactly what she appeared to be: a twenty-eight-year-old computer geek from a family of military heroes and cops.

"Yep, boss?" Aggie said when she picked up the phone.

"Dunning with the FBI was detained after SAPD found sixteen kilos of coke in his truck. I need everything you can find about the case. There has been a strain between our departments ever since the FBI took down a corrupt cop who worked for Rollins."

"Nate? Nate Dunning?" Aggie was clearly surprised. "What did he say?"

"It's not his, he doesn't know how it got there, and I believe him. But I can't get involved—SAPD will cut me off because they know Nate's a friend." As he navigated lunchtime traffic, he told her briefly about the history with Eric Butcher and why SAPD wanted to play this one by the book. "One problem: Sean Rogan has been arrested for murder in Houston and Lucy and Sean need Nate's help."

"Wow. What can I do? Tell me—anything. Lucy is a goddess in my book, anything you need."

"We play by the rules—but find the line and ride it hard. I need everything you can get about this bust. You're friends with Zach Charles at the FBI?"

"Two peas," she said.

"See what you can get from him, on the q.t. I want to know how the FBI is handling this. I'm pretty certain they'll keep Nate from being booked, but there's going to be an investigation. And second, I need everything we can get on the drugs themselves. Tests, exact quantity, packaging, I want to know where they came from. Photos—I know these people, and virtually every gang running around town has a signature. The fact that the sergeant on scene isn't bringing in Jerry Fielding—who knows more in his little finger about the San Antonio drug trade than any other SAPD cop—tells me this is personal. Whether it's personal against Nate, or it's personal against the FBI because of the Butcher bust, I need to know."

"I'm on it."

"Keep this between you and me for now, okay? Just until I know what's going on. And watch your back."

"Sir?"

"Don't do that."

"Okay, can I speak my mind?"

That made him smile. "You always do."

"So you basically told me that Sean is in jail for murder, Nate is being questioned in a major drug bust, and then to watch my back. What else is going on? You think this is all related, don't you?"

"Could be."

She snorted.

"Okay, yes. Something fucked is going on. I can't wrap my head around what it is, though. Sean's brother went missing in Mexico while tracking human traffickers. Is that also connected? Nicole Rollins is dead, and this isn't her game play. She killed when you got in her way, but she wasn't an idiot. She wouldn't plan this elaborate takedown unless there was something much bigger on the table. Yet Nicole's half sister, Elise Hunt, is crazy, smart, shrewd, and stupid all at the same time. You need to read her file, get up to speed. But she's only eighteen. Could she pull something like this off? She'd need a lot of help. I don't see it."

"You don't see it, but you hear the song."

He had no idea what she meant.

"Your instincts, right? You don't see her involvement, but you can't shake the feeling that she's behind this."

"Exactly," he said. "I have sources I can tap."

"Look, boss, if you're worried about me, I don't even know these people. I wasn't even here when this all went down. You should be worried about you. You're the one who needs backup."

"I'm coming into the office now. I'm fifteen minutes out because I forgot about the damn construction on the 410. See what you can learn before I get there."

"I'm on it."

Aggie Jensen immediately called Zach Charles on his cell phone. They'd become friendly because even though she was a sworn agent and Zach was an analyst, she'd taken on primarily an analyst role and they'd worked together multiple times. It didn't bother Aggie, to be honest. She liked being in the field, but she loved working with data. Technology was her playground. And when she was in the field in the tactical truck, it was the best of both worlds—being in the middle of action while monitoring the command center.

She'd wanted to be in the Dallas resident office—also an offshoot of the Houston DEA division—because the only thing she didn't like about San Antonio was that she was four hours from her family. But after eighteen months here, she realized that this was the best thing she could have done. For the first time she was truly on her own. She had a big family—big enough to populate a small town when she counted her aunts, uncles, and cousins— and she'd never been without friends and family to back her up. And while she missed her kin, she'd found a place here. She'd earned her stripes, so to speak. Everything she earned was because she did a damn good job. No one owed anything to her dad or brothers or her uncle, the congressman. Only Brad knew about her uncle Bill, and he agreed to keep it to himself.

Her war hero dad and his three brothers and two sisters, and the collective twenty-three kids they had between them, all with amazing jobs and many with clout, none of that mattered here in San Antonio. All that mattered was her own hard work and skill. That the boss trusted her so much and gave her so many opportunities to succeed meant everything to her. She would not let him down.

"Aggie?" Zach said. "I'm kind of in the middle of something, but is this important?"

"My boss wants to help Nate."

"Hold on."

She heard movement, then a door close. "What do you know?" Zach said, his voice quiet.

She told him the basics of what Brad had told her, then said, "He thinks he can trace the drugs, find out who's behind it."

"SAPD won't let our people anywhere near the case."

"Has Nate been arrested?"

"No. The ASAC and Rachel are both with him now talking to the assistant chief of police. They're working out something, but I don't know the details. No one is back, no one is returning calls or texts, and I have a bad feeling. With Lucy out—oh."

"I know about Sean."

He sighed in relief. "I don't know what I can do. I doubt they'll let us within a hundred yards of this case. They'd reach out to your office first."

"They haven't, nor have they pulled in Narcotics and Vice, which seems odd."

"You said it yourself, it's about that fucking prick Eric Butcher."

She'd never heard Zach swear before.

"SAPD knows that Brad and Nate are tight, they're not going to share anything. Where can we get the forensics report? Anything you can get, but Brad specifically asked for photos."

Silence.

She feared he was going to tell her he couldn't help. "Zach?"

"I know how to get them. I'll call you." He hung up and Aggie released her breath.

She could get them, too, if she violated federal law and hacked into the police database, but Brad said everything up *to* the line, and she knew what she could and could not legally do. Zach had far more contacts than she did, so she was happy he was going to help.

She turned back to her computer and ran through the rumor mill, as she called it—virtually every piece of information that agents collected was put into a closed database. Dealers, alliances, who was dating who, family connections, who was arrested, who was released, how they connected to other players on the street, international contacts, gang relationships, anything that might be useful when they had a big case. They tracked arrests and detainments outside of their jurisdiction as well, because it might connect to one of their cases. Any chatter also went into the database, rumors ranked by veracity. Most agents didn't know how to pull out any data in a relevant way. Raw information was confusing to most people, but Aggie saw patterns where most people saw chaos and knew how to pull out what she needed.

She went with the assumption that someone had planted the drugs on Nate. She liked Nate a lot, he had a good rep among people she respected. Didn't mean he couldn't be corrupt, but if Brad had such faith in his integrity that was good enough for Aggie.

If someone planted the drugs on Nate, why sixteen kilos? Maybe a baggie wouldn't be enough to get him in trouble, but a kilo stuffed in the glove box would cause him problems. But then he might find it . . .

Under the truck liner, Brad had told her. That meant someone had access to Nate's vehicle. It wouldn't take much time to pop the liner and plant the coke, but they'd need at least five or ten minutes uninterrupted. Where did he live? Was his truck accessible to the public? She really wanted to talk to him, that would help her find out when and where the drugs were most likely planted. Maybe there were surveillance tapes, something to look at. A potential witness.

But the big question was, who would be willing to give up sixteen kilos of coke to frame a cop when one kilo would be more than sufficient? It had to be someone with access. Someone who could afford to lose a quarter million in gross profit.

No one wanted to lose a quarter million dollars . . .

Brad was right—if they could see how it was packaged and test the drugs, they might be able to trace it. They could find usable prints. With SAPD taking lead, she wouldn't be able to get those reports.

Aggie skimmed through the rumor mill, figuring that the drugs were planted within the last week. That might be a faulty assumption, but Brad had hinted that this could be connected to Sean's arrest, so Aggie was confident in her theory.

And then she saw it.

A rumor, nothing provable, but it was so unusual that it jumped out at her.

Ten days ago, in Travis County, just outside Austin, a drug house was hit by a rival gang. The sheriff's office responded, found no one, and had no probable cause to search because the neighbor who called it in said the shots came from the property, not the house. She also said that everyone left quickly. The lease was in the name of Rosa Merides. She was the mother to known gang members, Raul "Blackie" Merides and his brother Stuart "Smidge" Merides, whose father had done two stints in prison before being killed in a prison fight. By the time they had a warrant to search, the residents still hadn't returned, and a possible crime scene was contaminated by bleach. No drugs were found.

Three days later, a man was admitted to a San Antonio hospital with an infection from a gunshot wound. He refused to talk. The police were called—SAPD—but no one had made the connection with the call in Travis County from three days earlier. Two completely different jurisdictions, but if Aggie had seen this earlier, she would have been suspicious.

The police had the bullet that the hospital extracted from the victim, Malcolm "Mitts" Vasquez, thirty-one, of San Antonio. He was released and ordered to come to a court hearing—scheduled for yesterday—but he'd never shown up and a bench warrant had been issued. He had a record—including time served for drug possession and intent to sell—but had been clean for a couple of years. Until now.

She made a note of his last known address and associates, and when she read his file learned he ran around with the Saints back in the day. The gang had more or less disbanded, but the nearly defunct Saints had been rivals of the Merides gang. The connection was as clear as day. The Saints had hit the Merides house, Vasquez was shot.

She didn't have a ballistics report, but that would be easy to get. They also might not have had a chance to test ballistics yet. They were running a two-to-three-week backlog if it wasn't a priority case. Even then, they'd be at least a week out.

This might not be related to the drugs in Nate Dunning's truck, but it was an outlier and it landed in her time window. Brad had taught her how to think like a criminal, and if *she* were a gangbanger who wanted to plant drugs on a federal agent, she wouldn't use her own stash—she'd steal it from someone else. Especially if by stealing it she'd cause trouble for people she didn't like, trouble that would benefit her.

She jotted down her notes and ran to Brad's office.

He wasn't there.

She glanced at her watch. He'd said fifteen minutes—sure, the construction could have delayed him longer—but it had been more than forty minutes since she got off the phone with him.

She called his cell phone.

It went straight to voice mail.

She tracked down Brad's administrative assistant. "Rena, I need to ping Brad, he's not answering."

Rena Abrams eyed her suspiciously. It was an unusual request, though not unheard of. Aggie often tracked agents when they were working, especially during a dangerous op. She could have done it herself, but she was trying to go through channels after being hand-slapped a few times for cutting corners.

"I'll take the heat if he gets mad, but he was supposed to be here, and he might be investigating something hot."

Rena didn't say anything, but she turned to her computer and started clicking. She frowned. Clicked again. Then she said, "His phone is not responding, it's off. But the last ping showed him a block away, on Desert Sands."

That was the back road into the DEA office, which was a nondescript building they shared with the sheriff's narcotics division. It wasn't a secret location, but it was tucked away without signage.

"I don't know what's going on, I need you to raise the threat level."

"I need to talk to the SSA. If Donnelly is really in trouble—"

"I'll talk to him," Aggie said. Brad's second in charge was Martin Salter, a quiet agent who looked intimidating, but was soft-spoken.

Martin was in his office. She explained what was going on as calmly as possible. Fortunately, Martin was sharp. He pulled his gun from his drawer and called two agents to accompany them. Even though the ping came from a block and a half away, they drove in a tactical truck to the location.

Brad's car was parked at an angle on the side of the road. It had a flat tire and the airbag had been deployed. *Why hadn't he called?*

Martin said, "Proceed with caution."

The two agents approached the car and Aggie stayed back with Martin, watching the surroundings. She noticed that there was a security camera on the corner of a small, fenced utility building.

One of the agents retrieved a phone from the ground.

It had been smashed. It looked intentional, as if someone slammed their heel into it.

The other agent said, "Salter, sir, this tire was shot out. There's a small amount of blood in the car and Donnelly's service weapon is under the vehicle."

Salter immediately ordered them all to get in the truck in case there was a sniper. Aggie didn't point out that if it was a trap, they'd already had several minutes to get off a shot. Whoever had shot out Brad's tire was long gone.

But Aggie knew exactly what had happened. Someone had taken Brad Donnelly.

Chapter Ten

Elise Hunt was lying out by the pool drinking champagne—not because she liked it all that much, but because it said something to anyone who watched her.

A woman in charge.

A free woman.

A kick-ass woman who doesn't fail and if you fail she'll eat your balls for lunch.

She smiled, sipped the champagne. The heat of the afternoon sun made her sweat, but it felt amazing. She was free. Twenty-two months, two weeks in that fucking jail—*juvenile detention*—and she wanted to just shoot the bitch who put her there.

Fucking FBI Agent Lucy Kincaid.

Killing her would be *so* much fun, and Elise was all about fun. But she had to wait.

She hated waiting. Waiting was *not* fun.

Putting Lucy's asshole husband in jail was fun. He'd stolen her money and played them all for fools. Well, he hadn't fooled Elise, but everyone else didn't realize how smart he was.

Planting drugs on that hunky, sulking FBI agent was fun.

Torturing the man who killed her sister was fun.

She had to admit, when she could sit still long enough to contemplate all the possibilities, that her daddy was right. Revenge was fun, but if you didn't get anything out of it, it was a waste of time and resources.

She'd visited her dad first thing when she got out of juvie. The government even paid for her airline ticket to Los Angeles, and she'd sweet-talked the dorky clerk into upgrading her to first class.

"We can kill them, and they're dead, but we won't have what we need," her father had told her.

"They should be dead. They killed Nicole and Tobias." Elise didn't care much about her aunt Margaret— Margaret was mean to her and she killed her mom, even though her mom was crazy—and Joseph, Nicole's fuck-buddy, was a thorn in her side and he hated Toby. Elise liked Toby. He was fun and had great ideas.

"They damaged our operation, but they don't know everything I know. Elise, I need you to do exactly what I say, understand?"

"Yes, Daddy."

"Don't mouth off to me."

"I'm not."

And what could he do about it? He was still in prison, and she was sitting here free *talking to him. She could walk out and never come back.*

She'd thought about it, the walking out and never looking back part, for a long time. Especially when Daddy said she couldn't kill Lucy Kincaid, the cop who could read her mind. She'd thought about not doing everything he wanted because it was a lot of work and she couldn't kill Lucy.

But he was her daddy, and he was her only family, and she wanted to prove to him—and to dead Nicole—that she was smarter and better than all of them.

She wasn't dead, was she? She was free, wasn't she?

"*Do you understand the plan, Elise?*"

"*Yes.*"

"*When you leave here, there can be no deviations. I need to trust you.*"

"*You can, Daddy. Didn't I do everything that Toby told me to do? Everything! And it wasn't* me *who screwed up.*"

"*You've always been a good soldier.*"

She wasn't a soldier. She was a leader. Toby always told her that she was smart enough to be in charge someday.

But she liked that her daddy trusted her. Without her, none of his plans could work. Without her, he would be in prison for the rest of his life.

She didn't want to be alone. She missed Toby more than anyone. At least Daddy loved Toby like she did.

"*So what is the rule, Elise? You have to tell me you understand.*"

"*I can't kill Lucy Kincaid. Yada yada.*"

"*You need to take this seriously. I'm getting out of this place, and I have to know that* you *know that Kincaid's safety is a deal breaker. You touch her, I'll lose everything. We'll both be dead.*"

"*I know.*" She rolled her eyes and wished her dad would stop treating her like a child.

"*Did you get the emergency numbers?*"

"*Yes.*"

"*We won't be able to talk until I'm free, but it's only a matter of weeks. If anything happens, if anyone comes close to you, go directly to the safe house.*"

"*Oh, you mean the house you let your fuck-buddy Portia have? No thanks.*"

"*Hey, that's uncalled for. It's safe and it's mine. I don't want you to end up dead like your brother and sister. Understand?*"

Elise pouted. "*She hates me.*"

"She doesn't, but it's your house as much as mine. And no one else knows about it."

"Portia does."

"She's not going to betray me."

"She's not family."

"Elise, please."

"Fine."

"No deviations from the plan. No games."

"You're no fun. And it's not fair that I can't kill Lucy. She's psychic."

"She's not psychic."

"You haven't met her. She knows things she shouldn't know."

"She's just a cop. But I promised her safety—we lose everything if she dies. Do you understand me? She lives, we get all the money her husband stole from us. All of it. That's the agreement. She dies, we get nothing and we'll be hunted."

She sulked "Fine."

"When all is said and done—and after time has passed, a year or two, tops—you can take her down. But this is the one time where you have to exercise patience."

"Okay." At least she had something to look forward to. And a year or two might even turn into a month or two.

Yes, she was looking forward to torturing and killing Lucy Kincaid. Elise smiled as she finished her champagne.

"Ms. Hunt?"

It was Donny, the puppy dog. The boy who did everything she said and never questioned her. He was cute and loyal. She liked him. She liked people who did what she told them to do. If she told him to kill someone, he killed them. If she told him to steal a car, he stole a car. It was fun. And all he wanted was to get into her pants. She hadn't let him yet, but she would when it benefited her. It was the promise that it would happen that kept him in line. That and money and fear of her daddy.

Donny should fear her more because her daddy was still in prison.

But he'd realize that soon enough.

"Sit," she said, patting the lounge chair next to her. They had rented this house before she was out of juvie. Cute Donny and bitchy Clara and stupid Pablo had been taking care of business for months.

But she was in charge and they all knew it.

He didn't sit.

"The DEA agent is still unconscious."

"I know, so?"

She really hated people repeating things.

"Pablo called. He and Clara were unable to get the kid."

She frowned. "I don't like that answer."

"He was taken out of school before the end of the day. They were in place, but he didn't come out. They learned that Agent Kincaid picked him up early."

"Why would she do that?"

"Clara thinks that once Rogan was arrested, they pulled him."

"Well, that's stupid." Clara always tried to make Elise seem stupid, like she couldn't plan a simple kidnapping. "The kid was icing. We'll get him later," Elise said. "He can't be locked in that house all fucking day and night, right?"

"Jimmy said—"

"I *know* what my daddy said. I helped him come up with this plan!"

Yes, they wanted the kid, because kids were better leverage. Well, *she* wanted the kid. He wasn't part of the original plan, but Clara and Donny didn't know that, and if they thought it was *her* plan, and not her daddy's plan, they might not obey her.

"I have an idea, if we can't get him by tomorrow morning." She jumped up and clapped her hands. "Let's go play with the fed, okay? That'll make me feel better."

"He's unconscious."

She winked. "Not for long."

Donny stared at her scantily clad body. She *knew* she was cute. And young and pretty and she had big boobs that guys liked. So she used them to her advantage.

She wrapped her arms around Donny and gave him a fat, sloppy kiss. She felt him tense, push toward her, instantly aroused.

She stepped back, enjoyed his torment. "*That's* for being the only person I can really count on, Donny. When we're done with this whole thing, we'll have time for a lot more fun and games. I *promise*." She touched his dick, because she could and it would drive him crazy, then she skipped into the house and to the soundproof studio. The owners had been musicians, they had a whole little recording studio set up in part of a tandem garage.

How nice of them to give her a kill room. Or a torture room. Or a room where she could do whatever the fuck she wanted.

Daddy said to kill him, but he didn't say she couldn't make him suffer first.

Chapter Eleven

Lucy told Jesse everything that she knew. He deserved the truth. Not only because he was nearly fourteen, but because Sean had promised Jesse he would never lie to him—even when the truth was difficult.

They were alone in Sean's den. While the police had been mostly respectful of their house, they had still left many things out of place. Lucy couldn't worry about that now. She was glad that they hadn't taken more than they had, and in the back of her mind she wondered why they had such a restricted warrant. Did they not want to ask for too much and have the whole thing tossed?

Ultimately, it wouldn't matter. If one of the guns they found was the murder weapon, they'd be back with an expanded warrant, including for Sean's computer.

She watched Jesse. He looked so much like Sean, it melted her heart. She wanted to protect him more than anything, but life wasn't always pretty. He didn't say anything at first, and Lucy didn't have anything to add. She didn't *know* much and it was driving her up a wall. She wanted to be *doing* something, not sitting here waiting for permission to see her husband.

She wanted to reassure Jesse that his family would fix this, but she couldn't.

Especially since she had doubts.

Small doubts.

Not about Sean's innocence, but that they would be able to prove it. And that troublesome voice in her head that kept telling her what was happening to Kane, Nate, and Scan were all related. That someone was out to destroy them.

She couldn't tell Jesse that. She *shouldn't* tell him that.

But was keeping him in the dark more dangerous?

"What are you doing?" Jesse asked.

"Everything I can."

"Which is?"

"I told you. Jack is in Mexico working on something with Kane, and Nate's on his way—he was detained. Nate will stay here with you." She didn't want to tell him Kane was missing. She'd already put a huge weight on Jesse's shoulders. "Jack and Kane will be here as soon as they can. Hopefully by tomorrow." She really had no idea. Maybe Sean was right—full honesty was the only way to go. But to tell him his dad was in jail and his uncle was missing in Mexico? It was too much.

"I want to go with you to Houston. I want to see my dad."

"I don't think that's a good idea."

"Yes! Please, Lucy?"

How did she explain it? Maybe just tell him what Sean was feeling. What she knew Sean would be feeling.

"It would tear your dad up if you saw him in jail. This is hard on him—really hard."

"Have you talked to him?"

"No. They wouldn't let me. I'm working on going to visit, it might not be until tomorrow."

"And why can't I come? I want to tell him I believe him."

"I'll tell him."

"It's not the same thing."

"Jesse, we don't have a lot of details right now, and it's safer for you to be here."

"It's not fair."

"I know. I'm hoping all this will be resolved quickly."

"You don't think he did it, do you? Killed that woman?"

"No." She shouldn't ask him questions, but she couldn't help herself. "What happened on Monday? Sean went to Houston—did he tell you why?"

"He said he had to do something and to have leftovers for dinner, and he might not be home until late. I tried to stay up, but went to bed at ten. I didn't hear when he came in."

"He was here when I got home at eleven ten."

"I can say he was here."

"No," she said emphatically. "Jesse—you cannot lie. It's better to remain silent than to lie. But you're not going to have to talk to the police. I won't allow it, and I don't think they can compel you. Don't say anything to them related to this situation or even something you think is totally innocuous."

"But you believe he's innocent?"

"Of course I do."

"Then why are you asking questions?"

He was genuinely worried that she thought Sean might be guilty.

"Because if I'm going to find out who killed Mona Hill and get Sean out of this, I need all the information I can get."

"I want to help."

"I know."

Jesse looked at his hands.

"What is it?"

"Is he okay? I mean—there are bad people who hate my dad." His voice cracked. He was worried. He'd lost so much in his young life; Lucy couldn't stand for him to lose anything else.

"JT and Rick and everyone at RCK and the FBI is working to keep Sean safe. I trust them. You need to trust them, too."

"Then why aren't Jack and Kane here? What's so important in Mexico that they can't drop it and come when we need them the most?"

"Kane and Siobhan just rescued six young girls from a human trafficking ring. There were some complications, so Jack's there. They'll be here as soon as possible."

"But they're okay, right?"

"As far as I know." She hated obfuscating the truth.

He stood up. "I still want to visit my dad."

"I'll tell you what. I don't think they'll let him out this weekend, but I think our lawyers are really good and he'll get bond on Monday. If something happens and he doesn't? I'll take you to see him.

"Promise?"

"Yes."

I hope it doesn't come to that. Please, God, don't let it come to that.

Jesse went upstairs to his room and Lucy didn't know whether she'd made the situation better or worse. Bandit, who'd been asleep on his dog bed, immediately jumped up and followed Jesse.

Her cell phone rang and the number was unfamiliar, but she answered anyway.

"Kincaid."

"Lucy?"

She didn't recognize the young female voice and demanded, "Who's this?"

"Aggie Jensen. From the DEA."

Lucy rubbed her eyes. "Right. Of course. How can I help you?"

"Brad was kidnapped an hour ago, a block from DEA headquarters. I would have called you sooner, but it's a madhouse here."

If Lucy wasn't already sitting, she would have dropped on the spot. Brad . . . missing. "What happened? Do you know who's behind it?"

"Not yet. Martin—SSA Martin Salter—he's not listening to me. Well, that might not be fair. He's weighing all the facts in the situation, but we don't have any evidence that what happened to Sean and Nate is related to Brad's kidnapping, so he's running the investigation from the wrong angle. He's a good agent, but . . . well . . ."

"I know Martin. He's by the book and very honest, which is why Brad brought him on the team. Are you sure—"

"Yes, Brad was taken, his tire shot out, his gun kicked away. This can't be a coincidence, right?"

"No. The big question is *why*. And how did they know he would be there at that exact time?" They'd ambushed him, but Brad wasn't a novice. How'd they get the edge on him? Had he missed a tail? Or was it a tag team? Had they waited for him?

"Brad asked me confidentially to look into Nate's situation. I don't have anything solid, but a drug house was hit last week outside Austin. The house was run by the Merides brothers, known dealers. Three days later a gangbanger came in with an infected gunshot wound. They cut him loose, he missed his court date yesterday. So now there's a warrant. He was part of the Saints, a rival gang."

Lucy knew all about the Saints.

"And you think the drugs taken in this raid were planted on Nate."

"I don't think anything at this point, I'm still gathering information, but I was wondering why sixteen kilos? It's a quarter-million-dollar bust. Most gangbangers aren't going to want to give up that weight, even to frame a cop, unless they take it from someone else, or get paid even more than it's worth to plant it. Honestly, it's overkill. A kilo would have netted the same result."

Aggie was right. "Where are the Merides brothers now?" Lucy asked. "Jail?"

"In the wind, no active warrants for either of them. The police didn't connect them to the shooting of Mitts Vasquez—the Saints gangbanger—but Mitts is in the wind as well. This is my theory."

"Can you send me what you have?"

"Aren't you kind of busy?"

"Helping Nate helps Sean."

"We might have caught a break," Aggie said. "There were security cameras on a warehouse right outside where we found Brad's car. Martin sent two agents to retrieve copies from a digital warehouse. We should have them within an hour."

"Good. Show them to me, if this is connected to the Hunt family I might recognize some of the people."

"I'll do what I can. Oh! I forgot, I reached out to Zach—on the q.t. I don't want to get him in trouble. But he's been trying to call me and I couldn't talk to him with Martin around. Brad wanted to look at the evidence from Nate's truck. Different gangs have different signatures, and if this is a major gang, he might be able to ID where the drugs came from. I have to go into a meeting right now."

"I'll call him. Thanks, Aggie. I appreciate everything. I want to find Brad, but I have to go to Houston." Brad had dropped everything to come over here when she called after Sean's arrest. And now she felt torn, like she was letting everyone down.

"Anything you learn, let me know. I'll do the same."

"Of course."

"And I reached out to Nate. I'm going to pick him up

at SAPD. He doesn't know anything more than we do, but I'm going to give him this information in person, not over the phone."

"Thank you, Aggie. I appreciate everything."

Lucy hung up and dialed Zach's cell phone. It wasn't that she didn't want the office knowing she was calling him, but she didn't want him to get into trouble for sharing information with her.

"Zach, it's Lucy. I'm calling from home."

"How's Sean?"

"I don't know. I can't see him yet. I just talked to Aggie Jensen."

"You heard about Brad Donnelly."

"Yes. Brad was here before he was kidnapped. He was looking into the origin of the drugs that were found in Nate's truck."

"I can't get anything from SAPD, but I got the photos, which Donnelly wanted. Not going to do us any good now."

"Send them to Aggie. Watch yourself. Someone is coming after us."

"Isn't that a stretch?"

"No." Jack had made her paranoid about talking on the phone. While their phone was clean, what if Zach's wasn't?

Now you're being far too paranoid.

"I wish I could do more for you guys," Zach said. "Rachel had a staff meeting and made it clear that we can't use FBI resources to help Sean. That's not our job, all that stuff. But she also said that Sean had a lot of friends. I don't know what that meant—like, can we help him as long as we're not using resources?"

"It means that he has friends in the FBI—not just here, but other places. I'm not worried about Sean's innocence—I know he didn't kill Mona Hill. I'm worried about him being in jail over the weekend. There are people who want him dead, and jail would be a great place to get to him."

She had an idea.

"I have to go, Zach—you can help Nate, so focus on that. I'll help Sean."

She immediately called Rick Stockton, an assistant director in the FBI. She could go through channels, she could try other people, but she needed a huge favor, and if anyone could do it, it was Rick.

It took her several minutes to get through to him, but she wasn't surprised. The national FBI headquarters had been raked over the coals of late—some of it justified, some of it not—but even though Rick's division had gotten through the controversies unscathed, he had to take on additional responsibility as a result.

"Lucy. I meant to call you earlier about Sean, but I've been swamped."

"I know, I didn't want to bother you, I knew JT was going to call, but I need a favor and I wouldn't ask if I didn't think it was important."

"Name it."

"Sean didn't kill Mona Hill, but they're not going to release him, not until Monday when he's arraigned. His lawyer basically said as much. Meanwhile SAPD found a large quantity of drugs in Nate's truck, which are not his. And Brad Donnelly was kidnapped less than two blocks from DEA headquarters."

"I heard."

That was fast.

"Sean is going to be in a Houston jail, and I fear for his safety. Can you do anything to get him transferred into federal custody?"

"This is a Houston PD case. I spoke with the chief of police personally, and she is aware of who Sean is, and that he has had a bounty on his head in the past. She doesn't want anything to happen to him while in their custody, and has assured me that she and her corrections department will go above and beyond in protecting him. They're considering putting him in the Houston administrative jail—it's federally controlled, it's probably the safest place for him. I'm helping facilitate that."

"Rick, there is something else going on here."

"If so, I don't know what it is. We need to let the system work. If Sean is innocent, Houston PD will prove it."

"If?" She didn't expect that from someone she trusted. Who Sean trusted.

"You know what I mean."

"No, I don't. Sean didn't kill Mona Hill, justified or unjustified. But someone is making it seem like he did, and chances are the gun they found in his plane will match ballistics."

"I know you're upset."

"It's not just Sean! It's Brad, Kane, Nate! Everyone is in danger or trouble, this isn't a coincidence, Rick."

He didn't say anything.

"You know it, don't you? Are you not telling me something?"

"I don't know anything more than you do," he said. "I'll keep in contact with Houston, make sure they fully understand that I will have everyone's head if Sean is injured. I have to go. I'm sorry."

He hung up.

She wanted to throw the phone across the room, but didn't. Why was Rick so . . . *ambivalent*? Yes, he was an assistant director in the FBI and he had to follow rules, but he could have said that he knew Sean was innocent.

If.

There was no *if*. Sean wouldn't kill anyone in cold blood.

Not like her.

She put her head on Sean's desk and closed her eyes. She had killed before. In the line of duty, but she didn't count that. To protect the boys in Mexico, she had killed those who held them captive. And she didn't count that.

But nearly ten years ago, she had killed her rapist in cold blood.

He was unarmed.

No one blamed her for killing Adam Scott. He'd killed dozens of women and eluded the authorities for more than twenty years.

But she didn't have to pull the trigger six times.

It haunted her.

No, it doesn't.

What haunted her was that she didn't regret it. Adam Scott had stolen so much from her. He'd facilitated multiple rapes. Humiliated her. Hurt her. Tortured her brother Dillon. Put her brother Patrick in a coma. Expected her to come with him, to replace a woman he had killed years ago.

She was glad he was dead. No regrets.

It had taken her years to learn that she wasn't broken. Years to accept that she was worthy of love, worthy *to* love. Her brothers had trained her, helped her heal, taken care of her, but it was Sean who gave her a future. Melted her icy interior so she *could* love.

A man like Sean would never kill in cold blood.

She had to prove it. If the evidence was overwhelmingly against him, she had to prove who really killed Mona Hill.

And someone took Nate and Brad off her team. So you're alone. Isolated.

Yes, it was connected. And maybe that would be their downfall.

Whoever *they* were.

Chapter Twelve

The booking process was hell.

They'd taken his belt and shoelaces, though he wasn't put in prison attire.

They'd taken his phone, his wallet, his wedding ring.

They'd photographed him front and side. Printed him. Took a sample of his DNA.

He was demoralized, reduced to a number. But even after all the humiliation, the worst was when they walked him down the hall to talk to his attorney. He overhead one cop say "That's Banner's collar, the john who whacked a prostitute. Wife's a fed."

A john. Killed a prostitute. The narrative destroyed him inside. It was untrue, and he was usually good about not caring what others thought of him.

But not today. Not here. Not now.

He was cuffed to the table. "Your lawyer is here, she'll be brought in momentarily," the guard said, then left.

He hadn't been allowed to call Lucy. They said *later*. When was later? He needed to explain to her, tell her everything. He hated that he hadn't told her about Mona on Monday night. He should have. Why didn't he? Why didn't he just *say something*?

Because you weren't sure this wasn't a trick, a trap, a scam of some sort.

Yet Sean believed the note was real. Which meant that Elise either killed Mona herself, or had someone do it for her.

To frame him. To destroy him—and destroy Lucy.

The guard brought in a woman. She was petite and wore four-inch heels. Still wasn't tall. Dark skin, dark hair, dark eyes . . . and walked as if she was an Amazon, not a leprechaun.

"Sean Rogan, Felicity Duncan," she said in a Texas accent. Not too thick, but definitely native Texas.

"Take the cuffs off him, Benny, will you?"

"Policy is that murder suspects require—"

"Take the cuffs off."

Benny complied. Sean's eyes burned.

He would not cry, but he hated the cuffs even more than he was going to hate the cage.

"Thank you," he said when the guard left.

"He's following procedure, but he knows I can go over his head and get my way, why fight me on it?" She smiled, but it didn't reach her eyes. She put a folder on the table in front of her and sat down.

"What happened, Mr. Rogan?"

"I was arrested for Mona Hill's murder. I didn't kill her. I need you to believe me."

"No, you don't. You need me to be the best damn defense lawyer on the planet, and I'm close to it, understand?"

He told her everything, beginning to end. He had to— only then would she understand why he couldn't tell the cops everything.

"That wasn't so hard, was it?" she said.

He glared at her. She meant well, she was trying to be supportive, but the more he ran through that night, the more he realized he'd been set up. Was Mona herself party to setting him up? Not to her murder—she valued her life. But maybe . . . maybe she had known more than she'd told him.

He rubbed his eyes. Speculation wasn't going to help him right now.

"I am going to push hard to have you arraigned and released tonight," Felicity said. "But it's not going to happen. Not on a capital case where you have the means to run."

"I'm not going to run."

"Irrelevant to Banner. And he believes it, so they plan to arraign you on Monday. They think they'll be able to work a no bail deal, but I'm not going to let that happen. Bail might be high, but RCK is good for it, and I know you have the means to cover it if necessary. They might ask for an ankle monitor, I'll give in on that provided you're allowed to return to San Antonio. They'll push for house arrest—I'll fight that, it'll be fifty-fifty."

"I'm innocent."

"I'm telling you what they're going to do, and what I'm going to do. You'll be out Monday."

Sean appreciated her confidence, but this was a setup. There was a reason he was here, today, a reason he was being framed for murder. Either they would find a way to keep him until trial, or he'd be dead this weekend.

"I'm being framed."

"Our job is not to prove *who* killed Mona. Our job is to prove they don't have a case against *you*. You need to tell the police the facts. Answer their questions."

"No."

"Sean, it's in your best interest to be as forthcoming as possible. I'll make sure they don't stray off track. That's my job, to protect your interests. But you're suspected of a felony murder. You were with the victim during the likely time of death. You need to tell them why."

"No."

"Sean—"

"They don't need to know why. All they need to know is that she was alive when I left."

"And if that gun they found in your plane is the murder weapon, what you say isn't going to matter much to the jury."

"I didn't fire it. I haven't fired a gun in over a week—last time I was at the gun range, Lucy was practicing before her requalification with the FBI. Nearly two weeks ago—two weeks on Sunday. I was trying out some different guns there. I didn't even shoot my own gun." He frowned. Could one of those guns he'd used been the murder weapon? His prints might be on it. Yet . . . they were regulated. No one could walk off with it. And latent prints were really hard to get off a gun. Maybe a shell casing . . . but the range was owned by a retired cop, they wouldn't let just anyone walk in there and collect the brass.

He was getting way too paranoid.

"There's no reason you can't tell the police why you were at Mona Hill's apartment. She called you because she felt threatened by Elise Hunt. You went to give her security advice. You left because she agreed to bring in a bodyguard."

"And they're going to ask why Mona would call me."

"We don't have to answer that. I know what I'm doing here, Sean. I understand this is a prickly situation." She sighed. "Tell me."

"What?"

"How you know Mona Hill and why she called you. I'm your lawyer, Sean. Unless you tell me there's a bomb planted somewhere or you know of a murder about to happen, I'm not going to repeat anything you say. Understand? But I need to know so I can better defend you. If you leave things out, lie to me, it's only going to make this case that much more difficult. I have a solid team of investigators who can corroborate information. They can do research. They can verify facts. Just tell me the truth."

"I need to see Lucy." God, he wanted to see her right now. Touch her, hold her, tell her he was sorry. He needed to explain.

"I'm working on it. They're going to question you pretty late tonight. I'll make sure that she's here in the morning."

"I want to see her now. Please."

"They're not going to agree."

"Can you call her? FaceTime? Anything? I need to explain why I didn't tell her I went to see Mona."

The lawyer stared at him for nearly a minute, then she nodded. "I can't leave my phone with you. I need to be here."

"Thank you. After I tell Lucy everything, then I'll answer all your questions, okay? But I'm telling you this flat-out: I did not kill Mona."

When Lucy saw Sean's face over her phone, she almost cried. He looked exhausted and worried.

"It's so good to see your face," he said.

"I'll be there tonight," she said, "as soon as your lawyer tells me it's okay."

"My lawyer says you won't be able to see me until tomorrow."

"Why?"

"I don't know. They plan to question me late. Just listen, please. Believe me. I didn't kill Mona."

"I know."

"I should have told you that I went to Houston on Monday."

"Yes. But that doesn't matter right now. JT says you called a guy, Nico, in L.A. to track Elise Hunt. Why?"

"I wish I'd just ignored Mona," he mumbled. "I went because she claimed someone from Tobias Hunt's network was back, and she was scared. I didn't believe her at first, but face-to-face—yeah, I believed her. She saw Elise Hunt twice last weekend. Once on the street and once in the lobby of her apartment building. Mona was scared, and you know as well as I do that woman has never been scared of anything."

"Why didn't you just tell me that?"

"Because I wasn't positive Mona wasn't playing some game. Or that Elise got her to jerk us around. She worked for Tobias before, but I didn't think she would do it again, especially since he'd at one time put a hit out on her. But if someone threatened her family—well, you know what I mean."

She did.

Sean continued. "I wanted more information before I talked to you. She had a note Elise allegedly left in her apartment. A threat. I told her to go to the police, she said she couldn't because she runs call girls, and we went around and around about that until she finally agreed to ask her bodyguard to move in for the duration, and I promised to find out what Elise was doing in Houston.

"I should have told you—but I still wasn't positive this wasn't Mona trying to, I don't know . . . leverage me. And you've been so happy . . . I know that's stupid, but I wanted accurate information before I dumped it on you. Nico got back to me that he found where Elise was living in Los Angeles—where her aunt had lived before she was killed—and he had eyes on her Tuesday afternoon. I asked him to keep her under surveillance. Thursday he was suspicious that she might have slipped away. I had a meeting scheduled with Elise's warden at the detention facility this morning—that's where I was going to go after I dropped Jesse off at school. It was scheduled at eleven."

It was already two in the afternoon.

"Why?"

"I wanted to find out who came to visit her, her call logs, her roommate, the whole nine yards."

"He wouldn't have given that to you."

"She. Kathy Pine."

"Pine? I heard her speak once. She's impressive."

"I can be persuasive. You need to be careful, Lucy."

"You're the one in jail, Sean. I talked to Rick about your safety."

"I'm okay. I'm going to be okay."

Lucy didn't want to tell him about Nate and Brad, but she had to. He listened. "And Kane?"

"Jack's in Mexico. He said he met up with Ranger and they have a lead on him."

"I should be there helping to find him. Dammit!"

"Jack will find him." She hoped.

"Where's Jesse?"

"Here. I got him out of school at lunch. He's safe and I hope Nate can stay with him this weekend. Or I'll take him to St. Catherine's."

"He shouldn't have to be dealing with this. Tell me what happened with Brad."

She did, Sean's expression over the phone going from concerned to very worried.

"I don't have to tell you to be careful."

He didn't. "I will be there first thing in the morning. I promise."

"I love you, Lucy. I love you so much and I'm sorry I didn't tell you everything on Monday. But there was no record of Elise Hunt or Elise Hansen traveling. She likely has another ID—she had a dozen when you caught her before. Please forgive me."

His anguish was real. "Of course I forgive you," she said. She did, though they would have to talk about this—when he was free. When she could hold him. He'd been protecting her, but he knew better than to keep information from her. Lucy had testified against Elise and that girl had played the judge and the psychologist who testified. The shrink insisted that Elise had been abused and forced to commit crimes. Lucy didn't know if Elise had been abused, but when she met her, that girl was running circles around everyone else. Her relationship with her psycho brother wasn't abusive, they played off each other. Elise was just as evil as Tobias, and as smart as her sister, and that made her doubly dangerous.

The only thing they had going for them was that she was young and impulsive. Which was both good and bad.

The people they cared about were in her crosshairs.

Like Nate.

"Planting the drugs is something she would do," Lucy said after a moment. "She wouldn't care about the price; it would tickle her to do something that bold."

"We have to go," Felicity said. "I'm sorry, Lucy, but they want to interview Sean, and I shouldn't have let him call you."

"Wait—just wait one second."

She ran upstairs with her phone and went into Jesse's room.

He jumped up. It was clear he'd been crying, but he pulled himself together.

"Your dad's on the phone."

His face brightened.

"He doesn't have long, one minute." She waited until Jesse wiped his face and then handed him her phone.

"Dad?"

"Jess? Hey, I'm okay. I promise."

"This sucks. This really sucks."

"I know, buddy. But I have the best lawyer in Texas with me. I need you to be strong and do exactly what Lucy and Nate say, okay?"

"I will, but are you going to be okay?"

"Yes. It'll look really bad if anything happens to me."

"That's not funny."

"I'm sorry. Yeah, I'm okay. I really am. I don't like this, I'll be honest, but I'm okay. I didn't kill her."

"I know."

"The truth will come out. But you have to be diligent at all times because someone is framing me."

"I promise, Dad. I'll be careful."

"I know you will. I love you, Jess."

"Love you, Dad." His voice cracked and he handed the phone to Lucy.

"I mean it, Sean—stay alive. We need you."

"Right back at you, princess."

The call ended.

"Thank you," Jesse said.

She hugged him, then she left and went to her room. She wanted to scream, but didn't. She swallowed it back, closed her eyes . . . and felt nothing.

No, that wasn't true. She felt everything too deeply. Rage. Love. Fear.

She couldn't afford to cry.

So she buried everything. Every emotion that threatened to take control.

The only way she could survive this—to prove Sean's innocence, to find Brad Donnelly, to remove the cloud over Nate—was to think like the people responsible. *Why?* Why was this happening? Revenge? Something more sinister? Maybe this was all to distract them from a darker plan.

If she was going to figure this out, she couldn't allow her own emotions to interfere. No emotions, no distractions, just a game plan.

The first thing she needed to do was meet with Elise Hunt's warden.

She went back to Jesse's room. "I need to follow up on a lead. I don't know when Nate will be here, but do not let anyone in, understand? Nate has the codes to the house. If anyone other than Nate comes, call me, then call 911. If the person is threatening in any way, call 911 and get to the panic room." After the house had been invaded last year Sean had a panic room installed. It was behind a false wall and could be accessed from downstairs or upstairs. Even the police hadn't found it. It wasn't large—downstairs was the size of a small closet with a ladder that went up to a ten-by-seven-inch space that stored weapons, a satellite phone, and rations for a week. Just in case.

Yes, Sean had gotten a bit paranoid, but if they needed it, they wouldn't think about that. They would know he had the foresight to protect his family.

Jesse hugged her. "Be careful. I don't want to lose another mom."

Jesse had never called her mom. He'd only lost his mother last year, and she didn't expect him to embrace her as a replacement. They had a good relationship, one she respected and cultivated. But for the first time, she thought of Jesse as her son. Not Sean's son, or her stepson, but *her* son.

She had to protect him with everything she had.

She didn't know if she was doing the right thing, but the only way she could truly protect Jesse was to find out who had framed Sean.

"I love you, Jesse. We'll get through this."

She went downstairs. Garrett was working at the dining-room table.

She said, "I'm going to the juvenile detention facility where Elise was housed. I'd like you to stay here with Jesse, but because I don't know exactly what's going on out there, I thought I could use the backup if you'd like to join me."

"I don't think you should leave."

"That's not an option. Are you going to stay here or come with me? The house is secure; Jesse is safer here than anywhere."

He closed his laptop. "Your brother would kill me if I let you go out alone, especially after what happened to Agent Donnelly."

Chapter Thirteen

Felicity put it on the record that she was filing a complaint about how the detectives had handled this case. She laid out the fact that Sean had high government security clearance, a wife and son, that his wife and sister-in-law were federal agents.

"You didn't have to arrest him. You have no case, only circumstantial evidence."

Mendez gave Felicity a half smile and shook her head as if the lawyer was a fool. From the beginning, there was something about Mendez that had Sean's instincts riled. She hated him, and it wasn't just because she thought he'd killed a woman. There was something deeper there, and he had no idea what or why—if they had any people in common, crossed paths and he didn't remember her.

Banner said, "Ms. Duncan, your client has the means to disappear and I am confident that I have the right man."

"Then why even question me?" Sean said. "Convict me and be done with it."

Felicity put her hand on his arm. He knew he shouldn't speak, and he knew that he shouldn't let his anger get the better of him. Now Banner knew how to get under his skin.

Felicity had told him to wait before answering any

question and not to speak unless asked a question. She told him to look at her first, get her nod before answering. It didn't matter, she said, if he knew she'd okay the answer, just that it was a way to slow things down and not say something in the heat of the moment that could be taken out of context.

They went over a bunch of preliminary questions that were irritating, but at least normal, so Sean found himself in a rhythm.

Banner asked, "Did you visit Mona Hill on Monday?"

Sean paused, forced himself to take a breath. Looked at Felicity. Now they were getting into it. "Yes," he said.

"What time did you get to her apartment and what time did you leave?"

Again, he paused, looked at Felicity, answered. "I arrived about six thirty, take or leave a few minutes. I don't know the exact time—I landed at five forty-five at the executive airport outside Houston."

Felicity tapped her pen once. Dammit, he was giving information they hadn't asked for.

"And what time did you leave her apartment?"

"It was just after eight P.M."

"How can you be certain?"

"I'm not certain, I said it was after eight P.M." He paused, looked at Felicity, then leaned over to whisper in her ear. "I have an Uber receipt for both trips."

She nodded.

"I took an Uber to and from the airport, the exact times will be on my receipt."

Banner made a note.

"Why did you visit Ms. Hill in the first place?"

Sean didn't answer. He looked at Felicity. She motioned for him to lean in, which he did.

"Tell the truth," she whispered. "It's a legitimate reason."

He didn't want to. But they might be able to learn the truth, and any lie would be impossible to prove.

"Ms. Hill called and told me that she had been threatened by a woman we both know and she wanted my advice."

Banner hid his surprise at Sean's answer, but not well enough. It's why Sean's friends in college hated playing poker with him—everyone had a tell, and Sean was very good at identifying them.

"Who threatened Ms. Hill?"

"Elise Hunt. Also known as Elise Hansen. She was released from jail three weeks ago and Mona saw her twice over the weekend, then found an unsigned note inside her apartment that she believed was from Hunt."

"Do you have that note?"

"No."

"Convenient," Mendez said.

"I told her to take it to the police," Sean snapped.

Felicity tapped.

Banner said, "What did the note say?"

"I took a picture of it. It's on my phone, I don't remember it verbatim. But it was clearly a death threat and signed, 'Your Worst Nightmare.'"

"How did you know that it was from Elise Hunt if it wasn't signed?"

"Mona told me she saw Elise in the lobby of her apartment the day before she received the note. The tone was similar to how Elise talked. Mona had no doubt that it was from her."

"What about you?"

"Relevance," Felicity said. "We've established that my client, a licensed private investigator and computer security specialist, was called in as an expert to offer advice to Ms. Hill on how to proceed after she received a threatening note."

Banner asked Sean, "What did you tell Ms. Hill to do?"

It was clear in how he asked that he didn't care what the answer was, because anything Sean said was irrelevant to the murder.

Sean glanced at Felicity, who nodded, and Sean said, "I told her to go to the police."

"Did she?"

"I don't know. She wasn't inclined to because she didn't trust the police—except for one officer who used her services."

"You're not going to rile me, Mr. Rogan."

"I'll telling you what she told me."

"Name."

"She didn't tell me."

"That's also convenient," Banner said.

Sean didn't smile, even though he enjoyed getting under Banner's skin. He was in no humor, and he just wanted to go home and protect his family.

Because he'd had all day to think about what had happened on Monday, and he now fully believed that Elise Hunt was somehow behind this, which meant Lucy was in danger.

"Did she call that alleged officer?"

"Not in my presence."

"Did you give her any other advice?"

"She informed me that she had a firearm on the property, and that she would contact a bodyguard she'd hired in the past. I suggested she contact him before I left and have him with her twenty-four seven until I could verify the threat."

"How were you planning on verifying the threat?"

He didn't answer.

"Relevance?" Felicity asked.

"Mr. Rogan, you have a nice, neat little story, but Ms. Hill was killed before her bodyguard arrived. Very tight window from when you left to when her bodyguard arrived. If she was so worried about this alleged threat, why didn't you stay with her until he arrived?"

Sean didn't answer. He didn't look at Felicity because he knew she'd want him to answer the question, but he didn't.

Mona had pissed him off and he'd walked out. But no fucking *way* was he telling the cops what she'd said, and he wasn't going to lie.

The cop stared at him for a long time. But Sean was even better at the waiting game. He wasn't going to be bullied by an arrogant cop who thought he had all the answers. He also knew that the best way for a cop to get a suspect to talk was to remain silent. Far too many people had to fill the silence with bullshit.

Sean wasn't one of them.

A full minute later, Felicity said, "If that's it? You have nothing, John. And you know it."

Mendez spoke. "How do you know Mona Hill?"

Sean didn't answer.

Banner said, "It's a valid question. She's in Houston, you're in San Antonio."

Sean didn't answer.

"We know that Ms. Hill lived in San Antonio for ten years before she moved to Houston, leaving town about six months after you moved there. In the six months that you and Ms. Hill both lived in San Antonio, did your paths ever cross?"

He didn't answer.

"Why did she call you, Mr. Rogan? Out of all the people in Texas, why *you*?"

"I told you. She believed the threat came from Elise Hunt, who I also know."

"But why *you*?"

He didn't answer.

"What did you plan to do? When Ms. Hill gave you this information, what was your next step?"

He glanced at Felicity, but not because he wasn't going to answer. But because he wasn't sure he *should* answer. Except . . . if they got his phone records and talked to Nico, they could easily find out. She nodded, but he still considered how to frame his response.

He finally said, "After I left Mona, on my way back to the airport, I called a private investigator I know in Los Angeles and asked him to locate Elise Hunt and confirm that she was still in L.A."

"Still? So you were tracking her even *before* Ms. Hill asked you to?" Banner made it sound like a crime.

"My wife was notified when Elise was released from juvenile detention three weeks ago. She was told that Elise was being flown to Los Angeles, where she had inherited property from her family—the only property that wasn't confiscated under asset forfeiture laws." That was a fact that Sean didn't have to mention, but it was relevant to the situation and would lend credence to Mona's fear of the teenager.

It was clear that Banner had no idea who Elise was or why this was important. He had a mostly good poker face, but Mendez didn't—and they exchanged a look that had Sean knowing they were completely in the dark—but they didn't care. The only reason they *might* care was because it was a fact they didn't know and hadn't considered, or that this might be connected to a federal investigation.

"What did your private investigator tell you?" Banner said.

"That's confidential," Sean said.

"So, you want us to believe that Ms. Hill hired you to find this Elise Hunt but you won't give us your alibi?"

"My client is not stating that Elise or the PI can give him an alibi," Felicity said.

"How do we know you even called the PI?"

"I can give you his name and contact information," Sean said.

Felicity put her hand on Sean's arm. "What else, John? You don't have anything solid against my client. You know it, I know it. You need to release him."

"I'm not done," Banner said.

"We are," Felicity said. "Unless you have solid physical evidence that my client killed Mona Hill, you arrested him without cause. Believe me, I will take it up with the court."

"We know he was in her apartment near time of death. We know that she was murdered—shot twice, once in the chest and once in the back as she tried to run. We know that the first shot was close range—less than ten feet. The .45 we retrieved from Mr. Rogan's plane has been recently fired, and we're rushing ballistics but as you know, it'll take a couple days. Mr. Rogan has the money and talent to flee the country, and I'm not giving him that opportunity."

"I didn't kill her," Sean said.

"We found no 'threatening note' in her apartment," Mendez said, her voice unnecessarily snide.

"I'll show you the image on my phone."

"You could have written it yourself," she snapped. "You have not answered my question. How do you know Mona? Were you one of her clients in San Antonio? Is that why she called you?"

Sean noticed that Banner winced at that comment. They had clearly thought it, discussed it, but he hadn't wanted Mendez to say anything.

He remained calm, or tried to. In a firm voice he said, "No."

"Then how did you know her?"

He didn't respond.

He had told Felicity about the first time he met Mona Hill, and she agreed with him that it wouldn't look good if he admitted it.

"If you're asked in court, under oath, you'll need to tell the truth, but during interrogation you don't need to answer."

"John, all you have established is that my client was with the victim prior to her murder. You don't have any evidence that he killed her."

Banner asked Sean, "Our witness claimed that he heard a male voice arguing with Ms. Hill when she called him just before seven thirty. He stated that she mentioned the name Rogan. You have already indicated that you were with her at that time. Was that you and Ms. Hill arguing?"

"It may have been."

"What did you argue about?"

"I told you."

"Remind me."

"I told her to call the police because of the threat. To put it on the record. We went back and forth about that for a bit, I think I convinced her. It was during that time that she called her bodyguard."

"You're claiming that Mona hired you to find this person yet you didn't know she was dead? You never contacted her with an update in four days?"

"I never said Mona *hired* me. I said she asked for my help, and Elise Hunt is a common threat. I told Mona if she received another threat or saw Elise to call me. I reiterated that she needed to tell the police to get the threat on record, and that she needed a bodyguard."

"You expect us to believe that you," Mendez said, "out of the kindness of your heart were helping a prostitute?"

Mendez was angry. Bitter. The way she spat out "prostitute" . . . there was something there, but Sean couldn't figure it out.

"I have nothing else to say," Sean said.

"We have more questions," Banner said.

Felicity motioned for Sean to lean over. "Let them ask, they don't have anything. Don't give them anything. Keep your cool. I'm working on this, okay?"

So Sean answered their questions—the ones that were relevant—over and over. They were asking the same thing in different ways, trying to get him to slip up, to contradict himself. But now that he realized they had shit, he didn't give them anything extra.

Thirty minutes later, a clerk came in with a file and handed it to a very frustrated Banner. He opened it, looked inside. At first Sean thought that this was a ploy—that he'd pretend it was the ballistics report or something incriminating.

Banner looked at him and said, "A rag was found with the gun we found in your plane. That rag had what appeared to be blood. I now have that confirmed. It's the same blood type as Mona Hill's. This is all I need to fry you, Rogan."

Sean had had it. "Do you think if I had killed *anyone* that I would keep the fucking *gun* and *bloody rag* on my property?"

Felicity put her hand on his arm. He bit back his next comment, but he could see the frame job as clear as day.

"I think," Banner said, "that if you were angry, Mr. Rogan, you arc capable of anything."

"You idiot. I'm being set up!"

"Sean—" Felicity said.

Banner interrupted. "Every man and woman I've arrested has told me, in the face of hard physical evidence, that they're being framed. That someone's out to get them."

He clenched his teeth. He needed to get out of here. He felt trapped.

"You were a client, weren't you?" Mendez said. "Traveled all the way to Houston so your wife wouldn't find out? And you killed her when she threatened you, threatened to tell your wife. Maybe she was blackmailing you, and you snapped."

Sean stared at her and did not respond. That's what they thought? *That* was their theory?

"I'm done," he said.

"We've been in here for three hours," Felicity said. "Give us a fifteen-minute break."

Banner didn't want to leave, and he was angry with Mendez. Good. He should be. He grabbed his file and walked out.

Felicity made sure the recording was off and said, "Sean, you need to pull it together."

"That's their theory? That I was being blackmailed by a prostitute? I'm not going to entertain that fucking idea."

"And your anger is going to be taken as a sign of guilt."

"You think if your husband"—he gestured to her wedding ring—"was accused of hiring a prostitute that he would just laugh it off? Or would he want to deck the accuser?"

"I understand that your reaction is normal, but you need to dial it back, okay?"

"They're not going to let me out tonight, you and I both know it."

"Finding Mona's blood in your plane gives them the evidence they need."

"They didn't have it when they arrested me."

"They would have. They were thinking they were in the process of getting a warrant. I agree they jumped the gun, but thinking as they were, they thought you might be able to destroy the evidence or that you might run if you heard they were searching your plane. Their gamble paid off."

He stared at her. "You're a defense lawyer. You have defended guilty people and innocent people. I have a lot of respect for defense lawyers because I know that the system doesn't always work, that cops get an idea in their head and the only person on your side is the lawyer to defend your rights. I know that there are some innocent people in prison, as well as the guilty. But I'm only going to tell you this one more time, Felicity: I did not kill Mona Hill. Whoever killed her, planted the gun and the rag in my plane. Elise Hunt is behind this—whether she pulled the trigger or not. My family is in danger, which is why this is happening. My wife. My son. My brother. I don't think you understand what the Hunt family is capable of!"

"Don't raise your voice, Sean," Felicity said. "Especially not to me. I am on your side."

He bit back his anger. He hadn't meant to yell, but he was so damn frustrated he could cry. "I'm sorry."

She let out a long breath. "I understand what you're going through. The physical evidence is difficult for us, but it's not insurmountable. The airfield where you store your plane isn't secure, there isn't staff on site twenty-four hours a day."

Sean felt so trapped. He had no control, and Felicity was his only line to the outside.

"One weekend, Sean. They don't have enough to stop you from posting bond. I will fight tooth and nail for you. We'll agree to an ankle monitor if we have to. Or house arrest. One weekend. Less than seventy-two hours."

She was trying to make him feel better, but it wasn't working.

He had a sick feeling he wouldn't be alive in seventy-two hours. He didn't kill Mona, but someone had wanted him arrested. They'd done everything to ensure it.

"When they come back, give them brief yes or no

questions whenever possible. Do not offer anything, and don't let them get under your skin again, okay? They want you to get angry, because they think you'll slip up, admit to a crime or contradict yourself."

"I need to make something very clear," he said, keeping his voice low for fear of snapping at Felicity again. It wasn't the lawyer's fault someone framed him. "Everyone I love is in danger right now and I'm stuck here and can't protect them. It's killing me. If anything happens to Lucy—to my son—I just, dammit!" Tears threatened. Tears of rage, of frustration. Sean had always been the problem solver. He'd always been able to fix things. Computers. Cars. Situations. It's what he did. He was compelled to, probably because of some deep psychological reason stemming from his childhood, but he didn't care . . . all he knew was that he couldn't fix this. He couldn't prove his innocence. He had to rely on others to do so.

He trusted Lucy . . . but how involved could she be? He trusted Nate, but Nate had his own problems right now. Jack . . . yes, Jack would move heaven and earth to fix this, but what if he couldn't find Kane and get back in time? What if there was all this circumstantial evidence and he was forced to go to trial? Would he survive that long? It would tear apart his family—the family he'd painstakingly built. Jesse . . . would Jesse still believe him? Would anyone?

Someone had killed Mona Hill in the twenty-five minutes between when he left and her bodyguard arrived.

But the police thought she was dead before he walked out her door.

"Let me do my job," Felicity said. "I'm very good at it. I have one of the best investigators in the state working for me. I know you want this all to go away on Monday, and I'll do what I can, but barring proof of your innocence or another suspect—we'll still need to work this like any other capital case."

His stomach lurched.

Capital case.

Death penalty.

"They're probably going to offer you life in prison in exchange for a confession."

"I'm not confessing to a crime I didn't commit."

"I just want you to be prepared. Because if this goes to trial—"

"It's not."

"If it does," she said, "your life will be an open book."

"Then you're not good at your job, because I didn't kill her."

But Felicity was right. If it went to trial, he would lose everything . . . even if he was proven not guilty.

Chapter Fourteen

Garrett thought it was a bad idea for Lucy to talk to Elise
Hunt's warden, but he joined her.

"You can't investigate this murder."

"I'm not," she said. He knew it was a lie, but she was
glad he didn't call her on it. She was the only one who
could do this. No one in law enforcement was going to
believe—with maybe the exception of Tia Mancini—that
Elise Hunt was a dangerous sociopath. The detectives in
Houston weren't going to talk to her warden, the guards
in her dorm, her friends. They weren't going to bring her
in for questioning by a trained forensic psychiatrist. Lucy
needed evidence, and this was the place to start.

"Sean said that Mona received a threat from Elise. The
police won't understand the significance."

"Unless her prints are all over it, it's likely untraceable."

"We don't know, because we don't have the note. Do
the police have it? I suppose that's something Felicity can
find out once Sean talks to them."

Garrett leaned back in the passenger seat, but she noticed that his eyes were constantly looking around, not
just behind them, but at every intersection.

"You were a cop?"

"Fifteen years. Here in San Antonio."

"Too few to retire."

"My knee was shot out during a hostage situation. A year of rehab and PT and I still can't run and going up stairs is hell. Went to law school, but hated it. I passed the bar, but much prefer being an investigator. So I'm a lawyer, but other than trying to protect my firm's clients during situations like warrant searches, I much prefer working the investigative end."

"It doesn't pay as well as being a lawyer."

"If you weren't an FBI agent, if you couldn't do it because of an injury, what would you want to do?"

"Be a CSI."

"That doesn't pay as much as the feds, does it?"

"No, unless you run the lab. Which I would — eventually."

"I like your confidence." He was looking in the side-view mirror.

"SAPD is still following us, aren't they?"

"Yep."

It made her angry; she quashed that feeling down quickly. She couldn't afford the anger; she couldn't afford any emotion clouding her judgment. She also couldn't lose them without breaking the law, and she didn't want to give them a reason to pull her over.

"It would help if you could do some research for me while I drive," Lucy said. "Do you know the warden, Kathy Pine?"

"No." He pulled out his smartphone and looked up the juvenile detention facility. Lucy knew where it was.

"I've met her once briefly, when she gave a report to a joint gang task force," Lucy said. "Back when I was working with Brad on active warrants. She's smart, she's been in this business for a long time, I don't even think Elise Hunt could bullshit her."

"Would she have had much interaction with Elise?"

"I don't know. I only know a little about her management style. What little I heard, I liked."

Garrett found an article and skimmed it, then summarized it for Lucy. "Her philosophy is based on mentorship," he said. "She works to get these girls out of the cycle they've found themselves in so they don't land in prison once they're out of juvie. She makes a point to know their histories, so when they're released she can match them with employers or school programs or rehab centers or whatever they need. But the biggest problem is the gangs, and it's hard to get the kids out once they've joined."

"True," Lucy concurred. "It's really hard when you have old friends trying to pull you back in."

Garrett nodded. "They often don't have parents, or their parents are in prison or part of the drug culture."

"Elise isn't a gangbanger, but she would join if she needed something from them." Like stealing sixteen kilos of coke to plant on a federal agent. That sounded like Elise, the type of grand, bold plan that was as much a crime as theatrics.

Garrett said, "Pine sounds like the real deal—she's tough when she needs to be, but believes in second chances. Since she's been here—five years next month—the recidivism rate has dropped nearly in half, staff retention is high, and the percentage of eligible girls getting their GED before leaving is a hundred percent."

"That's—wow."

"If you're eligible for a GED and earn it, you can reduce your time with court approval. So instead of getting out at eighteen, you can get out at seventeen if you apply yourself, do your work, pass the test. Definitely gives them a leg up."

Lucy ignored the SAPD officer who parked on the

street next to the administrative parking lot of the detention center, and entered the building.

She didn't have an appointment, but talked herself and Garrett into Kathy Pine's office. It took nearly twenty minutes, but then the warden called her in.

"I remember you, Agent Kincaid," Kathy said. "You came to my presentation for the joint gang task force."

"Good memory."

"You had good questions. You said your husband had an appointment with me this morning. That would be Sean Rogan?"

"Yes. He's sorry he couldn't make it and was unable to call." She decided not to mention he'd been arrested. "I tried to get here earlier."

"I told him over the phone that I couldn't give out information about Elise Hunt or anyone else here, but he insisted on meeting. Wanted to show me a threatening letter that Elise sent to someone. Do you have it?"

"No. It was sent to a woman who has been since murdered. I testified against Elise."

"Yes—I remember reading your name in the files."

"And I felt she should have been tried for crimes as an adult, including racketeering, kidnapping, accessory to murder, murder, unlawful imprisonment, and escaping from custody."

"Serious charges."

"Of which I am certain she was guilty, but we'll never know because she pled to lesser charges and was sent here. Elise is a game player, and she manipulated the court-appointed psychiatrist."

"Her files were sealed when she turned eighteen and was subsequently released. They will be expunged when she's twenty-one if she maintains a clean record."

That was news to Lucy. "I thought they were already expunged."

"No. Those were the terms of her release."

Lucy hadn't known, though she didn't know how it might help her. "But she's not on probation."

"Not exactly."

"You're going to have to explain."

Kathy chose her words carefully. "There are times when the court will listen to the warden in cases with unusual circumstances."

"And you spoke against her?"

"I spoke to certain circumstances where I felt Ms. Hunt might not be rehabilitated to the standard we have become known for," Pine said carefully. "If she steps out of line, her files can be opened by law enforcement with court approval."

"What did she do to merit such untraditional probation?"

Pine was clearly weighing how much to tell Lucy. "Well, the terms are public record, so I'm not talking out of line by telling you that. However, the reasons are confidential and sealed. If you suspect Ms. Hunt of a crime, you can petition the court to unseal them."

Lucy tried another approach. "What *can* you tell me about Elise's time here? Were there problems?"

"I can say that Ms. Hunt's time here wasn't challenge free."

That wasn't helpful. "Would you let me talk to the guard who had the most contact with her?"

"Even if I did, she wouldn't be allowed to share anything." Kathy hesitated. "I will tell you this only because I couldn't prove it and thus it's not sealed. It's my personal belief—opinion—not anything I would swear to in court. I believe Ms. Hunt found a way to sneak out. Not impossible, I'm certain—we are a minimum security facility—but I never figured out how she did it."

"Why do you think so?"

"She had items that she couldn't have gotten in here. Especially since she had no visitors and no mail in the almost two years she was here."

"None?"

"Only her court-appointed psychiatrist, who came once a week. And as far as I know, she never gave Elise anything. I know that the girls can smuggle items in here—they smuggle makeup, weapons, drugs, food—but one day Elise came to class with her hair dyed. Not just dyed, but professionally done. Highlights, cut—and she sported a new tattoo. She had one coming in, on the small of her back. This was on her arm. And it was clearly new and professional. It's like she went out and had her own spa day."

"And someone in here couldn't have done it?"

"Not that level of quality. These were two different days, about two weeks apart. I questioned her and she didn't budge. Lied to my face that she did her hair herself, that one of the girls—she wouldn't say who because she said she wasn't a snitch—gave her a kit. Even a top hair professional couldn't have done that good of a job on themselves. I questioned the tattoo and she said another girl did it—and did give me her name. And it is a girl who has given tats to the girls, even though she's been forbidden to do so. But the girl's quality is far inferior to what Elise was sporting. I questioned the girl, and she lied to me. I felt in my gut that she didn't care if I knew she was lying. My best guess is that Elise left at lights out and returned at shift change, which is right before we get the girls up. She had eight hours to do whatever she wanted."

"Why did she come back?" Lucy asked, almost to herself.

"I wouldn't know."

"Could one of the guards have been helping her?"

"I questioned all of them. I believed them when they said they weren't helping her.

"Can I talk to them?"

"I'm not going to let you—I have privacy and legal issues to worry about. However, there was one guard who quit and I'm positive it was because of Elise, but she didn't say so. In fact, she refused to tell me why, and Erica had been here longer than me. She was one of the best I had, dedicated, firm, but kind. I'll give you her number, maybe you can find out what went on."

"I appreciate that." She took down Erica Anderson's contact information. "Is she working at another prison?"

"I haven't heard. If that's all—I have a staff meeting in five minutes."

"Two things—was there anyone that Elise was particularly close to?"

"Elise made friends easily. But I had the sense that she made friends with people she had a purpose for. She didn't have a close friend, or someone she confided in, for example. We usually know what the hierarchy is— put a handful of teenagers in a room and by the end of the day it's pretty clear. Elise was an outlier. She wasn't in charge, but she was not a subordinate. And the tough girls didn't harass her like I expected, especially with her attitude."

"Was she friendly with anyone from the Saints? They're a defunct gang."

"I'm familiar with the gang. Yes, actually. Marie Ynez. A good kid—I mean that. She got in a bad situation because of her brother, who ended up doing serious jail time. Their time overlapped by about six months, but Marie was released before Elise. And she's doing well."

"I'd like to talk to her, see what she might know about Elise's plans."

While Kathy was clearly skeptical, she agreed. "She's

sixteen, lives in a group home, and is going to school. I don't expect to see her back here." She gave Lucy the group home number and address.

"If you can think of anything else, please call me," Lucy said. She made sure that Kathy had her contact information before they left.

As soon as they got back into the car, Garrett said, "You have a knack for getting people to talk."

"Kathy wants to do the right thing and if she could give me Elise's records, she would. At least we confirmed her Los Angeles address—and one more thing. She didn't have any visitors. Not one, other than the psychologist who testified on her behalf."

"Maybe we should talk to her. Dr. Oakley, right?"

"She won't talk to me. She refuses to see Elise as who she is. Insists that she's a terrified, abused teenager who was used by her family. Even when Oakley was confronted with the truth—that Tobias was her half brother, not the foster brother she claimed, and all the stories she told about being abused in the foster system were lies, she refused to assign any blame to Elise, claimed that the lies were Elise's way of protecting herself."

"That could be true."

"It wasn't," she snapped. "She lied about everything. She set me up to be killed. She takes pleasure in torturing people. She will say and do anything to get what she wants when she wants it—and that might be the way we get to her. Because she is young and impatient." She paused, considered everything Kathy had said. "Though the warden said Elise made no calls, criminals sneak in phones all the time. Notes could be passed to guests of other inmates. So I have to assume she had a way of communicating outside the facility."

"Reasonable," Garrett said.

"I need to talk to the corrections officer who resigned.

She might not have told Kathy why she was quitting, but I have to find a way to convince her to talk to me. And the girl from the Saints . . . that one might be harder, but I have some ideas."

Ideas that Jack wouldn't like, but Lucy didn't care because Jack wasn't here to stop her.

"Do you know what's happening with Sean?" she asked, trying to keep the emotion out of her voice.

"He's still in interrogation, as far as I know."

Keep your cool, Sean. Please. I need you back.

Aggie had never contradicted a direct order. Martin Salter was a good agent, just like she'd told Lucy, but in this case she thought he was being too cautious. He listened to her, but then dismissed her assessment that Brad's kidnapping might be related to the Hunt family and corrupt DEA agent Nicole Rollins.

Why wouldn't he have even considered that Brad's kidnapping was retribution for killing Rollins?

Aggie agreed with Lucy that all three cases were connected—probably because Brad had already planted the idea that Nate's and Sean's situations weren't a coincidence. Aggie hadn't been here during Nicole Rollins's reign of terror, but she had heard stories, not just from Brad but from the staff who had stayed on after Houston DEA cleaned house. Brad was nearly untouchable, Martin reminded her, because he had institutional knowledge coupled with his ability to close tough cases. But he was a maverick, took risks, and had more autonomy than most ASACs in the DEA.

"I know Donnelly hand-picked you and you have a strong sense of loyalty to him, but we need to be cautious and careful. Because Donnelly is a good agent, he has made a lot of enemies, and I don't want to be the one to tell your family that you're dead."

She tried to justify her decision to sit outside the SAPD waiting for Nate Dunning to emerge as not actually violating a direct order so much as not asking for permission. She'd done everything she could in the office, and they were waiting for the digital recordings from the warehouse to see if it showed anything that would be useful in tracking Donnelly's kidnappers.

She didn't want to get Zach in trouble, but she had been communicating with him, and he seemed to want to help. He'd been told to steer clear of Sean and Lucy, but given no orders related to Nate, so they were playing the "better to ask for forgiveness than permission" approach. He sent her photos the crime scene investigators had taken of the drugs on site. Nate's vehicle had been impounded and the drugs were at the crime lab pending verification.

Most work sent to the lab on a Friday wouldn't be dealt with until next week, if then. The Bexar County crime lab handled multiple different law enforcement jurisdictions and was one of the best in the state, but like any lab, they were backlogged. Nate was going to be without his truck for at least three days, if not longer.

It was after four that afternoon when Nate emerged from the facility. Aggie watched in her mirror as Nate listened to Rachel Vaughn, his direct supervisor. Nate wasn't speaking. Rachel was clearly emphatic about something, but Aggie couldn't read lips. A minute later, Nate turned and walked directly toward her small truck. He looked angry. Aggie froze as Rachel watched him approach her pickup. Had he told her that Aggie was picking him up? Did Rachel remember who she was? Would she think it was weird? Aggie had only met her twice, but she didn't want her to call Martin and rat her out.

Nate opened the passenger door and got in. "Thanks,"

he mumbled. When she didn't immediately drive, he said, "Go. Now."

She turned the ignition and sped off. She always drove too fast, but she'd been taught by her oldest brother, the cop, and she had to keep up with her siblings. She, at least, had only gotten one ticket—each of her brothers had more than three before they were twenty-one. She certainly wasn't the one who forced their parents' auto insurance rates to go up.

Truth be told, she had talked her way out of many more tickets. Was it her fault she was young, cute, and sassy?

"What do you know about Donnelly?" he asked. "Zach told me he was grabbed outside DEA headquarters four hours ago. I've been fucking fighting with SAPD all day to let me leave."

"What do I need to know?"

He glared at her, then looked back out the window.

"You don't know me well, but Brad asked *me* to help him with *your* case. No one else. Brad trusts me, you need to trust me."

He turned to her and almost looked . . . amused. "Need?" Maybe if he hadn't just spent most of the day being interviewed by SAPD he would have laughed.

"How about, you should trust me. I've been talking to Lucy—she's the toughest person I know. Considering what she's dealing with right now, she had a lot of great information."

"Like?"

She realized Nate wasn't going to trust her until she proved herself to him. So she told him what Lucy said about Elise Hunt, what Brad had wanted her to do, and that Zach was helping on the q.t.

He was thinking. He had a blank face, but he looked just like her brother Dave—who was career military— when he was deep in thought.

"Did you get the security footage outside DEA?"

"We looked at everything on our cameras, but Brad was grabbed out of range. We're tracking down private security now. If Salter calls, I'm going to have to hightail it back to the office. But so far, nada." She glanced at him, told him the rest. About the Merides brothers and the Saints and the shooting. "Mitts Vasquez had been a member of the Saints before it collapsed." She explained why that was important, and that the Saints had worked for Nicole Rollins when she was still DEA. That it could be the connection to Elise Hunt that they needed.

"You have proof?"

"I have a theory based on the evidence. I see connections where other people don't. I look at all the data and things just move into place. And my gut tells me the drugs stolen ten days ago are the same drugs that were found in your truck."

"And you want to track down Vasquez."

"Yes, but I really want to track down the Merides brothers because they have a greater incentive to talk."

"Why the Merides?"

"They lost sixteen kilos of coke, and looking at the pictures from SAPD it hasn't been cut yet—which means it's probably worth a helluva lot more than a quarter mil."

"They're not going to talk to a couple of feds."

"Don't be so sure."

"You're not going to waltz in and have them eating out of your hand because you bat your eyes or flash your dimples. You'll get yourself killed. I can't let you do that."

"Let me?" She laughed as she smoothly passed a minivan that was doing a turtle's pace. Damn driver was going to get rear-ended one of these days.

"Those aren't my drugs and I'm not going to prison over this. SAPD are just being assholes."

"Technically, they're doing their job."

He growled.

"Look—we need to find these people not just to prove that the drugs were taken from them, but to find Brad."

"Now you lost me."

"The Merides brothers know who stole from them. They're looking for Vasquez as well. Whoever stole the drugs are most likely the same group of people who grabbed Brad—because *if* this is all orchestrated by Elise Hunt, that means that her people stole the drugs, planted them on you to take you out of the picture while Sean Rogan is in prison. Maybe to get you fired or arrested or hell if I know. And Brad is high on their list because he killed Rollins. Revenge? Maybe all this was planned as revenge on everyone who messed with the Hunt family."

"You are up to speed."

"I told you." She weaved in and out of traffic—she loved driving, but she hated slow drivers.

"Why not kill Brad?" he wondered out loud. "They could have easily assassinated him right there."

"I don't know," she admitted. "I said as much to Lucy and she got all quiet, then mumbled, 'There's always a reason.'"

Nate didn't comment.

She pulled off the freeway into Olmos Park, where Lucy and Sean lived.

"Why isn't Lucy in Houston?" Nate asked.

"The lawyer said she can't see Sean until tomorrow." She glanced at him; Nate was thinking again. She said, "In addition to figuring out where the drugs came from, I've been looking at how they got in your truck. I drove by your apartment—"

"How do you know where I live?" Damn, he sounded suspicious.

"Brad told me." Not exactly true, but she'd gotten

the information from Brad's office, and knew that he wouldn't mind that she did. Nate lived simply. He had a one-bedroom apartment in a borderline sketchy area of San Antonio that was convenient to FBI headquarters. "I didn't see any security cameras."

"There aren't any."

"Which tells me they easily could have planted the drugs right there. I took some pictures of your carport, and there's a couple of apartments that have a good visual of it."

"I know when they did it."

"How?"

"My truck has an alarm. No one could have planted the drugs at my apartment, not to mention they would have made noise and I'm not a heavy sleeper. The carport is right under my bedroom window."

"So where?"

"Tuesday. Three days ago. I woke up and noticed a semi-flat tire and a nail in the tread. I took it to a tire place near my apartment, Lucy picked me up there because we had a case. They replaced all four tires because I was due anyway. I didn't think anything of it, but I'd never been there before. Yet, they couldn't have known that's where I would take my truck."

"They followed you."

"I don't get followed."

"You said it was near your apartment. They wouldn't have been on your tail long. They could have put in a tracker. And they probably put the nail in your tire."

He didn't say anything.

"After Lucy's, we'll go over there. And I have a couple ideas where Mitts might be hiding out.

"I'll take care of this. You don't need to be involved."

Now she was getting angry. "I *am* involved. Brad

tasked *me* with clearing your name, I'm not going to let him down. And by tracing these drugs, we'll be on the path to find Brad."

"And you want to look for the gangbanger? Don't you think that the Merides brothers will know where to look for him as well?"

"No. Because I'm not going to the obvious places. His ex-wife, his ex-girlfriend, any of the former Saints. He's going someplace where the Merides won't even think of looking for him."

Nate didn't say anything.

"I know you don't trust me yet, but you will."

"Oh?"

She pulled up in front of Lucy's place and didn't respond.

He would. When she proved herself.

That shouldn't take long.

"And where are you going to look for Vasquez?" he asked.

"Come with me, and I'll tell you."

"No way in hell am I letting an analyst go out into the field, not dealing with these people."

"What the fuck makes you think I'm an analyst?" she snapped. Then inwardly winced. If she was swearing that meant he had really gotten under her skin.

He looked at her. Really looked at her for the first time, she realized. In more than a security assessment kind of way.

"I'm a field agent, just like you, Agent Dunning. I just happen to be really good at analysis, which is a bonus as far as I'm concerned, making me an even more valuable *field agent*. And honestly, I don't need your permission to investigate. Brad is my boss, he gave me the intel, and I'm going to follow through whether you come with me or not."

* * *

Jack was angry. When he got angry, he didn't yell, which somehow made it worse—except that Lucy wasn't taking it from him.

"You should have stayed put," he said.

She was sitting at Sean's desk, alone. Garrett Lee was in the dining room working; Nate had texted her twenty minutes ago that he was on his way. And when Jack called, she'd hoped he'd found Kane and was on his way to San Antonio; unfortunately, they had lost the trail, but Ranger was out talking to a source.

What Lucy shouldn't have done was tell him what she'd learned. Except that she'd wanted information, and that meant telling Jack what she knew.

"It was vital I find out everything about Elise Hunt that I can. You know she's orchestrating this! But she can't do it alone. She's working with someone, but she didn't have any visitors. I'm going to start looking at staff connections—"

"I told you not to leave the house."

"Don't talk to me as if you're my father."

"Dammit, Lucia!"

"Don't coddle me, Jack."

"You think that's what I'm doing? *Coddling* you? I don't want you dead. Sean is in jail and Brad Donnelly is missing. Why the fuck did you let him leave your place? He was safer there!"

She felt like Jack had punched her in the stomach.

"I told you to stick with him," he continued. "You're both at risk."

She didn't back down. "Donnelly is the ASAC of the DEA. You think he's going to hide in my house all day because there's a threat?"

"There was, and he's probably dead."

That hurt.

"I'm sorry," he said, as if he could read her mind.

"Don't," she said. "Don't apologize. You think he's dead. Why?"

"I . . ." He paused, and she feared he had more information than she did. Then he said, "I think if they wanted him dead, they would have killed him on sight. It would be demoralizing to an office that has already endured a traitor who killed their boss. But I can't think why they want him alive. He's not going to talk."

Lucy needed to think like the people who grabbed Brad, but she didn't know who they were. And because she didn't know, she might get Brad killed if she read the situation all wrong.

And Jack was right. If they wanted Brad dead, he'd be dead. So why? What did they need him for?

"I know you're worried about Sean." Jack's tone softened. No one else, other than Lucy, would be able to pick up on that. "We need to be on the same page. I trust Garrett, but he's not a bodyguard. You leave, you need to be with Nate until we know what we're facing."

"Garrett is good backup. I'm a trained FBI agent. I'm going to handle this—"

"Listen to me," Jack interrupted. "Someone is taking out our team. Not killing—not yet at least—but taking us off the board. Sean. Nate. Brad. Kane. Even me because I'm down south looking for Kane. Our core. You're part of the core. I need you to be smart here."

"I am. I'm not reckless. You're have to trust me."

The alarm system beeped twice. Lucy looked at the security tablet she had open on Sean's desk; Nate and Aggie were approaching the front door.

"Nate's here. Let me know when you find Kane."

"Lucy—"

"I love you, Jack." She dropped the receiver in its cradle before Jack could say another word.

* * *

Ranger was watching Jack closely as they waited in a bar in Saltillo, Mexico. "Lock it down, Jack. We can't afford for your focus to split."

Jack didn't say anything. He should be in San Antonio keeping his sister safe.

Ranger stared at him over the bottle of beer he'd been nursing for the last hour. "Buddy."

"I'm fine." Jack sipped his beer. They were waiting for Ranger's contact. They had a lead, but needed to make sure it wasn't a trap.

Hell, even if Ranger's guy said they were clear, there was no trap, Jack didn't know that he would believe it. The more he thought about Kane's disappearance, the more he thought the hostage rescue had been a setup from the beginning. A way to get Kane south of the border. RCK had been tracking Peter Blair for years. A couple of times they'd almost gotten him, but he'd become much better at covering his tracks of late. They had no confirmed sightings—only rumors—and the only time they knew he'd moved anyone was after the fact.

He'd gotten so much better at being a criminal over time.

In fact, they had no recent intel, but everything aligned this week when they got an alert about seven girls who had been grabbed three weeks ago. They'd had the girls on their radar, hoping to find them before it was too late, and one had escaped. She'd gone right to a church, and the priest there was friends with the Sisters of Mercy. Everything made sense . . . except now, in hindsight, it was too easy.

Yes, they'd rescued the remaining girls. That was a win. But at what cost?

What if they had been the bait? There were people who would be happy to release a few girls—knowing they could get more whenever they wanted—if they could lure Kane Rogan into a trap.

"He's here," Ranger said, barely moving his lips.

Jack was suspicious, but Kane was still missing, and this was their single best lead.

Chapter Fifteen

Lucy understood Jack's concerns, but she couldn't hide in her house waiting for other people to find the truth about Mona Hill's murder. The cops in charge thought Sean was guilty and they weren't looking at anyone else.

By the time she stepped out of Sean's office, Nate was already inside and Jesse was running down the stairs.

"Nate!" Jesse hugged him tightly. "I'm so glad you're here. You're going to help prove my dad didn't do this, right?"

"Of course," Nate said, though he was looking at Lucy. Nate looked as worried as Jack had sounded.

Jesse stepped back. "You all want to talk and you don't want me here."

"That's not it," Lucy said. "We have to compare notes and decide our next step. Jess—I wish I could tell you not to worry. I hate this, and I'm doing everything I can to fix it."

"I know. I—okay." He patted his leg and Bandit, who was sitting next to Nate looking up at him adoringly, immediately went to Jesse's side and followed him back upstairs.

"I'm going to wring that girl's neck," Lucy said as she watched Jesse leave. She didn't have to explain that she was talking about Elise. Jesse had been through hell over the last two years and she hated that he was now scared about Sean's fate.

Lucy made introductions to Garrett Lee. "He's an investigator and attorney with the law firm who is representing Sean."

She motioned for Aggie and Nate to sit down at the dining table. "Garrett, I need to be blunt with Nate right now. If you don't want to be part of this, you need to leave."

"I'm not leaving," he said.

"You did your job—you were here for the warrant."

"And are you going out tonight to track down that corrections officer?"

"Yes."

"Then I'll stay. I'll help, as much as I can. Jack texted me not to let you out of the house. That I can't do, but I can back you up."

"Thank you." She turned to Nate. "What happened at SAPD? Did they clear you?"

He scowled, shook his head. "The SAC himself reamed the chief of police and ultimately, I'm not being arrested, but I can't leave the county and I'm suspended pending investigation."

"Nate, I'm sorry," Lucy said.

"I want these bastards," he said. "Aggie has a theory."

Lucy listened to Aggie's analysis, and immediately when she mentioned the Saints, she said, "Elise befriended a girl, Marie Ynez. She was affiliated with the Saints."

"I thought they were all but gone," Nate said.

"They're not organized," Aggie said, "but they're around. Brad has been watching former members, it's been quiet, but that doesn't mean they aren't working for whoever will pay them. That's what I think Mitts is—for hire."

"And you know where this girl is?" Nate asked.

"Yes. I need to talk to her and to a corrections officer who spontaneously quit."

Lucy told Nate and Aggie about Elise sneaking out of the prison, and about her nontraditional probation. "Elise didn't leave just to get a tattoo and her hair done," Lucy said. "And she returned because that's part of some plan—the same plan that has Sean in jail and Brad missing and drugs planted in Nate's car."

No one disagreed with her, even though it sounded incredible.

Lucy had read Marie Yncz's file on the way back from juvie, and shared the information with the others. "Marie had a messed up life. She was sexually and physically abused, her brother and mother are in prison, her father was killed in prison, her other brother is dead. She wants out of the cycle. She's in a group home, gets good grades, and the warden doesn't think she would be involved with a crime, but I don't like the fact that Elise befriended her—especially since her brother was part of the Saints." Lucy glanced at Aggie and realized she might not be the best person to talk to Marie. "I think Aggie should talk to her."

"Why?" Nate asked.

"Because Aggie doesn't look like a cop and she's smart enough not to be manipulated."

"Thanks," Aggie said, sounding surprised. "And she might give us a lead on Mitts Vasquez."

Lucy concurred. "I would join you," she said, "but Elise may have told Marie lies about me. Elise never met Aggie."

"She's not going alone," Nate said.

"I'm right here," Aggie snapped.

"Nate, you would intimidate the girl," Lucy said.

"I'll stay in the background, but if we're dealing with anyone associated with the Hunt family, no one goes anywhere alone. They grabbed Brad—they had to know his routine, because he's too good to be followed. And they could know about Aggie, even though she's new."

Lucy frowned. Jack's words came back to her.

They took out our core.

"What?" Nate asked.

"Jack and I were talking before you arrived. He said someone is taking out our core. It's Elise and whoever is working with her. But . . . revenge isn't the motive. It's *a* motive, but this is too big and too elaborate to be the *primary* motive."

"The Hunts are crazy," Nate said bluntly. "Especially Elise. Revenge is a perfectly viable motive. And didn't Nicole plot revenge against the DEA? Just because she was found out?"

"No—I mean, yes, she did damage to the DEA out of spite, but her *primary* motive was to disrupt the system so that she could get her confiscated money. She was cold and calculating, she would never have stayed in town if she had the money to get away."

"And Elise is young and wild and it makes sense that she'd want to get back at everyone who took out her family."

Something shifted in her thoughts. "We didn't get everyone."

"What do you mean?"

"Her father. Jimmy Hunt."

"He's in prison," Nate said.

"In L.A. What do you want to bet the first thing Elise did when she landed in L.A. three weeks ago was to visit her father?"

She didn't know why she didn't think of it before, except that she hadn't been involved in the Jimmy Hunt extradition and prosecution, had never met him, didn't work any aspect of his case.

She needed to know if Elise talked to him. It might not mean anything, but if Elise and Jimmy had talked even once over the last three weeks, maybe he was the one orchestrating her moves. It made sense. She'd taken direction from Tobias, her half brother. She would be more apt to take direction from her father than coming up with something this elaborate on her own.

And maybe then it really *was* just about revenge. They had killed his wife, his niece, his son. Would he use his only living daughter to get it?

Yes . . . she thought he would. And Elise would be more than happy to do it.

"I'm going to contact the agent who was involved in that investigation," she said. "Hopefully, she can get the information first thing in the morning."

She looked at her watch. "Okay, you guys get going and we'll meet back here when we're done, no matter how late. Garrett and I are going to talk to the corrections officer who resigned." She looked at the lawyer. "I assume you're coming."

"Jack would kill me—literally—if I let you go out alone. I have to say that I feel you're interfering with a police investigation and this could come back to hurt you."

"The police aren't looking at Elise Hunt, at least not yet."

"What about Jess?" Nate said. "He shouldn't be by himself."

"Leo Proctor called earlier and said he'd help any way he could as long it wasn't about Sean's case," Lucy said. Leo was a senior agent and the SWAT team leader. He was also the lead hostage negotiator and Lucy had been working closely with him for the last year. "But can you stay for the weekend?"

"You don't even have to ask. But I'll have to deal with this drug situation if they call. I'll ask Leo if he can help if that happens."

Lucy agreed with the plan and sent Leo a message. He responded immediately. "Leo will be here in fifteen minutes. I'll wait for him, you and Aggie go talk to Marie Ynez."

She hugged Nate because she needed a friend, and he was the best friend she and Sean had here in San Antonio. Maybe ever. He was a rock and she loved him.

"Be careful," she said. "If they're watching what went down today at the courthouse, they might not like that you were released."

Nate and Aggie left, then Lucy went up to talk to Jesse. When Leo arrived, she secured the house, then she and Garrett left. This time, Garrett drove—which was fine with Lucy.

This time, the SAPD officer didn't follow them. She was about to mention it to Garrett when her phone rang.

"Kincaid."

"Lucy, it's JT. I talked to Nico, our PI in Los Angeles. He hasn't seen Elise since Wednesday afternoon."

"Forty-eight hours ago?"

"He and his team have been watching since Tuesday morning. He first laid eyes on her Tuesday afternoon. She left Wednesday morning, went to the mall, the gas station, a salon, then was home that afternoon. He confirmed she entered the property. There are two ways in and out, and they had them both covered. But since he hasn't seen her, he's been checking his surveillance film and believes she left in a delivery van that arrived Thursday morning. That's the only way she could have eluded him, unless she went out on foot in the middle of the night, which is a possibility."

"She knew she was being watched."

"I'm emailing you and Nate photos of everyone who has gone in or out of the property since Nico has been monitoring the situation. Rick is working on identifying them, but you need to keep their faces in your head. Rick is having Blair Novak go to the prison to talk to Elise's father, Jimmy Hunt. She's the agent who liaised with the DEA in extraditing Hunt from Mexico."

"Nate and I were just talking that Hunt might be behind this. How'd you think of it?"

"I didn't. Rick did. He's been on top of this. He told me you called, he knew you were upset with him."

"I shouldn't have been. He's under a lot of pressure right now—"

"No apologies. We all love Sean, Lucy. He's family. He shouldn't be going through this and we're going to get him out."

"Thank you."

"But what I really wanted to tell you is that Rick already had the prison logs checked. It helps to have the assistant director of the FBI making the calls himself. Elise Hunt visited her father the day she landed in Los Angeles, three weeks ago. It could be that he gave her marching orders, or told her what was happening. He's in prison for life, and we can make his life hell if he doesn't cooperate."

"Thank you," Lucy said.

"I don't know that we can trust anything Hunt says, but Novak is good, and she was instrumental in pulling together evidence once the FBI extradited him back to the U.S. from Mexico. So give her a chance. Megan is flying down tonight to join her."

Megan Elliott was Jack's wife, an FBI agent based in Sacramento.

"Why Megan?"

"Why? Because we're a family, blood or not, and no one is going to let either you or Sean fend for yourselves. We're going to get to the bottom of this. I promise."

JT's reassurance gave Lucy hope that they would. That by Monday, Sean would be home and they'd know who killed Mona Hill and framed him. That they'd find Brad safe, clear Nate's name, and put an end to whatever revenge plot Elise had concocted with her father.

In the back of her mind, though, she couldn't help but fear that the worst was to come.

Chapter Sixteen

While Aggie and Nate were driving to Marie Ynez's group home, she got a message from Brad's administrative assistant that Salter had the video of Brad's abduction.

"I need to make a stop," she said. "You have to stay in the car."

Nate looked at her without comment as she sped toward DEA headquarters.

"Fine, come in, I'll be suspended for disobeying Salter's orders not to get involved in your case."

"I don't need your help."

"Yes, you do," she snapped. "But go ahead, play maverick, get Marie to talk. Because she won't tell you anything, and you know it. She's a sixteen-year-old girl stuck in juvie for being forced to help one of her brother's miserable friends."

He didn't say anything, but he didn't get out of her small truck when she pulled into the parking lot.

"I won't be long. I'm going to grab a copy because Lucy or you might know one of the suspects."

She was surprised that Salter wasn't there when she walked in. It was well after five, but with Brad missing he should be here working the case. She found Rena Abrams at her desk outside Brad's office. She was one of the few people still here from before Nicole Rollins betrayed them. She'd been the staff secretary for years, and Brad promoted her to his admin when he took over the ASAC mantle. She was loyal and devoted to him, so devoted that she postponed retirement to help Brad set up the new office.

Rena had been crying; her face was red and splotchy, and the makeup she'd had on earlier in the day had been wiped away.

Aggie went over and gave her a hug. "I should have been here, but—"

"I know. You are doing what Brad told you to do."

She didn't know what to say.

"Do you think anything goes on with Agent Donnelly that I don't know about?" she snapped.

"I'm sorry, I—"

She handed her a DVD. "I made you a copy. Agent Salter is at FBI headquarters putting together a task force. I know you're working with Agent Dunning and Brad thinks highly of him."

She almost denied it, but Rena wouldn't believe her if she did. So she kept her mouth shut. "Anything happen since I left?" She'd only been gone three hours. It felt like all day.

"Agent Salter was on a conference call with Houston, they called in the FBI, we're getting all the help we need, but no one thinks he's alive. But they didn't kill him on that tape." She said it emphatically, needing to believe he was still alive even after more than six hours.

Aggie asked, "Is Martin looking for me?"

"No. He's in over his head. He's a good agent, methodical, and focused, but he's not good in a crisis, I'll leave it at that."

She took the DVD and told Rena that she would call later.

"Find Brad—but be careful."

"Ten-four," she said and left.

She told Nate what Rena said about the FBI and the task force. She grabbed her laptop from the small space behind the driver's seat, booted it up, and popped in the DVD.

Heads together, they watched the black-and-white recording. It started thirty seconds before Brad's car stopped. They couldn't see him—just the front of the car as it skidded to a stop and four masked men in black rushed the vehicle. Two had come from the direction of the warehouse and two had come from out of range, across the street. The actual abduction was mostly off-screen, with only one man visible—holding a gun on Brad's car—then two men came into view dragging a semi-unconscious, struggling Brad across the street and out of sight. Aggie thought that was it, then ten seconds later a black windowless van flashed by. It turned up the street directly across from the camera. She couldn't read the license plate, but it was visible. With enhancement they should get the numbers.

As if Nate knew what she was going to say, he said, "The FBI will be all over the plates and tracking it. I'll call Zach and see if he'll give me the information. But this confirms that Brad was alive when they took him."

The van turned right at the intersection, a small dot now on the camera. She closed her laptop and slid it back behind her seat.

She had nothing to say. Seeing Brad manhandled like that disturbed her. She was an agent, she'd gone through training, she'd been Tasered and shot with pepper spray and put into a variety of scenarios so she'd know what to expect if it happened to her.

But seeing a friend—a mentor—dragged away like a sack of potatoes, they couldn't prepare you for that.

She sped out of the parking lot, going faster than even she usually drove, trying to work through the frustration. Nate, fortunately, didn't comment, nor did he grab the chicken stick.

She was beginning to like him.

Okay, she'd always liked him, but she was glad he was with her now because she didn't know what to expect. While she was confident she could handle most anything thrown at her, she feared Brad was dead. That they wouldn't find him in time.

She drove to the group home, south of downtown, in an older neighborhood that looked nice, but bordered one of the highest crime precincts in the city. If she were running a group home, she wouldn't put it in walking distance to a big drug center. But the house itself was well-maintained, clean, with a lawn and wide porch. It looked homey and safe.

Coming here was iffy. Lucy had given her all the information about Marie Ynez, but if the director of the home didn't allow them to speak to her, they didn't have a warrant or even an active investigation. She had to wing it.

She said to Nate, "Go with me on this."

"I'll follow your lead," he said. "But if I say jump, you jump as high as you can, understand?"

She blinked. She wasn't quite sure what to make of his comment. "O-kay," she said slowly.

He said, "I have your back, Aggie. Take lead, but I have to know that you'll do what I say if I see a threat."

That she understood. Nate might not trust her—yet—but she trusted him.

It was a start.

She rang the bell. Less than a minute later a teenager answered the door. "May I help you?" she said, though she didn't open the locked screen.

Aggie showed her badge. "I'm Agent Jensen with the Drug Enforcement Agency. I'd like to speak with Hannah O'Dell or Rose Hernandez."

"One moment, please."

The girl didn't seem scared or worried. Based on Lucy's notes, there were twelve girls between the ages of thirteen and eighteen who lived here at any one time. Hannah and Rose were licensed social workers who ran the home through a private nonprofit and contracted to the city. They had a solid record and only three of their charges had gotten into trouble with the law within a year of living here—and none while they were in the program. Out of more than one hundred ten girls who had gone through this house, those were terrific numbers.

A moment later, the door opened and a petite Hispanic woman who looked younger than Aggie answered. "I'm Rose Hernandez," she said as she stepped out. She closed the door behind her. "May I please see your badge?"

Aggie showed her badge and identification. Nate had his ID, but because of his suspension he didn't have a badge. He showed his ID, and the woman didn't ask for more.

"How can I help you?"

"We'd like to speak with Marie Ynez."

"Regarding?"

"When she was in juvie, she was roommates with a girl named Elise Hunt. Elise aged out three weeks ago, and is now wanted for questioning. We haven't been able to locate her at the address on file, and the warden indicated that Elise had become friendly with Marie. We're hoping that Marie might help us find her, and might have additional information regarding Elise's plans."

"I don't understand," Rose said. "What plans?"

The woman was not going to be a pushover.

Aggie remembered something Lucy had told her

months ago. *"Be honest, as much as you can. People know when you're lying to them, and they're not going to help if they think they're being played."*

"Elise is the younger sister of Nicole Rollins, a former DEA agent who was working with the cartels. Rollins murdered my boss." Slight fib—she'd still been at the academy at the time. "Rollins was shot and killed after her escape from prison, and Elise was arrested at that time. We have information that Elise may be seeking revenge on certain law enforcement officers in the DEA and the FBI who were involved in the operation that ultimately ended in Rollins's death. We can't find her, and we're concerned because a DEA agent is missing."

All of that was true. Rose looked concerned, but she also wanted to protect her young charge.

"What do you think Marie can help you with?"

"Warden Pine indicated that Elise and Marie were close while they shared a room. We don't think that Marie is involved in any way, but we're hoping that Elise might have shared information with her. Any information can help. We're on a clock, and fear for our agent's life."

Rose looked from Aggie to Nate, then settled on Aggie. "I'll let you speak with her, provided that I am present, though this is unusual. Usually when law enforcement wants to talk to one of our students they request an interview and we schedule it."

"I would have gone through proper channels except that this is extremely time sensitive because a federal agent's life is in immediate danger."

"All right. And Agent Dunning I hope you don't take offense to this, but I would appreciate if you could wait out here. Marie has been sexually and physically abused for most of her life and your presence would unduly intimidate her. Not just Marie, but several of the girls here have been sexually abused, and this is a safe place for them. For some, the only safe home they have ever known. We don't allow men inside."

"No offense taken, ma'am, I will wait out here."

"Thank you."

Rose led Aggie inside.

The house smelled of stew and cinnamon and Aggie smiled. "Are you making apple pie?"

"Two of our girls love baking. We encourage them to pursue what interests them. But the stew is my mother's recipe. Feeding a house of fourteen isn't easy, but I have nine brothers and sisters, so I have a handle on the kitchen."

"The warden sang your praises," Aggie said.

"Kathy is one of the reasons we're successful. She finds us the girls who need us the most. Marie was one. She's been here for three months, and already I see how much she has improved."

They walked to the back of the house, where a small room had been converted to an office. "Please wait here."

A moment later, Rose returned with a tall, underweight girl with very short hair and big brown eyes. "Marie, this is Agent Jensen with the DEA. She has some questions for you about one of your roommates at juvenile detention. You are not in any trouble, and I'm going to stay with you, okay?"

Marie nodded and smiled, revealing two deep dimples. "I'm okay, Mrs. H. I promise. I know I haven't done anything wrong."

"Good. Agent?"

Rose and Marie sat down and Aggie said, "You can call me Aggie, okay? Do you remember Elise Hunt? She also went by Elise Hansen."

Marie nodded. "She came in a few weeks after me. She was nice to me. Not everyone is nice."

Aggie shared with Marie what she'd told Rose about

Elise's background and why they were concerned. "Did Elise share with you what she planned to do when she was released? Did she share any anger or resentment she had toward law enforcement?"

Marie frowned.

"It's okay," Rose said as she rested her hand on Marie's arm. "Whatever you know might help."

"Elise was good to me. I got picked on a lot—lots of reasons, stupid, mostly, but Elise defended me, and she didn't have to. And she didn't expect anything from me, so I'll admit I feel a little like I'm betraying her by talking to you. I want to do the right thing, but she never told me that she was going to commit a crime or anything like that."

"I appreciate the fact that she helped you," Aggie said. "And if we could have found Elise this week we'd never have come here to talk to you. But we can't find her, and prior to her incarceration, she threatened specific people. So we're a little worried that we don't know what she's up to."

Marie looked at her hands, then looked at Rose. "She was very nice to me—stood up for me, but . . ."

"Go on," Rose pushed gently. "This is a safe space, you know that."

Marie nodded. "There was a girl who *really* picked on me—I don't know why, I don't know what I did, what I said, but Danielle hated me from day one. She'd push me, she'd take my food, say . . . well, they're just words. Just really mean words. But Elise . . . I don't know for certain, because I didn't witness it. I didn't lie to the warden when she asked me, I really didn't see it. But I knew it was Elise."

"Knew what?"

"One night Elise snuck out of our room. She had a way of getting wherever she wanted, I don't even know how. I even think she left the grounds sometimes, but she always returned before anyone knew. Well, that night I woke up when she came in. I asked her where she'd been, said that she was going to get in trouble. She said she was too good to get in trouble, but Danielle wouldn't be a problem anymore. The next day, Danielle wasn't there. But this is juvie, rumors spread faster than anything. And word was that Danielle attacked a guard, nearly killed him, and was being transferred to a psychiatric prison for evaluation. I don't know what happened, if Danielle did it or Elise or what, but Elise had that cat got the canary look, you know?"

Aggie knew. "Did Elise talk to you about what she planned to do when she got out?"

"No. Not really. Well—she talked about seeing her dad again. I asked why he didn't visit, and she said he was out of state. But they had plans to start a business together. That's what I took from the conversations, I don't remember the details."

Aggie didn't tell Marie that Elise's father was in prison.

"We know she didn't have any visitors during her two years in detention. Did she ever ask you to deliver a message to anyone? Mail a letter?"

"No."

"I know I asked you this, but did she talk about any of the agents involved in her arrest? In her sister's death?"

"She didn't really talk about anything personal, other than her dad. And she missed her brother. She said he was murdered. Oh. And she talked about a psychic a lot."

"A psychic? Like someone who knows the future?"

"Yeah. She talked about this psychic named Lucy. I thought, maybe, she kind of had a crush on her, like this Lucy knew everything and Elise was amazed. But then I got the feeling she didn't like her at all. I don't know, that doesn't make sense. I'm trying to be helpful, really. I want to do the right thing."

It was helpful, though odd, and Aggie didn't know what to make of it. "You are doing the right thing, Marie." She looked at her notes, what Lucy had told her to ask.

"Did Elise talk to you at all about your family?"

Marie frowned, looked back at her hands. "Do I have to talk about my family?"

"No," Rose said and gave Aggie a look that would have made her feel guilty if it came from her mom.

Aggie cleared her throat, asked again. "I mean, we know your brother was part of the Saints gang. We have reason to believe that Elise might have reached out to someone in the Saints, and because of your association, I thought maybe you hooked her up with someone."

Marie shook her head. "I have nothing to do with that gang, with any gang. Ever. I didn't want to do what I did, I didn't have a choice!"

"I'm not here to get you in trouble."

"I don't think you understand what they do, how they hurt people, hurt me, made me do things . . . the police don't even understand, as if I had a choice! No one has a choice, not when you have nothing and no one to help."

"I don't blame you for anything you did, and I'm so glad you have a place like this to help you find your path. But honestly, Elise isn't like you. She's not like the girls here. I think she used you, and if it wasn't for your help, it was for information. Do you know Mitts Vasquez?"

By her expression, she did. "Why?"

"Because he's wanted for questioning, and it's possible Elise hired him to commit a crime."

"Elise? Mitts wouldn't work for a girl. He's . . . well, he thinks we're all stupid and only good for sex."

"You know him."

She nodded. "I haven't seen him in years. He ran with my oldest brother—my brother is dead because of people like Mitts. Not that my brother was a good person, but . . . well . . . he protected me, too, when I was little."

Suddenly, Marie straightened. "Oh my God. It . . . I didn't really think about it, but . . . Elise once said she'd met my brother. He'd gone to prison the year before I was put in detention. I guess I reacted weird. I love my brother . . . but I hate him, too. That sounds bad."

"It doesn't," Aggie said. "He's your brother. You love him. He does bad things, which you hate. I get it."

"Yeah. Yeah, that's it. And Elise backtracked, and we started talking . . . she asked questions, and I guess I needed to talk to someone. I told her everything, about how I got into detention, all about my brothers, and she kept asking questions. Like she was interested in everything I had to say, like she was interested in *me*. And I was talking because I never talked about this before, and . . . well, I think I told her about Mitts. That he was the last of the old-time Saints. So many of my brother's friends were killed. Drugs—God, I hate drugs. They ruined my family, my parents—my mom's a total addict. It's why she's in prison, but I don't think she'll ever stop. Well, Elise listened and said the right things I told her everything. I didn't realize . . . maybe she was pumping me for information. I don't even remember everything I told her, but I just felt like someone understood what I'd gone through and how conflicted I was about my life and family."

"Do you know where Mitts would go if he wanted to hide? Not from the police, but from a rival gang?"

She bit her lip. "I really don't. But there was this woman—an old woman, mean as anything, who kind of took the Saints in if they needed it. My brother used to say she was their alibi whenever they needed one."

"Do you know her name? Where she lives?"

Marie shook her head. "They called her Aunt Rita, but I don't know if that's her name or if she's still alive. The rumor was that the police killed her husband in a shoot-out and she hates cops, but that's all I know."

"That's more than I knew coming in here," Aggie said. "Thank you, Marie. I really appreciate your help. If Elise contacts you in any way, let me know." She handed cards to both Marie and Rose. "But don't engage with her. She's unpredictable and dangerous, and I don't want to see you hurt."

Chapter Seventeen

Lucy had Erica Anderson's last known address, a small house near the Air Force base. Garrett drove while she read everything she could find on the corrections officer—which wasn't much. She had a solid fifteen-year record in corrections. Prior to that, she'd been in a variety of jobs. Divorced, two kids. Her ex-husband, Bill, lived only a few miles from Erica. He was an electrician and co-owned a business with his brother.

It was after six on a Friday night, so Lucy expected Erica to be home. She wasn't. The house was dark and there was no sign that anyone was inside.

Lucy convinced Garrett to stay in the car and she went to the neighbor's house—a large house with a well-kept lawn and dozens of kids' toys—bikes, trikes, scooters—out front. A dog barked before she even rang the bell.

She learned from the neighbors that Erica was rarely home; they didn't know where she was working and since she quit the corrections department, she'd been aloof and antisocial. But Lucy did get the address of Erica's ex-husband, which the family had in case of emergencies.

She went back to talk to Garrett, gave him the address, told him about Erica's change of behavior.

"You want to talk to the husband?" Garrett asked.

"Yes. According to the neighbors, they had an amicable divorce, were friendly, and until she quit the kids were here nearly every weekend. Since then, the family hasn't seen the kids more than once. They tried talking to her a few weeks ago and Erica brushed them off, said she was working a private gig."

"Which is probably true."

"Then the husband will know how we can find her, right?"

Garrett drove off without comment.

The private sector often paid more than law enforcement, though law enforcement had perks like retirement and generally good health benefits. Also, Erica had more than ten years in service, so would be vested—leaving when she did seemed odd. Law enforcement was stressful, but there was nothing in her record that said she'd had any problems until three months ago when she quit without notice.

Maybe there was nothing going on with her. Maybe it was personal. Maybe it had nothing to do with Elise Hunt.

Or maybe your instincts are right on the money.

Garrett pulled up in front of Bill Anderson's house less than ten minutes later. He lived three miles from his ex-wife, down the street from a middle school in a house that was distinguished from its neighbors by a huge tree in the front yard. The roots must be deep otherwise a big storm would put that tree right across the roof of the single-story house.

The neighborhood was a typical middle-class San Antonio neighborhood where kids played on the street and a baseball game was being played at the park on the corner. It reminded Lucy a lot of the neighborhood she grew up in. Modest homes in a clean, well-loved neighborhood.

Lucy began to doubt herself. Maybe she was on a wild

goose chase. Even if Erica left because of a confrontation with Elise—if that's what it was—would she know anything to help Lucy get Sean out of jail?

Her head ached. She hadn't eaten since coffee and a bagel this morning before she left the house, When everything was normal, and Sean had kissed her good-bye.

She wanted that back.

"Do you want to join me?" she asked.

"I just want to remind you that if you learn something that is important to the investigation, you'll need to tell the authorities."

She didn't comment. She got out and didn't care if Garrett followed her; he did.

She knocked on the door. A moment later a tall, broad-shouldered man in a T-shirt, jeans, and bare feet answered. The amazing smell of some sort of pasta and tomatoes hit Lucy and her stomach growled.

"Mr. Anderson?"

"Yes."

She showed her identification. "I'm looking for your ex-wife, Erica. She wasn't at home and her neighbors said she hasn't been home much since she quit. Her former employer—the warden, Kathy Pine—asked me to check on her because she hasn't been able to reach her."

A fib, but bordering on the truth.

Bill frowned, then stepped out onto the small porch and closed the door behind him. "I don't need the kids to hear this."

"We just want to make sure she's okay. When was the last time you spoke with her?"

"A couple days ago she called me to cancel her time with the kids. Again. This wasn't the first time. She's canceled all but one weekend with the kids in the last two months. I'm pissed. We've always gotten along, even after the divorce. Well, I guess you could say that we learned to get along after the divorce, and things were fine. We both love the kids, and we have a custody arrangement that works for us, and the kids adjusted. In two years she's never canceled a weekend. Ever. And four in a row? It's not like her."

This would be the fourth weekend since Elise got out of juvie. Coincidence? Lucy didn't think so.

"Did she say why?"

"The first time she had an excuse I didn't quite believe—a job interview out of town. But I didn't question it. Then she stopped giving excuses. And quitting—that's another thing. Completely out of character. Erica is predictable. She likes routine and organization and a regular schedule."

"So she didn't tell you why she quit her job at corrections?"

"No, and it was the first fight we've had since the divorce was final. She has damn good benefits, the kids were on her plan. She said she'd cover them, but that's just bullshit, you know? I'm self-employed. My insurance is crap."

"Is she covering them?"

"Yes, paying through the nose for it, too, to keep the same plan through the COBRA program. I called her on it, but she just clammed up and said she was working on something."

"And you don't know where she is or where she's working?"

"No. If she calls, I'll have her call you, that's the best I can do."

"Does she have any other family? Someone who might know where she is or where she's working?"

"No. She doesn't get along with her dad, he's in Indiana now, I think. Her mom is dead. She has half siblings she never talks to."

"Did Erica say anything or can you think of any reason why she's acting odd? Or why she quit her job? Was she seeing someone?"

"I don't know, to be honest. She could be seeing someone, though we agreed that if either of us brought a regular person into the lives of our kids, we'd tell each other. Just so we have everything on the up-and-up, you know? And that's worked for us. Quitting was out of character, canceling on the kids, me not being able to reach her." He frowned, looked worried. "Is she in trouble?"

"No, but the warden is concerned, same as you, so I promised to track her down." Lucy handed him her business card. "If she calls you, please give her my name and number and tell her I can help her with anything that's going on. If she doesn't want to call me, if you can just let me know if she reaches out?"

"Of course. Should I be worried?"

"I can't say, I just need to talk to her. Did she tell you why she quit her job?"

"No. She was having problems with an inmate, but I thought she'd fixed it."

Lucy's heart skipped a beat. "Do you know which inmate?"

"Elise. A girl named Elise. I know Erica couldn't wait until she aged out because she dreaded going in and seeing her."

Lucy was so surprised she couldn't hide her reaction. "She talked to you?"

"Not about why she quit, but she had been complaining about this girl for months. Then she stopped complaining, a couple months ago, and I thought Elise had left the system. But then she quit her job . . . I suppose that could be why."

Except Elise didn't age out until three weeks ago.

"Thank you, Mr. Anderson," Garrett said before Lucy could pump him for more information.

Back in the car, Lucy said, "I wasn't done."

"You were treading into dangerous territory. This isn't your investigation. Just because Erica's ex-husband mentioned her name doesn't mean anything."

"Like hell it doesn't!" Lucy forced herself to calm down. "It's not enough, but it's one small thread and we *are* going to pursue it."

She was about to drive away when Bill Anderson came running up to her car. She rolled down the window. "Is there something else?"

"I just told the kids I had to run an errand. I'm really worried about Erica—I have the keys to her house. Like I said, we're on good terms. Would you follow me over there and . . . well . . . if she's there and something's wrong, I would just feel more comfortable with you there, if that's okay."

Lucy nodded. "Absolutely, Mr. Anderson."

Ten minutes later, they were back at Erica's house. Bill walked up to the door and knocked. "Her car's not here," he said to Lucy and Garrett, who were standing behind him, "but . . . well, just in case." Through the door he called out, "Erica? It's Bill. You there?"

Silence.

Bill opened the door and walked in. Lucy motioned for Garrett to stay back—he might have been a cop before, but he wasn't one now, and they didn't know what to expect.

"Would you mind if I did a quick search?" Lucy asked Bill.

"Please."

Lucy looked at Garrett to make sure he heard that Bill had authorized her. He didn't react. He was probably thinking that just because Bill had the key didn't mean he had a lawful reason to enter, but at this point, Lucy was concerned about Erica's safety—and possible involvement with Elise Hunt.

Elise had blackmailed, threatened, and manipulated dozens of people into helping her. She could have done the same to Erica.

Lucy walked quickly through the small, meticulously organized house. The kids' rooms had the most personality and clutter, but the master bedroom and the living area were immaculate. Nothing looked out of place, and she didn't find a body or sign of a struggle.

She came back to the living room where Bill stood. Garrett came into the room and closed the door.

"Can you tell if anything is missing?" Lucy asked Bill. "Did she have luggage, could she have gone on a trip?"

"Three months ago, I would have said she'd never leave without telling me. But now? Hell if I know."

He walked down the hall to her bedroom and Lucy walked over to a small desk in the kitchen. Mail was organized in a small wooden box. She opened a desk calendar, which appeared to be sparingly used. Physicals for the kids were scheduled in June. She had her "annual" in August. Last October was a week vacation "Disneyland w/Bill, Paula, George." She had birthdays listed, and her work schedule until she quit.

There was nothing on her calendar after she quit the first week of February except a birthday of a friend, but the calendar had all birthdays for the year marked in the same red pen.

Bill said, "Her suitcase is in her closet, but she has a matching overnight bag that I can't find anywhere. I just don't understand any of this."

Lucy knew she shouldn't, but she would argue that a welfare check meant that this was a lawful search.

They didn't know where Erica had gone, why she wasn't talking to her kids, why she'd quit her job, what she was doing.

She opened the desk drawer. Out of the corner of her eye she saw Garrett frown, but then Bill walked over and started going through Erica's things.

The drawer was also organized, with pencils in one tray and pens in another. Notepads and extra phone chargers and keys without rings. Suddenly Bill turned and walked briskly down to the bedroom.

Lucy didn't see anything in the drawer that might help. Then Bill said, "Well, shit."

She went down the hall. "What?"

He was in her closet. A small gun safe was open. "Her guns are gone. She owns a .357 revolver and a .45 semi-auto."

"Did you open the safe?"

"Yes, it used to be in our house, both of our thumbprints can unlock it."

"Those were the only two guns she owned?"

"Yes. At least that I know of."

Mona Hill had been shot with a .45 caliber.

"Did she regularly carry her firearms with her?" Lucy asked.

"No. I need to call her."

Lucy didn't stop him, but it was clear he didn't reach her when he left a message. "Erica, it's Bill. I need to talk to you tonight. Call me."

He frowned. "I don't know what else to do."

Lucy looked around the small closet. It, like the rest of the house, was well-organized. She had three uniforms all hanging in dry cleaning bags. She hung her T-shirts and pants. She owned only a few dresses, several pairs of comfortable work shoes, sneakers, and two pairs of heels.

Garrett spoke up. "Bill, you should file a missing person's report. That you haven't heard from your ex-wife since whatever day she canceled her weekend with the kids."

"Should I?"

Lucy glanced at Garrett. Erica wasn't missing, she was working on something—and likely for Elise. Lucy didn't know why—but there was always a reason. A threat? Money? She didn't have a good read on Erica. Her ex-husband seemed to get along with her, but she didn't have custody of her kids. That seemed odd.

But missing? Nope.

Bill nodded. "I'm going home, I'm going to try calling her again. If she doesn't get back to me tonight, I'll call the police. Thank you."

Bill locked up the house and they left.

Lucy got behind the wheel of her car. There was something very odd about Erica Anderson's behavior. She needed to find her, sooner rather than later.

"You shouldn't have gone in there," Garrett said.

"I had permission."

"He's her *ex*-husband. He *may* have permission, but that doesn't give him the right to bring law enforcement inside for a warrantless search."

"I didn't search. She's missing a .45. That's according to Bill, not *my* search."

"The police have the weapon they believe was used. They found it in Sean's plane."

"And it's not Sean's!"

"You can't possibly think that a corrections officer with no ties to the victim or your husband killed a woman in cold blood to frame him."

"I'm not saying or thinking anything. I'm letting the evidence speak for itself." And right now, the evidence was quiet. Because Garrett was right: *why?* Why would

Erica kill anyone? Even if Elise had something on her, something that could hurt her or damage her career or her custody agreement, would Erica actually *kill* anyone for her?

Maybe. If Elise threatened her family. Or for money.

Lucy needed to find Erica, talk to her, convince her that Lucy was the only person who could help her against Elise.

She called Kathy Pine, who answered on the second ring. "Kathy, it's Lucy Kincaid. I was doing a welfare check on Erica Anderson, and talked to her ex-husband—"

The warden interrupted her. "Agent Kincaid, did you think I wouldn't find out that your husband was arrested for murder?"

Lucy didn't know what to say.

"That's not—"

"Are you doing an end-run around Houston PD? I don't like being lied to."

"I didn't lie to you, Warden."

"I just got a call to send over Elise's files to Houston PD. I asked why, and learned that your husband claimed that she'd threatened the woman he's accused of murdering. And you didn't think that was important to tell me?"

"It's complicated."

"It's not complicated. You used your badge to get information from me not in your capacity as an FBI agent, but because your husband is in jail."

"Elise Hunt is dangerous and I think that Erica Anderson is in trouble because of her."

"I want nothing to do with this, Agent Kincaid. You crossed a line. If you want anything from my office, you'll go through the proper channels. Good-bye."

She ended the call.

Garrett had heard everything—Kathy had not been quiet.

"You have to back off," he said.

"No!" Lucy wasn't going to be deterred. She was onto something, she knew it, and the police weren't going to follow up on Erica Anderson's odd behavior or Elise Hunt.

"You could lose your badge, Lucy."

"I didn't do anything wrong or unethical." Borderline, maybe.

"That's not my call, nor is it yours."

But Lucy was only half listening to Garrett.

"We're being followed," she said.

Garrett looked in the side view mirror. "The dark Honda?"

"Yes."

It was dusk, and visibility was poor.

"Erica's neighborhood. They weren't parked on her street, but when I turned out of the neighborhood onto the highway, they were behind me." She hadn't been suspicious at first but she'd intentionally slowed down and they hadn't passed her.

Lucy had been followed before, and last year she and Jesse had been run off the road. She wasn't going to let that happen now—though a Honda that was the same basic size and shape as her car wasn't going to be much of a threat, unless they were armed.

She wasn't going to lead them home.

Who is following you? How did they know you were going to be at Erica's?

Maybe they weren't following her because they knew who she was, but had been watching Erica's house and were suspicious.

Lucy exited the highway and turned immediately into a gas station. She parked near the doors that led to the mini-mart and said, "Keep your eye on the car, it pulled in at the pump, but the driver isn't getting out. The windows are tinted and at this angle I can't see the occupants."

Lucy got out and went inside. She grabbed a water bottle and energy bar, then stood at the counter and waited for the lone person ahead of her while keeping an eye on the driver outside. The driver was partly visible, male. Young. She could see that there was someone in the passenger seat, but she couldn't make out any distinguishing characteristics.

As soon as she reached the clerk, she put her items down and showed her badge. "I need the license number on that vehicle," she said and gestured to the black Honda on the security screen behind him.

Without commenting, he enlarged the image, but didn't say anything. She wrote down the number, paid for her items, and was about to go back to her car when she saw the passenger door open.

Elise Hunt stepped out.

Lucy froze for a second. As she watched on the security screen, Elise stretched as if she didn't have a care in the world.

Lucy ran out of the mini-mart, her water and energy bar forgotten. She walked right past her car, straight for Elise.

"Why are you following me?" Lucy demanded.

Elise stared at her.

"Answer the question."

Elise frowned, looked around as if she were trapped. It was an act. Lucy had gone through this with her many times.

A guy filling his truck up was watching them. "Is there a problem?" he asked.

Lucy pulled her badge and flashed it at him, but didn't take her eyes off Elise.

"Driver," she called, "get out of the car."

"Wh-what do you want?" Elise said, sounding like a scared child.

Elise Hunt was no child. But right now, she looked and acted younger than her eighteen years.

"I know exactly what you're up to, Elise. It's not going to work."

"You're scaring me. I haven't done anything."

"Driver of the black Honda! Get out of the vehicle now."

Even as Lucy spoke, she realized she was escalating this situation when she should have called for backup.

Backup? Who would back her up? She wasn't supposed to be investigating Mona Hill's murder. She didn't have any active cases. But she wasn't officially suspended, she was simply told to take time off.

Garrett Lee had emerged from Lucy's car. "Garrett, call SAPD." To Elise she said, "It's a crime to follow a federal agent." Not exactly.

"I wasn't following you! I wasn't! I-I—stop, please stop, I served my time, why are you harassing me?"

The Honda's driver emerged. Lucy diverted her attention to him. Male, Caucasian, under six feet tall. Mid-twenties. "Keep your hands where I can see them."

"What did I do?" he asked, but kept his hands on the roof of his car.

Garrett walked over and said, "Lucy, you need to let them go."

"Did you call SAPD?"

"No, you don't want to do that."

"They were following us."

"We weren't!" Elise said.

"Your innocent act may fool your shrink, but it has never fooled me."

The guy with the truck finished fueling, but he didn't leave.

The driver said, "Are you arresting us?"

Lucy said, "I'm going to prove you killed Mona Hill. You're not as smart as you think, Elise."

"Kill? You're going to kill me?" Elise acted hysterical.

"That's not what I said, and you damn well know it," Lucy snapped.

"If you're not arresting us, we're leaving," the driver said. "Get in the car, Elise."

"Do not move," Lucy said.

But now she was stuck. She couldn't arrest them. She had no cause. And she couldn't prove that they'd followed her from Erica Anderson's house. She had noticed the vehicle as she emerged from the neighborhood . . . but that was the most likely route to take from Erica's house back to the highway. Elise was supposed to be in Los Angeles, but there was nothing keeping her in L.A. She wasn't even on probation.

"You hate me, I haven't done anything to you, but you hate me." Elise was crying. She'd forced herself to cry on cue in the court, what did Lucy expect? That Elise was going to confess to her?

"Elise, now," the driver said. "That cop is crazy."

"Don't shoot me!" Elise cried.

Lucy didn't even have her gun out, but she'd had her hand on the butt of her gun during the conversation.

Elise jumped in the car, and the driver got back in and left.

"She's a piece of work," Lucy said.

The customer who had been watching them gave Lucy a look, then he went into the mini-mart.

Garrett said, "We need to go, Lucy, now."

Lucy didn't have a choice. But Elise was not going to get away with this. "You heard her. She made a scene, she did not respond to what I said, but only said what she wanted others to think I said!"

"You're not making sense."

"It's how she operates!"

"I agree, she wasn't making sense, but you intimidated her—that's what the witness observed. You intimidated a young girl and she was scared."

"She was faking!" Lucy slammed her door shut and hit her hand on the dashboard. "You weren't here two years ago, Garrett. You don't know what she did—how she manipulated people, including her shrink. And the courts! The judge was Eleanor Axelrod. She was in the pocket of the cartels, and we couldn't prove it!"

"You need to watch what you say. Judge Axelrod is still on the bench."

Maybe Lucy handled it wrong. But Elise was here in San Antonio and had followed her. Whatever game she was playing wasn't going to work. She was going to slip up. She had before. She was impulsive and would make a major mistake. But could Lucy be there to catch her at it?

Elise killed Mona Hill—or ordered Mona's death. She framed Sean for it. Lucy had to prove it.

Lucy should report this to her office, but now she was stuck. She wasn't exactly sure what she should do, so she called JT Caruso as she drove home. JT had resources, he could track Elise. While she talked to him, she made sure that no one—the black Honda or another vehicle—followed her.

She told him that Elise Hunt was in the vehicle, and another male that wasn't in the photos he'd sent to her earlier.

"You confronted her?"

"She got out of her car thirty feet from me. What was I supposed to do?"

"And?"

"And she made a scene, then left. She's up to something—I *know* she's behind this. She followed me out of Erica Anderson's neighborhood, JT."

"You need to back away from this investigation. Let things settle down—"

"No one else is investigating," she said. "Houston PD thinks Sean is guilty and they're not going to pursue other possibilities."

"You don't know that."

"I do. Look at everything that happened today." She didn't want to argue with JT and she had a headache. She'd left her food in the mini-mart, but she didn't care. She just wanted to see Sean and figure out what was going on.

"Give me the license number."

She did.

"I'll look into this, see what I can do. I know standing down isn't in the Kincaid genes—but right now, that's all you can do. This whole situation is volatile right now."

Then she thought of Jack.

"Do you know something about Jack and Kane? Are they in trouble?"

"Jack has a lead on Kane, that's all I know. I'll call you later."

JT ended the call and Lucy forced herself to breathe. JT was right. Hell, Garrett was right. She shouldn't have pushed so hard, but she couldn't stand knowing Elise was behind this and not being able to stop her.

What was Elise's endgame? To mess with her? Revenge for the SWAT action that claimed her sister's life? Kane had killed Elise's brother—is that why Kane was now missing? Could Elise have had something to do with Kane's disappearance?

If so, she had more people under her thumb than they could even imagine.

No, her father. Her father has the contacts in Mexico. They're in this together, it's the only explanation.

By the time she got home, it was after eight. She was exhausted and her headache had gone from bad to worse. Her stomach was all twisted and she couldn't stop thinking about Sean. Where was he now? What was he doing? Was he safe?

Please, God, please keep him safe.

She didn't see Aggie's truck out front, and Leo was still there. He and Jesse were playing video games.

"There's pizza in the kitchen," Leo said. "We were hungry, but I got plenty."

"Thank you. Have you heard from Nate?"

"No," he said.

Jesse frowned and looked concerned. "Was he supposed to be back?"

"No," she said, not wanting him to worry. "I haven't talked to him since he left, but he has Aggie with him. Thanks for coming over, Leo. I really appreciate it."

"Anytime," he said. "I'm free all weekend if you need me—I'm not even on call. Mind if Jess and I finish up this battle?"

"Stay as long as you want."

She left them and went to the kitchen, where Garrett was drinking a water bottle. "I hope you don't mind."

"Of course not."

"Are you okay here?" Garrett asked.

"Yes," she said. "Leo's still here and Nate will be back soon."

"You're not going to leave the house tonight, are you?"

"I don't plan to."

"I guess that's good enough. I'll be back in the morning to take you to Houston. Felicity sent me a message—Sean is at the Houston Administrative Jail. This is a good thing. It's a federal facility, but they often keep local prisoners there before their court date, so the city uses it as well. It's the safest place he can be."

The best place he could be right now would be home, but Lucy didn't say that.

Garrett continued. "Visiting hours are from ten until four tomorrow. It's a three-hour drive—I'll be here at six thirty?"

"Thank you."

"Lucy, I understand what you're going through."

She doubted that.

"And I know you're a trained agent. But you have to back away from this investigation. I didn't hear the entire conversation, but that girl clearly wanted the witness to hear what she said, and you didn't come off looking good."

"What is that supposed to mean?"

"She barely looks eighteen. You are an armed federal agent. You approached her and made demands—she's not a wanted criminal. If you get a call about it, anything—call me. Don't talk to anyone, just call me and we'll work through it. I was there, I can testify to exactly what I heard and saw, but it felt like a setup."

She knew Garrett was right. "It's her MO. She convinced her shrink that I had threatened her, and because she spoke so quietly on tape, the tape didn't catch what she said. She's an actress. She set me up and I walked right into it. Dammit!"

"Tread carefully, Lucy."

Leo came out of the video game room shortly after Garrett left. Lucy was trying to force a slice of pizza down, but her stomach was so twisted she was afraid she was going to throw up.

Leo gave her a hug. "Jess is fine, he's a great kid. Worried about his dad, but he's doing good, okay? Do you want me to hang out until Nate comes back?"

"No, I'm okay. I need a shower; I have an early day tomorrow."

"You need me, just call. Anytime, I mean that."

"I really appreciate it."

"Oh—someone named Duke called Jess, he's talking to him now."

"Sean's brother."

"Jess seemed glad that he called. You have a great family, Lucy, you're going to get through his. Sean is going to clear his name. He's a good man."

"Thank you." She was on the verge of tears and she didn't want to cry.

She walked Leo to the door, then reset the alarm and went up to Jesse's room.

He was just hanging up his phone. "That was Uncle Duke."

She sat on the edge of his bed, scratched Bandit behind the ears. Sean didn't like Bandit being on the furniture, but the dog seemed to know that Jesse's bed was the exception.

"Duke doing okay?"

"Yeah. He wanted to make sure we were okay. Said that everyone is fighting for Dad and he knows he didn't kill anyone. That the truth will come out."

"It will."

Jesse scratched Bandit, too. "I fed him. He misses Dad."

They all did. Sean was the life of the house. Without him . . . no, she wasn't going to go there.

Jesse asked, "Did you learn anything?"

"Yes and no."

"Where's Nate?"

"He and Aggie aren't back yet. Are you hungry?"

He shook his head. "Leo got pizza, but I wasn't hungry. It just didn't taste good." He looked at her, serious, worried, a young version of Sean. Her heart was breaking.

"I'm scared, Lucy."

She leaned back into Jesse's bed and hugged him. "I'm scared, too."

Chapter Eighteen

Nate didn't like working with Aggie in the field.

They were staking out an apartment building in a sketchy area and Aggie was certain that if Mitts Vasquez was in town, this was where he was staying. She was positive that "Aunt Rita" was Marguerita Fernandez de Garcia. The DEA had a file on her. She'd never been arrested, but she'd been questioned in several investigations that involved her late husband, who was suspected of running a meth lab ten years ago. He'd been killed in an explosion in his lab that he may have intentionally set when he was alerted that the sheriffs were on their way to arrest him.

She owned this eight-unit apartment building, and lived in a unit on the top floor. She wasn't home—at least, the car registered in her name wasn't on the street or in the carport behind the building.

Nate wasn't confident that Aggie was right that Aunt Rita would give Mitts refuge, but she'd made a compelling argument, so he was willing to give her the benefit of the doubt. She'd taken the information she knew about the Saints, what Marie Ynez told her, and information she'd pulled from Mitts' extensive rap sheet.

Nate wasn't sure why he had a problem with Aggie.

He'd been thinking about it all afternoon and into the evening—it was after nine—ever since she'd picked him up at SAPD.

It wasn't that she was young or female. Aggie was Lucy's age, and Nate didn't have a problem working with Lucy. He preferred it, because she was smart and focused and well-trained. Plus, he liked her.

Aggie was smart, but in a different way. She was tech-savvy and analytical. But she was chatty and couldn't stay still.

And Nate had never worked with her.

There was a trust that he'd built up with Lucy and even Brad. A trust he'd built with Sean and Jack and Kane. When he was in the Army, he learned to trust his squad. He *knew* them, inside and out. It was so deeply ingrained he knew when one was in pain, or his commander had doubts, or when they looked at each other and knew they were going back to save a civilian even in the face of danger.

Trust took time. It took working together and learning the other person. How they would respond to any situation. How they thought and processed intel.

He'd never worked with Aggie. He'd met her a handful of times—the talkative geek analyst at the DEA.

Agent. She's a DEA agent *and you'd better remember that.*

But agent or not, he'd never worked with her. He felt protective because that was his background. Protect the weak, the innocent, the civilians. He didn't know her skill set or how she would react in the face of adversity. Which meant that he was on edge; tense and watchful.

And Aggie fidgeted constantly.

It was annoying. And a little endearing, if they weren't on a long stake-out. She'd taken her long white blonde hair down from a messy bun and braided it down her back. Then ten minutes later she'd undone the braid and wrapped her hair on the top of her head. He'd threatened to cut it off if she couldn't keep still.

"He's not coming," Nate said after more than two hours.

"He will. I should have bought more food. I'm starving."

He couldn't imagine she had any more room in her stomach. They'd had hamburgers and fries from Whataburger, then she'd stopped at a mini-mart for water, chips, sunflower seeds, and bananas. Everything was gone.

"You don't know that he will. It's a guess."

"An educated guess."

"What about the Merides brothers?" he said. "Earlier you said they would be more apt to talk, and I concurred."

"I don't know where they are. I have some ideas, but we don't have the manpower to check them all out. Mitts will be here. He doesn't have many places he can go."

"Unless he left San Antonio all together."

"Possible. Unlikely."

"Why?"

"Because this is all he knows. He doesn't have contacts all over the state or country. He's American through and through, he'd be eaten for lunch in Mexico if he tried to work something with the cartels. He's going to stay in his comfort zone."

She sounded positive, not one doubt. Nate wasn't so certain, but this was her job. He had to try to find a way to trust her. Lucy had brought her in. Brad trusted her.

Aggie continued, her mind clearly working through all the possibilities. "Mitts stole the drugs and planted them in your truck because he was hired to do so—not because he was *in* a gang, but because he was one of the few left. Meaning, whoever hired him only knows the Saints." She was nodding to herself.

She made a lot of sense, especially if Elise Hunt was behind this.

But a stakeout could take all night. Days. They'd been here for three hours now and hadn't seen anything but two drug deals.

"We need more information and a better plan," Nate said.

"He'll be here. It's the only place he can go that is off the radar of the Merides brothers and law enforcement. He's probably been going in and out for the last few days, he'll get cocky because no one has found him. He'll show."

So he sat and waited. He didn't move. Stakeouts were like being in the Army. You had to sit and wait and ninety-nine times out of a hundred nothing happened when you were on your post. But when the shit hit the fan, you had to be ready to act.

A car drove up to the decrepit apartment. The building was one long unit on a narrow lot, two stories, four units top and bottom, sagging stairs, and broken railings. An empty fenced lot to the right, a larger but equally broken apartment structure to the left.

The unit they were watching was in the front upstairs corner.

He kept an eye on the car. At first, nothing happened. That made Nate nervous. Drug deal? Drive-by? Had they been spotted?

A minute later, the passenger door opened. Mitts Vasquez got out of the car and before he could walk up the stairs, the driver left.

"It's him," Aggie said, excited.

Her hand was on the door.

"Wait."

"We need to get to him before he gets inside. We don't

know who's in there, what kind of weapons they might have. We don't have a team for the back."

She was right. "Follow my lead."

She didn't argue.

Nate had already disabled the dome light, so it remained dark when they simultaneously opened their doors.

Before Mitts even stepped on to the bottom stair, the downstairs apartment door opened.

Nate didn't hear anything before the gunfire. Mitts went down fast, three bullets ripping into his body. Nate had his gun out and was behind the truck. Aggie dropped to her knees and had her gun out as well.

The shooter hadn't seen Nate or Aggie—at least Nate didn't think that he had. He left the dark apartment, fired one more bullet into Mitts's head, then turned and walked briskly down the street toward the main road.

"Call it in!" Nate ordered Aggie. He went after the shooter.

"Freeze! FBI!" Nate shouted.

The shooter didn't look back. He went from fast walk to sprint. He was young—early to mid-twenties—and looked scared. A tattoo on his neck stood out, but at this distance Nate couldn't tell what it depicted.

Nate was an excellent shot, but he couldn't risk collateral damage in the residential neighborhood. If he missed, his bullet could go through a wall or window, injuring an innocent inside.

The shooter rounded the corner onto a busy street. A stoplight ahead was red and before the runner even registered his plans, Nate knew what he was going to do.

Damn damn damn!

"Freeze!" Nate shouted as he ran.

The shooter ran to the driver's side of the first car at the light and pointed his gun at the driver's face. "Out or I shoot!" Nate heard as he ran toward the intersection.

A slow-moving car clipped Nate as he ran diagonally into the street to cut the guy off.

The driver opened her door. The shooter pulled her out of the car and threw her to the ground, then jumped in, driving through the red light before Nate reached the intersection. Two cars screeched to a stop to avoid hitting him.

Nate helped the middle-aged woman stand. He wanted to berate her—why'd she open her door? She'd been safe inside the locked car, she could have driven off, but he didn't say anything. People not trained for situations like this didn't always know the smartest move.

She was shaking and he walked her over to the sidewalk, where he sat her on a bus bench.

"Are you okay? Do you need an ambulance?"

"I—I—I'm okay."

She began to silently cry. Nate called Aggie. She answered immediately.

"He carjacked a woman at the corner of Blythe and Mission."

"I'm on the phone with SAPD dispatch. Do you have a description?"

"Blue Honda Accord, license BH8-G. I missed the last three digits." He turned to the woman. "Do you know your license plate number?"

She shook her head. "My insurance cards are in the car . . . they say to keep them in the car . . . I need to call my husband."

"What's your name, ma'am?"

"Holly Johns."

He gave Aggie her name. "Have them run the name, get the plates. He was going south on Mission Road. Hispanic male, five foot ten to eleven, one sixty, between the ages of twenty and twenty-five. Wearing dark jeans, a white T-shirt with a logo on the front, and dark gray hoodie. No facial hair. Neck tattoo, indistinct."

"Got it. I'll call you back."

Nate didn't want to leave Aggie alone, but he also couldn't leave the witness. A minute later, he heard sirens. Aggie called him. "Mitts is dead. SAPD is on their way. Nate, you can't be around here."

"Like hell."

"You don't have a badge right now. You're suspended."

"I'll deal with it. I have a witness; I've talked to her. I have another driver approaching me now, he saw what happened. I'll get his statement, send an officer here to make it official. And no way in hell am I leaving you here in the middle of this."

She didn't say anything.

It wasn't that he disagreed with her, and if he didn't have this woman who had seen him, who he'd talked to, he might slip away undetected. He didn't want to talk to anyone at SAPD, and he didn't know how his working with Aggie was going to impact his situation—or her job. But dammit, he didn't run from trouble. He never had, he never would.

Aggie was talking.

"What?" he said.

"Will you follow my lead this time?"

"What?"

"I asked you to help me. You were just on a ride-along. This is my case, assigned by my boss Brad Donnelly. Understand?"

"Understood."

"They were waiting for him," she said. "They knew he would come here. Rita set him up."

"So she's working with the Merides brothers?"

"I don't know."

"If someone stole sixteen kilos of coke from me, I wouldn't kill them until *after* I got my drugs back."

"What do you think?"

"Whoever hired Mitts Vasquez to steal the drugs in the first place didn't want him fingering them to the cops."

Aggie concurred. "I think you might be right."

"I know I am."

Chapter Nineteen

By the time Sean was transferred to the administrative jail
Friday night, it was late. All prisoners were in their cells.
He had been taken to the jail alone in a police van, in cuffs.

He'd gone through the booking process at Houston
PD—turning over all his personal items, mug shot,
prints, orange jumpsuit. He complied without mouthing
off or disrupting the process. He was so weary . . . so
frustrated . . . so *humiliated*.

His attorney told him to keep his head down and
she would do everything in her power to get him out on
Monday. He knew that creating problems wasn't going to
help him and he would try to keep a low profile, while
still being on high alert all night, all weekend.

*There are a lot easier ways to kill you than to set you
up to go to prison.*

In reality, the frame job was solid, but the police
shouldn't be able to prove he killed Mona because he
hadn't. He'd been there, he'd argued with her, but he hadn't
killed her. They had to prove he did it—he didn't have to
prove he didn't. At least, that was how the system was supposed to work.

Whoever killed her knew you were there—and when.
Someone had been watching Mona, knew when Sean

arrived, knew when he left, killed her. She'd been expecting her bodyguard . . . just how clean was he? Had he killed her?

That doesn't explain the pizza guy getting no answer at Mona's door.

He had to take that testimony at face value at this point. He could have been bribed, but that would likely not hold up in court, especially since there were security cameras that could confirm the time line.

So the killer either avoided the cameras, hacked into the cameras, or had a legitimate reason for being in the building. Sean trusted Lucy to work the case, but she was out of her jurisdiction and wouldn't have access to all the information Houston PD had. If it were him, he would want to interview the pizza delivery guy. Maybe he had been bribed—maybe he had gang affiliations—maybe he'd been threatened. Or maybe he'd seen something and didn't realize the import.

The corrections officer was silent as he led Sean to his cell. Most of the men didn't pay any attention to Sean; everyone was already locked in. It was after hours in a medium security facility, and most of the men here were waiting for court dates. They hadn't been convicted. Most were guilty. Some weren't.

Like Sean.

"At oh-six-hundred, the doors will automatically unlock, but wait in your cell until the announcement before you step out and line up for breakfast."

"When are visiting hours?"

"Ten A.M."

"Thank you."

He wanted to stay on the good side of the guards. If something happened in here, he wanted them to help him. If he caused problems, they might not be as inclined to jump to his defense if he needed it.

Less than thirteen hours and he could see Lucy. He hoped between the two of them, they'd find answers to get him out.

Mostly, he needed to tell her he was sorry. To tell her face to face that he was innocent. He knew she believed him, but explaining the situation over the phone wasn't good enough.

The lights turned off automatically at ten P.M., only minutes after he was put in the cell.

He lay on his bunk in the seven-by-nine-foot room and stared at the dark ceiling. Sounds everywhere. Quiet talking. Snoring. One guy far off, sobbing. Steady footsteps of the guards patrolling.

The smell of fear, of acceptance, of despair.

His heart raced, knowing he was trapped, knowing he couldn't leave if he wanted. He sat up on the thin mattress and willed his pulse to slow down. Panic wouldn't help him.

You're in prison. Your life is not your own.

He put his head in his hands and for the first time in years, Sean wept. Silently, his body shook as he fought to control his pain, his fear.

And the realization that he might not be getting out—on Monday, or ever.

Erica Anderson rolled over and wrapped her arms around the man she loved.

It was almost over. Three months of hell.

"What's wrong, baby?" Tim turned on the nightstand light. "It's late, I thought you were sleeping."

She had barely slept this week. Hell, she'd hardly slept in months.

"Bill left three message on my voice mail today. A federal agent wants to talk to me."

Tim sat up. "Why didn't you tell me?"

"Because what can we do? I talk to her, they'll kill you, they'll go after my kids."

"Tell Bill to get the kids out of town. Maybe—"

"What? Maybe what? We got ourselves in this mess, we can't talk our way out."

She'd tried. When she realized what Elise Hunt was up to, she tried to get them out of this disaster. But they were already in too deep. Tim had committed a crime—a felony—because of her. She wasn't going to send him to prison because he was trying to fix a mess she got them into.

But the bitch who ran the operation made it clear that there was no turning back.

So Erica and Tim took the money and worked any job required. She had no other choice. And it wasn't like any of these people were saints. So what if a prick got jammed up for murder? From what she'd been told about Sean Rogan, he was no better than Elise herself.

At first, it was about the money. She was tired of being broke all the time, and what Elise asked her to do was no big deal. She'd opened up an account for the kids for college. Bill didn't make enough money and her babies were smart. Smart enough to go to college—something neither she nor Bill had ever been able to do.

The jobs went from borderline illegal to actual felonies. But by that time, she and Tim were in way too deep to get out clean. First time she complained, the bitch in charge showed Erica pictures of her kids walking home from school.

She hadn't said a word since. Just did what they asked. Everything, pretty much, short of murder.

"Tomorrow," Tim said. "One last assignment and we're free."

"Are we? If her federal agent wants to talk to me, maybe she knows something . . ."

"No one knows anything."

"You don't know that."

He turned her to look at him. Waves of emotion washed over her. She loved this man so much and he shouldn't have to pay for her mistake. But he was, and she was, and that was fucking life. Because life sucked.

"When this is over, we go away. Disappear for a while."

"My kids . . ."

"Just for a while. Just lay low and make sure everything dies down."

"I'm scared."

"I have it covered. I love you, Erica. I love you more than anything."

She held him tight. They made love, hard and fast and desperate. Then slow and hard until she was so satisfied that she could hardly move. She had to remember every muscle in his body, the way he touched her, the groan he made when he was about to orgasm. She had to remember the way he made her feel because she feared this would be the last time.

Chapter Twenty

Torture was mostly ineffective.

This was a truth Brad knew from a half dozen years in the military and nearly two decades fighting the drug cartels.

Mostly because human beings were resilient and could be trained to withstand physical pain and psychological pressure.

But emotional torture accompanied by well-planned physical torture could turn even the strongest of men to mush.

It was the games Elise played that had him on edge. Psychologically, he could withstand it. She hadn't even asked him for information. It was like cat and mouse—he was the mouse and Elise was a psychopathic cat who wanted to see how long he would last with her claws at his throat. Why he wasn't dead baffled him, but clearly there was a *reason*.

After he'd been grabbed only blocks from DEA headquarters, he'd been unconscious for hours. There was no clock in the dark, windowless room where he was being held, but one of the men who checked on him had a digital watch. It helped him keep track of the time, because once he had a starting point, he could mentally keep count.

At three thirty-four P.M. he saw Elise Hunt for the first time. He suspected that they'd injected him with drugs and he was still mostly out of it. She talked and he tried to listen, but it was as if she was at the end of a long tunnel. The room was hot and stuffy, but he felt cold and his every muscle was sore from being tied up for so long. But he wasn't dead, and he had to hold on to that.

At seven ten he felt more himself; whatever they'd drugged him with had passed through his system. His head ached, his mouth was parched, but he was alive and needed to regain his strength.

Then bright lights came on, nearly blinding him after being in the dark for so long. Instinctively, he fought against the restraints, but they were secure.

"Take off his shirt and roll him over," Elise said.

His survival instincts had him fighting, but to no avail. Hands that belonged to faces he couldn't see grabbed his shirt and tore it off, then pushed him facedown on scratchy, thin carpet. It smelled like oil and cleanser. "Hold him still, I don't want to kill him yet."

The pain that seared into his back made him scream and she laughed.

"Scream as loud as you want, sugar. No one can hear you."

It wasn't until she was done and he felt the throbbing from her knife that Brad realized Elise had carved an *H* into his back. Branding him. Marking him.

She talked almost the entire time. She was excited, energized. She talked about Lucy.

"She can't touch me," she kept saying in a singsong voice. "I knew she'd go crazy. Maybe *I'm* the psychic one!"

Then she'd slapped him.

"*You killed my sister!* Do you know how that scarred me? For life? Watching my sister and aunt die so violently?"

He didn't believe it for a minute. The girl was insane.

Lucy said she's a psychopath, plain and simple. Not legally insane. She enjoys these games and knows right from wrong. She loves doing bad things. Inflicting pain, humiliation.

What had Lucy said? She was impulsive and unpredictable. So Brad didn't bait her. He couldn't afford to be so seriously injured that he couldn't escape if presented the opportunity.

She kicked him in the balls and the pain was so sharp that he couldn't breathe for a long minute. He felt men tugging at him, Elise giving orders, but he couldn't distinguish the words over the ringing in his head.

By the time he gathered himself together, the lights were out, the room was empty, and his feet were chained to a metal desk. His hands were free. He tried to get out of the chains as soon as his fingers stopped shaking, but they were secure.

He hadn't seen anyone since then. They hadn't fed him or given him water, but every once in a while bright lights would blind him unexpectedly. Not a basement— there were few basements in Texas, especially in this area—but it felt secure. Like a storage room or a garage or reinforced shed or something similar. Thick walls, and when he leaned against them they had some give, as if there were padding to them. Soundproofing.

Scream, no one can hear you.

The first time someone threw firecrackers into the room, he thought it was gunfire and he was dead. Elise laughed hysterically outside the door.

Not bullets. Fireworks. Just fireworks.

The second time firecrackers were set off in the room, one got so close to him it seared his skin. He was pretty sure it was the young guard this time—a kid named Donny, not more than twenty-three—because Brad recognized his voice. He'd said something when he opened the door, like, "You sure?" Then he tossed in several firecrackers and closed the door.

It was Donny's watch that gave him a good basis for tracking time, and he figured it was between nine and ten about now. Maybe a little later.

His back ached from where Elise cut into him. If they didn't kill him, he'd probably die from an infection. Elise had used a pocketknife, laughing that she was branding him for her family.

He tried to shake his chains, see if he could get loose, but the connection was solid and the desk he was tied to wasn't budging. He moved around as much as he could. The chain was about ten feet long, and there was a small bathroom right next to him. No electricity but the bathroom at least provided him water—metallic tasting water that dribbled out of an old sink, but it was better than nothing and he had to keep up his strength. When Elise had been down here carving his back, he'd memorized the layout. It looked almost like a den—nothing inside, everything built into the walls. There was padding on the walls—soundproofing—but it looked old, like it had been installed years ago. A window looked out into another smaller room—dark. No chairs, no pictures, no windows. Beyond that was a door. He hadn't been able to see on the other side of the door, even when they opened it. The other room was dark, but based on the smell he thought it might be a garage.

A residence? Whose? Donny's? A property they'd missed when they seized of Nicole Rollins's holdings? Were they still in San Antonio? Out of town? It was an older home in a quiet area—he didn't hear traffic or kids or neighbors. They hadn't gagged him, which told him Elise was right and she wasn't worried about any sound he might make. Possibly because of the soundproofing.

Possibly because they were in the middle of nowhere. Or both. Besides, screaming would deplete his strength, and he needed every ounce.

Other than the bathroom, he couldn't reach anything else in the room, including the door that was locked from the outside. He didn't have a mattress, blanket, or pillow, but he didn't care about comforts. He'd already searched the bathroom—it was bare. He'd felt around for anything he could use as a weapon—there wasn't even a towel rack attached by the sink and the toilet didn't have a water tank.

He didn't hear *anyone* unless they came into the room.

He was cold because he was still mostly naked. At one point an hour ago he heard the AC turn on; it was still on and he was even colder. Did they want him uncomfortable? Or were they not even thinking about him anymore? Drug withdrawal also might have affected his body temperature. They'd taken his shoes and his belt, though he didn't remember when; he still wore his pants. He could tell by the lack of weight in his pockets that he didn't have his wallet, badge, or gun. He vaguely remembered pulling his gun when his car was shot at, but he didn't remember what happened to it. Everything was fuzzy.

He drank some more of the foul-tasting water, then sat down. His back smarted. But that was the least of his concerns.

What the *hell* did she want?

He heard someone talking—not Elise—it was a male voice and another female voice. He couldn't see them, and he wondered if he was imagining things. He heard words here and there, but couldn't put them in context.

He must have dozed off for a while because he woke to a click of the lock, then blinding light. He blinked, couldn't see who'd come in. His body was sore, telling him he'd been asleep for some time.

There were at least two of them in the room, maybe three. He narrowed his eyes, but was still nearly blind from the light.

He heard voices, one definitely Elise's.

"Ready, set, go!" she said.

Suddenly, a sharp, stabbing pain hit him all over. He had no idea what the hell happened, but it was like every nerve burned him, and he couldn't help but scream out. It was so sudden, so unexpected . . . another bright light, this he now knew was a flash, and then icy cold water was poured over his body.

A moment later, the room went dark, the door shut, and the lock engaged. The last thing he heard was Elise's laughter.

Chapter Twenty-one

Aggie acted far more confident than she felt as she explained to SAPD officers the events leading up to the murder of Mitts Vasquez. Fortunately, no one questioned Nate's presence, and none of the cops who had searched his truck earlier were there—a different precinct coupled with a different shift. Nate even chatted with one of the cops he'd worked with in the past.

She stuck with her story that her boss, Brad Donnelly, had assigned her to locate Mitts Vasquez, who had an active SAPD warrant and Brad believed he had valuable information about drug shipments in the area for another case he was working. Observe and report, she said, call in if she spotted him. Yes, she knew that Donnelly was missing, but were they supposed to stop working? It was a potentially important case, and she didn't want it to fall through the cracks.

No one questioned her. She didn't lie about her interest in Aunt Rita, or the shooter coming out of the downstairs apartment—which they now knew was vacant—nor did she lie about Nate's pursuit of said shooter. There was no reason to, and *technically* she didn't really lie about her assignment. Brad *had* asked her to work on the drugs found in Nate's truck, and the cops didn't have to know that her stakeout of Mitts Vasquez was related to *those* drugs. Besides, that was *her* theory, one she hadn't had a chance to share with Brad before he was taken.

By the time they were done and cleared to leave, it was after ten at night. She was tired and worried and starving even after all the snacks earlier. "Want me to drop you off at Lucy's?" she asked Nate.

"You're staying."

"Excuse me?"

"I don't think you should go home right now. If one of the players was staking out the apartment, they could have seen you, figured out you work with Brad, might go after you. Until we know what the hell is going on, we stay together. There's plenty of room at Lucy's house."

Aggie didn't think that was necessary, and she was about to argue with him, when he continued. "When the shit hits the fan," Nate said, "we need everyone together and on the same page. Brad would have my hide if we didn't put you under our protective wing."

That irritated her. "I didn't take you for a sexist, Nate."

He stared at her so intensely that she almost stepped back. He looked genuinely insulted. "Lucy is a woman and my partner and I fucking respect her as much as anyone on the job. But we watch each other's backs."

She shouldn't have said it. Nate was right. She'd seen no sign that he treated Lucy different than he treated Brad. "I didn't mean it like that, I'm sorry," she mumbled.

"Look, Aggie, we don't know what's going on. Vasquez was gunned down in front of us. He had answers; he's never talking. Brad is missing. We have Sean in prison and who the fuck knows what's going on with Kane and Jack right now. You've been making calls and talking to people, you're in the middle of this now. Okay?"

"Okay," she mumbled. "Can we stop by my place so I can pick up a bag and feed my cat?"

"Sure." Then he smiled, just a bit. "Cat?"

"I wanted a dog, but my work hours are crazy, and Solo came with the house. When I bought it, I realized the owners had left him behind."

"Solo?"

"I'm a Star Wars fan, have a problem with that?"

"No, ma'am. Let's go feed Solo the cat."

An hour later, Lucy listened to Nate and Aggie report on their evening. The death of Vasquez hit her hard—whoever was orchestrating this . . . *attack* for lack of a better word . . . on her friends and family didn't have any qualms about murder. Vasquez might have been a drug dealer and thief, but he'd been killed because of what he knew.

Which meant Brad Donnelly was in grave danger. The same people had him, and they wouldn't think twice about killing him when they were done with him.

You have to accept the fact that Brad might be dead. Just because they didn't kill him in the street doesn't mean they didn't kill him later.

Why take Brad in the first place? Why plant the drugs on Nate? Nate should be able to get out of it . . . he had no history of drug use and his record was clear. Decorated veteran, established FBI agent, SWAT trained, well respected. Did someone just want to tarnish his reputation? Try to force him out? Keep him off the job for a few days?

It's a game, and you know how much Elise likes to play games.

The security panel beeped. Lucy looked at the tablet, saw a familiar figure walking up to the door while a taxi disappeared from view. She blinked, unsure if her eyes weren't deceiving her.

She ran to the door, flung it open just as her brother knocked.

"*Patrick?*"

"Lucy." He stepped in, closed the door, and hugged her. "I would have been here earlier, but I was flying standby and stuck in Dallas waiting for a transfer. I almost rented a car and drove."

She couldn't believe he was here, standing here, in her foyer. She hadn't seen him since Thanksgiving—six months ago. They'd had a great weekend, but they didn't get to see each other often enough.

"Why are you here?"

"Why? Jack didn't tell you I was coming?"

She shook her head. "I haven't talked to him since he landed in Monterrey to search for Kane."

"When he found out that Nate was in trouble, he asked me to help. I'd do anything for you and Sean, you know that."

Tears threatened, but she pushed them back. She led Patrick to the kitchen, where Nate and Aggie were cleaning up after their impromptu dinner. "You remember Nate."

"Of course."

"Aggie, this is my brother Patrick. Aggie Jensen is with the DEA. She's been working the drug angle. Her primary suspect was gunned down tonight."

"I talked to Dillon before I left D.C. He'll be here Monday night if Sean doesn't make bail. He's testifying in a trial and can't get out of it since he's the expert witness."

"Sean will make bail. He's innocent."

"I know."

Lucy didn't know why she was so relieved to hear that.

"But even so, bail on a capital case isn't guaranteed. Did you see him today?"

"He was questioned all day—his lawyer told me

tomorrow. Visiting hours start at ten. Rick Stockton worked with the Houston chief of police to make sure that Sean was in the federal administrative jail for the weekend. It's safer for him—not only because it's a federal facility. If someone set him up because they wanted to kill him, he's not going to be at the jail they'd expect."

"Good. I'm here to do anything you need. Jack said Jesse needs protection. I assume that's why Nate is here. I can drive you to Houston tomorrow."

"My lawyer was going to—he's friends with Jack, a former cop. I'll be there all weekend."

"Because you're going to investigate Mona Hill's murder."

"Of course I am. Houston isn't going to do it."

"Then you need backup, and a lawyer isn't going to cut it."

"Thank you." She hugged him again, not realizing how much she needed her family right now. "I'll call Garrett and tell him."

The security panel beeped again. Nate looked at the display. "SAPD," he grumbled. "Two cops and a suit."

It was close to midnight. What were they doing here?

Lucy feared the worst. That they were coming to tell her that something happened to Sean in jail. That he was hurt . . . that he was dead.

She ran to the door and flung it open, Patrick right behind her.

"Agent Lucy Kincaid Rogan?" one of the officers said.

"Yes. What happened?"

The "suit" as Nate said was a tall female impeccably dressed. She said, "I'm Delia Fortuna with the district attorney's office. I'm here to inform you that there is an emergency restraining order against you for the next seventy-two hours. You cannot contact Elise Hunt, or go within one thousand feet of her person."

"What the hell?" Patrick said.

The ADA asked, "Who are you, sir?"

"Her brother."

"Agent Kincaid," Fortuna said, ignoring Patrick, "Ms. Hunt claimed that you harassed her and threatened her at a gasoline station, and she produced a witness who corroborated her story."

"That is not true."

"Ms. Hunt's lawyer and her psychologist also submitted sworn statements that you threatened her in court and during interrogation when she was being questioned two years ago, and that you have consistently threatened and intimidated her over the last two years. I have written up the accusations."

"I'm an FBI agent. I questioned Elise in the course of a murder investigation."

"Judge Axelrod signed the restraining order, you can go before the court on Monday to contest it, otherwise it will be extended for a year."

Axelrod. She was suspected of being on the take, had been for years. She'd given Elise her original sentence of a group home—she escaped en route—and then Axelrod bought her bullshit story that her brother Tobias had forced her to escape. She was then given not even two years in juvenile jail! Lucy saw red. She didn't know how to convince these people that Elise was a pathological liar and a cold-blooded killer and that she was intimately involved in everything that had happened today.

"She followed *me*!" Lucy could not *believe* this. Had this been Elise's game? To tie her down here in San Antonio? "Do not be fooled by her age," she continued. "Elise Hunt is a sociopath and a liar. Talk to my lawyer; he was there. He can corroborate everything I said."

Patrick had his hand on her arm. "Thank you, Counselor," he said. "Do you have the documentation so we can read it?"

"Of course."

Patrick took the papers. "Thank you," he said again.

"This is bullshit!" Lucy said.

"Good night," Patrick said and closed the door. "Lucy, you need to calm down."

"Calm down? Really? She followed *me*. She confronted *me*. I didn't threaten her. This is her playbook. She's going to do something and now I can't go after her!"

"You're not the only cop in San Antonio," Patrick said.

"I'm the only cop who understands Elise Hunt!"

She brushed past Patrick and went to the kitchen. This was . . . unbelievable. Just a mess.

Patrick followed her. "Right now, our focus is Sean."

"But she's planning something!" Why could no one see that girl for who she actually is?

"We'll be in Houston tomorrow," Patrick said. "Nowhere near her." He handed Lucy the papers. "This says you need to be in court at three on Monday."

"No," she said. "I'll be in Houston bringing Sean home." Still she looked at the papers, getting angrier by the minute. "She's supposed to be in Los Angeles!" She pulled her cell phone out of her pocket and called Garrett Lee—she didn't care that she woke him up.

She told him what had happened, and said, "According to the papers, I'm supposed to be in court at three on Monday. You were there today. You know I didn't threaten her."

"Yes, I was, and no, you didn't, but I need to read the report. Fax it to me. We'll talk in the morning."

She walked back to Sean's office and faxed everything to Garrett. Then she sat down at Sean's desk and stared at the papers.

Lucy Kincaid Rogan is a sworn federal agent and used her badge and weapon to intimidate Ms. Hunt.

Ms. Hunt fears for her life.

What was her endgame? To keep Lucy in San Antonio because of something going on with Sean in Houston? Lucy had to be there, with Sean, when he was arraigned. He would be granted bail—he *had* to be granted bail. She couldn't abandon him to defend herself against trumped up charges!

Garrett would stay. He was her lawyer, he could speak for her, right? He'd been there at the gas station. He didn't like everything she'd done today, but he knew that she hadn't followed Elise, and none of the other events were relevant to *this*. If he swore to the court that Elise followed *them* and that Lucy hadn't threatened her, they would believe him, right?

She didn't know. She didn't know which end was up.

Patrick came into Sean's office and closed the door. "You okay?"

"No." She slapped her hand on the papers. "She has Brad Donnelly. I know it. There's a reason she did this—she set me up. She *lied* to get this ridiculous restraining order. But why?" She wanted to talk to Dillon, but it was far too late in Washington.

"Let's focus on what we can control. And right now, that's helping Sean."

"But I can't control what happens to Sean! He's in jail for a murder he didn't do. So many things are up in the air. They think they found the murder weapon in his plane. They really believe he killed her. It's . . . it's . . ." She was going to say *too much*. But she'd faced worse in her life. She'd faced a greater evil than a little sociopathic bitch.

But the truth was, she would rather face evil head-on than the unpredictable Elise Hunt.

"You need to sleep."

"I can't sleep."

"You *can*. You need to get a couple of hours or you'll

be worthless to Sean. We'll leave at five, okay? Beat traffic and get to Houston long before visiting hours. You're not in this alone, Lucy. And if we have to investigate Mona's murder ourselves, that's exactly what we will do."

She had someone on her side. Someone who loved Sean, had faith in him. Someone who believed in the system, but also knew that the system could be corrupted. Someone who had been by her side her entire life.

Tears threatened. "Thank you," she whispered. "I—I don't know if could do this on my own."

Patrick walked over to where she sat at Sean's desk and hugged her. "*We* are going to get through this, Lucy. You, Sean, Nate, Kane, Jack, Megan, me—no one can defeat us, not when the Kincaids and the Rogans work together. Never forget that. You will never be alone, Lucy."

Then the tears came. For the first time, the tears came and wouldn't stop.

Her brother held her tight.

Chapter Twenty-two

Jack was up before the sun, cleaned up the small camp they'd made, and had eaten his rations and cold coffee before Ranger came back from his recon.

"I caught his trail." He handed Jack a small black bag.

"His phone?" Shit. Kane had lost his sat phone, which is why he couldn't check in.

Ranger nodded. "But it was hidden and marked."

"He planned to return. Idea of how long?"

"Less than twenty-four hours."

They had an internal code system that worked in the field, especially on long, complex ops with multiple teams. Less than twenty-four hours meant that Kane had dropped the phone sometime after sunrise yesterday morning. "We'll put it back on the way, leave a message. Ready?"

"Yep." Jack put on his pack and handed Ranger his. Checked his sidearms even though he'd checked and rechecked them both last night and this morning.

Ranger's contact yesterday was adamant that Kane hadn't been recaptured, but that he was still pursuing Peter Blair deep into the steep mountains southeast of Monterrey. It was dangerous because Kane was persona non grata in this part of Mexico. And the whole thing stunk like a trap. Why had Kane pushed so far into hostile territory?

When he was grabbed Thursday, Ranger called it in, but Ranger's contact was certain that Kane had escaped and was still in pursuit. Why hadn't he pulled back? This whole thing made no sense; that Kane hadn't called in to say he was alive was problematic, and made Jack question Ranger's source of information.

Maybe this was a trap for Jack and Ranger as well. Take out Kane, leave a few crumbs to think he's still alive, draw in the rest of the RCK team. Without Kane's or Ranger's leadership, RCK operations south of the border wouldn't survive long.

Jack had to think about all possible contingencies. He told Ranger to hold up. He pulled out his sat phone and called JT to give him a report and their exact location. JT didn't say much—there wasn't anything to say—but indicated that he had mobilized a second team that was waiting for instructions in Hidalgo. If Jack needed it, they could parachute to any location near them in two hours.

Jack hoped it wouldn't come to that.

He asked about Sean.

"Let me deal with Sean. You find Kane. Out."

Shit, that wasn't an answer, which meant the situation was bad.

Jack secured his phone and motioned to Ranger that he was ready. They hiked nearly a mile southwest when Ranger stopped and hid Kane's bag back in its spot, with a message in the bag that said when they found it and to make contact.

Silently, they continued. Kane either marked his path because he'd need help finding his way out, or he'd expected Ranger to follow.

Jack knew Ranger was upset because Kane had been

grabbed in the first place when they had been paired off. He blamed himself, and that wasn't going to help them in the long run. Guilt made good soldiers do stupid things. But he hoped that Ranger's experience and training had him coping with the situation.

He let Ranger lead not only because he knew this area better than Jack, but because he needed the focus. They stopped for water and a one-minute rest every hour, and to confirm their location, even though Ranger knew exactly where they were and hadn't gotten off course.

Nearly four hours later, Ranger put his arm up, fist closed; Jack froze.

They were on the edge of a small village far from any other town. So small that Jack could only see three structures, all appearing unoccupied. He knew where he was on the map, but he'd never been on this side of the mountain. A dirt road could be seen through the shrubs, and in the distance Jack heard an approaching Jeep. He and Ranger maneuvered closer to the road, then crouched so they could observe unseen.

Two Jeeps approached their spot. The first had three men, all in pseudo-military gear. The second had two men including Blair, the man Kane had been tracking.

Kane was here somewhere.

If he hadn't been recaptured.

He wasn't in either Jeep. A good sign?

If Ranger's contact was right, Kane had escaped and was intent on pursuing Blair as long as it took to stop him. Jack couldn't help but wonder if Kane was motivated by a darker purpose.

While it was true that Peter Blair was bad news, a notorious human trafficker who had ruined the lives of countless people, Kane's job had been to rescue the girls, that was it. Though Jack wouldn't lose sleep if Blair ended up dead in a ditch, he also had powerful allies, and Jack didn't think that Kane had quite thought this through. RCK did not assassinate the bad guys. Unless Kane knew something that he hadn't shared, his actions didn't make sense.

Yet, Jack had the utmost respect for Kane Rogan and all that he'd given to protecting the innocent. He didn't act on anger or for revenge. He risked himself solely to save lives.

Yes, Kane knew something they didn't.

When the trucks passed by, Ranger whispered, "There's only one place they can be going. That's where Kane is. There's a creek bed on the other side of the road we can follow—safer than using the road. If we hoof it, it'll take an hour." Ranger took out an energy bar and water bottle; Jack did the same. They waited another two minutes, made sure no other vehicles were coming, and crossed the road.

Jack let Ranger lead and hoped his old friend was right.

Chapter Twenty-three

Sean kept his head down during breakfast. No one talked to him; he was fine with that. He didn't feel much like eating; his stomach was twisted up in knots. But he forced down toast and scrambled eggs so dry he drained his orange juice (five percent real juice) in one long swig.

At the end of breakfast, he lined up with the other prisoners to head back to their cells for a head count. Then at nine they'd be taken to a common area.

All Sean wanted was to see Lucy.

Sean was still sitting in his cell—staring at the wall but not seeing anything—when his door buzzed open. A guard with the name PORTER on his chest said, "Rogan, follow me."

"Why?"

"You don't ask the questions."

"But—"

"Do you want to be written up? I can make your life easy, or I can make it hell. Your choice."

If he was in prison for any length of time, he'd be written up often. He didn't fall in line with authority easily. Never had.

It was only seven thirty. Lucy wasn't here—unless she pulled strings and was able to get in earlier. That was possible. Or his lawyer was here with news. Good or bad. Hell, just getting out of the cell was a plus.

Porter motioned for Sean to walk ahead of him. Sean complied, and they headed to the end of the hall. The guard manning the door unlocked it from the other side of the glass and buzzed them through.

They went through this four times, including an elevator ride down. They ended up in the same holding area where Sean arrived yesterday.

"What's going on?" Sean asked.

Porter didn't answer. Instead, he handed the guard manning the main desk a file folder. "Rogan, Sean Tyler, Prisoner 4J55591, cleared for transport."

"Transport where?" Sean asked.

He didn't answer that question, either.

The desk guard looked at the paperwork, signed the folder. "We have a bus going to Beaumont in twenty."

"No," Sean said. "My lawyer is meeting me here this morning."

Porter finally looked at him. "I have paperwork to take you to Beaumont, that's what I'm doing."

"I'm being arraigned on Monday; I'm supposed to be here until then. I need to talk to my lawyer. I'm not going anywhere until I talk to my lawyer!"

"One more word and you'll be in solitary when you get to Beaumont. Turn around."

This wasn't right. Someone had screwed up somewhere, because he wasn't supposed to go anywhere. "You don't understand," he said.

The guard forcibly turned him around. Sean pushed back, startled.

The guard took out his billy club and hit him hard on the back of his thighs. That brought him immediately to his knees. "Do not move." To the desk guard, Porter said, "Who's running the bus?"

"Beaumont. They're here to pick up a prisoner who had a late court date yesterday. They can take one more. But if anyone else is going, we'll have to send one of our people with them."

"This is the only one," Porter said. "Get up, Rogan. Slowly."

Sean complied. He didn't have a choice. He knew this was wrong, but the more he argued with the guard, the worse off he'd be.

Porter and the desk guard put shackles on his ankles and a belt around his waist, they cuffed his hands to a short chain.

Then to the desk guard, Porter said, "I have to get the prisoner's belongings, can you watch him for five?"

The desk guard motioned for Sean to sit on a bench. "Don't move," he said, then went back to his desk.

Porter left.

"Sir," Sean said.

"Don't talk, either," he said and went back to reading a file on his desk.

"There's something wrong with this transfer. I'm being arraigned on Monday. I can't go to Beaumont."

"The paperwork says you can."

"I can't. My wife is a cop."

That had the guy looking at him. "Here?"

"San Antonio." He didn't say FBI. Some local cops didn't like the FBI.

"I'm sure no one here knows you're married to one of us. So don't go flapping your mouth to the inmates." He looked back down.

"Sir, she's going to be here for visiting hours. Can we postpone this? Until I talk to my lawyer and get this straightened out? Call the Houston police chief. She worked with the FBI to get me here, rather than county lock up, because there's some people inside who would like to see me dead."

"You're full of stories, aren't you?" he said with a half smile, not looking at Sean.

"Please, just call someone and verify the transfer."

Sean must have sounded scared or serious or sincere, because finally the guard looked at him again, then typed on his computer. "The transfer was authorized by the warden, with a return Monday morning."

"Are you sure?"

Now he'd lost the guard. The guy went back to his work and said, "Zip it, Rogan. You're not the first prisoner who thinks the system is fucked, you won't be the last."

Porter returned. "Is the prisoner giving you a bad time, Joe?"

"Just chatty."

Porter shook his head at Sean. "I see from your file you have no record, you're going to have to learn real quick how to survive in here."

Sean didn't say a word.

Porter shook his head. "Get up."

Sean complied. Arguing wasn't going to do anything except piss off the guards.

They walked down two secured corridors to the garage. Two corrections officers with the Beaumont prison logo on their sleeves were drinking coffee and talking with the desk guard there, who was behind bulletproof shielding in a control room. A small bus labeled TEXAS PRISON AUTHORITY was parked in the wide space. Another prisoner—in his sixties with short, thick gray hair, shackled like Sean—sat on a bench against the wall.

Porter handed the paperwork and Sean's belongings to one of the guards. He looked it over, signed something, and handed it back to Porter.

No one questioned the paperwork. Why would they? Transfers from the administrative jail happened all the time.

Don't panic. Remain calm.

Sean didn't do well in cuffs or behind bars. When Lucy got here, she'd figure it out. She'd talk to his lawyer; Felicity knew what she was doing. She would get him back here today. There had to be a mistake.

He had to believe it.

Forty-eight hours. You'll be out of this mess in forty-eight hours.

Unless he wasn't granted bail.

Unless he couldn't prove he hadn't killed Mona Hill. He didn't have the same faith in the system that Lucy had. He knew that circumstantial evidence could sometimes convict innocent people. But this was worse—someone was framing him. The gun they found in his plane . . . it might as well have been smoking. Someone had planned this. And the only person could be Elise Hunt.

An eighteen-year-old psycho planned this?

No . . . there were others involved. Who had taken over for the Hunt family after their network was destroyed? Was Elise working with them? Why come after Sean and his friends? That said revenge.

But this was a lot of work for revenge when he would have been easy enough to kill. He took a lot of precautions with his security, but nothing was foolproof.

They don't want you dead. If they did, you'd be dead.

They had a bigger plan. In the end it might mean killing him, but until then . . . what?

Lucy was in danger. His son. Who was with them? Who was protecting them? Nate? Who else, with Jack and Kane stuck south of the border? Would Duke come? JT? Kate? Patrick?

Someone had to protect his family when he couldn't.

"We got the clearance, let's go," one of the Beaumont guards—Sheffield—said.

And with that, they led Sean into the bus and attached his handcuffs to the bar in front of him on the seat. The other prisoner was put across the narrow aisle from him, also cuffed to a bar. One guard drove, separated by a steel grate. The second guard sat on a jump seat sideways. There were six rows of benches in the small bus, but only Sean and this old guy were inside.

As soon as they were cleared, the garage door rolled up and the bus backed out.

Sean couldn't shake the fear that he was being taken to his execution.

Chapter Twenty-four

Megan Elliott Kincaid had had enough of the runaround. Yesterday she'd talked to three people at Victorville, where Jimmy Hunt was incarcerated, and finally she got the assurance that she could interview him first thing this morning. She and SSA Blair Novak arrived at six in the morning and at first, everything went well. They were escorted to an interview room usually reserved for lawyers and their clients; fifteen minutes later, Megan walked out and asked the guard about the delay. "We called, we had this set up, Hunt should have been waiting for us."

"I don't know why there is a delay," he said.

"Find out," Megan snapped.

He bristled, and she realized she should have been more diplomatic. But she was as worried about her husband as she was about Sean and Lucy. Jack was somewhere in the middle of Mexico on a dangerous mission to find Kane and she'd only spoken to him briefly last night, just long enough to know that he was alive. She'd hardly slept and had to be up at three in the morning to drive down here. Dealing with bureaucracy was the last thing she wanted to do right now.

She returned to the interview room and told Blair the

status. "We'll give it five more minutes," Blair said, "then I'll call the warden. I know him pretty well."

"You were involved in this case?"

"Not directly. It was a DEA case, we assisted."

"Why is he in a state prison if it was a federal case?"

"The state prosecuted first. His federal case is pending. At first they were talking plea, but then he started playing legal games."

"Why didn't we get him first?"

"That's way above my pay grade. But it had to do with the murder of an undercover LAPD cop. So he's not getting out even if nothing happens with the federal case. My part of the investigation was documenting the search and seizure of property at the Hunt compound. When Margaret Hunt was killed, we went through everything. She'd destroyed much of the evidence, but we found enough that helped the state in their conviction, and some evidence of corruption in LAPD. I helped remove two bad cops from the line of duty. Not my favorite thing to do—but dammit, I hate when our job is tainted by these guys on the take."

She glanced at her watch and pulled her phone out of her pocket. Before she could locate the warden's number, a man walked into the room accompanied by a corrections officer.

"Agent Novak? Elliott? I'm Assistant Warden Josh Steiner." He extended his hand, which they both shook. He motioned for them to sit and opened a file folder he was carrying. "I'm flummoxed about why this information wasn't in our computer system, I could have saved you the trip. Jimmy Hunt was transferred two weeks ago."

"Where?"

"Beaumont."

"Texas?" Megan said. "Under what authority?"

He pushed the folder toward her. She looked at the paperwork, but it didn't make a lot of sense to her. Steiner explained, "The DEA requested the transfer because Jimmy Hunt planned to turn state's evidence on an active investigation."

"He doesn't need to be transferred for that," Megan said.

"They needed him to testify in court."

"Why didn't you tell me this yesterday?"

"It wasn't in the computer—I mean, it is, but it wasn't logged properly. He was transferred temporarily and will be returning here once he is done with his testimony. The AUSA who approved the transfer is there—you can contact him and find out what's going on. I'm sorry you came all this way for nothing."

On the surface, it all looked legit. But the timing was more than a little suspicious.

"Is there anything else I can do for you?"

"Logs," she said. "I want to see everyone who visited Hunt, talked to him on the phone, sent him mail. Every. Single. Contact."

While they were waiting, she sent a message to Rick Stockton.

Hunt transferred to Beaumont two weeks ago per AUSA Neil Barnes to testify in a DEA trial. I requested all logs. Please advise.

Chapter Twenty-five

Jack stayed hidden in an abandoned barn that looked ready to fall at the slightest breeze while Ranger confirmed that the trucks they'd seen two hours earlier were at the compound in the center of town. Town being relative, as there were few structures, no maintained roads, and they hadn't seen anyone other than Blair and his men.

There was no reason that Kane couldn't have alerted them that he was safe. Jack had been thinking about it for the last twenty-four hours, and if Kane had told Ranger that he'd escaped, Jack wouldn't have had to come down here. Instead they learned through Kane's actions—he'd left them a path to follow, but Jack was certain Ranger could have tracked Kane on his own.

But it was always safer in numbers.

Jack was worried about Lucy. He considered Sean as close as any of his brothers. He wanted to be there not just to support them, but to protect his family. That he couldn't be was troublesome on multiple levels.

And he really didn't like not knowing what was going on.

Ranger returned after forty minutes.

"There's a meeting. Two other vehicles came while I was observing. I didn't recognize any of the players, but they look mid-level cartel. Village is abandoned, but looks like a regular meeting spot."

"Kane?"

Ranger shook his head. "If he doesn't want to be found he won't be."

"Damn straight."

Jack and Ranger both had their guns out at the sound of footsteps, but didn't fire. Kane walked into the barn.

Ranger breathed an audible sigh of relief, but Jack was irritated. "You fucking broke protocol, Rogan," Jack said.

"It couldn't be avoided. I knew Ranger would learn I escaped—Peter Blair and his people are used to keeping young girls in line, not trained soldiers."

"Sean's in trouble."

"I know."

"Know? How do you know? He was just arrested yesterday."

Kane looked surprised. "Arrested?"

"What kind of trouble are *you* talking about?"

"It's why I went after Blair. When they had me in the root cellar, they were chatty. Sound carries. Blair told his people that Sean would be under their thumb soon, that everything was on schedule. I sent Sean a message as soon as I could to give him the heads-up, but I needed more information. There's no reason that Sean should be on their radar. Maybe to leverage me, but that didn't seem to be the context of the conversation."

Kane looked from Ranger to Jack. "Why was Sean arrested?"

"Killing Mona Hill."

"I don't know who the fuck that is."

Jack reminded him of Mona Hill and her connection to the Hunt family and their drug cartel. "Sean's in jail in Houston until he can be arraigned on Monday. Donnelly was grabbed outside DEA headquarters and is currently

MIA, and Dunning's been suspended after SAPD found sixteen kilos of coke in his truck. Sean had Nico Villanueva down in L.A. investigating Elise Hunt, but didn't tell anyone. We only found out after he was arrested."

Kane didn't say anything. He walked out of the barn.

Jack didn't follow. He knew his friend well enough to know that Kane needed a minute to process the new information. Kane Rogan had an uncanny way of seeing the bigger picture. Not to mention he usually had more information than anyone else.

It didn't take him long to return. "Peter Blair was in the States three weeks ago. Wasn't that the same time that Elise Hunt was released from prison?"

"Yes."

"This is a setup, but I don't know who the primary target is—me or Sean."

"We need to go back."

"First we get Blair."

Jack disagreed. "Lucy is in trouble, Rogan! Sean, Nate, Brad—they've all been taken off the field. That leaves Lucy and Jesse vulnerable."

"Nate's not in prison, is he?"

"No."

"He'll stay with Jess. But Blair knows the bigger plan. He will talk. Why would Sean be under *their* thumb? Blair's a freelancer. He could be working for anyone. He can go in and out of the country with ease, he has people all over the fucking place. He's worked for the Hunts in the past, before the shit went down. I wouldn't be surprised if Jimmy Hunt was running his operation from prison. Hell, they could have built an alliance that we don't know about yet, people we didn't shut down two years ago. Blair knows details. We make him talk. We need his information or we can't do shit to help Sean or find Donnelly."

Jack hoped that Kane was right. He trusted him, even though he thought this was a fifty-fifty proposition.

Kane looked at Ranger. "What do we have?"

"Us, a bag of weapons, standard equipment. There's at least a dozen men at the compound."

"Seventeen. Four factions trying to come to terms on territory. Blair is leading it, and he'll get what he wants. He didn't tell anyone that we rescued the girls, nor did he tell anyone about me—just his core group. Which tells me my capture was a separate job from this excursion. I've been tracking him since I slipped out. I heard him tell someone that the girls were en route to El Paso as planned."

Ranger shook his head. "I've been in contact with the Sisters. They've already moved the girls to a safe haven in Monterrey, and they'll be reunited with their families as soon as possible—Siobhan and Dyson are leading the effort."

"His lie tells me that he either doesn't care or is buying time. But we need more information about Sean's situation; Blair has it."

"And you expected to do it alone?" Jack said.

"If I had to, but I trusted Ranger would find me. You're a bonus, which puts us in the driver's seat."

"Three against seventeen," Jack muttered. Sometimes, Kane's idea that they had the upper hand made Jack nervous.

"I have a plan."

Jack didn't doubt it, but he was getting too old for this shit. So was Kane, but he'd never admit it.

"So all your talk about retirement was just bullshit," Jack said.

"Not at the time," Kane said with surprising seriousness. "I get it. You and JT think I need to walk away. And I thought I could. But when the Sisters called Siobhan about the girls, I realized there was no one else they could call. There's others that do what we do, but not many and not in the same way. They rescue these girls after they've already been abused. There's not enough of us, and there's too many of them, and damn if I'm going to let these girls be repeatedly raped and drugged until they die before they hit twenty-five. I'm in the unique position to act quickly to certain situations. I'm not going to say no when I can say yes."

Jack used to be the same way. What changed?

Family. Commitments. Age.

Kane was going to have to come to the same realization himself, though Jack accepted that Kane might never get there. Maybe because Siobhan had a big heart, maybe because Kane didn't know any other way to live.

Jack couldn't fault him for it. Hell, he admired him even more. How did Kane turn it around? Jack had been ready to throttle him for chasing after Peter Blair and breaking all RCK protocols, yet was now ready to join his dangerous crusade?

"You have a plan?" Jack said. "Hope it's a good one."

One side of his mouth twitched up. His blue eyes practically sparkled. "It is."

Kane went over the plan and Jack thought it was fucking crazy.

But it was so crazy and so smart that Jack thought that it just might work.

Chapter Twenty-six

Lucy woke up Jesse before sunrise to say good-bye. She didn't want to keep him out of the loop. Nate and Aggie were there, and if they had to leave, Leo Proctor would fill in.

Jesse understood. But he'd grown up far too fast in the last twenty-four hours. Why did he have to go through this? His stepfather had worked for the cartels, his mother was murdered last year, now his father is in jail? The kid wasn't even fourteen yet. She wished she could give him a real childhood filled with soccer and friends and simple pleasures. Instead, his life had been defined by danger and risk and worry. She didn't want that for her son.

It had been sudden, she realized, thinking about Jesse as her son instead of just Sean's son. She loved him as her own, and loved him because he was part of Sean. Not being able to have her own children had been a dark spot on her soul, and that would never completely disappear. But it had grown smaller because she had Jesse in her life. Accepting Jesse as her son had opened her heart up more to consider adoption. She and Sean had always planned to at some point—but she'd always envisioned it in the distant future. It had only been recently that she'd wanted to bring a child into their family. She loved babies but she didn't need a baby. There were so many young children who needed a family to love and care for them.

But not now. Clearly, they had some huge hurdles to overcome. Getting Sean out of jail was only the beginning.

As Patrick drove them to Houston, leaving before the sun had even come up, she asked him about the young family that Elle, his longtime girlfriend, had been working to keep together. Patrick and Elle had brought the three kids with them for Thanksgiving, and Lucy had seen another side of Elle, who she had butted heads with over the years. For the first time, she could see what Patrick saw in the criminal defense lawyer. A strength and deep compassion that had her fighting for the underdog.

Patrick seemed surprised that she'd asked.

"The kids are doing well, thanks," he said. "Elle found them a foster family and they're together. She's still working with the older girl because of the repeated arrests—that kid is her own worst enemy sometimes. But Elle got her into a community service program instead of doing time in juvie, and as long as she keeps her nose clean, her record will be expunged when she's eighteen."

"You were great with them," Lucy said. "Both you and Elle."

"They drew the short straw with their parents," he said. "We were lucky, Lucy. Mom and Dad weren't perfect—Dad was tough on everyone, except maybe you—but they gave us exactly what we needed and they loved us."

"Dad was tough on me," she said quietly. Not while growing up—one of the benefits of being so much younger than her brothers and sisters was that she had been a bit spoiled and she didn't have the same restrictions they did. But as an adult, she sometimes felt like she'd constantly disappointed her father and worried her mother. It wasn't because she was a cop—half her family were cops—but because of other choices she'd made. Her dad was still was angry with her for pursuing the cold case into her nephew's murder. And some of the things he'd said . . . they still hurt.

"Hey, you okay?"

"Yeah, just thinking."

"We're going to get Sean out of this."

At least she could change the subject away from their family. Patrick was right: they had had an amazingly wonderful childhood. They were hardly rich—her dad had a terrific career with the Army, but they lived on a single government salary. Her siblings had been raised as Army brats, but not her. Her dad took a permanent post in San Diego when she was three, so she only remembered that house, not moving around from base to base like her brothers and sisters. Growing up she'd often felt left out when they talked about the different bases and schools, things they did together as a family. But she cherished the relationship she had with them now.

Especially now when she needed them the most.

"Elise Hunt set this up," Lucy said, "but she's not working alone. I can't figure out who is helping her. She doesn't have money to hire people. I might concede that she has contacts here, but they would be her sister's contacts, not hers. She was only in San Antonio for a few weeks before we arrested her."

"But her family has contacts. Her father."

"They've been out of commission for two years."

"I don't have to tell you that criminals can run their enterprise from prison."

True, Lucy thought. Jimmy Hunt could be orchestrating the whole thing from California, using Elise on the ground.

"That restraining order is serious," Patrick said. "You're a federal agent and it could go on your record."

"I know. I already have a message from Rachel, my boss, about it. I texted her that I would explain later, but I can't do it now. I have to focus on Sean."

Her phone rang and it was Rick Stockton. "Director," she answered formally. She was still upset with him from yesterday and the feeling she couldn't shake that he wasn't sold on Sean's innocence.

"I just got off the phone with Megan. Jimmy Hunt was transferred to the Beaumont prison. He testified against a known cartel hit man, Michael Thompson. The DEA arranged for it, and since they're the ones prosecuting Thompson, I didn't hear about it."

This was no coincidence. Jimmy was in Texas; Elise was in Texas.

"When?"

"He was transferred two weeks ago from Victorville. The trial was this week, and he's being transported back to Victorville on Monday. Megan is on her way to Texas to interview him. I'm telling you for your information, but do *not* try to talk to him. I heard about the restraining order."

"News travels fast," she snapped.

"I understand what you're going through, but you have to play by the rules."

"I was. She followed *me*, Director. There's a corrections officer from her juvenile detention facility who is missing. Erica Anderson. She canceled the last three visits with her kids. Her ex-husband is worried, and she was last seen three days ago by her neighbor. She's acting out of character according to her neighbors and her family. I think she knows something and is hiding from Elise, or she's working for Elise."

"You have nothing to back up that accusation."

"And no one else is looking! Houston PD has no idea that Elise Hunt is behind this, aren't even looking for evidence because they're convinced that Sean is guilty. Because of that, she's walking around doing whatever the hell she wants with no consequences! You don't know her like I do. We *need* to track her down and keep her under surveillance. She'll lead us to the heart of this conspiracy, and until you and the powers that be recognize that, we're all screwed. We'll find Brad Donnelly's dead body and Sean will be in prison for the rest of his life!"

She stopped, her heart racing, her face heated. She had never talked to a superior like that before in her life. A superior and a friend.

"There're some choices I can't protect you from, Agent Kincaid. I'll call you once Megan has a report."

He ended the call.

Lucy could barely contain her frustrated scream. Who was investigating Elise? Maybe if they followed her they'd find Brad, or find the people who took them.

This was all just too much. Rick was right—he couldn't protect her. But she didn't care. Saving Sean was more important than her career.

"Lucy," Patrick said.

"Don't say it."

She sent Nate a text message.

Someone needs to find and covertly track Elise Hunt. She's the key, she'll lead us to answers.

"I know what's going on here, Patrick. Elise followed me, set up the confrontation, and got the restraining order. I was firm in court, and Elise played the 'woe is me, I'm an abused kid' card. That kid was never abused. She was born bad, into a bad family, and she enjoys hurting people."

"I'm not the enemy here. But if you're not careful, you'll lose your badge."

"I don't care!"

She looked out the window. They were not even halfway

to Houston. She willed Patrick to drive faster, though he was already exceeding the speed limit.

Several minutes later, Nate called her. "I talked to Leo. He's going to spend today here with Jesse. Aggie has a lead on the Merides brothers. And as soon as I find Elise Hunt, I'll follow her."

"Thank you. If you find Erica Anderson, you might find Elise."

"Aggie has been doing some work on that angle. Brad kept detailed records of every one of Nicole's contacts. Most are dead, in jail, or underground. But there are a few who slipped away on technicalities, and a few who are affiliated with some of her old contacts. Aggie wrote a probability program that ranked them as to most likely to be working with Elise Hunt."

"I knew she was good."

"She is," Nate concurred. "The way she processes information and remembers details is a lot like Sean, actually."

"Thank you for everything, Nate. I don't know what Sean and I would do without you."

"No thanks necessary, Lucy. I'll keep you updated."

Lucy ended the call and closed her eyes. Considered her options, which were becoming fewer by the minute.

She called Megan. Her sister-in-law answered immediately.

"I'm at the airport. I'll be in Houston in a few hours," Megan said.

"Have you heard from Jack?"

"Last night, briefly. He and Ranger are secure, tracking Kane."

"Tracking Kane? How? Who has him?"

"Jack didn't share details, just wanted me to know he was safe and tracking Kane. I honestly try not to think too much about what Jack and Kane do. Are you okay?"

"Not really. I just talked to Rick."

"There are things going on at headquarters that have nothing to do with you or Sean or any of us. Rick has a lot to juggle."

She knew that, and it was hard to put aside her anxiety and worry to remember that national headquarters was going through a major reorganization. "I don't think he's confident in Sean's innocence. But that's not why I called you. When you talk to Jimmy Hunt—tread very carefully."

"I didn't know you were involved in his original investigation."

"I wasn't directly, but I know the family. Hunt was in charge, but he was removed from the day-to-day management because he was hiding out in Mexico after the state indicted him. He lost control, and he knows it deep down, but I doubt he has acknowledged it to himself or to people who work for him. Remember—according to what we learned about Nicole Rollins, Hunt orchestrated every move in her early life so she could infiltrate the DEA for the purposes of building their family drug operation. He's not stupid, he thinks multiple steps ahead. Family is very important to him, use your maiden name. Don't let him know you're a Kincaid—you won't get anything out of him, and you'll put yourself on his radar."

"Point taken. I still use Elliott at work and it's on my business cards."

"Good. While he's smart—cunning, methodical, a detailed planner—he's also a narcissist. He's blind to his faults. His primary fault is that he's a coward. Not in the traditional sense—I don't think he would shy away from violence or from making bold moves—but remember that he fled the country to avoid prosecution, leaving his family to pick up the pieces. No one knew about Nicole, but his wife was left having to deal with the FBI, the local cops, the IRS, a whole host of issues. And he was in Mexico having fun and running his drug empire from afar. I think he prefers that than to running the business day to day. And we destroyed it."

"He's angry."

"Very. He's in prison, which makes him bitter. The agreement with the DEA to testify against this hit man? He's not doing it out of the kindness of his heart. He's not even doing it for a reduced plea—I looked at his record, he's serving life in California because he was convicted of conspiracy to kill a peace officer. He didn't pull the trigger, but he ordered it done. There's another reason for him to testify, but I don't know enough about the case to know what it is. Revenge? Maybe. But it makes me very nervous that he's in Texas right now, even if he's behind bars."

"I have all the files from the recent trial, I'll look for something. I'm meeting with the AUSA when I get to Houston, he seemed cooperative when I talked to him. My flight's boarding, I need to go."

"Be careful, Megan."

"You too, Lucy. For what it's worth, I'm confident that we'll prove Sean innocent."

"Thank you. I needed that."

Chapter Twenty-seven

Beaumont was ninety miles from Houston, but they were stuck in traffic getting out of the city. Once they reached the city limits, they cruised comfortably.

If being shackled and chained in a prison bus could be considered comfortable.

Scan had gone through every possible scenario as to why he was being transferred and nothing made sense. His lawyer would have told him if it was a possibility. If there had been a threat against him, someone would have said something, right?

He didn't know. He could barely think. He hadn't slept. He was tired and scared.

He hated being scared.

Sean stared out the window. There was minimal traffic on I-10. A narrow frontage road—probably the old highway—ran parallel. Lots of open space, farmland. Green. Freedom.

Sean didn't know how he would survive prison. The idea of being behind bars for days . . . months . . . *years*. He couldn't. He couldn't do it. Even if he survived his enemies . . . and Kane's enemies . . . he would die inside. His freedom meant more to him than anything. How could he raise his son, love his wife, if he was locked up?

You'll get out of this. You have to believe it.

He didn't believe because he didn't *know*. He'd never lacked confidence. Sean had always been the one who was convinced he could get out of any trouble, because he'd proven he could. Most of the time. Even when he was expelled from Stanford after hacking into his professor's computer and exposing him as a pedophile, he didn't spend more than a night in jail. Of course, his brother Duke had banished him to MIT and he'd been angry and resentful, but he had still managed to make something of his life.

What would you have done yesterday if you'd known the police were coming for you?

He wouldn't have made it easy for them. Would he have run?

Running makes you look guilty.

But this was a frame job. If he had just gone to his plane, he would have found the planted gun. If he hadn't gone to see Mona in the first place . . .

He remembered what she said on the phone.

"If you're not going to come here, I'll fucking knock down your front door. We have to talk, Rogan. This is serious!"

He hadn't wanted her to come to San Antonio. Not because he planned on keeping the information from Lucy, but because he didn't want her anywhere near his family. Not Lucy, not Jesse. So he went there.

What if he'd told her to come to him? Would it have changed anything? If the people who killed her wanted him to be framed for her murder, where she was killed was irrelevant—it was simply that she was killed immediately after he talked to her.

His head pounded and he wished he could have slept last night, because he needed to think. To plan. To figure out what he was going to do if he couldn't get out on bail.

The only thing he knew was that he couldn't spend the rest of his life in prison. He would rather be dead.

He closed his eyes.

You can't think that way. What about Lucy? What about Jesse?

He couldn't kill himself. But he could escape. It might take a while, but he could escape.

And then he'd be on the run for the rest of his life. Without his family, without his wife and son. Without anyone to help him.

All this speculation was only going to make him sick. He had to take it day by day. Get through the weekend. He'd have more information on Monday.

The problem was he couldn't see the end. He didn't have important information *now*. He didn't know what anyone was doing, or how they would prove he hadn't killed Mona Hill.

He regretted very little in his life, but he regretted with all his heart and soul not telling Lucy about his meeting with Mona. Lucy thought that he was trying to protect her, and in some ways he was. He knew how Elise had gotten under her skin two years ago, and how upset she was when Elise was released from juvie. He also knew she despised Mona. That Mona had done the right thing in sharing information when she had it—when he pressed her—was lost on Lucy, because in the end she saw them on opposite sides.

He'd wanted to make sure he had facts, not Mona's paranoia, before he went to his wife. In hindsight, he was wrong.

And his mistake could end up hurting him more than anyone.

The bus jerked violently and he opened his eyes. They were still in the middle of nowhere on the road to Beaumont, but they passed a sign that said WINNIE 3 MILES.

He had no idea where they were. They'd been driving maybe an hour.

The driver swore, and the guard next to him—Sheffield—said, "Did we blow a tire?"

The driver was doing everything he could to control the bus, but said, "I gotta get off here. Call it in."

Smoke surrounded the bus, heavier in the rear. Out the window Sean saw a sign that said EXIT 822. There was nothing here, it merged onto the frontage road. As they pulled off, Sean noticed a clearing ahead to the right—an old slab foundation and weathered piles of wood and concrete off to the far side.

Sheffield picked up the radio, but as he did the bus swayed wildly. The driver wasn't slowing down as he exited.

"Fuck!" he said.

Sheffield clicked the radio. "It's out, Dave."

"Shit! Shit! Hold on!"

They were going too fast, and the bus veered toward the slab as the driver downshifted and braked and tried to slow the out-of-control bus.

They bumped violently over the foundation and into thick vegetation, then hit a low wall. The back of the bus came up and Sean hit his head on the seat in front of him. The bus teetered and Sean thought they were going to completely flip. He held his breath, trying to relax his tense body in case they rolled, but then the bus righted itself. The engine smoked, then the sound of sparks and Sean saw flames. The fire would only get worse and spread to the dry grass around them.

He glanced at the other prisoner; he had hit his head like Sean. He was bleeding but alert.

Almost immediately, Sean heard something odd . . . then realized they were shouts. At first he thought civilians had come to help them, but then he heard a gunshot. Two, three, four shots fired. The door was forced open.

"Out!" one of the gunmen said.

Sean glanced at the other prisoner. He had a key in his hand and was unlocking his shackles.

He'd planned this escape. Who the hell was this guy?

Sheffield got out of the bus. The guards weren't supposed to leave—especially in a situation like this! Sean couldn't see what was going on because of the smoke. Someone must have seen the out-of-control bus. They'd have called 911. Help had to be coming.

The bus driver was talking on the radio, but Sean couldn't hear any response.

The other prisoner was already out of his chains. He reached under the seat in front of him and pulled out a gun.

Not only was this planned, it was an inside job.

The prisoner smiled at Sean, but there was no humor in his eyes. "You're coming with us."

"No fucking way am I going with you," Sean said.

The prisoner put the gun in Sean's hands, which were still locked to the bar in front of him. He aimed the gun toward the driver.

Sean jerked his hand, and as the prisoner pulled the trigger, the bullet went wild. The prisoner elbowed Sean in the jaw, then forced the gun level and fired twice in the back of the guard's head, still holding Sean's hands tight around the grip. Sean stared, wide-eyed. What the hell? What was this guy doing?

"You're now a cop killer, Sean Rogan. You're coming with me or you're dead."

How did this old man know his name?

Two masked gunmen boarded the bus and aimed their guns at Sean.

The prisoner unlocked Sean's shackles and pulled him up. He was strong for being in his sixties. Sean fought, knowing he couldn't go with them. He just had to buy time. Wait for the police.

You're now a cop killer.

No one would believe it. They would investigate. Realize this was an inside job and Sean had nothing to do with it. There had to be a witness. There was a camera in the bus—they would know Sean wasn't a willing participant, right?

The radio was out. Maybe the cameras are out as well.

Even with all the smoke, Sean fought against leaving the bus. The prisoner hit him on the top of the head with the butt of the gun. Sean immediately saw black and fell to his knees.

"Drag him out," the man said. "Time."

"Eight twenty-five, sir."

"Right on schedule. Secure that bastard."

Sean's vision was clouded, but as the two gunmen dragged him out of the bus, he watched the prisoner conversing with Sheffield as if they were friends. Then the prisoner shot the guard in the calf. Sheffield fired multiple times into the bushes beyond the bus. He heard the prisoner mention his name, and Sheffield said yes, but Sean didn't know what was said or agreed to.

Sean was dragged across the slab. The two men picked him up and pushed him into the back of a windowless cargo van. Another gunman in the back zip-tied Sean's hands behind him, and pushed him against the metal floor, then climbed into the driver's seat.

Sean cut his cheek on a bolt, but his head already hurt like hell so the injury only added to the cacophony of pain. The two gunmen who'd boarded the bus jumped in behind him and closed the doors.

The prisoner opened the passenger seat door, climbed in, and asked the driver, "Everything on schedule?"

"Yes, Mr. Hunt."

"Then get us out of here."

Mr. Hunt.

Jimmy Hunt.

He was in prison in Los Angeles.

Except he's not.

Sean had never met Jimmy Hunt; he'd never had need to. Hunt had been in Mexico when Sean had helped take down the rest of the family in Texas.

Hunt turned and stared at Sean, a shit-eating grin on his face. Sean wanted to look defiant, but he was scared. Hunt had just kidnapped him, but the police would think it was a breakout. A cop had been killed. Would they believe Sean when he told them that Hunt had killed him? That Hunt forced Sean's hands on the gun? Why would they believe anything Sean said when he had been arrested for murder himself?

He felt like a pawn where he had no control over anything. A sinking feeling filled his chest, a huge weight dragging him down because he saw no way out.

"Sean Rogan," Hunt said with a half growl. "I have wanted to kill you for some time, ever since you stole my money. Now, I have use for you. You will do exactly what I tell you to do, or your kid's dead. I will kill him just like your brother killed *my* son. Do not doubt me, Rogan. My reach is far greater than you can imagine."

Chapter Twenty-eight

It wasn't the first time that Jack thought he was getting too old for this shit.

Even so, a familiar thrill ran through his veins, focusing him on the task at hand. It was the same controlled adrenaline rush he felt when he served in the Army; the same focus he had when he ran his own mercenary squad, before he partnered with Rogan-Caruso. A heightened sense of awareness—of himself, of his squad, of his surroundings.

He might not spend as much time in the field as he used to, but there were some things so ingrained in the psyche that you never forgot. The muscle memory that allowed him to assess a situation accurately and react quickly to any change or threat.

There was something wrong with this entire operation. If the girls were bait for Kane—and that was something they all concurred with—were they just stupid in enabling his escape? They'd captured him, and this was Kane Rogan. His enemies knew that he was dangerous and resourceful, not easily contained. The whole thing just felt . . . off.

They'd been watching Peter Blair and his men for the last two hours. They were meeting in an old farmhouse—

the leaders of four separate factions. Each faction had two men inside, and two men patrolling, plus Blair had one extra man who was in charge of the security— seventeen hostiles. Three against seventeen. Even Kane recognized that they couldn't handle that, not with their limited supplies.

His plan seemed solid, however. When the meeting broke up, the four groups would be going in different directions. Blair would be with four men, and three against five were odds Jack would take any day of the week, especially when his partners were Kane and Ranger.

"They're moving," Ranger said quietly from his spot ten feet to Jack's left.

First one Jeep of four left, quickly followed by a second group of four. Blair wasn't among them. That left nine on site, but there was no other movement.

They waited.

Kane signaled over the radio. "Blair's going out back with two. Distract the others, I'll get him."

Jack wanted to argue—this wasn't the fucking plan— but it was too late. Once Kane shifted focus, they all had to shift focus.

Without discussion, Ranger and Jack moved from their position to the gulley across from the farmhouse. Ranger had his hand up, counting down with his fingers.

Three. Two. One.

A small explosion ignited from where they had been. The men out front took cover. No one went back inside, but instead hid behind the Jeeps.

"Where are they?" someone shouted

"Find them!" someone ordered.

"No, no, no, we stay here."

"Who the fuck?"

"Where's Blair?"

"Follow orders . . ."

Ranger hit the second detonation, which they'd set on the south side of the property, then immediately after he set off one to the north. The six men who were still here didn't know where the attack was coming from, so they stayed put and within sight.

Still, Kane hadn't checked in.

Jack should never have let him watch the back alone.

Blair's men were randomly firing toward the explosions, a waste of ammo, but even wild shots could hit a live target, so Jack and Ranger stayed low and didn't give their location away.

The gunfire stopped. There were shouts, but no one advanced toward their position.

Less than five minutes had passed since Kane alerted them, but it felt like fucking forever, and Jack had hoped they could handle this quietly. He should have known better.

Kane finally beeped over the radio.

"Have target, acquired vehicle. Rendezvous mark B."

"Roger," Ranger responded.

"What the hell?" Jack said. How were they going to get to the pick-up spot undetected by the free-firing assholes across the road?

"You've been out of the game a long time, buddy," Ranger said with a grin.

"You've been hanging with Kane too long, buddy," Jack responded. He'd known Ranger since basic training and trusted him, so let him take the lead.

"Head down, give it a minute."

As Jack and Ranger watched, the shooters backed into the house. They weren't trying to get away. There was talking and shouting, but Jack couldn't make out what they were saying.

"Now," Ranger said. "Stay low, head south."

Jack followed Ranger and within minutes they were standing on a narrow dirt road out of sight from the house.

Two minutes later, Kane drove up in an old pickup truck. Other than a cut on his arm, he appeared uninjured.

Peter Blair was hog-tied in the bed of the truck.

Kane said, "Hop in, we have a lot of questions to ask our guest and need a secure location. I have one in mind." As soon as Jack closed the door, Kane drove off.

Chapter Twenty-nine

Patrick made good time and they arrived at the administrative jail at quarter to nine that morning. They were walking up to the lobby when Lucy's phone rang. She didn't recognize the number.

"Kincaid," she answered.

"Agent Kincaid, this is Felicity Dyson, Sean's lawyer. Don't go to the jail."

"I'm already here."

She turned immediately and went back outside before she went through security. "What's wrong?"

Patrick followed her, concern etched in his expression.

"I don't know what happened, no details yet, but a friend of mine from the jail just called me. Sean was transferred to the Beaumont prison this morning. There was an accident on the highway. No one told me about the transfer, I'm on my way to the jail to get answers."

Ice ran down Lucy's spine. "Beaumont?"

"It's federal, maybe this was arranged by your boss Stockton or something and they just didn't get the message to me."

"No. No—this is all wrong. Are you sure?"

"I'm not sure about anything, to be honest. I'll be there

in fifteen minutes, but I don't want you to be cornered by the press or Houston PD."

"Jimmy Hunt is at Beaumont. Hunt hates my family. Someone set this up!"

Felicity didn't say anything and Lucy thought her panic had scared off the lawyer.

"How do you know that name? Did Banner already talk to you?"

"No, I just got here—what's going on, Felicity?"

"There was another prisoner on the transport bus with Sean. Jimmy Jay Hunt. How do you know him?"

"Oh God. Oh God." This was revenge, pure revenge. Fear ate at her stomach. How in the world could Jimmy have orchestrated something so elaborate? To have all the stars align so perfectly that he and Sean would be on the same transport bus? "Hunt framed Sean. Got him some-how on that bus with him. This is the end game."

"We don't have anything confirmed yet."

"This is not a coincidence. Hunt set this up!"

"That seems impossible."

"Do you know *who* Jimmy Hunt is?" Lucy asked.

"Basics—"

"Do you know that Sean's brother Kane killed his son? That he is Elise Hunt's father? That he ran his crime family from Mexico for the five years he was on the run?"

Felicity frowned. "I didn't know about Kane."

Lucy took a deep breath and told Felicity everything that she knew about the Hunt family. There was a lot. Vio-lence. Drug running. Murder. "After Rollins's escape, she and her people killed multiple DEA agents, includ-ing her former boss. They learned that Sean had been the civilian consultant for the FBI who helped seize their bank accounts. They kidnapped him, forced him to steal money electronically, but he tricked them and alerted the FBI to his location. That's when we got them all—so Jimmy Hunt lost most of his family *and* millions of dollars because of Sean. Everything—it's all revenge. Brad. Nate. Kane."

"I—"

"These are extremely dangerous people. Sean wouldn't escape custody, he wouldn't be party to this or to helping Hunt. He was in this jail for what? Twelve hours? How could he have orchestrated any of this?"

"I need to make some calls, get all this verified—"

"You don't believe me?" Lucy knew she was losing it, but she knew Sean was in immediate danger.

"I believe you, Lucy, one hundred percent. But Banner isn't going to believe you. I need someone above both of us to talk to him. Someone above reproach. I'll be at the jail, outside the main doors, in fifteen minutes. Until then, lay low."

It was fifteen minutes of hell.

Lucy called JT Caruso and gave him all the information she had; she trusted him to get more. She called Nate next, filled him in. She tried Megan, but her phone was off. She sent her a text message and hoped she got it as soon as she landed.

Then she called her sister-in-law Kate.

"I just got off the phone with Rick," Kate said. "I'm heading out now. To Houston."

"Do you know anything?"

"Rick said Sean is missing, suspected to have escaped with Hunt. One officer is dead, one is wounded."

"Oh, God. Sean—"

"Is *missing*. He's not there. Neither is Hunt. We don't know what happened, but first responders arrived on scene twenty minutes ago and no one wants to talk to the feds right now. But because it was a federal prison transport, we have jurisdiction. The Houston FBI has been alerted and they're taking lead. Marshals have been called in. And they know that Sean is a potential victim in this."

"Hunt set this up, Kate."

Lucy was relieved that Kate didn't tell her something asinine like *we don't know that*. Because Kate understood people like Jimmy Hunt.

"I'm going to find out exactly what happened. Sean wasn't supposed to be transferred anywhere. He was supposed to be in lockdown at the administrative jail all weekend. Someone screwed up."

"This was done on purpose."

"Rick got me on a military transport, I really have to go."

"Thank you, Kate."

"Hang tight."

Kate hung up. Lucy told Patrick what she'd said, and then saw a petite Black woman, her curly hair pulled back into a shiny ponytail, slick on her head, thick in the back, wearing impossibly tall heels that Lucy was certain she'd break an ankle in if she took two steps.

She looked like a lawyer on a mission. "Felicity?" Lucy said.

Felicity extended her hand. "Felicity Duncan. Lucy?" She had a Texas twang and sharp eyes.

She nodded, introduced Patrick.

"I don't have much more information for you."

"I do." Lucy told her what Kate said. "Kate is the cybercrime expert at Quantico. She's going to find out what happened, and having her here on site is a bonus."

"Banner is on his way here. He knows you planned to talk to Sean at ten. I don't want anyone inside to alert him that you're early. We need to figure this out."

"I don't have to talk to him."

"It might be in your best interest to do so."

"It's not in Sean's best interest. Neither Sean nor I had anything to do with this—Jimmy now has Sean as his prisoner." He wouldn't kill him—not yet. Because if he wanted him dead, he would have killed him and left him on the bus.

Why keep Brad and Sean alive if they planned on killing them? Money? Torture?

"You said that Hunt is Elise Hunt's father, correct?"

"Yes. And she's in Texas. She followed me yesterday."

"I heard. I talked to Garrett this morning."

"So you know that she lied in order to get a restraining order against me."

"I think that's the least of our concerns right now. You need to stay away from this. I know that goes against every instinct you have, but you're only going to hurt yourself."

Felicity looked at her phone. "I have to take this. Wait here, okay? I'll be right back." She answered her call as she walked to the far side of the building.

"I'm calling JT," Patrick said. "This is bullshit. We can't be kept out of the loop on this. We have to figure out a way to get our people on the inside."

"Kate's coming."

"She not here now, and a manhunt is serious. Who's in charge in Houston? What do we know about the detectives investigating Mona Hill's murder? We're flying blind, we need information or we're going to remain in the dark."

Patrick walked away and Lucy was alone. She was actually relieved; she needed time to pull herself together. She had to put aside her fears and focus on finding answers so she could track Sean and bring him home safe.

Felicity returned quickly. "That was Garrett, no news. He's working on having the restraining order tossed so you don't have to be in court on Monday. I have a room for us inside—a friend of mine is a guard here, he's going to get us in quietly."

Lucy motioned to Patrick that she was going inside. He nodded and continued with his call.

Lucy had to turn in her weapon at the security office, then she and Felicity walked down a corridor to a small room. "It's not an interview room," she said. "No cameras or recording devices. There's going to be press all over this place in a few minutes, I don't want you to have to deal with that. We can go out the back when we're ready to leave."

"What happened? Everything, Felicity. Don't coddle me."

"I don't know much, but I'll tell you everything I know." Felicity motioned for Lucy to sit down. Lucy didn't want to, but she did. Felicity sat across from her. "At approximately seven thirty this morning Sean was put on a transport bus with Jimmy Jay Hunt and two guards, heading to Beaumont. Hunt was here because he testified in a federal trial, on behalf of the state, with no promise that he would be given leniency in his own case."

"Which is suspicious on its face."

"It happens quite frequently. Especially when the defense will pull the 'he's lying because he's getting ten years off his sentence' or some such thing. The defendant is a hit man and won't talk, even though he was offered twenty years if he gave up the person who hired him."

"What did they need Hunt's testimony for?"

"Tying two cases together, in San Antonio and Houston. Hunt testified that he hired the defendant in a cold case, and that case is linked to the Houston case and possibly others."

"Hunt was probably given immunity for his part in hiring a hit man."

"It's still irrelevant," Felicity said. "Hunt has life in

prison in California on the conspiracy to murder a peace officer. There are federal charges pending. But this is all I know about the DEA case."

It was fishy as far as Lucy was concerned—if only because it brought Hunt to Texas. To the same prison that Sean was in.

"Hunt was scheduled to be transported back to California on Monday. The only thing I know about the breakout I already told you. The FBI is taking over the investigation, and Houston PD is not happy about it."

"FBI and the marshals," Lucy said.

"Word gets around."

"I need to know everything about the investigation into Mona Hill's murder."

"Banner isn't going to tell us. I'm Sean's lawyer." She looked at her phone. "Damn, this is Garrett again. I have to talk to him."

"Go."

Felicity stepped out and Lucy called Nate. She told him everything she knew.

"I should be there," he said. "This damn SAPD farce of an investigation."

"That's what the Hunts wanted, Nate. To keep you tied down. But they don't know I have Patrick, and Kate's on her way."

"Maybe I should stay with Jesse."

"You and Aggie find Brad and Elise. I trust Leo, and Elise could very well lead us to her father—and to Sean."

"Are you okay?"

"No. I'm not okay because I know that Sean is in very real danger. They won't let me anywhere near the search for Sean, but if I can get the Mona Hill files, I can prove he's innocent of murder."

As she spoke, the door opened. "Don't be so sure of that."

Lucy glanced up and saw Detective John Banner with a woman Lucy assumed was his partner based on the fact that she glared at Lucy as if she were the criminal, and she had a badge clipped to her belt.

"I have to go," she said to Nate and ended the call.

She didn't want to talk to them now, or ever. Her fear for Sean grew with each passing minute, but she was trapped at the jail, waiting for Patrick to return with answers, waiting for Felicity.

Banner said, "I have news about the transport."

"And?" She wished she didn't sound so desperate.

"One corrections officer dead, one wounded. The wounded officer gave his statement. I think you might want to come with me."

"I'm fine here." Dammit, where was Felicity?

Formally, Banner said, "We're still conducting the investigation. The officer gave a statement before he went into the ambulance that a blowout—and he believes the tire was shot out— resulted in the bus being forced off the road. The radio was out, they couldn't call for help, and the bus crashed as they exited. One prisoner had a key to unlock the shackles, and one prisoner had a gun that evidence suggests was taped under one of the seats. That prisoner shot and killed the driver. That prisoner was your husband."

Lucy stood. She started toward the door and Banner blocked her way. Trapping her.

"I'm not done!" Banner said.

Lucy didn't speak. She couldn't. Sean would never kill a cop. He would never plan an escape like this.

"I can have you arrested as an accessory," he said.

Lucy laughed, otherwise she would scream. He was baiting her. He wanted her to get angry, to yell at him, to "slip up" and incriminate her husband. To show fear.

And dear God, she was scared. If the cops thought that Sean had killed a cop, he was in danger from the authorities *and* from Hunt.

Felicity walked in through the door. "Move out of my way, Detective," she said. She was the smallest person in the room but clearly commanded authority.

He stepped aside.

"Do not talk to Agent Kincaid," she said.

"She's not a suspect, I can talk to her. Or are you claiming spousal privilege?"

"She has spousal privilege," Felicity snapped.

"She's a sworn officer, she has a duty and obligation to report any crime she knows about even if it's her husband who's guilty."

"Screw you, John," Felicity said.

"He killed a cop!"

"Allegedly. Do you know who the other prisoner is?"

"That's irrelevant."

"Jimmy Jay Hunt. It's more than relevant."

Banner wasn't swayed. "Officer Sheffield gave a statement that Rogan shot his partner in the head, so I don't care if the other prisoner was Charles Manson, Rogan is a cop killer."

"Do your homework, John, because there is something more than a little fishy about this entire thing."

"I need to talk to Agent Kincaid. Are you representing her?"

"Our firm is, yes."

"She might have relevant information about where her husband is. I will get a fucking warrant if I have to, but she needs to tell us what she knows."

"And your warrant will be bullshit because the FBI has taken over this case, and you damn well know it."

Banner fumed.

His partner said to Lucy, "Woman to woman, are you okay that your husband killed a prostitute? A prostitute he was having an affair with?"

Lucy couldn't even think of a comment.

"You don't have to remain silent, Agent Kincaid. You can do the right thing and help us. You worked in sex crimes. You know how this goes."

"You're out of line, Mendez," Felicity snapped. "Move out of my way, or I'll have you both written up for intimidation and harassing my client, and if you think I won't, Banner, you don't know me."

"You're on the wrong side of this one, Felicity."

"Not this time, John."

But he moved and Felicity grabbed Lucy's arm and pulled her out of the room. She didn't even see where Felicity was leading her until they reached the edge of the lobby and Felicity sat Lucy down on a bench.

"You're pale. Are you okay?"

She nodded. "We need to investigate Sheffield. He was paid off or threatened. There has to be some way we can prove it."

Felicity motioned for her to keep her voice down.

"You can't do anything, Lucy Haven't you been listening? You already have a restraining order against you—"

"Which Elise set up. She knows I have to go to court on Monday. That means she knows when and where I will be at a specific time. They have Sean and he can't even find help because he's now considered a cop killer. The wrong cops get to him first, he'll be beaten or dead and you know it!" She took a deep breath. She had to calm down, but this situation had long ago spiraled out of control.

She needed someone who understood the severity.

"Lucy, I talked to the FBI here in Houston. You need

to give a statement. Just that you didn't know anything about the escape, that you haven't spoken to Sean since yesterday, the whole nine yards."

"They need to look into Sheffield. And into who authorized this transport in the first place. There's no reason for Sean to have been sent to Beaumont. None!"

"I'm looking at your future, Lucy. You obstruct this investigation and you will kill your career."

"You think I care? I don't give a *shit* about my career when my husband has been kidnapped by a man who wants him dead." Why didn't Jimmy Hunt just kill him then and there? That didn't make sense . . .

It always makes sense. There is a reason for this whole charade. What is Jimmy thinking?

"Oh, no. I know why he took Sean." Lucy realized that it was a repeat of what had happened nearly two years ago. It was as clear as day. "He wants Sean to steal money for him."

"Like a bank robbery?"

"Sean is a computer security expert. He can break into any secure system. He's hired by governments and businesses to test their security. He legally hacks in and then writes programs to improve their security. That's his *job*. And Hunt knows this. He could have Sean hack into any system electronically and steal the funds . . . then he'll kill him. And Kane—that's why Kane is missing. Maybe they have him already, to use as leverage. Then they'll kill him, too." She sounded crazy, like a conspiracy theorist, but she didn't care because she knew she was right, or close to it. "They've had two years to plan this, and if I don't stop it, they'll win and I'll lose everyone I care about."

"Lucy, stop. Take a deep breath."

Easy for her to say . . . but Felicity was right. Lucy had

to reclaim her calm so that she could find Sean and get him back.

And if they had to run from the cops and from Jimmy Hunt for the rest of their lives, so be it.

Running forever was better than being dead.

Chapter Thirty

Even though Nate trusted his SWAT team commander more than anyone else in the FBI, he was nervous about leaving Jesse with anyone. He loved the kid like the little brother he'd always wanted, and knew that Sean and Lucy were counting on Nate to protect him should the shit hit the fan.

But this was Leo—a former sniper in the Marines, one of Nate's closest friends, and his superior on the FBI SWAT team. He was more than capable of protecting Jesse if necessary. Nate had given him a full security briefing about what was going on, and Leo took it seriously.

"You're worried about Jesse," Aggie said as they headed to where they believed the Merides brothers were now living.

"He's my responsibility," Nate said. "I feel like I've passed the buck."

Lucy trusted Leo, too. But Nate still felt like he was the best at making sure that Sean's son was safe.

"He's a good kid. Smart," Aggie said. "Do you really think that Elise and her people will go after him?"

"I think Elise can and will do anything she damn well

wants," Nate said. "Sean's house is secure—but nothing is one hundred percent."

Nate would never forgive himself if anything happened to Jesse.

"You're good with him," Aggie said.

Nate shrugged. "I like him."

"It's more than that."

"Maybe."

When Nate left the Army, he was lost. He hadn't wanted to leave, but a series of events that culminated in his best friend getting blown away by a roadside bomb had Nate rethinking his life choices. His commanding officer—a man Nate respected more than anyone on the planet—urged Nate to take his years, his GI Bill, and become a cop. In college he was recruited by the FBI, but he often wondered if he should have stayed in the Army. He'd been lost Stateside for years . . . until he met the Rogans.

Sean wasn't military, but he understood Nate's mindset, and with Sean came Kane Rogan and Lucy's brother Jack. They, more than anyone, had helped him fully integrate back into civilian life. As much as soldiers-at-heart could be civilians. Nate embraced his SWAT duties, enjoyed the investigative work, and tolerated the paperwork necessary to close cases. Because of the Rogans and the Kincaids, Nate finally felt like he had a place, an anchor. When Sean learned he had a son, Nate de facto became one of Jesse's uncles. Or a big brother. He would die for the kid.

"You want kids someday?" Aggie asked.

"No."

Aggie seemed to want more of an answer, but Nate didn't feel inclined to talk. Finally, she asked, "Why?"

"The world sucks."

"I don't think so."

Nate shrugged. There were so many kids out there today who had nothing. No family, no hope. There was danger, heartbreak, and agony. Nate had lived it. He didn't care to bring a child into the world to share in that pain.

"Did you have a shitty childhood?" she asked.

"No."

She waited.

"And?"

"You're nosy," Nate said.

"Not really. But you're like my brother Tommy. Also Army. One-word answers. But I can usually get him to talk."

"Because you're his annoying little sister, I'm sure."

She laughed. "I can be."

She wasn't really prying, so Nate said, "My childhood was ordinary and quiet, I guess I'd say. My parents adopted me late in life. They had one kid themselves—my sister. She's twelve years older than me. They couldn't have more, were on a waiting list to adopt, got me when my mom was forty-two. I think they forgot they were still on the list; they really didn't know what to do with me. They loved me and gave me everything I needed, I have no complaints."

"Did you ever look for your birth parents?"

He didn't like talking about it. But what could he say, that he didn't want to talk about it? "My birth mom is dead. She was a teenage drug addict, didn't know who my father was. I tracked her down when I was eighteen; she'd already been dead for years. Overdose."

Thankfully, Aggie didn't say anything about that. Didn't suggest he get a DNA test. Nate didn't want to meet his birth father. Didn't care. His parents weren't perfect, but they were solid, law-abiding, middle class folks who cared about him, even if they didn't quite know what to do with an active boy after raising a studious girl.

Aggie pulled off the highway just past New Braunfels, northeast of San Antonio. Late last night Aggie had tracked the mother to this house; odds were her two sons would be here as well.

Nate was uncomfortable with their plan, but Aggie was confident. She felt that they'd talk. The goal was to identify who else was with Mitts Vasquez when he stole the drugs. Nate was skeptical that they'd tell cops anything, but so far Aggie's instincts had been solid.

He cleared his mind. He went back to his core training. He couldn't think about the people he cared about; he had to focus on the potential threats. Protect his partner, gain intelligence. That was the goal.

It was still early; before nine. The property was ten acres, an old farmhouse barely standing up in the middle of a wide-open pasture. Nate was surprised it had withstood the storm last year. Perhaps some of the older homes were so well built they could survive anything, even if they looked like crap.

"I don't like this," Nate said. They had no cover.

"We approach this the way we discussed," Aggie said.

"We need backup," he mumbled.

"That'll take hours to put together, and I don't think Salter will go for it. I can't always explain exactly how I reach my conclusions. People don't see the same things I do in the data. But it's there. Brad trusted my instincts, but it took me a while to prove myself."

"Clearly not that long. You've only been on staff for eighteen months."

She smiled and her light green eyes sparkled. "Being right is the best persuasion."

"We do it your way—again," Nate said. "And again—if I take over, don't argue."

"Never," she said.

He grunted.

She'd been right yesterday. Vasquez had shown up where she thought he'd show, based solely on her analysis of data that everyone else had access to, but didn't interpret in the same way. That made Aggie Jensen very valuable to any agency she worked for.

But cockiness was dangerous.

They drove up the long, bumpy road to the house. It was a permanent trailer, raised several feet off the ground, which had probably saved it from the flood last year. The roof was patched in multiple places, and junk filled the carport—an old doorless refrigerator, three couches that should be burned, dead plants, a multitude of car parts. Five—no, *seven*—cars and trucks were in various states of disrepair in the open space next to the house. Two dogs barked and ran at them from behind the house. Aggie froze. Nate stepped in front of her. The dogs looked vicious, but they stopped several feet back, baring teeth. They didn't attack.

Yet.

Nate kept his hand on the butt of his gun.

The dogs alerted the residents of their arrival. A small, skinny woman of indeterminate age—anywhere between forty and sixty—opened the screen. Her skin was tanned and weathered, making her appear like she'd seen everything and didn't give a shit about anyone.

"Brutus! Carter! Quiet!"

The dogs growled, but surprisingly stopped barking.

"What do the cops want with me today?" the woman said.

"Rosa Merides?" Aggie said with an odd smile, unable to tear her eyes from the canines.

No answer. Of course not. She wouldn't admit who she was even if there was a warrant—which there wasn't; Aggie had checked. And she wouldn't talk if Aggie didn't get her bearings and forget about the mutts.

There was a warrant for one of her sons, but it was a failure to appear on a DUI, and Nate wasn't going to ring the guy up for that—not if they shared the information they needed.

The dogs seemed to intimidate Aggie, and she wasn't acting as confident as she normally did. Nate decided to run with her plan, but he took over the questioning.

"Mrs. Merides, I'm FBI Agent Nate Dunning, this is my partner. We're not here to jam up you or your sons. We just need some information, then we'll be out of your hair."

She stared at them from the doorway. She didn't come down to them; Nate didn't make a move to approach her.

"Have a warrant?"

"No, we just have questions. We're not here to arrest or detain you."

She made a point to look around the land. "I can see that, it's just the two of you."

"Do you know Mitts Vasquez?"

She scowled, her face darkening. "So what?"

"We know he stole something from you. Two weeks ago. In San Marcos."

She just glared at them.

"Who was he working for?"

"How the hell am I supposed to know?"

"Mitts and his team came in and stole sixteen kilos of coke right out from under your nose. By the looks of things, just delivered, uncut. Probably cost you a ton of money. I don't give a shit about the drugs. Gunfire was exchanged. Mitts was shot in the leg, needed medical attention, disappeared before the cops arrested him. Now he's dead—killed by his own people." They didn't know that for a fact, but it was a logical guess.

"That's what I care about," Nate continued when Rosa didn't say anything. "I want the killer. You help me there and I'll pretend I was never here."

"And if I don't help you?"

He didn't say anything. This wasn't someone who would care about threats. According to Aggie's research, the Merideses had owned this house for some time under a corporate name. The only thing that tied them to it were utility bills. They might have other property in other names. They hadn't been killed by their supplier for losing the sixteen kilos, which told Nate they were high up themselves, had the resources to weather the storm, or had the ability to make it up.

"Hypothetically, if someone stole from me, I wouldn't give a shit about them if they were arrested by the cops. But I'm not going to put a target on my back so you all can come in here and nail me and my boys. I'm not an idiot."

"No, you're not. You've been in this business too long to be stupid."

"Why thank you," she said, almost humored.

"So I'm going to tell you something I shouldn't, but I really need the name of the people with Mitts that day two weeks ago." Nate made sure Rosa was looking him in the eye, then said, "I'm suspended. I shouldn't even be here. Anything you tell me can't be used against you because technically, I don't have a badge today. I want those people because Mitts' isn't the only life they destroyed." He didn't know if they killed anyone else, but if he didn't figure out what the hell was going on with the planted drugs, if he couldn't clear his name and find Elise Hunt and save Brad, then yes, more people would die. And Rosa Merides was not party to that. She was a high-level drug supplier. Bad news, and Nate hoped the

DEA could eventually make a case against her. But it wasn't his job, and he wasn't arresting anyone today.

"Oh, you're being a bad boy, aren't you, Agent Dunning?" she said with a smile.

Aggie was tense next to him. The dogs had inched closer to her and Aggie had inched closer to Nate.

"Names, and we're gone."

"Mitts is a fucking asshole, he used to work for me, when the Saints got whacked and arrested a couple years back. There were only a few of them around, and Mitts was desperate. And what does he do? Bites the hand that feeds him, that's what. He's dead? Good. Deserves worse, the fucking traitor."

Nate didn't say anything.

"Not saying what's what, but *if* Mitts came over, he doesn't have a lot of friends. His best friend is Pablo Barrios. Not the sharpest tack in the box, but surprisingly, been off the grid for *two weeks*," she emphasized. "No fucking way could Mitts and Pablo have done anything like what you said they might have done, just telling you that straight up. Not on their own."

"Who do they run with?"

She stared at them, weighing what she should say. Whether she wanted to screw them. Aggie shifted as if she were going to speak, and Nate took a half step in front of her.

Rosa would tell him what she knew, but one misstep and she'd laugh in their faces.

Aggie picked up on his subtle hint and froze.

After a tense ten seconds Rosa said, "Word has it that Pablo is being led around by his dick. Couple months ago, he hooked up with this looker named Clara. What a looker like Clara wants with a buffoon like Pablo, what the shit do I know? And if Pablo and Mitts were to do something stupid like steal from me, they might have brought the looker with them. And she ain't no dumb bitch, I'll tell you that right now, because stupid fucks can't steal from me."

"I need more."

"Like her full name and address? Fuck. Don't have that shit. But let's just say that *if* she had a gun on my boys, and *if* I saw her, I *might* have seen a colorful skull and snake tat on her wrist."

Aggie perked up.

"And that's all the fuck I know," the woman said. She whistled and the dogs ran to her; Aggie jumped and unconsciously grabbed Nate's forearm. Rosa laughed. "Don't like my pups? They won't hurt you . . . unless I tell them to. You have thirty seconds to get back in your truck or you're puppy chow."

Aggie was shaking and Nate took her key and drove back to the highway.

"Spill," he said.

"Nothing."

Her voice cracked and she wished she could control her panic. This was so stupid! She was twenty-eight years old. She was a trained federal agent. And two dogs—mean, scary dogs—had her completely unhinged.

He pulled her truck over before the on ramp and she frowned.

"I know th-th-that I-I screwed up," she stuttered. Damn. Her heart would *not* slow down.

"I know a panic attack when I see one."

"It's. Not."

He didn't move, just stared at her.

She took a deep breath. Then another. Then another. The thudding in her chest quieted and she could finally think.

She pulled her polo shirt out of the waist of her jeans and turned her back slightly to Nate. He didn't bat an eye when she pulled up the shirt and exposed her back.

"Look," she said.

He did, then frowned.

She pulled her shirt back over the nasty scar that took up her left side. "Got more on my leg. I just—dammit."

"Tell me about it."

She didn't like talking about it, because she felt stupid. It was nearly twenty years ago! But hearing the dogs—hearing them more than seeing them—brought back all those fears.

"It was the summer I turned ten. My brother Teddy—he's a year old than me, he's a firefighter now—he and I were responsible for walking the dogs every morning. We had three—two golden Labs and this little dust mop named Frisky who *thought* he was a Lab. I usually carried Frisky half the way because he would get tired, but we couldn't leave him—he would cry if we walked the Labs without him.

"Anyway, we lived in this development in Dallas. When Dad was deployed, we lived on base wherever he was—I was born on the base in Stuttgart, lived there the first eight years of my life. But when I was eight, he was permanently stationed in Dallas, and my mom was glad. She wanted her own house, you know, not military housing. And my oldest brother was starting high school. He became a cop—did a stint in the military, was an MP, now is with Dallas PD. Anyway . . ." She stopped, realizing she was rambling because she didn't want to talk about it.

Nate didn't comment. He just waited.

"So. Well. We were walking, and there's a park about six blocks away. We went there to throw Frisbees with the Labs. Frisky wanted to play, but he couldn't even carry a Frisbee without tripping over it. We got him this cute little mini Frisbee . . . well, he got tired and so I took him to the fountain for water and these two dogs ran up from out of nowhere. One bit my leg and pulled me down and Frisky was barking and the other dog . . . just . . . grabbed him. And I screamed and kicked the dog that bit me, got him off me, I don't know how, and I went after Frisky. Teddy and the Labs were running to me, I'll never forgot the horror on my brother's face . . . and the dog that bit me, jumped on me, got me down on the ground, bit my side, I was protecting my face and . . . I . . ." She took a deep breath and wiped tears off her cheeks that she hadn't realized were falling until they dropped onto her shirt.

"Anyway, there were lots of people in the park and they got the dog off me. And, umm, Frisky didn't make it." She almost died, but she didn't say that. She *didn't* die, but her dog did, and though she knew deep down she couldn't have done anything to save him, the guilt hung over her head for years. "So. I don't really like dogs. I mean, dogs like that. And I'm sorry I panicked. It was a surprise, and I know that's bad, to be a trained agent and get surprised by stupid dogs, I'm usually better about it."

Nate started driving again. "You know, partner, I've always got your back."

He couldn't have said anything else that would have made her feel better.

"Bingo!" Aggie nearly jumped up and down for joy, except that she was sitting at her desk in the DEA and trying to keep a low profile, since she wasn't really supposed to be doing this.

Nate sat next to her. Martin wasn't in the office, and no one seemed to bat an eye that Aggie had brought Nate in.

She'd needed her computer and access to DEA data. It

didn't take long to find an example of the skull and snake tattoo that Rosa Merides described, and then to learn that it was affiliated with a gang in Los Angeles. Aggie cross-referenced known gang affiliations with the name "Clara" and up popped Clara Anne Valeria. She had a sheet, but no active warrants. No arrests since she was a minor. She was currently twenty-five and her address was listed in Topanga Canyon.

Nate said, "I know that address. That's Elise Hunt's house in Los Angeles."

"Really?"

Aggie dug deeper. She got a photo of Clara—it was older, but Merides was right, she was a looker. Naturally tan skin, long dark hair, dark eyes under long lashes. Perfect cheekbones. She could have been a model. Except her eyes . . . they were cold.

Clara had a younger brother, Donald "Donny" Valeria, no known gang affiliation, but he'd been arrested three years ago for possession with intent, pled, and been given six months' probation. He was now twenty-three, no known address, had an expired California driver's license. Aggie printed out his photo as well, and sent both to Lucy on the off chance that Lucy had seen them.

Next she ran Pablo Barrios. He had no recent record, a couple of dings when he ran with the Saints years ago.

She should have found him yesterday when she ran Mitts. But there was no Barrios as a known associate in his file. If she'd had time, she would have thought to run all the Saints and then cross-reference them to Mitts.

Stop.

Aggie knew she had a bad habit of second-guessing herself, especially when something seemed obvious to her now. She knew that it wasn't obvious to most people, and that the connections she made were based on intuition as much as evidence.

"I have an address for Barrios and two known associates. If Merides is right, he'll lead us to Clara and hopefully she'll lead us to Elise." Aggie frowned.

"This is a solid lead, what's wrong?"

"It's a lot of what-ifs. What if she was lying?"

"She wasn't."

"How do you know?"

Nate gave her a half smile. He was really cute when he smiled. "My guess is that she tried to find him, couldn't, and now wants us to destroy him. I can live with that."

Suddenly, he grabbed the DMV photo of Donny Valeria off Aggie's desk. "Who is this?"

"If I'm right, Clara Valeria is the 'looker' Merides told us about. Donny is her brother."

"This is the guy who killed Mitts Vasquez."

"Are you sure?"

"I chased him. Got a good look at him, gave a description to SAPD. But I didn't have a photo, and they haven't recovered the car he stole."

"How do you know?"

"I still have friends in SAPD."

"We need to tell them."

Nate hesitated.

"We have to," Aggie said clearly. "Nate, he killed a man. This will put pressure on him."

"You're right. Damn. That makes this an official investigation, and my suspension could fuck it all up."

"Let's cross that bridge when we come to it," Aggie said. "I'm not suspended, and Merides was my contact. I did the research, I found her house, I got the information." She looked at him. "Thank you, by the way."

"For what?"

"For realizing I was frozen because of those dogs and handling the interrogation like I'd suggested. You had more clout with her *because* you are suspended. She could very likely get any confession thrown out because of it."

"She didn't confess, not outright, and I don't care about her. She and her kids will screw up down the road and find themselves dead or behind bars. Either is fine with me. Right now, this is our best lead to finding Brad."

"Let's go."

Chapter Thirty-one

Two hours after they captured Peter Blair, Kane pulled up to an RCK safe house high in the mountains west of Montemorelos. It was remote and private, though Jack had never been to this particular property.

Ranger jumped out of the truck and inspected the property before he cleared it for Kane and Jack to bring in their prisoner. It was getting hot, though it wasn't yet noon. The adobe structure kept the building cool, at least for now.

Kane secured Blair to the stone wall, then Jack pulled off his hood. The hood had two primary benefits: first, it would make finding the RCK safe house more difficult for Blair, and second, it disorientated a captive, instilling a deeper sense of fear and panic, which helped to make them talk.

Kane did his own recon, then said to Jack, "No one's been here since me last year."

Jack didn't even ask how he could tell. The place was filthy from dust, storms, animals; mud had caked and dried in the corners from where a storm had blown through a broken door in the back.

Though the place was remote and would seem like nowhere to Peter Blair, they were only an hour from the city limits of Monterrey. But they were in the mountains, and going in virtually every direction, except east, would land their captive deeper into the jungle.

Kane had been particularly moody, and Jack realized that they weren't far from where his brother Liam had been killed—and where Liam had nearly killed Kane. Kane didn't talk about it, but Jack knew those events had nearly broken him.

Jack didn't have the same feelings, though he understood what Kane was going through. Jack hated Liam. He'd put Lucy in grave danger all because of money. Jack didn't have any remorse for his death.

But Liam had been Kane's family, even if estranged, and family was complicated. There was a time when Jack didn't talk to anyone in his family. His father had virtually disowned him and Jack couldn't forgive him for the circumstances surrounding those events. Jack still didn't have a good relationship with his dad—they couldn't quite get beyond those old hurts—but at least he had his family back. He was closest to Lucy and his twin brother Dillon, and had tried to rebuild relationships with his other brothers and sisters. It was, at least, better. He was married, and having Megan in his life gave him a peace he had never known before he'd met her. No matter what he did, how dangerous the job, Jack had a home and someone who loved him as much as he loved her.

He'd hoped after Kane married Siobhan four months ago that he'd realize there were more important things than fighting other people's battles. But Kane had been in the business longer than Jack; he'd taken longer to find the right woman; and leaving it behind was hard.

Especially when you were Kane Rogan, who thought he was the only one who could save the world.

Fucking jerk. Jack loved him.

And hoped this situation wasn't going to be his undoing.

Peter Blair stared at them, trying to look tough, but his fear betrayed him. "My men will come for me."

His voice was strong, but his body trembled, his eyes darted back and forth, looking for an escape that would not come.

Ranger was patrolling. Jack stayed with Kane to make sure he didn't go too far with Blair.

Jack squatted in front of their prisoner. His hands were zip-tied behind him. Jack tied his ankles together. Rats and rodents scurried, heard but unseen.

"I'd suggest you talk," Jack said, his voice low and deep. "Neither of us are in the mood for grandstanding or games."

"You got the girls, what's the problem? You want more?"

Jack punched him in the stomach. It took the wind out of Blair, even though Jack checked his punch to avoid doing serious damage to both Blair and his own hand.

He stood, walked to the only piece of furniture in the room, a table in the opposite corner. Jack pulled a water bottle out of his pack. Drained half of it in front of Blair, who watched, eyes wide. One thing Jack knew from his training, the hood made you thirsty.

He capped his bottle and put it back in his pack. Psychological torture was more effective than physical torture, but a combination of both usually broke most men.

Especially a soft asshole like Peter Blair.

Kane leaned against the wall, only feet from Blair, and didn't say anything.

Blair started talking. Not anything important. Empty threats. Then pleaded for his life. Then more threats against friends and family. The usual.

Kane ignored everything.

Jack had patience, but Kane had always impressed him with his ability to remain still and silent.

Finally, Blair said, "What the fuck do you want? If you wanted to kill me, you would have killed me. You have the girls. You killed two of my best men, what do you want from me?"

"Sean," Kane said. "Talk."

Blair looked confused. "What? Who?"

Kane didn't say anything.

Blair shook his head. "I don't know what you want from me!"

Kane pushed off from the wall and walked over to him. With Blair on the floor in the corner and Kane—though not a particularly large man—standing over him, Blair looked pathetic.

"The girls were a trap. I let you capture me to find out why. I took my escape, but circled back and heard you and your men talking about my brother. *Why?*"

Blair's mouth opened and closed like a fish as he processed the information.

Jack could deck Kane himself. He hadn't known he'd intentionally let himself be grabbed. You don't do that without backup! Kane couldn't have known whether Blair had been given a kill order. He didn't know if they might have incapacitated him. Drugged him. Shot him. Tossed him out of a fucking airplane.

Sometimes Kane made Jack crazy.

Kane's arm came out so fast that if Jack wasn't expecting it, he would have missed it. Kane punched Blair in the face. If he hadn't checked his swing, the bones from Blair's nose would have shot up into his brain. But as it was, Kane knew exactly what he was doing. Blair's nose was smashed, he was in pain, but he would live.

Blair started blubbering as blood poured from his face.

Kane pulled Blair's phone from his pocket and pushed his shaking thumb on the button to decode it. There was no reception here, but Kane scrolled through recent calls and texts. He frowned. Showed the phone to Jack.

Jimmy Hunt was in his contacts. They'd had extensive contact two years ago, then intermittent contact since— apparently through a surrogate. Kane went through more carefully.

"What's going down?" Kane asked.

"Fuck you! Fuck you!" Blair said, his nasally voice pained.

Kane put his fist up and Blair screamed, then started choking on his own blood. He spat out blood, coughed, spat out more. Kane watched.

He didn't ask again.

Blair began to sob. He put his head down on his knees and cried like a baby, muttering, though Jack couldn't tell what he was saying.

And still, Kane waited him out.

"He's escaping from prison, okay?" Blair finally said. "Sometime today. I don't have the details. I don't know when."

Hunt had been transferred to a prison in Texas, according to Megan. Beaumont wasn't far from Houston, but what did that have to do with Sean?

Sean was in prison in Houston.

Could he be in the *same* prison? Jack couldn't imagine how that would be possible. Sean was in jail, downtown, awaiting arraignment.

Hunt was testifying in federal court. He might be kept in the same jail . . .

Kane was doing his stare down, but Jack realized that Blair might not know exactly what was going on. He had some facts, but not all the details.

"Sean Rogan," Jack said. "Spill. Now."

"He's the guy who stole all their money two years ago, that much I know. I was told to grab you," he said to Kane, "to make him comply."

The way he said it, Jack believed him. And it made sense.

Sean was in jail.

Unless . . .

Jack walked out. Kane followed.

"I need to call Megan. Don't kill him."

"He planned to transport me, probably to Hunt."

"Why set it up like this?"

"Because we're weaker here than we are in the States."

"This is about the money Sean siphoned off from the Hunts—that money is long gone, in government coffers. Sean can't get it back," Jack said.

"Sean can get money for Hunt," Kane said. "It doesn't have to be *their* money."

Sean's hacking skills came in handy, but now they put him at great risk.

"We have to get him locked down."

"Sean isn't going to help even if he thinks I'm in trouble," Kane said. "I trained him better than that."

"It might not have been about you. Sean has other vulnerabilities. Nate is out of commission because of the drug bust, Brad is missing, and Lucy is likely in Houston because of Sean—which puts her at risk, even with Patrick watching her. It also means Jesse is vulnerable. Even if they can't get to Jesse, if they get to *you* Sean might believe they also grabbed Jesse, and he'll have no way to verify."

Kane clearly wasn't confident in Jack's analysis, but he nodded.

Jack pulled his sat phone from his bag and called Megan. It took her several rings to answer.

"Jack?" she said. Her voice sounded rushed and far away.

"We have information that Blair has been in communication with Jimmy Hunt and that Hunt is planning an escape."

"Hunt escaped this morning and took Sean with him. One corrections officer dead, the other wounded—but he made a statement that Sean shot and killed his partner. The police think that Sean orchestrated the escape, there's a manhunt, and they're interrogating Lucy right now. Kate Donovan is on her way here and I hope she can take over the investigation, because this is a mess—I heard that a cell phone was found in Sean's cell and the Houston computer system was hacked to put Sean on that specific bus."

"Blair knows that Sean is the one who took the Hunt money two years ago, which tells me that Hunt wants it back. Kane was targeted as leverage or revenge. Where is everyone right this minute?"

"Lucy is here, with her lawyer. Patrick is in the lobby. I only got here ten minutes ago."

"Nate?"

"I don't know, specifically. He has a lead on the missing DEA agent."

"Who's with Jess?"

"I don't remember his name. Lucy said he's SWAT and she trusts him."

"Leo Proctor," Jack said.

"That's it."

"Keep your phone on. I'm going to get more information."

He ended the call. Kane had listened, he didn't say anything, but walked back into the house.

Jack followed.

Kane stood in front of Blair, who was a mess. "Where were you supposed to deliver me?"

"I don't know, I don't know. I was waiting."

"Waiting for what?"

"Hunt to get out of jail and then he'd tell me."

"On this phone?"

"Yes."

"Then we'll wait."

He paused.

"Mexico, right?"

Blair nodded.

"And he planned to grab my brother on the way."

"He . . . I . . ."

Kane took a step toward him and Blair cowered. "What are you hiding?"

"Your brother isn't coming here. Hunt said someone else wants him. I don't know! I swear! All I know is that Hunt said he'd be down here twenty-four hours after the breakout and that I had better have you tied up with a bow."

Kane walked out. Jack followed. "We need him alive," Jack said. "He can confirm Hunt's escape plan and clear Sean."

"Only the escape plan. No one knows what happened in that bus except Sean."

"Sean would not kill a cop," Jack said.

"Not all cops are good cops."

"What the fuck is that supposed to mean?"

"There's one survivor. He's corrupt."

"You don't know that."

Kane didn't say anything.

"You're thinking they needed someone on the inside."

"More than one inside. And we sure as shit didn't find all of Nicole Rollins's contacts. But why grab Donnelly? Other than revenge."

"If that's the case, they already killed him."

"They might need him."

Jack wasn't as confident as Kane that Brad Donnelly was alive. He hoped, but he didn't think so.

"I think," Jack said slowly, "that Brad was grabbed solely for revenge, as you said. He killed Nicole in the SWAT raid. That would be enough."

"Then we would have already found his body," Kane said. "Blair knows more."

"Agreed."

Kane went back inside.

Jack didn't follow.

Sometimes, it was better not to know how his friend got the information he did.

Chapter Thirty-two

Sean looked for every opportunity to escape, but he was tied up and at least two men watched him at all times.

He couldn't see where they were going, but they'd turned left—south—about a quarter mile from the breakout site and had cruised steadily between fifty and sixty miles an hour. If they were heading south, they'd hit the Gulf pretty quickly.

He was right. He could smell the change in the air, and then the van veered to the right and the road became bumpy. The driver was forced to slow down, but Sean felt every pothole in the road.

He listened as best he could, but Jimmy Hunt wasn't talking much. No one was talking much. The tension in the van was thick, and he wasn't surprised. There would be a manhunt for them, and because a cop was dead, it would be put together fast. The guard Sheffield might be able to delay it, but not for long . . . as soon as they didn't arrive at the prison, or didn't check in on the radio, or if someone monitoring their GPS knew they had stopped, or if a driver on the highway saw the whole thing and called it in . . . law enforcement would be looking for them. They'd have access to helicopters, dogs, every state and federal agency.

Fifteen minutes tops, Sean figured, and they'd already been driving for thirty.

Hunt had changed in the van—he now wore military khakis and a black T-shirt. But Sean was clearly a prisoner, standing out in his bright orange jumpsuit with HDOC stenciled on the back.

Hunt and his people had a plan. Timing mattered because Hunt kept asking about their ETA. He was texting someone almost constantly. When Sean opened his mouth to ask a question—sort of akin to "are we there yet"—he couldn't get more than a word out before one of Hunt's goons backhanded him.

The van turned right again, then a sharp left, slogging through gravel, and then they traveled a deeply rutted dirt road. But not for long. A minute later, the van stopped, the driver slammed the vehicle into park, and turned off the ignition. "We have to jam. Cops on scene, they'll close off the ports in minutes."

Ports? Where the hell were they taking him?

"Haul him out, boys," Hunt told the men watching Sean.

One opened the back of the van while the other took a rope and wound it around Sean multiple times, binding his arms against his sides. They pushed him out and he fell onto hard-packed dirt. The blinding light made him blink rapidly, he could barely make out where he was. But he heard gulls and the sound of the ocean; they were at the Gulf of Mexico.

Two men pulled him to his feet and pushed him along. He tried to drag his feet, but he just fell, and they hauled him up again.

Hunt was leading the way. The second time Sean fell, Hunt stopped, turned around, and kicked Sean in the side. "Don't fuck with me, Rogan. You don't want to make me mad. You've already been a pain in my ass, and when this is over, I'll enjoy watching the bullet hit your skull."

Two goons pulled him up again and held him tight as they crossed the lot to a dinghy on a rocky beach. There were no people around—why? It was a Saturday in April. He squinted to see better in the bright light. This wasn't a full beach. There was some sort of barrier at the edge of the lot. Maybe they'd blocked it off for privacy; maybe it was closed for another reason.

The boat could only fit four people; two of the men stayed behind.

"Dump the van," Hunt ordered, "and get back to San Antonio. Elise has been on her own for too long, and when she starts to make her own plans, she fucks up. If anything happens to her, you are both dead, understand?"

"Yes, boss."

Sean was pushed down into the bottom of the boat. Hunt climbed in and kicked him. "Stay down," he ordered.

Water soaked through his jumpsuit. The two goons pushed the boat off the shore, then jumped in and started the motor. They headed out to sea.

Sean peered over the edge. If he threw himself off, he would drown. He was tied so tightly he almost couldn't breathe. He might be able to swim, even with the ropes, but they'd catch up with him. Shoot him or knock him out.

Maybe death would be better than this.

No. Alive, you have a fighting chance. Alive, you can think, plan, plot, get out of this mess. There's no coming back from dead.

He laid back down and looked at the bright sky through half-closed eyes. In minutes, they slowed down; a shadow cut across their dingy. Sean arched his neck— they had come upon a larger boat—practically a yacht. Hunt boarded first, then the two men lifted Sean on to the deck. One boarded, the other took the small motorboat back to shore.

But it wasn't just Hunt and his goon. Sean could hear other people on board. Voices. Footsteps. He couldn't make them out, not what they said or where they were going. Hunt's man and another grabbed Sean under the arms and dragged him down into the hull. They tied him to a support post and left without ceremony.

Less than a minute later, the engines roared to life and the boat picked up speed.

He was so screwed.

Chapter Thirty-three

As soon as Megan arrived in Houston, she stuck by Lucy. Patrick was working his own angle to get information about the escape, and Megan was the rock Lucy needed.

Of course she was solid, she was Jack's wife.

They were in a private room at the jail. The media was gathering outside, and Lucy had seen early reports— Sean's name had been released and her phone had been ringing constantly. She'd dismissed all the calls. She didn't want to talk to anyone about what was happening. She could hardly believe it was happening at all.

"Houston FBI wants to talk to you," Megan said, handing Lucy a bottle of chilled water.

"No."

"I think you should, if only to tell them you know nothing."

"I *don't* know anything!"

"This is a difficult situation, but anything you know may help bring Sean in safely."

"What I *know* is that Sean has been kidnapped by Jimmy Hunt and he's in grave danger."

"But he's not dead, that is a plus."

"For how long? Megan, I can't—" Lucy stopped that

train of thought. She couldn't think about what-ifs, not now.

Megan said, "Hunt wants Sean for something. Sean is the smartest guy I know. He's going to find a way out."

Felicity came in and closed the door. Lucy introduced her to Megan. "We should talk alone," Felicity said.

"Anything you can say to me you can say to Megan."

"With all due respect, she's an FBI agent."

"And my sister-in-law."

"She doesn't have any privilege."

"I trust her. And my other sister-in-law is on her way. I need them working on this."

"Kate Donovan. I know."

That surprised Lucy. Word did get around fast.

Felicity continued. "Houston FBI is up in arms that the national office is sending in someone to take over the investigation. They don't know she's your sister-in-law, however, so we'll keep that to ourselves until they discover it on their own." She paused. "She's not related to your husband, right?"

Lucy shook her head. "My brother's wife. Kate is one of the top cybercrime experts in the FBI. She teaches at Quantico. She can look at the data from the phone they found in Sean's cell and prove he didn't do anything. And what about his prints? Did they dust it for prints?"

"They're doing everything, Lucy." Felicity looked at her phone. "The SSA of Violent Crime is taking point on this. His name is Steven Pierce, he's been in the Houston office for more than ten years. He wants to talk to you."

"I know Steven," Megan said to Lucy. "We've met several times over the years. You can trust him."

"No, I can't," Lucy said.

"Talk to him," Felicity said, "and I'll make sure Sean's rights are protected. I promise you that."

Reluctantly, Lucy agreed, and hoped she wasn't making a mistake.

Steven came in alone, which Lucy appreciated. She already felt completely overwhelmed after Banner and his partner had talked to her earlier. After introductions, Steven sat down and said, "When was the last time that you spoke to your husband?"

"Yesterday late afternoon," Lucy said.

"Did he give you any indication that he planned to escape?"

"He didn't plan to escape."

Steven stared at her. It didn't faze her. She'd interviewed more than a hundred suspects, an FBI agent wasn't going to get to her.

The Houston cops did. You need to be focused, Lucy.

She knew that the FBI would want to bring Sean in alive. Houston PD, she wasn't so certain. So she needed to trust Steven Pierce—up to a point.

Steven shifted gears. "Where would Sean go that he feels safe?"

"If he can escape Hunt, he'll call Rick Stockton, assistant director of the FBI, and arrange to turn himself in."

"Does Sean have any friends in Houston? Anyone he trusts?"

He did, but Lucy wasn't going to share that information and bring a SWAT team into someone's life. Patrick was already talking to everyone Sean knew; better him than her, in case the police had her phone tapped.

"You're focused on the wrong thing, Agent Pierce," Lucy said. "Jimmy Hunt planned this escape. He took Sean against his will. Find out where Jimmy Hunt would go, who he associates with in Houston. Find his daughter Elise and ask her where her father is."

"We are following all leads," Steven said. "I'm trying

to help you. I don't want anyone hurt. I'm doing everything in my power to bring your husband in alive."

That blunt statement stabbed Lucy in the gut so hard she had to pause before she could speak.

"And I'm telling you right now, Sean will do everything in his power to free himself and turn himself in." She wasn't a hundred percent certain of that. Sean might run if only because he feared for his life. But for now, she was sticking to this. "Multiple people helped Hunt break out. Talk to the corrections officer who lied when he said Sean killed a cop. Sean would never kill a cop. Talk to the people Hunt was in prison with, whom he associates with, who would take a job from him. He ran a major drug smuggling operation for years, he infiltrated the DEA, he has people on his payroll, and if you don't focus on *that*, you'll never find them and Sean *will* be dead!"

Megan put her hand on Lucy's arm and said to Steven, "You have Hunt's files, correct?"

"Of course."

"Can I speak with you outside?"

"Megan, I don't know—"

"Steven, two minutes."

He stood. "Agent Kincaid, I'm sorry that you've been put in this situation, but I'm doing my job, and you want me to do my job. I'm very good at it. If you know anything about the whereabouts of your husband, you need to tell me."

She stared at him. "If I knew, I'd call in the Marines to save him, because he's a hostage, and you need to see him as such."

Megan and Steven stepped out and Lucy put her head on the table. She was exhausted and scared.

Felicity said, "You did fine. Megan's going to reinforce everything you said, make sure that Steven knows who Sean is and why he's at risk. Okay?"

"I just want him safe," Lucy said. "It's been nearly three hours. They could be anywhere. I can't stay here and do nothing."

"Let others take up the slack. You have a lot of friends and family helping."

"We're missing something. Whatever is going on with Jimmy Hunt and this escape, he's planned this for a long time. Mona Hill's murder, his transfer to Houston, testifying against the hit man, everything led to this escape. That takes money, time, resources. People."

"Megan knows that."

Patrick walked in. "Lucy, you need to eat."

She stared at him, confused. "Food? I don't want food!"

"Come on. You ate two bites of toast and drank a gallon of coffee."

Felicity said, "Lucy, go with your brother, take care of yourself. My colleague just texted me. Kate Donovan has arrived, I need to talk to her, talk to Houston PD and Agent Pierce, then I'm meeting with the AUSA about Michael Thompson, the hitman Hunt testified against. Okay?"

The last thing that Lucy wanted to do was eat, but she needed to get out of this room. "Okay. Fine."

"I'll call you the minute I hear anything," Felicity said.

Lucy followed Patrick outside. "I don't want to go anywhere."

"Shh."

She glanced at her brother. "What's going on?"

"Just follow me."

Patrick was definitely acting weird. But she followed him. They left the building and walked down the block. He'd parked on the street two blocks from the jail. "Get in."

"I don't want—"

"Trust me."

She did, so she climbed in. He tossed her a paper bag, then drove away.

She looked inside. A deli sandwich and her favorite jalapeño chips. "I can't—"

"Eat," he said. "I already ate mine. I have a lead."

"On Sean?"

"No. We can't get anywhere near that—you have to trust Megan and Kate to find him. I have a lead to pursue on the Mona Hill investigation."

It took Lucy a moment to switch gears. She took out the sandwich and unwrapped one half. Turkey, cheese, and jalapeños, her favorite.

"How does that help find Sean?"

"This whole thing started because Mona Hill was killed."

It took her a second to get on Patrick's wavelength. "Yes, so? That's kind of irrelevant now."

"The police think Sean is guilty, so it's *not* irrelevant. We prove he was framed and it goes a long way into proving that Hunt orchestrated the escape."

"It's an elaborate plan just to kidnap someone."

"But Hunt was in prison. He wanted out. Testifying against a hit man—probably a guy he hired himself—was brilliant. Once he knew when he was testifying and when he'd be in Houston, he had Elise frame Sean."

"There was no guarantee that it would work."

"Which tells me that Houston PD had Sean's name almost from the beginning. But they're not going to share any of that with the defense. But thanks to your friend Ryan—"

"Ryan Quiroz?"

"Yeah. Jack talked to him yesterday, gave him my number. He was a cop here, has friends here, and he got a copy of the original police report. Wouldn't give it to me, but he read it over the phone. Banner hasn't even *talked* to the pizza delivery guy. But the responding officer did, to confirm the bodyguard's statement."

"And?"

"We're going to talk to him."

"You have his name."

"I know his name, address, workplace, school, and the fact that he has no record."

"How does that help us?"

"The important thing is that the detectives haven't interviewed him. I want to know what he knows—they'll follow up eventually, but the fact that they didn't tells me they took his original statement on its face. I would have had follow-up questions."

"Like?"

"For started, did he see anyone outside Mona's apartment or in the lobby, go from there. But here's the thing—he arrived at eight thirty P.M. The *only* security cameras are in the elevator and in the lobby. There is only one public entrance into the building, which is locked at ten P.M. and you need a key. That much I got from the report. I want to see the place, figure out how the killer got in and out without being seen on camera. So we're heading there first. Ned Williams—the pizza guy—is a college student and works nights, but I checked his social media accounts and he is always at his dorm between one and three—leaves a little after three for a class."

"That is—wow. You've been busy."

"I have to keep busy, Lucy. I'm worried about Sean, and I'm worried about you. If I didn't have something to do, I would pull my hair out."

"I'm so glad you're here."

"So you've said."

"Really. I've missed you, Patrick. When I lived in D.C., I saw you almost every day. I took you for granted."

"You didn't."

"I did. I expected to have you around all the time, and then when I moved here . . . I didn't. You have Elle and are always busy."

"You have Sean."

"I know. And I probably didn't give Elle a real chance at first."

"You more than made up for it at Thanksgiving. Seriously—I know you and Elle don't see eye to eye on a lot of things, but you both tried over Thanksgiving to like each other."

"I like her. I'll never agree with some of her ideas, but I like her. And more? In her heart, she's a good person. More important, she loves you. And what she did for those kids, keeping that family together, really impressed me, showed me that her compassion is for real. Maybe I don't have enough."

"You have enough, Lucy. We've all lived different lives with different experiences that have shaped us. We need people like Elle in the world—and we need people like you."

Lucy sometimes lamented the fact that she often saw the worst in people. She didn't used to be that way. In fact, she used to be more like Elle . . . and maybe that's why she'd had a hard time warming up to her. Elle was the woman that Lucy could have been if she hadn't been kidnapped and raped when she was eighteen.

She shook her head, dismissing the negative thoughts. She had done so well putting the past behind her, but in truth, it was always with her—for better or worse. She had incorporated the pain and anger into a productive career where catching bad guys and finding justice for victims gave her satisfaction.

Patrick drove to Mona Hill's apartment. She lived in a classy downtown building.

"I called ahead, but not as a PI. Prospective tenant. Go with me on this, okay?"

"Of course."

The building was large enough to have a small management office. There was only one person in the office. Patrick smiled. "I'm Patrick, I called earlier about a vacancy?"

"Yes! I have the key right here."

"Great. This is my girlfriend, Lucy."

"I'm Diana Gomez, nice to meet you both. Would you like to see the apartment first or tour the facilities?"

"Tour would be great." He casually put his arm around Lucy. Yes, it was weird to pretend to be her brother's girlfriend.

"The best thing about this building is that we're new opened up three years ago. The appliances, the gym, everything is state-of-the-art. But in case something isn't working, we have full-time maintenance. They handle the common areas as well as any problems in your unit. We have one hundred and twenty units, all with their own private balcony and washer and dryer. The bottom floor units have terraces. Down here"—she opened a door that led to the common area   "we have a great room with a large screen television. We have movie parties, there's a pool table, games, and residents can reserve the facility for private parties."

She went on about the amenities, the pools, the gym, parking. Lucy focused on security while Patrick asked innocuous questions. She noted that there were security cameras in the lobby, but she didn't see any in the common area or outside the elevator.

After the tour, they looked at the apartment, which was not Mona Hill's—that might not have been cleared by police yet. The apartment was on the third floor. In the elevator, Lucy noticed the security cameras Patrick had mentioned earlier, but there were none in the hallway once she stepped out.

She asked, "I assume there are staircases? I like taking the stairs up and down."

"Yes, for fire safety there are four sets of staircases, one next to the elevator, one on the north wing in the corner, and two in the south wing."

Lucy made a point of opening the door to the staircase next to the elevator. No security cameras.

The two-bedroom apartment was spacious. The balcony looked out into the courtyard, which was about fifty yards across. She considered that everyone had balconies, and privacy was afforded mostly by the blinds—if it was night and lights were on, people would be able to see into each other's units if the blinds were open.

Lucy involuntarily shivered. She hated the thought of someone watching her.

But then she thought, had the police talked to the people who lived across from Mona Hill? Would they have seen anything?

"Do you have something a bit bigger coming up?" Patrick said. "I work from home for a computer software company, and Lucy is getting her master's and needs her own quiet room. We're saving up to buy a house, but we don't want to be miserable or cramped, either."

"All our three-bedroom units are on the fourth floor—we even have several four bedrooms. They're in high demand. I have a three-bedroom coming up in about a month . . . I don't know exactly when."

"Can we see it? Or are they still living there?"

"We, uh—well, there was a domestic situation. I shouldn't even tell you, but a guy killed his girlfriend, at least that's what we got from the police. They haven't let us into the unit yet, so I don't know the condition, and the police said there is no next of kin. So when they clear it, we will contact whoever is on the paperwork when the resident filed."

Patrick was holding Lucy's hand, and he squeezed it. Probably to make sure she didn't say anything to correct the woman.

"That's awful," he said. "I saw security cameras downstairs—but I guess you can't always know who is who."

"Well, the killer wasn't a resident. We run a background and credit check on everyone on the lease."

"And security?" Lucy asked, her voice sounding unnatural.

"We have cameras in the lobby, the mail room, and in the elevators. The main doors are locked at ten P.M. and then residents use a card key to enter—same key that opens the other common areas like the gym."

"Do you have security guards?" Lucy asked.

"No, but we record everything, and if there's a problem we can go back up to thirty days. I don't really know a lot about it, we have a company that stores and retrieves data. The only time we've ever had to use it—other than this situation with the police last week—was when some packages were going missing. I had to go through hundreds of hours of recordings from the mail room to find the culprit. It was the son of one of the residents. He didn't even live here, but used his mom's card key when he visited. Collected her mail, stole from others. We've changed the way we handle packages now."

"What about the garage?" Patrick said.

"Well . . . no cameras, but we take a photo of everyone entering and exiting. You need a card key to get in the garage."

They chatted a bit more, then Patrick thanked her for her time and said he and Lucy would talk about it and let her know.

"We have two other people interested," she said. "So if you can get your application in by the end of today, that would give you priority."

"Thanks, I'll definitely let you know." Patrick's smile was charming and easygoing, and the manager returned it. Lucy and Patrick walked out.

Patrick said, "Anyone could get into that building without much effort. I want to show you something."

They walked around back to the underground parking entrance. An arm swung up when you placed your card key on the sensor. They spotted the camera on the wall above it. "When you activate the sensor, it takes a photo. Anyone can walk in and out without triggering the camera."

"And if there are no security cameras on the staircase, someone could use the staircase to get up to Mona's apartment."

"Exactly." Lucy remembered that Mona called Sean after she'd seen Elise in the building. "The manager said they keep the recordings for thirty days. Elise was in the lobby last weekend. If we can prove that, it'll go a long way in substantiating Sean's statement."

"The police should have them, but we'll talk to Kate and make sure."

"The police here don't seem inclined to do anything that might exonerate Sean." But Kate would. Agent Pierce would follow up. This was one small piece of evidence, but it would help.

"Hold that thought." Patrick glanced at his watch. "Time to talk to the pizza guy."

Ned Williams was a tall, skinny Black kid with glasses and an award-winning smile. He held a video game controller in one hand, and had headphones draped around his neck when he opened the door of his dorm room.

"I'm Patrick Kincaid," Patrick said, "a private investigator looking into the murder of Mona Hill last Monday. This is my partner, Lucy. Do you have a minute to answer a few questions?"

He shrugged. "Sure." He looked in his messy room. "Umm, there's no place to sit."

"That's okay," Patrick said, "this won't take long."

Ned smiled again, motioned for them to come in. Patrick glanced at the game he had paused. "Fallout. I love that game."

"Oh, man, the expansion pack is totally dope."

"I can play for hours. That and Rainbow Six Siege."

"Totally. I have a group of buddies from high school, we still play."

"My best friend moved to San Antonio and sometimes that's the only time I get to talk to him."

"I know, right?" He smiled, looked again from Patrick to Lucy. "So, what can I help ya'll with? This about the woman over on Hudson Street?"

"Yes, Mona Hill. Do you deliver regularly to the building?"

"All the time. It's on my route."

"And Ms. Hill orders often?"

"Well, she uses the name Odette. But yeah, at least once a week."

"An Officer Reynolds spoke to you the day after the murder, correct?"

"Yeah, thought I was in trouble—and I didn't do anything, I mean, I work thirty hours a week at the pizza place—mostly deliveries at night, some of their events and stuff. And I have a full load of classes and tutor at the math lab twice a week. I don't have *time* to get into trouble. But it was just about my delivery."

"I have a copy of Officer Reynolds's report, I just want to confirm the facts, okay?"

"Sure." He leaned against his dresser.

"The order came in at seven thirty Monday evening."

"Yeah. At least, that's what the receipt said."

"Did she pay by credit card?"

"Usually, I guess." He shrugged. "And she always tips well. Five bucks, no matter what, and that's even on top of the two-dollar delivery charge. If she orders a lot, like for a party, she tips even more."

"No one answered the door when you arrived at eight thirty?"

"No. Which was weird, because she isn't one of those jerks, you know? I called the number on the receipt, and it went to voice mail. So I left. Ran into Christian in the lobby, knew him because he was over there a lot, he's paid a few times, and he took care of me then. Tipped well, too. I thought he was her boyfriend, but the cop said he was a bodyguard, and I'm like, no shit? Then I read that she was a prostitute. Wow. Just didn't see that. She was nice, that's all I cared about, you know?"

"Nice" was relative, Lucy realized. Ned didn't know that Mona Hill used to blackmail powerful men and women to keep her business running, or had supplied women to a brutal cartel leader. So what if she had turned over a new leaf and kept her business mostly on the up-and-up?

But she didn't say anything. Ned was friendly and co-operating.

"So Christian Porter, her bodyguard or friend, took the pizza and tipped you?"

"Ten bucks. He said she was probably in the shower. He went up and I left. And that was it until the cops came the next day to talk to me."

"Did you see or hear anyone in her apartment?"

He shook his head. "It was quiet."

"Did you see someone getting in or out of the elevator? Maybe while you were waiting for it?"

"No." He cocked his head to the side. "Well, when I got off there was this chick walking toward the elevator. I held it for her, but she just walked by, didn't say a word. Just went to the end of the hall. I just thought whatever, you know? And walked the other way."

"So she was coming from the direction of Ms. Hill's apartment?"

"Hmm, yeah."

"And she just walked to the end of the hall?"

"I heard the staircase door close. Sometimes I go down the stairs, especially if it's busy. There's only one elevator. But there's a staircase at the elevator, though it only goes to the lobby. The others go all the way down to the garage."

"Do you remember what she looks like?"

"Not really. Why? I thought they caught the guy?"

"I'm a private investigator," Patrick said, "I'm looking at all possibilities. You said 'chick.' Was she young? Old? In between?"

"Young. Teenager. Twenty, tops."

"What was she wearing?"

"Dark hoodie, her hands in her pockets, you know, very pulled in, like not friendly and all. I'm friendly, I don't get it, but I guess I do. Petite white girl sees big Black guy and just walks by, it is what it is." He shrugged.

"You remember a lot more than you think. We now know that the girl was white, petite, in her late teens, wearing a dark hoodie—I assume the hood was over her head?"

"Yeah, it was."

"Did you see her hair?"

"Blond. Hey, you're right, I do remember a lot." He grinned.

"Could you tell if it was long or short?"

He shook his head. "It was all tucked under the hood,

but she had these long bangs that came out, that's how I know it was blond."

"That's great. You said petite, but you're pretty tall. So how short?"

Ned glanced at Lucy. "Shorter than you. Like, a lot shorter. I'd say five three, take or leave an inch. She was pretty short."

"Was she carrying anything?" Lucy asked. "A purse or backpack?"

"Nothing. Her hands were in her pockets, like I said."

Patrick asked, "Had you ever seen her before in the building?"

Ned shrugged. "Can't say, probably not. Most people say hi to me because it's like my territory, I'm there almost every night, sometimes five or six times a night."

Lucy asked, "Did anyone else talk to you about that night, other than Officer Reynolds? Someone in law enforcement or anyone else?"

"Nope. The officer said one of the detectives investigating the murder would probably come and talk to me, just to verify everything I said and whatever, but no one did. I thought because they'd caught the guy. It was on the news yesterday. I mean, I talked to people I worked with, if that counts, because no one said not to say anything, you know?"

Patrick handed Ned his card. "If you think of anything else, please call me."

He looked at the card. "Sure."

"The detective will probably be back to talk to you as they work the case, make sure you tell him everything you told us."

"Of course. Hey, my brother's a cop in Galveston, that's where I'm from. I totally respect those guys, so anything I can do to, like, you know, help, I will."

"We appreciate that, Ned. Thank you."

They left and Lucy almost didn't wait until they left the building before she said, "Elise Hunt is five foot three and a half and blond. She dyes her hair frequently, but she was blond when I saw her yesterday."

"If she used the stairs, that means she knew where the cameras were and that there were no cameras on the staircase. She went all the way down to the parking garage to avoid the lobby," Patrick said. "I'm going back to Mona's apartment and checking with all the businesses and neighbors. There's something here, I'll find it. I'm going to take you to the hotel."

"I want to go with you."

"No."

"What do you mean *no*?"

"Lucy, you are married to their prime suspect. You can't be involved at this point. You shouldn't have even been there when I talked to Ned, but now that we have something, I have to cut you out. I'm sorry. I have to be careful as well, but if I can find one small lead I'll push that arrogant cop to do his job or go over his head. Because the truth is here, I know it."

"I can't just sit around! Sean is out there, in danger, and every cop in the state will be after him unless we can clear his name and prove Hunt orchestrated this entire thing."

"You don't have to tell me that, Lucy. I know what's at risk. I think the best place for you is at home, but I know you won't do that, and the media is going to be all over the jail—eventually someone will figure out who you are and hound you. I don't want you to go through that."

Lucy didn't know *what* to do. She'd woken up this morning knowing the situation was bad but believing that she'd see Sean and together they'd figure out how to clear his name.

But it didn't happen.

"So the hotel is the next best option," Patrick said. "RCK got a suite, I'll be there as soon as I get answers."

Erica Anderson was fucked.

A cop was dead. Her lover was in the hospital. How could this situation have gotten so out of control? This wasn't supposed to happen!

She didn't want to show her face at the hospital, especially now, but she couldn't get any information from the nurses over the phone. If Tim died, all this bullshit would be for nothing. Everything she did, every crime she committed, would be for nothing if Tim was dead.

Sometimes, she didn't even know how she'd gotten to this point.

She still had her old corrections ID. She was supposed to turn it in, but she hadn't because she'd needed it. She wasn't in uniform, but half the cops who were here weren't in uniform. She showed her badge to the information desk and asked about the cop who was brought in that morning with a GSW. She was given a visitor's pass and directed to the second floor, where he was being prepped for surgery.

She found a young nurse and showed her visitor's pass. "My fiancé is here. He was shot, a corrections guard?" Tim wasn't her fiancé, not yet, but if they survived this they deserved to be together. "Tim Sheffield?"

"He's being prepped for surgery."

"I just want to see him, one minute, please, just to tell him I love him." This was true. She needed to see him. Because she had to find out what the fuck went wrong that his partner was killed and he was shot. Had Elise and her people betrayed them? Was Tim supposed to *die*? She had to find out what was going on and whether she needed to get her kids out of town.

"Let me see what I can do."

The nurse walked off and Erica paced.

Her cell phone vibrated.

She almost ignored it. But it was her contact, Clara. A smart bitch, but a bitch nonetheless.

"What?" she answered.

"Where are you? You're supposed to be back at the house to take care of *the situation*."

Erica closed her eyes. Elise Hunt had killed someone and Erica needed to dispose of the body.

How the *fuck* did it come to this?

First she was paid to falsify some paperwork. No big deal. Then running stupid errands and making sure gang-bangers did their fucking job. Annoying, but not difficult. Then planting a gun in a plane. Sure, why not? No skin off her nose. Tim had done worse, been forced to do things they both knew would get them in serious trouble, but he had to clean his slate. Make sure that one mistake didn't come back to bite him in the ass.

But now body disposal? When was it going to end?

"Erica, where are you?" Clara demanded.

"Houston," she said.

"You're fucking three hours away?"

"I'm leaving now."

"You'd better be, because this is not the time to get cold feet."

"I'm fine," she snapped.

The nurse was approaching. Erica hung up on Clara without another word.

"I can give you two minutes, that's it," the nurse said. "I'm sorry."

"Two minutes is perfect," she said. "Thank you so much."

She followed the nurse down the hall to a small alcove with a sheet draped across. Tim was lying on a gurney, already prepped for surgery. The nurse hooking up his IV finished, then said, "I'll be right back, give you two a minute. But he's going to be fine," she told Erica and patted her on the arm.

That made tears well up in her eyes. Erica was not a crier, but seeing Tim so . . . *helpless* . . . was her undoing. He was a big man, a strong man, and he looked defeated.

She took his hand. "Baby, what happened?"

He turned his head. He was on painkillers, she could see it in his eyes. "Just part of the plan."

"What? Getting shot was part of the *plan*?"

"Shh," he said. He squeezed her hand but his grip was weak. "To sell it. Shot me in the leg. Not fatal. But the bullet got lodged in my bone. They'll get it out."

"Your partner—he's dead."

"I know."

"That wasn't supposed to happen."

"I know. Just—shh. Don't worry. Everything is going to be fine."

The nurse came back and told Erica she needed to leave, the doctor was ready for Tim. Erica kissed his forehead and walked out in a daze.

Something was very wrong. Maybe it was the drugs, or maybe it was her eyes finally being opened.

Tim didn't seem to care that his partner, a man he'd known for more than a decade, was dead. Had he *known* that killing Dave was part of the plan?

Everything had gone off the rails, and Erica didn't know what to do.

Except one thing.

She left the hospital and called her ex-husband. "Erica! Where are you? I've been trying—"

"Shut up, Bill. Shut up and listen to me. Get the kids out of town. Don't ask questions, don't ask me anything. Just get them safe *right now* and don't do anything else until you hear from me. I fucking mean it, Bill. Those kids are all I care about in this world and if anything happens to them . . . just do it."

She ended the call. If anything happened to them it would be on her, because she was the one who blew it. She'd never forgive herself. Those two kids were the only truly good things she'd accomplished in her life. And Bill . . . well, he was a good man. Not perfect, too cautious in everything he did, but a good father. He would take care of them whether she was dead or in prison.

Erica didn't want to die. She didn't want to go to prison. But if she was going to avoid both, she had to survive the rest of the day.

Chapter Thirty-four

Aggie was more nervous than Nate that they were outside Bexar County. SAPD specifically told Nate that he couldn't leave the county, and Nate had agreed to abide by the terms. They could actually arrest him now. But Nate wasn't concerned. He couldn't be now that they had a real lead on the people who planted the drugs in his truck. The people who could lead them to Elise Hunt.

"What if we're being followed?" she asked.

"We're not."

"But SAPD was sitting outside Lucy's all night."

"They're still there."

He'd checked with Leo every hour since they'd left. All was well, but how long would that last? He'd read the news—Sean was in serious shit—but Nate had always been the type of cop to focus on the facts and immediate situation. Lucy had keen intuition—that "gut" that a lot of cops talked about. Nate didn't. He had a strong sense of security issues—he could walk into any room and immediately assess the threat level, know every escape route, and exactly where he would take cover if someone started shooting. But that wasn't the same as understanding criminal psychology. Nate didn't understand why people did the shit they did. He understood soldiers—

fighting for a cause, fighting for your country, protecting the innocent—he just didn't understand how some people hurt others for no fucking reason.

It made him double down on his commitment to not bring children into the world. He'd lost friends, he'd lost people he cared about. And now his best friend was at great risk and he couldn't do anything about it—except find Elise Hunt.

But he wasn't going to let the damn SAPD and this phony drug seizure stop him from finding the bitch who set it all up. He was only five miles as the crow flies across the county border.

"Nate," Aggie said, "this is serious. You could permanently lose your badge. You could be prosecuted."

"I'm willing to take that risk. Nothing you say is going to change my mind, so stop trying."

They were parked on a long road off Highway 46 north of San Antonio, somewhere between Boerne and Spring Valley. The houses were spread out, everyone had some land—two, five, twenty acres. There were a lot of horses, too; the terrain was greener as the elevation rose. Nate liked the Hill Country. He wouldn't mind getting a place out of town—his apartment was functional, but he'd rented it three and a half years ago when he was assigned to the San Antonio office, and he rarely spent time there. It was a place to sleep. He spent more waking hours at Sean and Lucy's.

Nate had been conflicted about whether he would stay in the FBI. On the one hand, Leo Proctor was only a few years from retirement and had already talked to Nate about taking over leadership of the SWAT team. San Antonio had one of the best-trained FBI SWAT units in the state, and Nate would be honored to lead them and build on what Leo had started. That would mean staying and maybe buying a house. But on the other hand, he never quite felt like he fit into the office. He kept waiting for something else, but he couldn't quite define it. Partly it was that he missed his old unit, the men and women he'd worked with, fought with, laughed with. Partly because he was still there, in the past. It was hard to explain to anyone who had not served, especially for the length of time he had.

Having Jack and Kane around really helped, he realized.

Maybe he should focus on making a future here, not thinking about the past, not thinking about moving on. And if he were going to buy a place, he'd buy somewhere up here, out of town. Have a little space. Get a couple of dogs.

Violating direct orders not to leave Bexar County wasn't a problem for him. Right now, he was the only one who was looking for Elise Hunt.

He had already assessed the terrain. Sitting out here on this country road wasn't an option. Though the houses were few and far between, they'd be easily spotted if they parked for too long. They'd driven close enough to the target property to determine that there were no external security cameras; while Nate drove, Aggie had looked up property information and learned that the house was owned by an out-of-state investor and managed by a local company. A couple of calls later, and she had confirmation that the house had been rented on a month-to-month basis, since February 1, to Clara Valeria. She'd moved here two months before Elise had been released from juvie. The same week that Erica Anderson had quit her job. Coincidence? Unlikely.

When a neighbor drove slowly by them, Nate drove away and found a place to pull over and figure out the best way to approach and assess the property. Nate looked at satellite footage of the area.

"I got it," he said.

He turned the tablet around so Aggie could see it. "If we drive down here, go up this street, which is parallel to the target, here's an entrance to a state preserve. We park there and then cut through the preserve. We'll only have to cut through one parcel of private property to hit the rear boundary of Valeria's place—then we can recon."

"Do we need a warrant?"

"To search. But we're not going to search. If we stake out here"—he pointed—"the trees will shield us. I have binoculars and we can assess whether any of our subjects are on the property. If we get eyes on Donny Valeria, we call it in." His boss wasn't happy that he was working with Aggie on this case, but Rachel hadn't told him to stand down. SAPD already had their description of Valeria, and that Aggie had ID'd him through DEA photos. No one else had a lead on his whereabouts. "You have cause to talk to Pablo Barrios, so if we see him and not Valeria, then we talk to him about the sixteen kilos."

"What do we say when they ask why we're out here?"

"Just checking up on an unverified lead. Look—you don't have to be here. We're in the gray area and could both be reprimanded or worse. I'm okay with that. But I don't expect you to give up your career to follow me down this rabbit hole."

She bristled, her eyes narrowing. "That doesn't say much about how you think of me, does it?" she snapped. "I'm doing this because my boss, a man I respect and admire, is missing and very well may be dead. Our office was torn apart because of the Hunt family, and I'm not going to sit by and wait to find his body. They must have taken him for a reason—to torture him? To get information? To draw away resources? I have no idea, but one thing Lucy said was that Elise Hunt does things that don't make sense because she thinks it's fun or disruptive. It's like yelling fire in a crowded theater and enjoying the chaos. Maybe Brad's kidnapping is part of that chaos, or there really is a bigger plan."

Nate admired Aggie's fire and appreciated the fact that she didn't back down. He didn't encounter many people like Aggie in federal law enforcement. Rules were important—but so was doing the right thing.

"We stake out the house, get confirmation, call it in. Agreed?"

"Agreed."

He turned the ignition and headed to the state preserve.

Chapter Thirty-five

GULF OF MEXICO

For the first hour that Sean was tied up in the hull of the yacht, he panicked. He worried about what Lucy would think when the guard told authorities that he'd been the one to shoot his partner. He worried about what the police would do when and if they found him. How would he be able to clear his name?

The second hour, Sean found surprising calm. He couldn't do anything to help himself if he only focused on the bad . . . he had to find a way out of this mess. He had no idea where they were taking him. He had a good sense of time, but on the boat he didn't know the direction they were going. Toward Beaumont? He doubted it. Toward Corpus Christi? More likely. Or heading to a boat deeper in the Gulf. But then they'd have to worry about the Coast Guard.

They would be docking somewhere. He had to find the strength to make his move when the opportunity came. He stretched and the ropes tightened.

Think!

He couldn't see anything; the hull was dark. His hands were numb so he started working his fingers back and forth, little stretches, trying to keep his blood circulating. It took several minutes, but he was able to move better.

When he regained control of his fingers, he started feeling the knots on the ropes, trying to picture how they were tied by touching each curve. It took him a while—he relied on sight too much, he realized—but he developed a plan to untie them. He didn't know how long he had, but he worked methodically, carefully, shifting slightly now and again.

Thirty minutes later, the binds fell off. He shook out his arms as full feeling rushed back in. He then untied the ropes around his chest, the ones that tied him to the support beam.

Almost free.

The big problem were the shackles around his feet. Not only did they make noise when he moved, he couldn't run and if he jumped in the water, they would pull him down or make it extremely difficult—and exhausting—to swim. Not impossible, but it would slow him down and they'd easily shoot or recapture him.

He could pick the locks if he had the right tools, but he had nothing.

Getting out of his binds had given him hope, and now he again felt lost. Dammit!

Think, Rogan!

The yacht reduced speed. It turned to the right, and based on the motion of the water, they were going over choppy waves. For fifteen minutes they maintained moderate speed, then the engines idled. Someone was maneuvering the boat through some sort of obstacle. Or inlet. Where they hell were they? Sean figured they'd been out on the water around three hours. How far could they have gone? Not to Mexico. If they'd gone south, they'd be past Galveston, he figured. But he didn't know the geography well enough to know the towns along the coast. Certainly Corpus Christi, the next major coastal city Sean could think of, would have taken longer than three hours by speedboat. If they'd gone east, they'd be somewhere along the Louisiana border, but New Orleans would be hours, if not a day or more, away. There were lots of places they could dock, but no major towns. They could pull up at a private dock where there could be a helicopter or plane waiting to take them to Mexico.

Finally, the boat stopped. Sean waited, tense. He wanted to go down fighting, but he didn't want to die.

Then the door above him opened and light blinded him. He closed his eyes and he heard laughter.

"Well, look at that, he got out of his binds."

"I told you he would," a voice said.

A very, very familiar voice he hadn't heard in two and a half years.

Sean stood outside Colton Thayer's hospital room and thought about leaving. Colton didn't want to see him. He'd refused all of Sean's calls over the last week.

But he was getting out of the hospital tomorrow. If not now, Sean didn't know when he'd ever have a chance to apologize. It was one of those awful situations—Sean didn't regret working with the FBI to take down a corrupt United States senator, but Sean really wished he didn't have to use his best friend to do it.

It was water under the bridge. What was done was done, and Sean just wanted to explain . . . or maybe not. What could he say? He had no excuse. Colton had been working for Senator Jonathan Paxton for good reasons—reasons Sean would have joined him in supporting ten years ago. But today? Sean had changed. While he understood the allure of white hat hacking, he was in love with an FBI agent and he wasn't going to risk his freedom, or Lucy's career, to go back to his old ways.

And, Sean realized over time, sometimes two wrongs didn't make a right. Sometimes, there were no winners in the battle between criminals and innocents. Sometimes people like Paxton were so corrupt, so selfish, so driven by their grief and narcissism that they didn't care who they hurt in the process.

But the last thing Sean wanted to do was hurt Colton. He didn't know what he was thinking—that maybe Colton would never learn that he had been working with the FBI? That maybe Colton would never figure out why Sean had infiltrated his group?

Yeah . . . that's what he'd been thinking from the beginning, that he could walk away without his longtime friend ever knowing the truth. He'd been lying to himself, but he wasn't going to lie to Colton, not anymore.

He walked through the door.

Colton was sitting up in his hospital bed. He was pale, dark circles under his eyes. The IV was still in his arm, and he had a bandage across his chest. Two bullets—one that hit half an inch from his heart. But he survived. And the FBI promised Sean that if Colton cooperated, he wouldn't do jail time. That was something, wasn't it?

"Hi, C."

Colton was staring at him. He didn't say anything.

"I heard you were being sprung tomorrow."

Again, silence.

"I, umm, just wanted to—"

"What, Sean? What do you want to do? Try to justify lying to me for weeks? To me—the man you said was your best friend? The man you said had saved you and given you purpose?"

Colton stared at him and Sean felt small and miserable.

"Jonathan Paxton was going to kill hundreds of people."

"Sexual predators. Ten years ago you wouldn't have cared."

"I never killed anyone."

"So that's where you draw the line? Murder? Good to know."

"Colton, I am really sorry."

"I don't want your false apology. I won't alleviate your guilt. You came back into my life and I thought we were brothers in every way except blood."

"We are—"

"No! We're not! You lied to me, used me, for a personal vendetta."

"It wasn't personal." Except it was, in a way. Jonathan Paxton had held a crime over Sean's head for the last six months and Sean had to clean the slate. He'd confessed to the FBI, he'd agreed to infiltrate Colton's team and gather evidence against the senator in order to erase his own black marks.

"You're a selfish bastard, Sean."

"Paxton knew about what we did ten years ago, Colton. You told him about that, C! That's the only way he could have known. He was holding it over my head. I didn't have a choice! I had to go to the FBI."

"We all have choices, Sean. You aligned yourself with the system. I aligned myself with doing the right thing."

"Maybe," he said quietly, "but they used you, Colton."

"You should know because you used me, too. We're done, Sean. I never want to see you again. Get. Out!"

Sean had left and sat in his car for an hour trying to control his pain and guilt. Would he have done it again? He didn't know. Maybe . . . maybe not. Colton nearly died. Others did die, people he had once cared about—even if they later made bad choices.

Everything Sean did he did because he thought it was right. What if he didn't know anymore? What if he didn't know right from wrong?

Because the pain on Colton's face was real. The emotional pain of betrayal. And Sean would never forget it.

"Colton."

Sean almost couldn't speak. He hadn't seen Colton since that day in the hospital when he went to apologize . . . it had been a dark time in Sean's life, but he had no other options. Not then.

Colton stared at him for a long minute. Hatred. Colton hated him so deeply he couldn't even hide the emotion in his expression.

Sean had wronged him, but Colton had gotten in deep into an illegal operation and if Sean hadn't been there, he would have certainly been dead or spent the rest of this life in prison. But Sean had still betrayed his oldest friend, and he'd never forgiven himself.

And clearly, neither had Colton.

Colton motioned toward the ropes Sean had left on the bottom of the boat then said to the men with him, "Tie him up, bring him out, we're on the clock."

He turned his back on Sean without another word.

Chapter Thirty-six

Jack walked over to where Kane was resting against a shade tree. It was hot, but not unpleasant, especially this high in the mountains. He handed Kane a water bottle.

"I talked to Leo," Jack said. "He's bringing in someone he trusts."

Kane had interrogated Peter Blair and learned that Jesse was supposed to have been grabbed Friday after school. Because Lucy picked him up early, that didn't happen—but it didn't mean it *couldn't* happen. Until they found Jimmy Hunt and Elise, Jesse was under house arrest. Jack talked to Jesse, made sure he understood the situation. He didn't want to instill fear in the kid, but right now they had to be doubly cautious.

Kane didn't say anything.

"We need to go back. Now."

"No."

"Dammit, Kane! Hunt has Sean, Jesse is in trouble, Lucy is vulnerable. And we're down here sitting on our asses!"

Kane opened his eyes, looked at Jack. "Hunt is communicating with Blair."

Jack had seen the messages. Kane had figured out the

code that Blair and Hunt were using, and so far it was working, Kane pretending to be Blair.

"I don't care, Kane. At this point, we're more valuable in Texas."

"Hunt will be here. As soon as we have the location, we'll meet him. It's only a matter of time."

"Time that Sean may not have." Why was Kane being so stubborn about this? "Are you not telling me something?"

"Sean makes RCK a lot of money."

"So?"

"I've been trying to figure out why Sean. Revenge—yes, but that's why Blair was tasked to grab me. I killed Hunt's son. But why Sean? Money is the only explanation that makes sense."

"Sean's not that liquid right now. He spent a small fortune on that panic room, which I think is overkill, and he hasn't been taking jobs out of town." Jack understood Sean's paranoia. His house had been breached last summer by an elite para-military team. Jesse's mother had been killed. Sean wanted his house to be a fortress, but sometimes you had to accept certain risks.

"Hunt knows Sean's skill set. I need Blair to get the information out of Hunt—the exact information about what's going on in Texas—without making Hunt suspicious."

It took Jack a minute to follow Kane's train of thought. "You think Hunt wants Sean to steal something for him."

"Not exactly. This operation cost a shitload of money. Blair isn't cheap—Hunt's been paying him for the last two years. Where'd he get the money? We wiped out his operation, the FBI seized his bank accounts, he has nothing. Someone is funding him. Blair thinks so too, but swears he doesn't know who."

"You believe him."

"Yep."

"And you want to use him to get the information."

"We can't help Sean or anyone until we know who's funding Jimmy Hunt." He looked down at Blair's phone, which was attached to a portable charger. "He's supposed to make contact within the next hour. I made a deal with Blair. He gets the information, he walks. He fucks us over, he's dead."

"You're going to let him walk?"

"We just took out his core operation. No one else is going to work for him, especially when I start the whisper campaign."

Jack would have laughed, if he wasn't so tense.

Kane was going to destroy Peter Blair by spreading a rumor that he was working both sides. It would probably get Blair killed. But at a minimum, it would stop Blair from sex trafficking. Jack would rather see him in prison, but they hadn't taken the time to build a case against him, and without evidence, he would walk.

Better Kane's way. This time.

Kane stared at the phone, as if willing a message to come through, and that was when Jack realized he was more than a little concerned about Sean. He just didn't know how to show it.

Chapter Thirty-seven

Elise did *not* like Bitch Clara. That was how she thought of her in her head—and a couple of times the nickname slipped out, but who cared? Elise was in charge. That *Bitch Clara* thought *she* was in charge was laughable. Only because Clara been living in *her* house for the last year. That she'd visited *her* father in prison. That she was older and all that fucking nonsense.

Age had *nothing* on brains, and Elise had brains in spades.

"Jimmy wants him dead and you're fucking playing games!" Bitch Clara said.

Elise put up her hand and moved her fingers in the blah-blah-blah motion while she mocked her. "'Jimmy wants him dead.'"

"You're fucking insane."

She laughed. "I'm just having fun. Really, we have nothing else to do here until tomorrow so lighten up."

"You were supposed to fuck him up and dump him with a bullet in his head."

"I *will*. And he *is* fucked up. Did you see what I carved in his back? He'll be fucked up plenty, then we'll dump him tomorrow morning when we head south."

Elise was really going to miss seeing Lucy in court on

Monday when she had to defend herself against the restraining order, but by then her daddy said she had to be in Mexico at the safe house because someone *might* have figured out she killed Mona.

Lucy already knew because she was a psychic, but no one would believe her because she'd *attacked* Elise at the gas station.

That had been Elise's brilliant idea and even her daddy would see it.

"Once I break out, they're going to be all-hands," her father said. *"And there might be someone you overlooked. A witness. A camera you missed. Fingerprints. We need to be cautious, and I'm not going to lose you like I lost Tobias and Nicole."*

Her daddy loved her, and that's why he'd forgive her for playing with the DEA agent who killed her sister.

"You're impossible," Bitch Clara said. "You'd better be ready to bolt because I don't like this. I don't like that you sent Donny to kill that ganghanger. He was almost caught. You had no *right* to do that."

"I have every right. Who's paying you?"

"Your father."

"Which means *me*. So fuck off."

Finally, the bitch walked out.

Elise went down to the garage and opened the door to Agent Donnelly's makeshift prison. She liked having her own prison. She would have to make sure she had one in Mexico so she could punish Daddy's enemies. It would be fun.

She flipped on the lights. He groaned, tried to move. He was hurting bad. He might just die without a bullet, but she'd put one in his head anyway just on general principles.

Elise walked over to him. She had stripped him to his boxers because it was humiliating, and humiliating a prick like Brad Donnelly was fun. Her big brother had taught her that.

"Alas," she said as if she were on stage, "you only have hours to live." She giggled. "You should thank me, Big Bad Brad, because I was supposed to kill you and dump you already. So be grateful you had an extra day on the planet. Say 'thank you, Elise!'"

He mumbled something she didn't understand.

"Aw, shucks, I know, it's been fun for me, too!"

She brought over a folding chair and sat across from him.

Everything she had planned was working Perfectly. *Perfectly* with a capital fucking P!

She couldn't discount Jimmy's advice. Her daddy was both smart *and* ruthless. Not as smart as Nicole and not as ruthless as Tobias. But Nicole and Tobias were dead, so being smart and ruthless didn't really matter when you were six feet under.

She kind of missed them. Tobias because he was fun and didn't treat her like a baby. Nicole because she could see ten steps ahead and always knew *exactly* what the cops were going to do. And she was always right.

Well, except for the day this stupid cop killed her.

"You know, Nicole should have figured out that Rogan was delaying, that he'd found a way to communicate with the outside. He tricked her. Her *and* Joseph, and they thought they were so damn smart. But now we have our own computer expert and he'll make sure Rogan doesn't trick us."

Well, he wasn't *her* computer expert. He belonged to the man her daddy had partnered with. But if they were partners, that made everything hers too, right? What's mine is yours and all that bullshit.

"I'm not allowed to kill Lucy—which I think is stupid, but it was part of Daddy's agreement—but she's going to suffer anyway. You'll be dead—I even got a ribbon to tie around your neck when I deliver you. Like, a really fucking big ribbon. And her poor husband will be dead. And the asshole who killed Toby will be dead and she'll never know when I'm going to get her, too."

Elise knelt in front of Brad. "You know, Nicole thought you wanted to get inside Lucy's pants. You had the hots for her. Did you? Did you, huh?"

He lifted his head. His face was bruised and blood had dried on his head and nose. He looked pathetic. "Fuck. You."

She laughed. "Oh, you can't think of anything else to say? So *boring.*"

Her cell phone rang. It wasn't a familiar number, but that didn't mean anything. "Hello?" she answered.

"I'm free."

"Daddy! Are you here? Are you coming?"

"We're still in Texas, heading to my partner's compound."

"Where? Here?"

"No, we're heading to—" She thought she lost the call then he said, "You don't need to know, just in case, but I'm okay. Everything is perfect."

"Can I come? Please? I'm so bored here, and tired of listening to Clara complain and bitch all the time."

"Elise, do exactly what you're supposed to. Go to the safe house tomorrow morning as we agreed. I'll be there sometime tomorrow afternoon; I have to collect my final payment first. You did what we agreed, right?"

"Of course."

Mostly.

"I have to go. Not much longer, Elise. Then we'll be back to business."

He hung up and she smiled. "Back to business!" she told Brad. "I guess our time together is ending. My sister always thought that you were smart, but you're not so smart."

She got up. A dead body was a lot harder to work with, so she figured as soon as the sun went down they'd toss him in the van, drive back to DEA headquarters (or maybe . . . Lucy's house?) and kill him there. Yeah . . . on Lucy's front lawn. That would *totally* mess her up.

She went into the garage and filled a bucket with ice, then filled it with water from the sink. She walked back into the "prison" and dumped it on Brad.

He screamed.

What a beautiful sound.

Nate heard a faint scream—distinctly male—from inside the garage.

He was already on the move. "Call it in *now*," he ordered Aggie. "Then wait for my signal that it's clear."

He had his gun out and ran from their hiding spot on the other side of a retaining wall only thirty yards from the garage. They hadn't seen anything for the last twenty minutes, when a van had arrived with two men they identified as Donny and Pablo. Aggie called in the sighting to SAPD and they were putting together a team, but Nate didn't know how long it would take for them to get here, and he wasn't going to lose Brad now when they were so close.

Nate entered silently through the side door of the garage, which was surprisingly unlocked. He was cautious, expecting a trap, but he entered without incident.

The garage had no cars inside and was smaller than it appeared on the outside because of an internal room in the rear. He waited a heartbeat, listened. He heard an adult male sputtering from the other room. He didn't know who else was inside the room, so with his back against the wall, he walked to the partly opened door and peered inside.

Brad was naked and chained to a desk, drenched in water. Ice cubes surrounded him. He was bloodied, bruised, and extremely pale.

Nate stepped in and gave a low whistle.

Brad struggled to look up. One of his eyes was swollen shut.

His voice was raspy. "Coming back."

Nate stepped inside the door and stood flush against the wall. Years of military and SWAT training made him calm; every sense heightened. Sound. Sight. Smell. He heard the door leading from the garage into the house open, a mere click of the lock, a faint scrape from the hinges. The footfalls were heavier than those of the petite Elise Hunt, so he prepared himself for what he now expected.

Donny Valeria stepped inside as he spoke, "Elise says it's time, we're—"

He noticed Nate far too late to do anything about it. "Shit!"

He had a gun in his hand and he brought it up, aimed at Nate, which was his fatal mistake.

Nate fired three bullets to his chest. Donny didn't get one off before falling to the floor, dead.

The takedown was too noisy, which put Nate at a disadvantage.

He kicked Valeria's gun away and peered out the door. He and Aggie had determined there were at least four people inside the house, but they hadn't been able to confirm the number.

He looked around for a barrier, anything he could put in front of Brad to protect him from flying bullets. There was nothing. The room appeared to be a music studio based on the soundproofing. Or maybe Elise had built it just so she could torture people, hell if he knew. But there was nothing here except a folding chair next to Brad and the desk he was chained too.

"Behind the desk," Nate ordered.

Brad struggled to move, but was making some progress to protect himself.

Nate looked back into the garage. No one was coming through either door.

He heard two gunshots inside.

He was not going to leave Brad unprotected.

He tapped his earpiece and called Aggie. "If clear, follow my path, I'll cover you as soon as you get inside."

"Roger."

Thirty seconds later, he heard in his earpiece, "Hunt is leaving in the van. I can stop her."

"No! Stand down! That's an order, Jensen!"

He didn't hear anything except the ignition turn.

Nate glanced at Brad, then left the room, closing the door behind him. He looked at the house door—no one was coming through.

He ran out the side door and heard Aggie shout, "Federal agent! Stop!"

Aggie stood at the corner of the garage, gun out.

Nate ran up behind her. Elise had backed the van out of the driveway so she had a direct line of fire at Aggie. She rolled down the passenger window and aimed her gun at them. She fired without hesitation.

Nate had Aggie on the ground immediately as he fired at the van.

Elise shot more rounds as she sped off. They went wild, one shattering a tile on the garage roof.

"Are you hit?" he demanded.

"No. I could have had her."

"You were completely exposed!"

"Dammit! She's gone, we can't catch up to her."

Nate was livid. Aggie needed more training or she was going to get herself killed. "Follow me," he ordered. "I have to clear the house."

They went into the garage. Nate opened the door to where Brad was being held. Aggie gasped.

"Stay with him," Nate said. "Call an ambulance."

He went into the house. Elise had left alone, but there could be someone hiding in here or leaving on foot.

He searched room by room. He found one body, female, deceased, in the living room. By the distinctive tattoo on her arm he determined she was Clara Valeria. He found the second body, male, breathing, gut shot, in the kitchen. He searched the man, who was barely conscious, and pulled two guns and a knife off his body. He cuffed him and then searched the rest of the house. No other victims or threats.

Nate pulled blankets off one of the beds and returned to Aggie and Brad. Aggie had taken off her jacket and put it around Brad's shoulders. By that time, he heard sirens in the distance.

"I don't have a key to get him out of these things," Aggie said.

Nate walked over to Donny Valeria and searched his pockets. He had been coming in to take Brad somewhere, so it reasoned that he had the keys to the shackles.

He did.

Nate unlocked them and Brad sagged to the floor.

"I was a dead man," he said in a raspy whisper.

Nate put the blankets on him. He saw that Elise had tortured him, cutting deep into his back. A big "H" followed by a message:

Elise was here.

"You're going to make it."

"Hunt."

"Don't talk," Aggie said. "Help is coming."

Brad shook his head and coughed. "Elise. Her father."

"Jimmy Hunt escaped from prison this morning," Nate said. "He took Sean with him. They're at large."

"He's still in Texas. Called her, told her. Don't know where."

"He called her?" She would have taken her cell phone with her.

Brad struggled to speak, but he clearly wanted to give them information. "He was hired," Brad said. He took a deep breath, then continued. "To get Sean. Someone with lots of money. She's supposed to meet Hunt in Mexico at a safe house. I have no idea where. Clara knows."

"Clara is dead."

"They hated each other," Brad said.

"Pablo Barrios is alive. I cuffed him inside."

"He's hired. Muscle only."

Brad was shivering uncontrollably.

The ambulance was closer. "Go meet them, get them here," Nate told Aggie.

She frowned, but did it.

Nate would apologize later. Maybe. He was still angry that she had put herself in the line of fire outside.

He squatted next to Brad. "What?"

"She said something I don't understand," Brad whispered, still struggling to breathe. "She's not allowed to kill Lucy. Someone paid them to frame Sean, and this patron broke Hunt and Sean out of prison. His partner. But I don't think Hunt's calling the shots. Elise is going to Mexico. A safehouse."

"Jack found Kane, they're in Mexico right now. They might know where the safehouse is."

"Can you reach them?"

Nate nodded.

"I owe you," Brad said.

"Never."

"Yes. They were going to take me to Lucy's house and kill me on her lawn to mess with her. That's all Elise could talk about, tormenting Lucy. She's not happy that she can't kill her, and I don't trust her not to."

Chapter Thirty-eight

Lucy was more than a little relieved that Brad was alive and would make it. He had been tortured and may never make a full recovery, but he was alive and getting the medical care he needed.

That gave her hope that they'd find Sean. The Hunts' plans were falling apart, Elise was on the run, and Brad could identify her. She wasn't getting out of this mess now. Pablo Barrios was going into surgery, but authorities would be talking to him soon.

So now she waited. Waited for news on Sean, information about where he was, what was happening in the search. Brad had made a statement about Hunt's plan to break out and force Sean to go with him. The police *had* to believe that Sean was a victim in all this, and not a killer.

She hated waiting. She wanted to be out *doing something*, looking for Sean, proving his innocence. But Patrick was right. She wouldn't be allowed to help the police, she could potentially blow the case against Elise—who, according to Brad—had been the one who killed Mona. And she might put Sean in more danger if there was a perception that she'd contaminated evidence or a witness statement.

So she waited.

And waited.

Her phone rang, and she grabbed it, desperate for news. It was an unfamiliar number, and her heart sank.

"Kincaid."

"Agent Lucy Kincaid?" a man said.

"Yes. Who's this?"

"Bill Anderson."

Erica's ex-husband. "Yes? Have you heard from Erica?"

"I'm scared. She called me, wouldn't explain, wouldn't say anything other than to get the kids out of town and someplace safe. I don't scare easy, but I'm packing my kids up right now because I *am* scared. I've been trying to call her back, but she won't answer."

"I need that number."

Bill gave it to her. "It's not her regular number. I don't know what's going on, Agent Kincaid, but this isn't like Erica. She's spooked."

"Did she give you any idea where she was calling from?"

"No. You have my number, please call me if you hear anything. I'm taking my kids to my dad's place, he lives in the middle of nowhere. We don't really get along, but he loves his grandkids and it's safe."

"I'll call when I know anything. Thank you."

Lucy called Kate. She told her exactly what Bill Anderson said. "Erica Anderson knows the prison system. Could she be behind Sean's transfer?"

"She's not in corrections anymore."

"But she knows people there. I can't find her; no one knows where she is." Lucy gave Kate the number Bill gave her. "Can you trace it?"

"I'll see what I can do, but it's going to take time. I'll call you back." Kate ended the call.

They were getting close . . . but not close enough.

A knock on the hotel room door made her jump. She looked through the security hole and saw her sister-in-law, Megan.

"I'm so glad to see you," she said.

Megan was carrying a large box, and she put it down on the desk. "I just spent an hour talking to the AUSA prosecuting Michael Thompson."

"The hit man Hunt testified against?"

"Yes. The AUSA—Neil Barnes—had Thompson dead to rights on killing a Houston council member last year, which was tied to a San Antonio case three years ago. During the investigation, which was a joint FBI/DEA/ local investigation because of the multiple jurisdictions and evidence of drug running, the DEA determined that Thompson had been hired for *both* murders. He refused to talk."

"San Antonio three years ago? That was right before I moved there. Was it connected to Rollins or Hunt?"

"There was no evidence at the time, but now they think the victim in San Antonio was connected to the Hunt family drug network. After the murder, they connected the victim to the drug trade. They had a description of Thompson and his vehicle—a rental. He had a fake identity, but they got his prints. Thompson disappeared for two years. When the councilman was killed in Houston, they found his image on security and a shell casing they recovered at the scene."

"Not a smart hit man."

Megan shrugged.

"He could have been rushed, or something distracted him. But the San Antonio victim is connected to Jimmy

Hunt, and Hunt claimed he took the hit out on him because he was skimming and thought that he'd been compromised to the DEA. The second victim—no connection to the drug trade."

"Do they know why he was targeted?"

"Not yet. After the councilman was killed, they identified Thompson, got warrants for his financials and learned he'd been paid $100K for each murder. That's the assumption—they can prove that the large sums of money were deposited into his account from an unknown source. Thompson files tax returns and claimed the income from a company called Fair Play Inc. Thompson hasn't spoken since his arrest. He pled not guilty, and that's it. He didn't testify in his defense and has no plans to. He wouldn't cooperate during the investigation. But somehow the investigators knew to talk to Hunt, and he was questioned while he was in prison. He said that Thompson had been hired to kill Davidson, a teacher in San Antonio, because Hunt's people believed that he'd been compromised and that the DEA was looking into him."

"Were they?"

"No, but they had been looking at a drug-related death at a local high school where the victim taught. Hunt claimed that he was a 'weak link' and feared he'd turn state's evidence."

"And Houston? What's Hunt's connection here?"

"Hunt has no knowledge of that murder, just the San Antonio crime."

"But what does this have to do with Sean and the escape?" Lucy asked, exasperated. "This isn't telling us anything—except that Hunt manipulated a current case to get transferred here, to Houston, at the same time as Sean was in jail."

"You're right, but I just don't know how or why. Hunt

himself went to the warden in California with information about the San Antonio case after he heard of Michael Thompson's arrest."

Lucy opened the box of files that the AUSA had given Megan. First thing she did was organize them—depositions, Michael Thompson's rap sheet, investigative notes, trial transcripts. First things first—figure out who Thompson was, why he was a hit man, who else they suspected he killed, to see if there was a pattern.

It was going to be a lot of work, but she was motivated.

If there was something here that they could use to prove that Jimmy Hunt had orchestrated this in order to facilitate the escape, they would be one small step closer to proving Sean's innocence.

There was a knock on the door and Lucy jumped. She hated being so antsy.

"Room service," the visitor said.

Lucy reached for her gun. "I didn't order anything."

"I did," Megan said. "You need to eat, and I ordered it when I got here."

"I'm not hungry."

"We *both* need to eat."

Megan answered the door and signed. RCK had reserved them a suite, so they'd be staying here tonight—Megan and Kate were sharing an adjoining room.

She'd ordered salads, soups, and sandwiches. "I didn't know what you wanted, but I went with healthy over junk food. I know you and Jack love spicy, so ordered the spiciest dishes on the menu."

"Thanks." She picked at a salad as she read over the information in Thompson's file.

Michael Thompson was born in Maine. He'd served in the military for six years, honorably discharged, then came home and worked for a construction company. Ended up starting his own business in Maine, married, and had two daughters. He left Maine seven years ago . . . and fell off the grid.

Something was missing.

"Megan, what happened seven years ago to Thompson? He had a wife and two kids, and then he fell off the grid."

Megan opened her laptop and did a more detailed background on him. "His older daughter was raped and murdered at the age of ten. How awful."

Megan skimmed the information she'd found. "The killer was their next-door neighbor, a repeat sex offender from New York who hadn't registered in Maine. Thompson became despondent and paranoid, his wife left him and took his younger daughter. He disappeared . . . until he got on our radar after the San Antonio hit."

There was something very familiar about that story, Lucy thought. Had she read about it? Studied it?

"What happened to his daughter's killer?"

Megan scrolled. "Roger Tyson. Convicted of all counts, life in prison. He was killed in a prison fight a year after he was convicted."

Lucy took a bite of a sandwich. Hmm. This was familiar . . . why did she know this case?

She continued reading, then turned to Megan and said, "Where did his wife go?"

"She took their younger daughter—then eight, now fifteen—to Colorado. Remarried last year to a cop, a widower with two kids. There had been a restraining order against Thompson in Maine, but she never refiled it when it expired."

"And we don't know where he went after he left Maine?"

"No."

"Can you dig deeper on him? Where he went to high school, whom he served with in the military, family connections."

"Why? What are you seeing?"

"I don't know. But there's something really familiar about Thompson, and I can't put my finger on it." She bit her lip. "I think I know him, but I don't know why. I don't recognize his picture, I don't think I've met him."

"I'm on it," Megan said. She started typing.

Lucy put Thompson aside and finished half the sandwich. She would pick up the file again after she studied the victims.

Gregory Davidson in San Antonio and Councilman Charles Gomez in Houston. Was there a connection between them? Davidson had been dealing drugs at the high school he'd taught at; there didn't appear to be a motive for Gomez's murder—no drug connections before his death or discovered during the investigation. What about the other alleged victims of Thompson?

"Where are the other victims?" she asked as she began flipping through files.

"Excuse me?"

"You said Thompson was suspected of killing several other men and women, likely murder for hire, but I can't find them."

"Because there was no clear money trail, and they couldn't make a clear connection using other factors. They're still looking into those cases, but they didn't want to give his defense attorney a reason to confuse the jury. These were the two they had proof of payment *and* physical evidence plus a witness or security camera tying him to the scene of the crime."

"I need that list."

Megan frowned, but picked up her phone and sent a text message. "Okay, I asked Barnes for it. What are you thinking, Lucy?"

"I don't know yet, I'm hoping that more information will help."

Megan looked at her phone, then said, "I'm forwarding you the memo."

Lucy downloaded the names and started looking at the victims. "How did authorities connect these other victims to Thompson?"

"Finances, though they weren't in the big dollar amounts that Davidson and Gomez were, and travel history. Thompson was in the same city as each of those victims when they were killed. All the crimes are unsolved, not all were shootings. Confidence and proof are two different things."

Lucy started looking closely into the other victims. A doctor. A teacher. A low-level county employee in Washington State. A twenty-four-year-old grad student? Why would a grad student be the target of a cartel hit man?

She rubbed her eyes, then picked up the Michael Thompson background file again. She was about to read it again when Megan said, "Here's the list of everyone in Thompson's unit when he was overseas." She turned her computer to face Lucy.

The name jumped out at her immediately.

Sergio Russo.

She jumped up. "I have to talk to Rick. And Kate. Right now. I know why these people were killed, and I know who hired Michael Thompson. It wasn't Jimmy Hunt."

Chapter Thirty-nine

After they left the yacht, Sean was moved to a small bus, but they weren't on it long. Ten minutes later, in the middle of seemingly nowhere, they left the bus for a twelve-passenger van. One of the guys that Sean thought of as Colton's right hand was driving. Whoever had brought the van to the location was in the passenger seat. Jimmy and his two guys were in the seat behind them. Sean was tied to the third bench seat in such a way that he could barely move, his back against the van wall. Colton and his other goon were sitting in the last bench seat.

He was still trying to wrap his head around why Colton Thayer was part of Jimmy Hunt's escape plan. It wasn't making any sense, so Sean decided to keep his mouth shut and watch for a while.

But Colton kept staring at him, and the way that Sean was forced to sit, he couldn't avoid his glare. The hate that rolled off him was real, it had been festering for two and a half years. Sean felt it that day in the hospital, and it was worse now. Colder. Vicious.

Too calm.

"C, what's going on?" he asked. "Why are you doing this?"

"Do not call me that. You betrayed me, Sean. Betrayed everything we ever believed in."

"I told you—"

"You put your security ahead of what's right. I should have seen it from the beginning."

"Do you know who this man is? What he's done? He killed a cop! Shot him in the back of the head! You're not like him, Colton. You don't—"

Jimmy turned around and slapped Sean across the face. "Shut the fuck up, Rogan."

Sean swallowed blood.

"Do not touch him again," Colton told Jimmy. His voice was . . . cold. Hard. This wasn't the man Sean had known, this wasn't his best friend from college. Something had happened over the last two and a half years that had hardened him.

Maybe it was you, Sean. You lied to him, betrayed him. Your reasons don't matter, not to Colton.

He watched the silent exchange between Jimmy and Colton. Jimmy scowled, but turned away under Colton's glare.

Colton wasn't working for Jimmy. He wasn't a guy for hire. He acted like he was in charge.

Very odd. Why would Jimmy Hunt be scared of Colton? His old friend was of average size and build, he wasn't a fighter—maybe he'd learned over the last few years, but Colton's strength had always been his brain power. His ability to analyze complex systems. He was as good—maybe better—than Sean in computer hacking.

But clearly, Colton was the top of the pyramid, at least in this vehicle.

What did that mean? Was this all retribution for what Sean did back in New York nearly three years ago? That didn't make sense. If Colton wanted to get to Sean, he could have done any number of things. Hell, if Colton had called him up and asked him to meet for drinks, Sean would have gone, no questions asked. Because the one regret he had was that he hadn't handled the situation with Colton right. He wished he could do it over again.

But you would have done the same thing, because you needed your crimes to go away. You did it to give yourself a clean slate, you did it for Lucy.

Did Colton think that Sean had picked Lucy over him? Maybe he had. And yes, he would always choose Lucy first. But this wasn't really a choice between an old friend and the woman he loved. Colton had been into serious crimes, way over his head. His borderline illegal activities—hacking that did good—had changed focus to blatantly illegal crimes. Breaking into a pharmaceutical company. Stealing information. Helping plan the murder of men who were doing their time in prison.

His head hurt. He didn't know what the hell was going on, but it was far bigger than Sean could imagine. He leaned back against the van wall and closed his eyes.

An hour later—maybe longer—the van pulled off the highway. They went over some side streets, then gravel, and finally stopped.

Colton told everyone to sit tight and left out the back of the van.

Five minutes later he returned with another man. "Chris, dispose of the van. Take him with you," he pointed to the guy in the passenger seat. "You two, take Rogan to the vehicle. Hunt, you and your men follow."

Sean was untied from the van, jerked up and half dragged, half carried to the third vehicle, his prison shackles making him stumble. It was an actual black stretch limousine. Hunt strutted, not realizing, maybe, that he wasn't in charge. When Hunt wasn't looking at him, Sean saw Colton glare at the back of his head.

Jimmy was a dead man walking. He was in over his head and didn't realize it.

They were in the middle of a plowed field. Other than that, Sean had no idea where they were. He didn't know if they'd gone north or south or west. Not east—that would have been the Gulf. They were still in Texas. It was late afternoon by the look of the sky. It would have been a beautiful day if he wasn't being held captive and wanted for murder.

A limo was . . . odd. Jimmy was impressed, made a comment to his two goons that this was the way he expected to be treated. The three of them talked too much.

Colton and his two men didn't talk. Sean couldn't see the driver, but already that meant Colton had five men working for him.

Probably more.

And they knew to keep their mouths shut.

Colton motioned at one of his men, then gestured toward Sean. The man pulled handcuffs from his pocket and cuffed Sean's hands in front of him.

"In," Colton told Sean. He awkwardly climbed into the limo.

Hunt said, "Can't we just put him in the trunk?"

Colton didn't say a word. He got in and sat across from Sean and stared at him.

Colton acted like the limo wasn't out of the ordinary, and Sean wished he'd known what his old friend had been up to since he'd last seen him. Maybe he should have kept tabs on him after their confrontation in the hospital. Maybe he should have reached out, when Sean's betrayal wasn't so fresh, and apologized again. Explain better why he did what he did, why he had to do what he did.

They'd been so close at one time, but Sean didn't know him anymore. He didn't know how Colton could work with someone like Hunt. Colton wasn't a violent criminal.

They weren't in the limo for long. Hunt and his men wouldn't stop talking, about nothing in particular, though Sean heard something about the DEA agent being toast. He prayed it wasn't Brad, but feared it was.

And Colton didn't act like anything was out of the ordinary, his face set, never taking his eyes off Sean.

Fifteen minutes after they got into the limo, it turned toward a gate that opened automatically. The property they drove through was expansive, acres upon acres of lush vegetation and mature trees. Based on the glimpses he'd seen, he only had a vague sense that they were somewhere in the middle of Texas.

Texas was a big state.

Logically, based on the drive from the coast and a sign he'd seen shortly after they got into the limo that said DALLAS 226 MILES, he figured somewhere north or northeast of Houston. They'd practically made a circle. But he saw the wisdom of the route—the police would be looking south, not north. They might eventually find the boat, or know which direction they'd gone, but they wouldn't naturally assume Hunt would circle back to Houston.

Escaped prisoners were almost always caught. Law enforcement wasn't going to give up looking for them. Sean *wanted* to be found, but he didn't want to be shot on sight—and he didn't trust that he wouldn't be. Not if they thought he killed a cop. But since he had a general idea about where he was, he could conceivably find help.

If he wasn't shackled or in prison orange.

The limo drove to the house, but instead of stopping at the wide veranda, drove past it and to a secondary gate that was attached to the massive stone and wood house. An armed guard stood there and waved them through as the gate opened.

An eight-car garage straight ahead with what appeared to be rooms above it—four wide dormer windows sticking out. A water fountain claimed the middle of the circular drive; to the left was a smaller building, and to the right the main house.

The limo stopped and the driver—also armed—opened the back door. Hunt, Colton, and the others climbed out.

"We're here, Sean," Colton said. "Don't make this more difficult that it needs to be."

Sean awkwardly moved over to the door since he was still cuffed and shackled. He put his feet outside, and Hunt's two goons hoisted him up.

They all went in through the side door—which looked like the main door of any mansion. This place had to be ten thousand square feet, minimum. And if all the land they'd driven through was part of the estate, it had to be at least a hundred acres.

They didn't put a hood or blindfold on him.

He'd been expecting to die since being locked in his cell last night. The constant fear had him in a heightened state of alert and panic. He began to shake and the more he tried to stop, the worse it became.

A large, heavily muscled armed guard silently approached. How many of these guys did Colton have on the property?

Colton turned to Hunt's two goons. "Reggie will assign you quarters."

"We stick with our boss," one of them said.

"Mr. Hunt is not paying you," Colton said.

So Sean was right. This wasn't Jimmy's operation. He was just one cog in the wheel. An important cog, perhaps, but not in charge.

"It's fine," Hunt said, waving them off. "Go with Reggie, good work, both of you—you deserve a break."

They left, and Sean wondered if he would see them

again. There was something surreal about this entire situation. If he wasn't a prisoner, he might have been amused.

"Colton, if you'd just—"

"Stop, Sean," Colton said. "Nothing you can say or do is going to change what will happen."

He motioned for Sean to move. They walked through the side entry room, a large game room, a butler's pantry, then turned down a hall with multiple closed doors, and finally ended in the main foyer. A beautiful carved staircase went upstairs, but they headed across the foyer to double doors.

Hunt stepped in front of Colton and was about to open the library doors. Colton put his hand up. "Wait here," he said.

Hunt glared at him. "You wouldn't even be here without me."

Colton didn't rise to the bait. He motioned to someone Sean couldn't see, and suddenly two armed guards—tall, broad-shouldered men who looked like former military just like everyone else that worked here—appeared. They flanked Hunt. He looked both angry and fearful.

Whoever Colton was working for had extensive resources. This remote, vast estate. The resources for the prison break. Bribing guards. A minimum of four trained security men here, not to mention those who drove him here. Colton also didn't come cheap, unless he was doing this for a cause.

What cause? What cause would have him breaking Sean out of prison?

Or setting you up to go to prison in the first place?

Colton said, "Take Mr. Hunt to the kitchen and ask Mrs. Yancey to prepare him a meal. We'll call for him when we're ready."

"That's more like it," Hunt mumbled.

Colton tensed next to Sean. He didn't like Jimmy Hunt. Hunt didn't pick up on the subtle change in Colton, which would be his downfall.

Sean looked at Colton. Fourteen years ago when Sean first met him, he hadn't tolerated violence. Even two and a half years ago, Colton wouldn't have killed anyone. Sean didn't think he had it in him—then. But today? Today Sean believed that Colton could kill. Coldly, methodically, without remorse.

He had changed.

So have you.

Colton waited until the two guards left with Hunt, then he opened the doors. Sean didn't move. Colton pushed him in. Sean almost tripped over the shackles.

Colton followed him, then closed the doors. The library was circular, one half all windows, the other half all built-in bookshelves filled with books and expensive art. A spiral ladder went up to the second level, which had more art and books, and there was a sitting area directly across from the windows. It was a room Sean knew Lucy would love and lose herself in; a room that the Beast would design for Beauty.

The desk stood directly across from the doors. The tall executive chair was turned away from the door, but Sean could see a man sitting in it, the back of his head—dark brown interspersed with salt-and-pepper—visible.

"Walk," Colton told Sean.

He did, the shackles rattling as he shuffled across the lush carpet. He stopped when he reached the desk.

The chair turned.

"I've been waiting to see you in an orange jumpsuit and chains for a long, long time, Sean Rogan."

Everything clicked. The boldness of this operation.

The money and resources. Colton's involvement. Hunt, not so much, but Sean would figure it out.

His blood boiled even as his fear grew.

"Paxton."

Jimmy Hunt didn't like being dismissed by Paxton's computer geek. If Jimmy didn't need Paxton's resources, he would have whacked the arrogant asshole as soon as they got off the boat, then hightailed it to his plane and would have already been to his safe house in Ebano by now.

He really hated anyone who thought they were smarter than him. He had built an empire that lasted for *years*. He'd infiltrated the DEA and created a supply chain that was unprecedented. And for *five years* he did it from afar because he had family he could trust to take care of business.

It wasn't perfect. Tobias had his problems with women. Nicole often acted like *she* was in charge. And even though his niece had been sharp as a tack, she had been *too* cautious. On the other hand, his daughter Elise wasn't cautious enough. She came up with crazy ideas that were either brilliant or off-the-charts stupid. She didn't take kindly to being told she needed to grow up or calm down. He had Clara keeping her in line, but Clara didn't like Elise, and his daughter knew it.

Clara was a smart bitch. But Jimmy always put his money on Elise to come out on top. He'd learned not to underestimate her long ago.

He accepted the meal Mrs. Yancey—a trim, older woman who apparently ran the household for the former senator—prepared for him. It was delicious, especially after two years of crappy prison food. He asked if she might have a beer; she did and poured it for him in a chilled glass.

He could get used to this. Even when he had plenty of

money and lived well in Mexico, he didn't have full-time domestic help. Portia cooked and cleaned and satisfied him in bed, but she wasn't really good at the first two. She did, however, do well in the sack.

And it wasn't like he was *broke*. He had some money hidden away—enough to keep Portia happy and begin to rebuild his network. What he didn't have were the contacts he needed in the DEA. They'd cleaned house after Nicole was killed, and no one in San Antonio or Houston was on the take—yet. He still had a mole deep in Los Angeles, but that guy was friggin' paranoid, so Jimmy wasn't certain he could trust him anymore. It took time—a lot of time, patience, and money—to create a traitor.

Plan B was to have Elise sell the house in Los Angeles and they could live on the proceeds quite well in Mexico for years. But then he would have to find something for Elise to do, because she got bored very easily. When Elise was bored, she got stupid. Give her a job, though, and she usually did it better than anyone.

And Elise didn't know the meaning of the word *discretion*. She'd be dangerous to have near him . . . because even when the Rogans were all dead, they would have to deal with the Kincaids.

Apparently, in the world according to Jonathan Paxton, anyone who touched a hair on Lucy Kincaid's head would die.

Right.

But for now, Hunt could live by Paxton's rules because they had a mutually beneficial relationship. Hunt testified against Paxton's personal hit man to protect his business interests, and Paxton helped Hunt get out of prison. And it was Hunt who came up with the plan to frame Sean Rogan for that whore Mona Hill's murder. First, Mona deserved it for leaving Elise high and dry and getting her arrested in the first place. Second, Mona had betrayed him.

No one betrayed Jimmy Hunt.

Paxton's plan had been more subtle, but without the added benefit of making Sean Rogan the most wanted man in Texas. The geek squad had been working on infiltrating his home security system with the goal of planting evidence of a major hack or some such thing, to get him arrested for espionage. But apparently Mr. Geek wasn't all that smart—not as smart as Rogan, at any rate—because he couldn't get inside his computer. At least not fast enough to satisfy Jonathan Paxton.

Though what the rush was, Jimmy didn't know. According to rumors, Rogan had screwed Paxton over a couple of years ago. Why the rush to destroy him now?

In the end, Jimmy knew he had the better end of the deal. Paxton gave him the resources to go after Kane Rogan and Brad Donnelly. One was waiting for him so he could whack him personally, the other was already dead.

Mrs. Yancey came in with a phone. "You have a call, Mr. Hunt."

He frowned. "Why are you telling me?"

"This is the emergency line, it's safe."

He didn't know whether to trust her, but answered. "What?"

"Daddy?"

"Elise?"

She only called him Daddy when she knew he would get mad about something.

"What happened?"

"Well . . . it didn't work."

"What is going on?"

"Everything else worked exactly as I planned. Get Donnelly. *Check*. Get that FBI agent suspended. *Check*.

Take care of loose ends. *Check*. Restraining order against the psychic fed. *Check*."

Why Elise thought Lucy Kincaid was psychic, Jimmy couldn't figure out. Something about how she could read Elise's mind. Which was just bullshit, but he couldn't seem to get that through Elise's thick skull.

"What's the problem? You killed Donnelly, right?"

"Well . . . no."

Dammit! This was when Elise made him angry. "I gave you explicit instructions."

"And I obeyed, mostly, except he's *fun*. And he deserved to suffer for killing Nicole. I liked her. She was smart, even if she wasn't fun. I was about to kill him, but that suspended agent came to my house. And he killed Donny. I liked Donny, he did anything I wanted."

Donny was dead? That was not good news. Clara would be on the warpath.

"Elise, you need to leave San Antonio. Right now. Don't talk to Clara. Don't do anything—Donny was Clara's brother. She's going to take it out on you."

"Oh, please. I'm not scared of her anymore. No loose ends, right?"

"What did you do, Elise?"

"It was me or her. Would you rather have Clara alive and me dead? Were you fucking her? I'm your *daughter*!"

She'd killed Clara. Not ideal, but better Clara than Elise.

"I have to take care of the bitch guard," Elise said.

"She did her job."

"And then she showed up at the hospital to see her fuck-buddy! I have people, Daddy, you always told me to have people in all the right places. Lucy can probably read her mind, too, and if she knows that bitch went to see her boyfriend, she'll *know* everything, and the little bitch will roll. So I have to find her and take care of her."

"No. It doesn't matter, Elise. The FBI is going to figure out she's involved with Sheffield, and that Sheffield put Rogan on the transfer orders. We have to assume that."

"Which means doubly she needs to die. Because she'll rat me out in a blink of an eye and then I'll be on the run just like you."

When was his kid ever going to learn? She was already going to be on the run because she lost Brad Donnelly!

"Elise, go to the safe house, as I told you, and stay out of sight. Donnelly is going to report this. What were you thinking? I told you to kill him."

"I was going to. I was just having fun. Why are you being so mean to me?"

He took a deep breath. "I'm not, sweetie. I'm just worried because I'm your father. I need you to be safe."

"I am, Daddy. I wish I could kill Lucy, though. I really will do it; I won't play with her like Donnelly. Wham bam, dead."

"Not now. But later. I promise, when everything dies down, you can do it."

"You really promise?"

"Yes."

"Okay. I'll go."

"Be safe."

He ended the call. Thank *God* he didn't tell Elise where he was or who had broken him out of prison. She was too wild, too impulsive, and while Jimmy Hunt wasn't overly concerned about Jonathan Paxton, he was a *tiny* bit concerned about what he would do if he got *really* angry.

Elise was his daughter and he loved her. She was the only family he had left. He didn't want her dead.

He finished his meal and his beer and Mrs. Yancey asked him if he'd like to freshen up. He would—it had been a long, exhausting day. She escorted him to a suite on the second floor.

When he was alone, he took out his burner phone and called one of his two men who were on site.

"Trevor, it's Jimmy. You and Paul being treated well?"

"Yeah—we have this apartment over the garage and there's a fucking full bar."

"Don't get drunk. Rest up, we're leaving before dawn."

Chapter Forty

Lucy had Megan with her in the hotel suite, and Rick and Kate were both on speakerphone. She was brief, because how she came to the conclusion was not relevant, but she wanted them to at least know she wasn't pulling this theory out of thin air. She went through the methodology of looking into Michael Thompson's past and why it had seemed so familiar to her.

"And when I saw that Thompson had served with Sergio Russo in the Army, I knew why his MO was familiar. He, like Russo, lost a child to a sex offender. Jonathan Paxton feeds off the grief and despair of these lost men. He turns them into vigilantes."

"*Senator* Paxton?" Kate asked.

"It's exactly how he operates."

"Lucy," Rick said, "this is a leap. There's no connection between Jimmy Hunt and Paxton—Paxton is a narcissist with a God complex who saw himself as judge, jury, and executioner. But he went after other criminals. Hunt is the epitome of everything Paxton hates about our system, and the reason he thought he had to take the law into his own hands."

"True, but Paxton is blinded by his rage, twisted by his grief and guilt over his daughter's murder. He worked with criminals in the past for what he saw as the greater good," Lucy reminded him. "Do you know how many times he called me Monique?"

There was silence, because they all knew that Lucy bore a striking resemblance to Jonathan Paxton's long-dead daughter.

"I know Jonathan didn't go to prison," Lucy said. "He cut a plea deal after his conspiracy to poison sex offenders in prison didn't work." She had been angry about the agreement, even though she understood the reasons. Paxton could have made a lot of people's lives extremely difficult if he ever stood trial. It would have come out that he'd orchestrated a conspiracy that targeted sex offenders. He could have easily become a martyr, a leader in a vigilante movement that would destroy society. People would follow in his footsteps.

Lucy, more than anyone, knew that the system sometimes failed. That some evil people evaded justice; the system couldn't catch or prosecute all of them. But without the system, they had nothing. No laws or punishment; no rules or morals. There would be a vacuum, and someone would fill it.

Their system, however flawed it was, was the best thing they had going for them. To protect the rights of the innocent, some of the guilty went free. They were not God; they couldn't see all. They didn't know everything.

Lucy believed in the system . . . even though the system, at this moment in time, thought her husband was a killer. Even when she knew that sometimes the law enforcers got it wrong.

"Well?" she said when no one spoke. "I'm not wrong."

"Why?" Rick asked. "What you're saying is incredible, to be honest. I'm not saying I disagree, but what would Paxton's motive be? Put aside the hit man—because yes, that is his MO. He finds men who have lost someone they love and twists their grief into vigilante justice. That Thompson served in the Army with Russo—who is still a fugitive—convinces me this angle is viable. But what's the connection to these victims? A drug dealer and a councilman who may have taken bribes? What's the connection to Hunt?"

"I don't know why Hunt. But I know why those victims. The teacher in San Antonio was caught with Rohypnol and Ecstasy. Two date rape drugs. Evidence gathered after his murder indicates that he sold these drugs primarily to high school students. His school had a thirty percent higher incident of reported rape and sexual assault than any other high school in Bexar County. Did he contribute to that? Very possibly. We would have to dig deeper there. Every single one of these victims was suspected of sex crimes. I don't have evidence on each and every one, but Jonathan wouldn't care about evidence, if *he* believed they were guilty. I could go case by case, but we're on the clock here—I need you to trust me on this."

"I believe you," Kate said over the speaker, her voice odd. Lucy knew this case would be difficult for her. Her partner had been a victim to the same killer who killed Paxton's daughter, Monique. She felt a kinship with Paxton on the one hand, and a hatred of him on the other because of how he'd used Lucy to justify his killing spree.

Rick said, "Send me everything you have. I'll look at it immediately."

Having Rick and Kate on her side was huge, but she still feared for Sean. Because she didn't know why Paxton would want to frame Sean and then break him out of prison. Or why Paxton would use a convicted drug runner like Jimmy Hunt to do it.

"I'll have a team in New York pay him a visit," Rick said.

"He's still living at his house?"

Rick hesitated. "He was after we reached the plea deal."

"I need to talk to him," Lucy said.

"We need to establish that he's behind this first. While I see what you're saying, I don't see how he knows Hunt. Like you said, Hunt's not the type of criminal he'd work with. And why would he go to these extreme lengths to get Sean?" Rick asked. "I'm playing devil's advocate, because there are easier ways."

"Yes, maybe, but this way puts a target on Sean's back. He's considered a killer. He then escapes and the surviving guard states that Sean killed his partner in cold blood. It would damage his reputation, even if proven innocent, and it hurts RCK and their business. Sean has the computer skills to facilitate the transfer in the first place, so on the surface it seems logical that he would do something like this."

Kate interrupted. "I have news about how the transfer was done. The phone found in Sean's cell didn't have his prints on it, and it wasn't used to hack into the system—though there was code in there that clearly was created to *look* like Sean had hacked in."

"Explain," Rick said.

"The code is a backdoor to get into the core system—so on the surface, it looks like Sean did it because the information was found in his cell. But when I reversed the trace, it was clear that the hack came from the Beaumont prison. I have it traced to the exact terminal and am waiting for security tapes to show who was at that terminal at the time the transfer was set. And it wasn't hacked—the phone makes it *appear* that the system was hacked, and the code *could* have hacked the system if plugged directly into any computer connected to the network, but it didn't. It was done in-house. But the key problem we have is that it *could* have been external, so we need to shut down that security risk ASAP."

"What you're saying," Rick said, "is that someone with the brains to hack into the prison system put the code on the phone to make it appear Sean did it, but they didn't actually break into the system to change the transfer orders."

"Exactly. If anyone else analyzed the phone, they would believe it. Because it's that good."

"Is this something Sean is capable of doing?"

No one said anything.

"So yes," Rick said.

"Sean didn't," Kate said.

"But the prosecutors will say he *could have*," Rick said.

"My analysis is impeccable, Rick."

"We need more."

"Let me interrogate Officer Sheffield."

"He just got out of surgery."

"He's lying," Kate said. "Sean would never kill a cop in cold blood. In the back of the head? That's not him."

"I believe you. I've known Sean since he was a kid, I love him like a brother."

For the first time, Lucy heard emotion in Rick's voice. She'd been so angry earlier that he thought Sean *could* have killed Mona Hill, that she lost sight of the fact that Rick cared.

"But," Rick said, "we have to find evidence before we confront Sheffield. Money. A threat. Blackmail. Whatever it is, find it, then talk to him."

"I need a warrant to search his house, including his phone records and his computer."

"I'll get it. But what I really want to know is who the hell is as good a hacker as Sean?"

No one said anything. Kate was as good as Sean. There were members of the FBI cybercrime unit who were as good as Sean. But who was as good as Sean *and* willing to be an accessory to killing a cop and frame Sean for two murders?

Lucy couldn't imagine.

She said, "Rick, when you confirm that Paxton is home, please let me talk to him."

"I don't think that's a good idea. I know your history with him, Lucy."

"I'm the only person he won't lie to."

"I'll think on it," he said reluctantly. "I've already dispatched the team. I'll call you as soon as I know anything. In the meantime, Kate—you dig into Sheffield. Everything you can do until I get the warrant. Megan— you talk to Thompson. See if you can get him to talk, knowing what we know. I'll clear it with the AUSA and get you in tonight. I'm going to contact the marshals who are in charge of the manhunt and tell them we have some new information. They'll listen to me, I'll convince them that Sean is a victim."

"Director," Lucy said when he was about to end the call, "Thompson isn't going to talk."

"You don't know that. If we can get him to turn on Paxton, we might be able to offer a reduced sentence."

"He's not going to turn. You know Jonathan Paxton, he's charismatic and charming and absolutely driven. The people who work for him will do anything to protect him. I guarantee that if Thompson thought the only way to protect Paxton was to kill himself, he'd kill himself. He's not going to be manipulated."

"I appreciate your analysis, but we have to try," Rick said. "Thompson is dangerous, he won't be back on the streets, but Paxton is even more dangerous because he can get people to do his bidding for him. We have to stop him, and I have no evidence against him. None. Honestly, I would never have even considered he was behind it except that you convinced me that the very tenuous connection between Thompson and Russo was suspicious. Getting a jury to believe it? I wouldn't even be able to call in every favor at the Department of Justice to get an AUSA to indict. We need more."

Rick ended the call, and Kate also signed off.

Lucy looked at Megan. "I'm talking to Thompson with you."

She didn't say anything.

Lucy leaned forward. "Megan, if I'm right—and I know I am—Thompson is working for Paxton, and therefore he'll know exactly who I am and why I'm important to Paxton. I can do this. I still don't think he'll turn against Paxton, but he might give us something we can use to find him."

Megan smiled. "Well, Rick didn't say you *couldn't* go."

Kate Donovan, warrant in hand, grabbed SSA Steven Pierce to join her to search Tim Sheffield's house. Steven wasn't pleased about being pulled out of the office, and while he wasn't as gung-ho as the two Houston detectives about Sean's guilt, he also wasn't convinced that he was innocent.

Fortunately, Kate had a solid reputation and she had the ear of Rick Stockton, which helped, so Steven came with her.

"When are you getting the footage from Beaumont? That would help."

"I sent people over to grab it," Steven said. "I'll know within the hour exactly who changed the transfer orders."

Tim Sheffield lived in a modest home outside Beaumont. A car was in the driveway but it was registered to Sheffield.

He wasn't married, according to his employer, but they preceded with caution. Knocked on the door.

"FBI, we have a warrant. We're coming in."

Kate didn't expect an answer, but she heard footsteps.

Steven heard them, too. They both had their firearms ready because they didn't know what to expect.

The door opened. Kate recognized the woman from a photo Lucy had sent.

"Erica Anderson?" Kate said.

"Yes. I have a lot to say, but I'm begging you—please protect me, protect Tim. We got in over our heads, I didn't realize it at the time . . . I can't imagine that he knew they were going to kill his partner. I can't believe he would condone that."

But she thought it was possible, Kate realized, based on her tone and body language.

"We have a warrant; we're going to come in."

Erica nodded. Kate searched her; then motioned for her to sit down at the dining-room table. Steven searched the house first for weapons or anything dangerous, and when it was cleared, he stood behind Kate, who sat across from Erica.

"Start from the beginning," Kate said after reading Erica her rights.

"Where?"

"How about how you met Elise Hunt, when you started working for her, and why you quit your job. Then end with what you know about the prison break and who was involved other than Tim Sheffield."

With tears streaming down her face, Erica Anderson told Kate everything.

Chapter Forty-one

It took hours to process the house that Elise Hunt had been living in. Two dead bodies, one critically injured, the room where Brad had been tortured, and of course both Nate and Aggie had to give statements to SAPD, the DEA, and the FBI. Brad had given a preliminary statement, but he was in serious condition and his statement was cut short.

Fortunately, his statement would clear Nate on the drug charges. A more detailed investigation would have to take place, but Brad had overhead enough at the house to believe that Pablo, Clara, and Mitts Vasquez had stolen the drugs, and Pablo and Donny and planted them in Nate's truck.

But that didn't clear Nate from violating his suspension.

He was summoned to FBI headquarters late Saturday evening and wasn't surprised to see ASAC Abigail Durant along with his boss, SSA Rachel Vaughn, sitting in Durant's office.

"Close the door, Agent Dunning," Durant said.

He did.

"You can sit."

"I'd like to stand." He always felt more comfortable standing at attention when giving an official statement. He didn't quite know why, but it felt more authentic to him, and he felt far more comfortable—even though he was no longer in the military.

"Nate—" Rachel began.

"He can stand," Durant said. "I read your statement. What did you not say?"

"I don't understand the question. I gave all information pertaining to how DEA Agent Jensen and I located the house and Brad Donnelly."

"Yes—I see that. You and Agent Jensen are clearly on the same page. Agent Jensen did the groundwork in identifying where the drugs came from, Agent Jensen located the house based on her sources and access to the DEA database, and Agent Jensen asked you to back her up."

"Yes, ma'am."

"Even though you were suspended."

"Yes, ma'am."

"Why didn't you call in a team earlier? You had clear and convincing evidence that Donny Valeria, who you identified as the shooter in the Mitts Vasquez homicide, was at that house. You should have called in SWAT and had them handle it."

"We did call in SAPD as soon as we had eyes on Donny Valeria and they were putting together a team, but Agent Jensen and I felt that there was a more than a fifty percent chance that SSA Donnelly was on the property, and we wanted to keep an eye on the situation until SAPD SWAT could take over. As I stated in my report, I heard a scream from the property and I feared that someone was in immediate danger. I ordered Agent Jensen to call it in and I went to assess the danger."

"Without backup."

"A life was at risk."

"You didn't know that."

"You didn't hear the screams," Nate said. He cleared his throat. "I apologize." He'd overstepped, something he didn't do. He was too well-trained to give more information than was asked, but Donnelly's pain had been so clear Nate could have done nothing but what he had done.

Durant didn't say anything for a moment. Then she wrote in his file, closed it, and looked back at him. "I'm suspending you for two weeks without pay," she said. "I know you won't care, nor will you care that this incident of disobeying orders will be on your permanent record. The next time, Agent Dunning, you will be up in front of the Office of Professional Responsibility."

"Yes, ma'am. Thank you, ma'am."

"But this is only one part of this meeting. You were ordered to stay away from Agent Kincaid and the investigation into her husband."

"Ma'am, I was ordered not to investigate, I was not ordered to avoid Agent Kincaid."

"Are you telling me that this pursuit that you and Agent Jensen were on had nothing to do with Sean Rogan?"

"We were investigating the source of the drugs that were planted in my truck. Because of the timing, as I stated in my report, Agent Jensen and I believed that the drugs were connected in some way to Agent Donnelly's kidnapping."

"You were told not to get involved."

"Yes, ma'am."

"Nate," Durant began, then sighed. "I know that Leo Proctor is at Lucy's right now. I know that you have been staying there. You're friends, I respect that, but I don't think you grasp the seriousness of the situation that Lucy and her husband are in right now."

"May I speak freely?"

"Yes."

"I proudly served in the Army for ten years. I knew

that my squad had my back, and I had theirs. When I came to the FBI, I felt a kinship because we are structured to have the same kind of support system. Until now. No one, other than Leo, has reached out to Lucy or to me during this time. I understand that you both need to protect the agency, I respect that. But my team—men and women I need to count on to have my back when we're in the field—have been silent. That is the environment that has been fostered here. Fear of retaliation, of suspension, I don't know, but how can I trust any of these people if they can't even support their own?

"Sean is my best friend. Lucy is my partner. Their son is in danger. I don't have to tell you that this arrest and Sean's subsequent kidnapping—"

"Prison break," Rachel said.

"Kidnapping," Nate repeated, "coupled with his brother being lured down to Mexico has left a young kid vulnerable. Leo offered to help and protect Jesse Rogan so I could get to the bottom of the planted drugs. I'm not going to apologize for standing by my partner or my friends in the darkest time of their lives."

Durant looked him in the eye, but Rachel didn't. That bothered him. But Durant said, "I respect that, Nate. But I don't think you understand the gravity of the situation that Sean Rogan is in. He's now wanted for two murders—Mona Hill and a corrections officer. He is considered a fugitive. You may be right—he may be innocent—but that still doesn't discount that there is evidence enough for both murders to keep him in custody. And when he's apprehended, you're going to have to accept that you cannot use this agency to assist him in any way. What you do on your personal time is your business, but if it comes back on the FBI there will be consequences over and above a two-week suspension. Do you understand?"

"Yes, ma'am."

"You may go."

Nate walked out. He didn't feel good about the conversation, but he didn't regret anything he'd said.

He drove immediately to Lucy's house. He glared at the SAPD vehicle still parked out front, but it wasn't their fault. They were doing their job.

Didn't make him feel any better about what was going on and that Sean was in such trouble.

Bandit greeted him as soon as he walked in and he hugged the dog. It helped calm him down.

Leo walked out from the kitchen. "I made dinner for Jess and me. There's plenty left. Spaghetti and meatballs."

"Thank you," he said automatically.

"Do you want to talk?"

Nate shook his head, got up from his squat, but kept his hand on Bandit's head, scratching his ears. "Thank you for being here for Jess."

"And for you, and for Lucy. I spoke to Jack Kincaid and I brought in a couple people to keep an eye on the place. There's confirmation that Jesse was a target yesterday, but they don't believe he still is. The patrol is just a precaution. Jack talked to Jesse, he was pretty blunt."

"Is the kid okay?"

"I think so, but he'll be glad to see you."

The house alarm beeped once. Nate looked at the security panel and saw Aggie walking up the front path. She looked exhausted but determined. He opened the door.

"You okay?"

"Suspended for a week for not informing my supervisor of my actions, but it could have been worse. Brad would be dead if we hadn't acted when we did so I'll take the suspension and sleep really well tonight."

Leo left, and Nate checked on Jesse. They talked for a bit, which was good for both of them.

It reminded Nate that he would do everything he'd done all over again, no regrets.

He went back downstairs to the kitchen, where Aggie had warmed up the food Leo cooked earlier. "I'm starving, I hope you don't mind."

Aggie was always hungry. "Not at all."

They sat down and Nate felt . . . comfortable. Aggie was comfortable to be around. She had grown on him, and he liked her.

Plus, she was cute.

They ate, and Aggie said, "Have you heard from Lucy? Do they know where Sean is? How he is? I can't seem to get any information."

"Lucy texted me that she had a lead and would call later. She has a good team with her in Houston right now, my job is to make sure that Jesse stays safe."

"I went to see Brad at the hospital. I wasn't supposed to—but after I was reamed by Salter, I just wanted to make sure he was okay."

"Did they let you in to see him?"

She had a sly smile on her face. "Not exactly. But I saw him for like two minutes." Now she frowned. "He was sleeping, on painkillers. I read his chart. That little bitch tortured him. There were cuts all over his back. She *branded* him. He'd been naked like that for God knows how long. Burn marks on his arms and legs. A cut on his face. His body temperature was dangerously low. Two broken ribs. A skull fracture and concussion. They only had him for thirty hours but he would have been dead if they had him much longer."

"That was their plan, Aggie."

She cleared their plates, rinsed them. She was working through something; Nate remained silent. He went into the freezer and found Lucy's stash of chocolate ice cream. He dished up two bowls.

"Hey," he finally said as she scrubbed a pot that was clearly already clean.

She glanced over at him.

He pushed a bowl toward her spot at the island. "Ice cream."

She turned off the water and came over. "I'm sorry."

"Don't apologize."

"I'm angry."

"I know."

"Thank you."

"No thanks."

"No, seriously, you saved my life. I wasn't thinking when I went after Elise. It was like all my training evaporated and I just wanted to stop her. I was so angry; I didn't see all the ways it could go wrong."

Nate put his hands on Aggie's shoulders. He felt a jolt, something he wasn't expecting. He said, "Your instincts are solid, Aggie. You need more training. I can help with that, if you want."

She looked up at him, her head tilted to the side, and then Nate kissed her.

He shouldn't have. He shouldn't kiss anyone; he wasn't relationship material. Too many demons battling inside him. And Aggie was the type of girl who was relationship material, not a casual fling.

But he wanted to kiss her, so he did.

She returned his kiss, wrapped her arms around his neck and pulled him in. He picked her up and placed her on the island so he could kiss her face to face, without bending down.

A small moan escaped her throat and his body went into overdrive.

He pulled back. Stared at her.

"What?" she said, breathless.

"Not now."

"I like you, Nate."

"I like you. A lot. But I can't tonight—not when I have a responsibility. I can't afford to be distracted." He touched her hair. It was soft and messy and he couldn't wait to take her to bed.

Just not tonight.

She didn't say anything. He kissed her again, so she would know that this wasn't about her, this was him. He took his responsibilities very seriously, and right now protecting Jesse was his job. Taking Aggie to bed— something he really wanted to do—could wait.

And sometimes, waiting made the reward ten times better.

"You're one of a kind, Nate Dunning," she said with a smile. "Let's eat that ice cream before it melts."

Chapter Forty-two

Talking to Megan grounded Jack, reminded him to be safe because he had someone he loved to go home to. Something he needed while he and Kane made camp for the night.

Megan explained Lucy's theory that Senator Jonathan Paxton was behind the prison break, though she was skeptical.

"Lucy hopes she can get Thompson to slip up," Megan said.

"When are you talking to him?" he asked.

"We're waiting for him to be brought to the interview room. Lots of hoops to jump through."

"Bureaucracy," he grumbled.

"Is everything about Paxton true? I mean, I know Lucy used to work for him, and that he was behind the vigilante group that was taking out sex offenders, but I didn't realize that Lucy looks like his daughter."

"Everything Lucy said is accurate, and more. I confronted him once and to my face he called Lucy *Monique*. That's his dead daughter. I've seen pictures, they do look alike, not identical, but enough where people would mistake them as sisters. But remember—Monique was killed before Lucy was born. Paxton grieved, which

I understand, but he turned his grief into rage, anger, and retribution. He was obsessed with Lucy and if he's behind this, there's something we're missing. I don't trust Paxton, but I can't see him hurting Lucy."

"How is what's happening here connected to you and Kane down there?" Megan asked. "What could Paxton benefit from this?"

"I don't know," Jack admitted. "And I don't understand why Paxton would work with someone like Jimmy Hunt. Hunt was the type of predator Paxton would put on his own hit list."

"Be careful, Jack. Both you and Kane."

"We are. Love you, Megan."

He ended the call and Kane joined him outside. Jack relayed everything he'd learned from Megan, then said, "What would Jonathan Paxton want with you, Kane? Why would he orchestrate this . . . trap?"

"Isn't Paxton on some sort of FBI watch list?" Kane asked.

"Yes. He was forced to resign, but the reasons were kept under wraps. Having a sitting senator exposed as the leader of a vigilante group would have had serious repercussions."

"I think the question to ask is, why did Paxton want Hunt to help him? To what benefit?"

Jack thought about that. "I don't know. Paxton would have the resources to frame Sean—if that's what this is about. Paxton would have the resources to set you up as well."

"But Paxton isn't a criminal."

"I beg to differ."

"What I mean is, his people believe in a cause—they aren't going to be gangbangers and drug traffickers or gun runners. They're killers, but they believe they're doing it for a noble cause."

"So you think he needs Hunt's network, his people."

"Exactly."

"I ask again: why frame Sean?"

Kane didn't have an answer. Instead he said, "Let's assume that Paxton needed Hunt's help for something. In exchange, Paxton gave him the resources to set me up, to frame Sean, to kidnap Donnelly. Sean helped the FBI seize Hunt's money; I killed Hunt's son; Donnelly killed Hunt's niece."

"It's all about Hunt's retribution," Jack said. "Still doesn't tell us why Paxton would work with him."

Kane concurred. "Why the fuck would Paxton care? I'm not seeing the connection."

Neither did Jack. Except . . . "Paxton wants Sean."

"Why? He frames him for murder then breaks him out of prison? That's a dumbass thing to do. A lot of things have to go right for it to work."

"But they did go right."

"He wouldn't need Hunt for that. Why would Paxton help Hunt take out his enemies? What does Hunt have that Paxton wants?"

That was an excellent question. Jack didn't know.

"And Hunt's son was a fucking predator. He raped dozens of women. Killed many of them. If Paxton knows that—why would he help him?"

Again, Jack couldn't answer that.

"Something doesn't add up," Jack said. "Hunt hasn't gotten back to Blair. Do you think he figured out Blair doesn't have you in his control anymore?"

"Possible, but unlikely," Kane said.

"I have an idea," Jack said. "We go on the offensive. We don't wait for Hunt to contact Blair; we go to Hunt."

"Blair claims he doesn't know where he was supposed to bring me, that he'll be told when and where when Hunt's on his way south."

"I have an idea there, too. Give me Blair's phone."

Kane did.

Jack read through a bunch of Blair's messages to get a feeling for how he communicated, then he wrote: *Situation hot here, have to move ASAP or cut him loose. Need safe house.*

It took several minutes, but Hunt replied.

My place in Ebano. Portia is there. Secure the cargo and wait for my arrival.

Jack showed the message to Kane.

"That's not far," Kane said. "Not even an hour, driving."

"Girlfriend? Associate?"

"Blair knows."

"Can we trust him?"

"He wants to live," Kane said. "I'll know if he's lying."

Chapter Forty-three

Sean forced himself not to react when he saw Paxton. The former senator had aged greatly in the two and a half years since Sean had last seen him. His age showed. The loss of everything. His career. His reputation. He had been banished to upstate New York, where he was from, lucky that he wasn't in prison . . . but probably thinking he deserved a medal rather than having his title, his reputation, stripped from him.

But he still had his money. And that, Sean realized, had given him the ability to enact revenge.

Did he blame Sean for Paxton's own bad decisions? Or did he blame Sean because Sean caught him in the act? That he'd gone undercover to find the evidence to destroy him? Happily, too, and he'd do it all over again if he had to. Paxton had blackmailed him, forced him to steal for him; he'd held Sean's past over his head so Sean had no choice. Truly, it was Paxton's own fault for all the events that had led to his fall. Because if he hadn't blackmailed Sean, Sean wouldn't have had a reason to take him down.

Except, of course, for his unhealthy infatuation with Lucy.

"Sit," Paxton said and motioned toward a leather chair across from his desk.

Sean didn't move.

Colton put a hand on his shoulder and pushed him into the chair.

"Do you want me to stay?" Colton asked Paxton.

Paxton shook his head. "Please make sure that Sergio is keeping a close eye on Mr. Hunt. If he so much as sneezes, I want to know about it. And let me know the status of the investigation. I don't want any surprises."

"Of course."

Colton left. Sean didn't have anything to say to him right now. He didn't think that his oldest friend could have been sucked in by Paxton's charm and rhetoric, but he was wrong. Colton clearly admired him . . . why in hell he would admire this bastard, Sean didn't know.

Yes, you do. Paxton has always fought for the underdog. Violently, illegally, and sometimes cruelly. But his mission has always been clear.

Colton was the same way. He'd always despised those in power who hurt those without power. Paxton had money. He probably funded projects Colton felt passionate about. Bought him off. Bought his loyalty.

And Sean had betrayed Colton. It didn't matter that what Sean did he did for the right reasons, that what he did was to protect Colton as much as Sean. He'd lied to his best friend and telling him he lied for his own good wouldn't get him anywhere.

Sean had once been the same as Colton. There were some things he did that he would never regret. Other things . . . Sean didn't regret so much as he knew he'd never cross certain lines again.

Because of Lucy? Partly. But mostly because he'd grown up. He valued his freedom too much to jeopardize it for a cause that he had little effect on. He would risk his life before he'd risk his freedom.

"Do you know why I brought you here?" Paxton asked.

"Revenge. A motive as old as time. I found the evidence that took you down. I would do it again if I could."

He sounded a lot braver than he felt. Sean recognized that Paxton held all the cards here.

Paxton shook his head. "That hiccup slowed me down, but didn't stop me. In fact, in many ways, I wouldn't be where I am today without your interference. I realized that had I been successful then, I wouldn't ultimately have changed anything. Those men were already in prison, and while they deserved nothing more than to die, it's the predators who walk free—who slip through the broken system—who deserve my wrath. I went back to the beginning, to my original mission, and it's served me well."

"If you're so noble, why the hell are you working with a drug smuggler like Jimmy Hunt? Do you know what he's done? Do you know who his son was? That he raped and killed dozens of women and Hunt covered it up? And yet you break him out of prison? Help him frame me?"

"I've given this plan a lot of thought, and I need to destroy you as you tried to destroy me. Sometimes, we have to align ourselves with the bad for the greater good. You know that better than anyone, don't you?"

"I'm not letting you bait me."

"Bait you?" He smiled. "I know everything about you, Rogan."

"If you think Colton knows everything about me, you're mistaken."

"Mona Hill was happy to spill everything for the right price. Long before she died, Colton paid her to find out exactly what you did that had her under your thumb. How you threatened her family. How you destroyed her blackmail business. How you used her for information. How you let her go when the police were looking for her. Cybercrime, breaking and entering, obstruction of justice . . . all very interesting."

"You don't know everything, Paxton." Sean wasn't going to explain himself. Nothing he said was going to change Paxton's opinion of him.

"It didn't take long to piece together all the information from Mona and what happened with Jimmy Hunt's criminal network. And because you kept in touch with Mona, it was really quite simple to set her up so she'd call you when she saw Elise. It all worked out wonderfully—except that the police took too long to arrest you. They had to be gently steered in that direction, but once they found the gun and bloody rag, it was a slam dunk. Just in time for us to arrange the transport. And the rest is history."

"The authorities will figure it out," Sean said. "No one is going to believe I killed Mona Hill, not when the evidence comes out."

"The evidence shows that you did. The prison break, which is clear that *you* orchestrated, is proof of your guilt."

"You've lost your mind."

"Do you realize that since Lucy met you, she's been in danger dozens of times?"

"She's a federal agent. It comes with the job."

Paxton slammed his palm on his desk so hard and fast that Sean involuntarily jumped. "No! She's in danger every day of her life because she's married to a *Rogan*. She was in danger in New York looking for *your* cousin. She was in danger in Mexico because of *your* brother Liam. She was shot in the back because of *your* brother Kane. And do you think I forgot what happened in New York when you were trying to destroy me? She was kidnapped because of *you* and *your* crimes. Do you think you've cleaned out all the skeletons? Do you think that your family can keep her safe?"

It dawned on Sean that Paxton had been watching him and Lucy for years. He knew far too much about things he shouldn't know—like what went down with Liam in Mexico. They had kept that information close to the vest. Paxton had to have people in the know. Maybe even someone close to Sean.

Sean absorbed what Paxton was saying. This was about his relationship with Lucy? Paxton was twisting everything . . . even though there was a kernel of truth in what he said. "Do you think *you* can keep her safe?" Sean said, sounding stronger and more confident than he felt. Because he couldn't escape the sick feeling that he was missing something. "That Lucy would even *want* you in her life? After everything you did to her?"

"Lucy is a strong, vibrant young woman. I'm so proud of her. She's only made one mistake in her life, and that was marrying you. I thought for certain when she learned that you had a son by another woman that she would realize you have always been, and always will be, unworthy of her. Alas, she was smitten."

Sean didn't respond. Didn't know if he could. When he learned about Jesse his fear was that Lucy wouldn't be able to get around the fact that he had a son—especially when she was unable to have children. But she had, and she loved Jesse.

"Killing Mona Hill was plan B," Paxton continued. "Colton, as good as he is, was unfortunately unable to execute plan A—which would have had you arrested for cybercrimes. He was impressed with your home security."

"So because Colton wasn't good enough to frame me for a cybercrime, you jumped into bed with a predator to frame me for murder. Lucy is going to figure it out."

"It won't matter if she learns the truth, because you'll be out of her life. Permanently. And she'll always have doubts about you. Added bonus."

"Then why didn't you just hire a sniper to kill me?"

"Because I want her to doubt you. I will *destroy* you in her eyes. The groundwork is already laid, it's only a matter of time. Oh, she might tell everyone she believes in your innocence, that she believes in you," he said with a flippant wave of his hand, "but when you disappear and leave a trail all over the world . . . she'll doubt. She'll think you are running, that your freedom is more important to you than anything, including her. And she'll choose more wisely next time."

"You're sick." Sean had no idea how he was going to get out of this. "You're working with Jimmy Hunt. They kidnapped a federal agent—Kane is missing and I know Hunt's behind it. You did that? You helped Hunt with his vendetta against my friends and family, all so he could frame me for killing Mona Hunt?"

"He doesn't realize it, but Hunt is as good as dead. Sean, really, do you think I would let him walk away from this? I just need him a little while longer. His network is . . . extensive and valuable."

"My brother has done more to rescue women and children from sex trafficking than anyone in the last ten years, he's stopped more drugs from coming into the U.S. than any other individual, and you're letting Hunt kill him? What does that make you?"

"You don't have faith in your brother, do you?" he said. "It was a risk I was willing to take, and I'm confident that Kane will find his way out of it. He's quite resourceful."

"He will hunt you down and kill you."

"No one is going to know I'm part of this. Oh, maybe they'll think Hunt did it because you stole his money, or maybe they'll think Hunt was getting revenge over his son's death, but there's nothing to connect him to me."

Paxton's phone vibrated. He read a message, typed, and a moment later Colton walked in. He handed Paxton a phone, and he listened to something. As he listened, his face reddened and the vein in his neck twitched. He handed Colton back the phone and said, "Bring him to me."

Colton left.

What the hell happened? Sean didn't dare speak, not right now. Paxton was furious about something—and Sean didn't want to take the brunt of his wrath. At this point, all he needed was to find a phone and call Lucy or Rick or JT and tell them Jonathan Paxton was behind this. They'd start investigating. They'd find him.

Sean had to find a way to escape. The longer he was here, the more danger he was in.

He could pick the shackles, but he needed access to something narrow, slightly flexible, and strong.

The grounds were patrolled by armed guards, there were cameras everywhere—Sean had noticed them coming in.

He might find a way to take down the security from within.

If he could get out of his shackles and find a computer hooked up to the network.

If Colton wrote the security system, Sean could break it. Colton was good, but he was basic. He never thought outside the proverbial box. Colton's strength was in planning and gathering information.

Which meant that Colton would know that Sean would try to get to a computer. Find a way to lock him out.

He might not have a choice. If Sean were creating a secure system, he would have a dedicated, closed security system that wasn't connected wirelessly. Only phone lines or T1/T3 cables backed up by a dedicated generator in case of power outage. Wireless systems were the easiest to hack. For home security it wasn't a problem for most people; for businesses or bad guys, they'd want the best security—which meant completely dedicated systems.

Sean had to find the main security hub. Which was most likely in a secure room. Guarded, with cameras.

But he had to get out of the shackles first.

While he thought about his limited options, he watched Jonathan Paxton. Though he appeared to have calmed down, he was still angry—his jaw remained tight and he had an almost desperate look in his eyes. Then he stared at a photo on his desk for several minutes and that seemed to calm him down. From where Sean sat, he couldn't see the image.

Then the door opened and Paxton rose from his desk.

Sean risked turning slightly in his chair so he could see who had entered.

Jimmy Hunt. He'd showered and changed. Overused cologne filled the large room.

"Mr. Hunt, I have a favor to ask," Paxton said, his voice deceptively calm. Sean's veins turned cold at the sound.

"Anything, you know that," Hunt said, gesturing to nothing specific. "We're partners."

Paxton smiled, and Sean realized he was setting Hunt up for something. And Hunt couldn't see it. How had this man run a criminal empire for so long?

He was out of the country. His sister Margaret ran the day-to-day operations . . . and Nicole . . . and they were both smarter than Jimmy Hunt.

"Would you please tell Mr. Rogan what our arrangement was?"

Hunt looked confused. "I don't understand."

"When my associate Colton approached you last year at Victorville. What did he ask?"

"Umm, he said he worked for someone who could get me out of prison when the time was right."

"And?"

"And I just had to testify that I hired a hit man to whack a low-level drug dealer."

"In exchange for?"

"Freedom . . . oh, and you'd help me get revenge on the Rogans for killing my son and wife."

"Exactly. Later, when we finalized the arrangement, I had a condition."

When Hunt didn't say anything, Paxton prodded, "I simply want Mr. Rogan to know that some people are off-limits, right? That certain people are protected?"

"Oh, yeah. Right. No one can touch Lucy Kincaid."

"Yes. That's right. You do remember."

Hunt smiled.

Paxton didn't.

He pressed a button on his phone.

Hunt's voice came through.

"I'm not, sweetie. I'm just worried because I'm your father. I need you to be safe."

"I am, Daddy. I wish I could kill Lucy, though. I really will do it; I won't play with her like Donnelly. Wham bam, dead."

Sean recognized Elise's singsong voice.

"Not now. But later. I promise, when everything dies down, you can do it."

"You really promise?"

"Yes."

Paxton ended the recording. Hunt waved his hand. "I was just telling her what she wanted to hear. If I didn't tell her she could kill that bitch, umm, the fed, she might have done it anyway. She's young and reckless. But I promised you we wouldn't, and you can trust me, Jon. I've done everything you wanted, and then some."

Jonathan nodded. "Just so we have that straight."

"We do, we do. I know the terms. I'm not going to blow this. It's too important, for both of us."

"Yes, it is." Jonathan smiled. "Thank you again for all your help." Jonathan extended his hand to shake Hunt's.

Sean knew what Paxton was going to do before he did it.

While holding Hunt's right hand, he flipped a butterfly knife that was concealed in his other hand, and stabbed Hunt in the gut all the way up to the hilt. Then he twisted the knife, pulled it out, and jabbed it back in at an angle, again twisted the hilt.

Hunt's mouth moved, but he didn't—couldn't—speak.

"You were never going to walk away, Mr. Hunt. From the beginning, I was looking forward to killing you. I wanted to wait, because I needed a few more things from you . . . but you threatened my daughter, and I cannot have that."

Daughter.

Sean felt the blood drain from his face.

He leaned over so he could see the lone photo on Paxton's desk.

It was of Lucy and Paxton, at an event years ago, when Lucy volunteered for Women and Children First.

Paxton had lost his mind.

Chapter Forty-four

It was after nine Saturday night before Michael Thompson was finally brought down to the interview room.

The tipping point was that Paxton was not at his estate in New York. According to his staff, he only visited periodically, and hadn't been there in months. They claimed not to know where he was, and gave the authorities a cell phone number they used to contact him. Rick called the number himself; it was disconnected. He was having Kate run a search on the number, but doubted they'd uncover anything of value without a warrant—and right now, they had no cause for a warrant.

Jonathan Paxton could be anywhere in the world. He had the money and contacts to disappear.

Thompson was barely six feet but walked as if he were taller, unlike most other prisoners, who seemed defeated to Lucy. He had a sense of peace surrounding him, as if he were comfortable with his fate.

Maybe he was.

If Lucy was right, then Thompson's mission—to rid the world of sex offenders—was so righteous that even the possibility of his death didn't faze him. In fact, he would be considered a martyr by many. And if she was right, he would never turn on Paxton, just like she told Rick.

He was a true believer. Like Sergio Russo, no one would be able to convince him that killing sex offenders was immoral or wrong. He would insist that the law against it was corrupt, that he was justified in his actions.

Megan stood and said to the guard, "You can take the handcuffs off Mr. Thompson."

"It's against protocol."

"I'll take responsibility," she said.

The guard complied, and motioned for Thompson to take a seat. He did. Megan extended her hand. "Mr. Thompson, I'm Supervisory Special Agent Megan Elliott, and this is Special Agent Lucy Kincaid, with the FBI. Thank you for agreeing to speak with us."

At the mention of Lucy's name, Thompson looked at her. She didn't know what she expected, but it wasn't this—a look of *reverence* was all Lucy could describe it as.

Megan caught it too, nodded at Lucy, then sat down.

Lucy extended her hand. "Mr. Thompson," she said.

He shook it, held it a second longer than necessary, but he didn't scare her. "It is very nice to meet you, Agent Kincaid. Agent Elliott."

He sat straight in his chair and looked at them with a serene, attentive expression. "What can I do to help you?"

Lucy had already told Megan that they couldn't offer Thompson anything in exchange for turning in Paxton. Thompson would die before he betrayed the man who gave him his mission. What they wanted was first confirmation that their theory was right; second, any hint as to where Paxton might be—and information about his plan with Jimmy Hunt.

Megan said, "You may have heard that Jimmy Hunt, who testified that he hired you to kill a drug dealer, escaped from custody this morning. We have evidence that Mr. Hunt lied on the witness stand and that he did not in fact hire you."

"I can save you time and energy, Agent Elliott. I'm not going to speak about my case."

"That is your right, but the trial is over. Closing statements are on Monday, and it's going to the jury. But I am compelled as an officer of the court to turn over the evidence that I have that Jimmy Hunt perjured himself. The prosecution will likely reopen the case. You will have standing to appeal."

"This is a first—an FBI agent working against her own government to help an alleged killer go free."

It was tricky, but Lucy wasn't scared of Thompson. She was more scared of what would happen to Sean if they couldn't find him. And she and Megan had agreed that the only way they could get Thompson to reveal anything was if he thought he was protecting Paxton.

"I'm more interested in the man who really hired you," Megan said. "I know you're protecting him, and I know why you're protecting him."

He didn't say a word. He didn't blink, he didn't look worried.

Again, Lucy thought: *This man is at peace.*

"Mr. Thompson," Lucy said.

"Call me Mike, please, Agent Kincaid."

He spoke to her kindly. He'd been professional all around, but there was a slight change in his tone when he addressed her.

"Had you heard of me before we met?" she asked.

He didn't answer the question and didn't lose eye contact. He knew exactly who Lucy was, and why she was important to Jonathan Paxton . . . but that revelation was subtle.

"I have a story to share," she said, deviating from what she and Megan had discussed earlier.

"Before I was born, there was a young woman who

looked so much like me, she could have been my sister. Her name was Monique Paxton. She was truly beautiful."

He didn't flinch at the name Paxton, but there was a subtle shift, from alert to hyperalert. He was waiting for something . . . but she didn't think he knew *what* he was waiting for.

"Monique wanted to be a nurse—she volunteered at her local hospital and read to the sick children every Sunday afternoon for three years. She was in advanced math and science classes. She was smart and studious. But, like many teenagers, she wasn't perfect. She made mistakes. But no one should pay for their mistakes with their life. Monique was murdered by her boyfriend—a boy no one knew she was dating. That boy got away with that crime and many more for twenty years.

"Even before I joined the FBI, I knew that violence hurts more people than the victim. Violence destroys families. To have a loved one stolen from you for no reason except another human being's sick needs, it tears you up inside. Especially when it's your child. It twists your heart. The grief. The anger. You can't breathe . . . you can barely think of anything but your child . . . even though you don't want to. Because when you see her smile in a photo and hear her laugh in your dreams, you can't help but flash to her last moment, her final breath, and feel the weight of your loss. That you weren't there. That you couldn't save her."

Thompson didn't move. His eyes were glassy, his face was flushed, but no tears fell. Lucy almost felt guilty for what she was doing to him. She knew his pain. Hers was different—she'd lost her nephew, but she'd been a child and didn't understand what happened until years later. But she'd also been a victim. She'd almost died. She'd also been a vigilante. She'd killed the man who hurt her.

She understood Michael Thompson. She felt for him, and because she felt his pain as it seeped through his soul, she wanted to stop.

But she couldn't.

"Jonathan Paxton suffered when he lost his daughter. His suffering never ended. He didn't know what happened to her. Adam Scott made her disappear, literally vanished her with chemicals, destroyed her remains, and it wasn't until twenty years after her death that Jonathan knew what happened to Monique. Twenty years to live with the unknown, the pain, the regret, the grief, the anger. What could he have done to save her? Every morning and every night he woke up with Monique.

"The truth didn't set him free. Instead, the truth twisted his grief even more. Yet . . . he has a spine of steel, an inner strength that draws people to him. It drew me to him. I worked for him for a year, while I was getting my master's degree in criminal psychology. I loved what he was trying to do as a senator. That he fought for crime victims. That he stood up for those who couldn't speak for themselves. No one cared as much as Jonathan. I knew I looked like his daughter, and maybe in the back of my mind there were warning signs, but I either didn't understand them or intentionally ignored them because I believed in Jonathan and his strong sense of justice.

"He is a master of charm and manipulation. He uses people—instead of helping them find real peace and forgiveness, he stokes their anger, milks their grief, and turns good people into killers. Good people like Sergio Russo."

He flinched. It was his only movement since she started talking.

"Good people like you.

"I know exactly what you're thinking, Mike. The people you kill escaped justice. They hurt others and saw no punishment for their crimes. The allure to end them is strong. They do not deserve to live. And you have convinced yourself of the righteousness of your cause. Because if not you, who will stop them before they hurt another child?"

Lucy took out her phone and opened her photos. She'd spent two hours compiling the photos and memorizing the facts while waiting for Stockton to arrange this interview.

"You were on trial for two murders, ostensibly you were hired to kill the men. But we both know that you weren't *hired*. At least not in the traditional sense. You are, essentially, on staff for Jonathan Paxton. But this wasn't about money. It's never been about money. It's about vengeance. It's about righting wrongs—a noble cause. Jonathan fueled your anger. You live with your dead daughter every day. You can never truly find peace, because Jonathan uses that pain to wind you up to kill for him."

She flipped to the first picture. "The teacher you killed in San Antonio. But Jimmy Hunt didn't hire you, and he wasn't killed because he was a drug dealer. You knew that he had facilitated rape through selling date rape drugs. And if I dig down? I'll find his victims. I'll know how he ended up on Jonathan's radar."

She showed the next photo. "Randy Corbin. He was killed in a hit-and-run in Michigan. A quiet little suburb . . . where he was a youth pastor for a church. Four parents went to authorities and filed reports that their teenage daughters had been raped by Corbin. Four victims. And one by one, they all recanted. The church did nothing. And one of those girls ended up committing suicide. What you didn't know was that there was an active FBI investigation into not only Corbin but other members of that church for sexual assault and the creation of child pornography. He would have been arrested. He would have been held accountable for his crimes."

Lucy flipped to the next photo. One by one she showed Thompson the photos of his victims. He had no reaction, at least on the surface. She recounted their suspected crimes—things she and Megan had dug up over the last few hours. Some unprovable, some rumors, but Lucy was certain if the FBI opened an investigation, they would find the victims of these people.

One by one until she'd finished. Then she waited until Thompson looked her in the eye. He didn't waver. She had rocked him—she could tell in his posture, by the tension in the room, the tightness in his jaw. But he didn't look away.

"Your victims weren't good people. But you created other victims. Among your known kills, they had thirteen minor children. Nine adult children. Twenty-six siblings. Three were married. Six had at least one living parent. Corbin, for example, had fathered two children out of wedlock, but the mothers were either too ashamed or too scared to name him as the father. He had a net worth of three million dollars, but they can't claim it now. They could have, had he been arrested and they came forward. You took that option away from them.

"I understand why you did what you did. It does not make it right or just. You think because Jonathan Paxton lost his daughter that he understands your grief? He doesn't. He used you. And your silence is going to allow him to use others.

"Honestly, I probably wouldn't care. I'm not going to lose any sleep because a pedophile and a rapist are dead. But Jonathan is a narcissist who believes that he is always right. That anything he does is justified. There are good men and women sitting in prison today because they refuse to speak against him. Loyalty is noble, to a point. But their loyalty is misguided. They suffer so he can be free."

She realized that wasn't a selling point as soon as she said it. Because Michael Thompson was suffering every day of his life. The pain from the murder of his daughter had never found a healthy outlet. You never got over loss, but you could find ways to survive it. You had to, or become a hollow shell.

"He's obsessed with me," she continued. *Keep it personal.* "He's called me Monique more than once. And not just because I look like his dead daughter, but because he wants me to love him as a father. He orchestrated the escape of Jimmy Hunt—a cruel and violent drug runner, the man who testified that he hired you. But he only did it because the Hunt family framed my husband for murder. If I know Jonathan Paxton—and I do—Jimmy Hunt is as good as dead. He used him to get to my husband, but he won't let him live. Hunt facilitated the rape and murder of a dozen or more women, all for his sick son. Jonathan would want that crime punished. So, why this elaborate plan, I don't know. That's the only thing I can't figure out—why frame Sean? Why kidnap a federal agent? My husband is not a predator. He's saved the lives of countless women and children through his selflessness and bravery. Yet Jonathan wants to punish him . . . or me. The only thing I've done to Jonathan Paxton is walk away from him."

"Mike," Lucy said, fighting to keep the emotion out of her voice, "you loved your daughter Sarah with all your heart and soul. I know you did. Would she want you to kill in her name? Would she want you to tarnish her short, beautiful life with these acts of violence? Is this how you want your daughter Whitney to remember you?"

A single tear slipped from the corner of Thompson's

eye. It slowly dribbled down his narrow face. He made no move to wipe it off, showed no reaction to it whatsoever.

"I don't know what grievance Jonathan has with my husband." Sean had certainly been party to Paxton's downfall, but so had she and several other FBI agents. Why single out Sean? "But I know that Jonathan is behind this entire thing. Working with Hunt and his daughter to frame Sean for murder. Getting into the prison system database to put Sean on the transport with Hunt. Orchestrating the escape. Sean will *die* if I don't find him. I love my husband more than anything in the world. So I am asking you, as one survivor to another, where is Jonathan Paxton?"

Chapter Forty-five

Jonathan Paxton ended the call from his house manager in New York.

This was certainly unfortunate.

Though the FBI agent who spoke with Margery said they wanted to talk to him about a current investigation in which he might be of help, that was a lie. For two and a half years, he'd spoken directly to no one in the FBI. When they wanted to communicate, they did so through his lawyer.

Visiting his house on a Saturday evening was certainly out of the ordinary.

It wasn't Hunt—he had no reason to blab, and he'd only known of Paxton's involvement recently. Jonathan trusted Colton more than anyone on his staff outside of Sergio Russo. Neither would make a tactical error. Thompson . . . he wouldn't betray him. He had wanted to kill himself when he was caught; Jonathan was the one who convinced him not to.

There is much good you can do in prison, he'd told him.

Thompson was eager to get started.

Then who?

Jonathan closed his eyes and replayed the last three years.

He'd kept tabs on Lucy. He had to; he loved her. He had grown increasingly worried about the danger she was in because of the man she'd mistakenly fallen in love with.

But he didn't interfere.

A good father never interfered unless their daughter was in immediate danger.

But he should have.

He should have found a way to stop Monique from dating Adam Scott.

He should have found a way to stop Lucy from moving in with Sean Rogan.

But he waited. Watched. Grew angry. Didn't act. He focused on his primary mission: to make sure no father, no mother, no family suffered as he had suffered. And if they did? They would find peace when the man (or woman) who caused the suffering was wiped from the face of the earth.

Thompson had been arrested. It was a fluke, a witness plus a good cop plus a small mistake. Who could have predicted it? Michael would have killed himself . . . Jonathan couldn't live with that. Not a good man, never a good man.

Then Colton analyzed the situation and came up with the idea to find someone to testify that he'd hired Thompson.

Because there were some money issues that might be traceable to Jonathan.

But who . . .

That's when Jonathan took the information he knew about Sean and was able to track down Jimmy Hunt. It was a bit of a tightrope exercise, but it worked.

And he'd kept his fingers mostly out of it.

So how did they know? And so fast?

How, dammit?

Then Jonathan realized he'd made one tactical error. His blind spot, his one weakness.

Lucy.

She wouldn't take the accusations against Sean at face value; she'd investigate herself. And he expected that, had planned for it—that's why the gun had been planted, why other information had found itself to the investigative team so they would believe that Sean was having an affair with Mona. Information that would eventually get to Lucy, so she would doubt.

Lucy was smart—smarter than most people Jonathan dealt with on a day-to-day basis.

If she was so smart, why hadn't she fallen in love with a man like Colton Thayer? A noble man, a man dedicated to doing the right thing always.

Instead Lucy had fallen for Sean, a womanizer and criminal who claimed to have turned over a new leaf, but had he? Lucy had been in danger because of him not once or twice, but *at least* five times. More, most likely . . . there were five that Jonathan knew about. What kind of man stayed with a woman when he put her life in perpetual danger?

It was unconscionable!

He had thought about killing Sean. Michael Thompson was more than willing to do it. Yet . . . Lucy might fall apart and grieve, and Jonathan didn't want to hurt her.

He wanted her love to turn to hate. He wanted her to grow a backbone and never settle for a man unworthy of her. He had to destroy Sean Rogan—so Lucy would see that he was rotten, deep down bad news.

The plan had somewhat gotten away from him. Simpler was always better, but he'd been convinced that killing Sean in prison—his second idea, after planting treasonous evidence on his computer failed—would make him a martyr to Lucy.

Jonathan had long had the idea that he and Lucy would make amends. She had told him she never wanted to see him again, but he'd hoped that when she realized that he had always looked out for her, had always had her best interests at heart, that they could do so much good together . . . yet she wouldn't speak to him. Without Sean in the picture, a few months from now, he would find a way to run into her. By accident. And she'd remember that they had once been friends, that he'd looked out for her, that he loved her as if she were his daughter.

She'd return to the fold.

It was a dream that kept him going, even though he knew the odds were slim. All the things he loved and admired about Lucy—her perseverance, her wisdom, her strength—told him she wouldn't easily forgive.

But couldn't she see that his way was the best way? Without Sean Rogan in the picture clouding her judgment, she would see the truth.

Yet . . . he knew that if she never came back to him, he would still protect her, as he was doing now. Protect her from her one flaw: the inability to see through men who were no good for her.

That might have to appease him.

Once Sean Rogan was gone.

Chapter Forty-six

"I thought he would talk," Megan said when they left the jail. "He was so close."

"I knew he wouldn't, but I'd hoped by appealing to his loss that he might give me something."

"Well, his reaction was confirmation, at least for me, that your theory is right. And we can convince Rick. But beyond that . . . I don't know."

They were heading back to the hotel. It was late; Lucy was exhausted. Talking to Thompson had been emotionally stressful; her head pounded. She didn't know how she would sleep. Not only was she worried about Sean, she hadn't heard from Patrick in hours. She'd told him about Paxton and he said he had an idea and would call later.

"Lucy?"

Lucy glanced at Megan. "Sorry. I hope he'll reach out after he thinks about what I said." She had given him her direct cell phone number, and Megan instructed the guards that if he wanted to make a call to let him—and to record it. He might not call Lucy, but he could call Paxton.

"You had me feeling sorry for him—you really understood him, showed him that."

"I feel for him. He lost his daughter and went through

a deep depression and paranoia. He didn't get any help, or if he did, he didn't stick with it. And sometimes, the guilt keeps eating at you. Paxton used that, turned him into a weapon. Thompson is a true believer in his mission and so I didn't get through to him. For a minute I thought . . ." She shrugged. She couldn't save Thompson. Maybe he was beyond saving.

Lucy continued. "We have to find Paxton. He could be anywhere by now—we don't know what his plans are. Why does he want Sean? What did Sean do to him? I mean, more than what anyone else did who took him down. I know he always disliked Sean, and the feeling was mutual, but to frame him for murder?"

"Have you talked to Dillon?"

"No. He's testifying in a major trial Monday morning, otherwise I'm sure he would be here."

"I think you're too close to this."

"What? Because Sean is missing?"

"That, and because you have a long history with Senator Paxton," Megan said. "Dillon might be able to look at the situation from a clinical distance."

Megan was right.

"I should have called him earlier," Lucy agreed.

"We didn't have all the information we have now."

Lucy glanced at her watch. It would be after midnight on the East Coast, but Dillon would take the call. "Okay, we'll call him as soon as we get back."

Ten minutes later, they walking into the hotel suite. Both Patrick and Kate were there, and both were on the phone. As soon as Lucy walked in, they ended their calls.

"We have news," Patrick said.

Lucy felt the blood drain from her face. "Sean?" Her voice was a squeak.

"No word on Sean, but after you called me about Senator Paxton, I changed my focus. The dead guard, David Dobleman, and the other guard, Sheffield."

Kate said, "After I had Erica Anderson's statement, I talked to Sheffield. He was groggy after surgery, but clearly said that Sean shot him and the other guard, that he'd worked with the other prisoner to escape. I then told him Erica had confessed to her part in setting Sean up, and that I had evidence that he'd been the one who changed the transport orders. He then shut up and asked for a lawyer."

Patrick said, "While I was skeptical about Paxton's involvement initially, I now think you're right, Lucy. At first, I had a hard time believing that a cop would lie to protect his partner's killer. He could have said he didn't see who shot Dobleman, but he specifically fingered Sean. The early forensics report shows that the gun was taped under a seat. But it wasn't Sean's prints that were found on the underside of the seat. They were Jimmy Hunt's prints."

"We just got that information," Kate said, "and Houston PD isn't being very friendly with us because they think we're trying to fuck with their case against Sean, but we have enough friends here who listen. Now, the prints are not foolproof that it was Hunt who knew the gun was there, or that he was the one who shot the guard, but it's one small piece of a bigger puzzle."

"Kate and I were looking at Sheffield. The guy appears clean, and all we have is Erica Anderson's statement. She's the one with the hefty bank deposits, not Sheffield. And while Kate has video proof that he was at the terminal at the time of the transfer change, it's still circumstantial."

"So," Kate said, "we began to think about how Paxton operates and who he targets, and wondered about the dead guard, Dobleman," Kate said. "Sheffield put him on the schedule for today. Told him that another guy had called in sick, and that it was his turn to come in. Which was a lie—no one called in sick."

"So Sheffield is corrupt," Megan said. "Erica Anderson didn't lie."

"Yeah, but not for the reasons we think."

It clicked. Lucy said, "Dobleman was a sex offender."

Patrick rolled his eyes. "Jeez, you stole my thunder!"

"How was he in law enforcement if he's an offender?"

"First, you're only partly right. He was an offender, but not a sex offender that we could find at any rate. He was suspected of domestic violence. His wife finally left him after *eight* visits to the emergency room in three years."

"How did he get to be a cop?"

"She never filed charges. She never named him. He'd been a cop at the time, in Austin. He had friends, and they helped move him over to Beaumont and into corrections. His wife changed her name and is living in another state."

"And you think that Paxton knew about this?"

"I don't know how Paxton knows half the stuff he knows—even when he was running the vigilante group in D.C., I didn't know how he got all his information."

"Key people in key positions," Lucy said.

"Or Sheffield found out."

"Sheffield sees the worst in people, but would expect the best in his colleagues," Lucy said. "Or he was working with his girlfriend Erica and Hunt's people said someone needed to die. So he found the corrupt cop to kill in the process, a win-win."

"Maybe. Or maybe Paxton has something on him. At any rate, I think Dobleman was a sacrifice, and stating that Sean killed him puts a target on Sean's back," Kate said.

"I need to call Dillon," Lucy said. "Thompson wouldn't talk, but it was clear from how he responded that he's working for Paxton."

"Do you have anything solid?" Kate asked.

"No," Megan said, "but I agree with Lucy. She affected him. He barely spoke, but there was something about his demeanor, and he knew Lucy's name when we introduced ourselves. What we can't figure out is why Paxton would work with a scumbag like Hunt, and why he would target Sean. Unless there's a bigger play here. Maybe he needs Sean's hacking skills."

There were other hackers out there, more willing to break the law and work for someone like Paxton.

Kate pulled out her cell phone and dialed. "Hey, babe, it's me. I know it's late . . . nothing solid, but we're making progress. Lucy wants to talk things through, can we Skype? Just want to make sure you're decent. . . . Okay, great. Love you." To Lucy she said, "He's going to his computer. He'll call when he's logged in."

A few minutes later, her computer beeped, and she opened her Skype. "It's so good to see your face, Dillon," she said.

Kate, Megan, and Patrick stood behind her. Lucy was getting a bit claustrophobic with everyone closed in on her, but she tried to contain it. Focus on Dillon.

"I'm so sorry you're going through this."

"I have no idea why. I need to tell you everything we've learned, and I need your help to figure out what Senator Paxton wants."

"Paxton? Jonathan Paxton?"

Lucy brought her brother, a brilliant forensic psychiatrist, up to speed as quickly as she could. Everything they'd learned, focusing on how they determined that Paxton was involved, Thompson's silence, and the new information about Dobleman.

"Paxton worked with criminals," Lucy said, "but he never worked with sex offenders. He would never work with someone like Jimmy Hunt. And for all of Paxton's flaws, I couldn't see him condoning killing a prison guard. It's not in his nature—even though he's a vigilante, he has a code he lives by. Kate and Patrick ran with that information and learned that the dead prison guard was suspected of domestic violence. We know the other guard, who said Sean killed him, and a guard at juvenile hall when Elise Hunt was there, were lovers. They were clearly working for the Hunt family, though the reasons are a bit sketchy."

Kate said, "I spoke to Erica Anderson this afternoon. Anderson was dissatisfied with her job, upset that she didn't have custody of her kids, had just started dating Sheffield, whom she met through an online dating app. She mostly did odd jobs for the Hunts, but she's the one who planted the gun in Sean's plane, and she's already made that statement."

"So you're saying Anderson and Sheffield worked together for the Hunts," Dillon said.

"Yes. Erica alluded to a crime Sheffield may have committed, that the Hunts had something over his head, but refused to give specifics. Houston FBI will continue to work on her."

Lucy said, "But why frame Sean for murder? When it was Elise Hunt, yes, I believe it. She's vindictive and unpredictable and Sean was responsible for stealing their drug money and giving it to the FBI. And knowing that she had been in contact with her father, I could see him pushing her to get retribution by targeting Brad and Kane. But they didn't have the resources. Not to hire all those people and put this all together. They had the vision— revenge—but Paxton paid for this. Which means it was his plan—Paxton wanted Sean. Why?"

Dillon didn't say anything for a long time—but Lucy knew him well enough to know that he had a theory and was trying to find the best way to share it.

He said, "You cut off all ties from Paxton after you learned he was behind the vigilante group in D.C."

"You know I did. I knew why he did it, but I couldn't prove it—so I gave him back Monique's locket. It's all he wanted."

"Paxton has always felt like you were his chance at redemption," Dillon said. "You look like his daughter, but more than that, you were strong. You killed the man who killed his daughter."

"I killed him because he raped me and planned to kill me," Lucy said, her voice cracking at the end.

"He saw it as an act of vengeance . . . of love . . . of redemption. You were strong and you fought back. It was the catalyst for everything he did. He has always used you to justify his actions."

She was horrified. On the one hand she knew it was true . . . Paxton had never regretted killing anyone. She wanted nothing of his plans. Nothing to do with the murder of anyone, guilty or not. She believed in the system, flaws and all. If she didn't . . . she didn't want to go there. She could have gone down that same path, but she hadn't. She had found a way to overcome what happened to her, to be stronger. To survive. And now, she felt like Paxton was stripping away every layer of protection she'd painstakingly built over the last ten years.

"Lucy," Dillon said, softening his voice, "do not even go there."

"I created a monster."

"If anything, I did."

"What the hell, Dillon? You did not have anything to do with this."

"I told the FBI ten years ago that it would be okay to tell Paxton what happened to Monique."

"You had to. She was his daughter; he deserved to know."

"But I should have been there; I should have done it myself. Who told him and how was he told? We know that it was after learning what happened to Monique—and after you killed Adam Scott—that he built his network, that he began to plot to kill predators who slipped through the system. He recruited men like Sergio Russo and Michael Thompson and others because he saw a kindred spirit—no guilt. He never recruited you—you were on a pedestal. You were untouchable. If he thought you would join his crusade, he would have roped you in, if only to keep you by his side, in his debt, as his daughter. Because that is ultimately what he sees you as—his daughter. And what does a father do for his daughter?"

She didn't know if the question was rhetorical or not. "I don't know what you want me to say."

"A father, above all, wants to protect his daughter. Don't give me that look, Kate," Dillon said. "I know what you're thinking. But you have to think like Paxton. Who he is, how he was raised, what he lost. His wife died of cancer when Monique was young, Monique was all he had. But he was a workaholic, a low-level politician and prosecutor who wasn't around because he was fighting other people's battles. Then his daughter disappeared. He had no idea if she was dead or alive. He searched for her until the day he found out that she was dead. Because he didn't *know*. Not knowing is almost as bad as knowing your child is dead. The hope and fear never goes away until you know the truth. By that point, the hope and fear had created a senator . . . a powerful orator with a natural charisma and a cause that people naturally gravitated toward. Because he spoke for them—their loss, their fears, their hopes. When he found out Monique was dead . . . and how she died . . . the grief and anger twisted until a vigilante was born. In fact, I don't think he's ever truly *grieved*.

"Paxton is not just any vigilante," Dillon continued. "Because he's smart and powerful and wealthy and has a strong sense of preservation, he's not going to pull the trigger—though he is capable of it."

"He killed Roger Morton," Kate reminded him. "We just couldn't prove it."

"That was personal for him. He is *capable* of murder, but he much prefers to build a network of like-minded people."

"Don't underestimate him," Lucy said.

"I'm not. You have."

"I have not. I know exactly who he is and what he is capable of."

"You've underestimated his obsession with you."

She frowned.

"He thinks of you as his daughter, Lucy. How many times did he call you Monique? He used to brush it off when you worked for him, but more than once after that he talked about you to other people as his daughter. Jack told me, when he was interrogating him in New York three years ago, that Paxton said he had to *protect his daughter*. That was you, Lucy, not a slipup. He was thinking about you, not Monique."

She hadn't known that.

"This plan—he somehow thinks he's protecting you."

"By framing my husband for murder?"

"He's never liked Sean."

"This is extreme, even for Paxton."

"Not if you think like he does. That's why I said you're too close to this. You're not in his head, Lucy, and the only way you're going to stop him is to think like him. So, a father protects his daughter. A father might think that no man is good enough for his daughter. Sean and Paxton have butted heads from the beginning. Paxton has *never* thought that Sean was good enough for you."

"But he's not my father!" she exclaimed.

Dillon didn't say a word. No one did.

She closed her eyes. He was right. From the beginning, Paxton had always treated her with affection—not sexual, but fatherly. They'd been friends, but she'd always kept him at arm's length. Partly because she didn't bring anyone into her inner circle as she still battled the trauma of being kidnapped and raped; partly because he was too nice to her. She enjoyed working for the justice committee in the Senate, but she didn't want any special favors. And she knew from the beginning that she looked like his dead daughter. She knew from the beginning that the man who'd hurt her had killed Monique.

You should have run far away from him long ago. How can you not be partly responsible for these events?

"Okay," she said quietly. "Think like Jonathan Paxton. He sees me as a surrogate daughter."

"Yes. And he thinks he would be a better father to you than your own. More, he thinks you made an unwise choice in marriage, but he wasn't around to guide you. It's a combination of guilt and regret. He blames Sean for taking you from him—and while what happened in D.C. wasn't Sean's doing, you were with Sean when you cut all ties with Paxton. He could easily convince himself that Sean told you to do it. He kept tabs on you, and you walked back into his life—in his mind—when you and Noah investigated the string of prostitution murders in D.C. before you joined the academy. He blackmailed Sean into retrieving the computer chip that had been stolen from him. And then what happened? Sean kept the chip. Not only that, but Sean went undercover to take him down."

"Many FBI agents were involved in that investigation. Noah, Rick, Suzanne—"

"But they were doing their job, right? Remember, he sees law enforcement as literal enforcers. He's not going to fault them for investigating him. But Sean? A reformed hacker who took his daughter from him? Sean—in Paxton's mind—is no better than any other criminal walking the streets. And yet Sean took him down. If Sean had never taken that chip, Paxton's plan to kill all those prisoners may have worked. And then after? Sean moved to San Antonio with you. You married him."

Dillon paused and was about to say something else when Patrick asked, "I don't see it, Dillon. He hasn't reached out to Lucy in all these years, he could have done a dozen other things to screw with Sean."

"We know that he kept tabs on Lucy when she was in D.C. I think we can assume he kept tabs on her when she moved to San Antonio."

She felt physically ill.

"Assume, Lucy, that Paxton knows what has gone on in your life—especially the high-profile situations. The situations where you were in danger."

"I'm a federal agent. My life is sometimes going to be in danger."

"It wasn't because of your job that Liam kidnapped you and took you to Mexico."

"For shit's sake, Dillon! Sean had nothing to do with that."

"He was Sean's brother. And you were in danger when Sean learned that he had a son. In fact, that would anger Paxton—that Sean betrayed you."

"Dillon, that's ridiculous. I didn't even *know* Sean when he dated Jesse's mother."

"Again, I repeat, you're not in his head, and if you're not in his head, you're not going to find Sean."

"But why did he take him? Why did he set him up?"

"It's obvious, Lucy. He set Sean up so you would see Sean as *he* sees Sean. A criminal unworthy of your love. I think Paxton sought Jimmy Hunt out. He might not have known everything about him, but he knew that the Hunts and the Rogans were in a war. He heard about what Sean did—from Hunt's perspective. That Sean had hacked in and 'stolen' his money. That Kane killed his son. Paxton would use that anger and vendetta to get Hunt to go along with this plan. Find a way to frame Sean for murder to put him *somehow* under Paxton's thumb. But mostly, so you would doubt him. And what better way to doubt him than to have Sean accused of killing a prostitute. A prostitute who was an informant for Sean, one who had a history with Sean, one who Hunt hated because she betrayed him. A win-win for Hunt."

"Why would Paxton think I would believe that Sean had killed her?"

"Evidence. The gun in his plane. The fact that he was the last person to see her alive. Even being in Houston helped him because you don't have friends and family there, people who might listen to you. Michael Thompson was incarcerated a year ago for killing the council member. That's when Paxton came up with this idea. He's always been about the long game. His hatred of Sean has festered for years. He misses you and blames Sean."

Megan said, "But isn't Lucy in danger from Paxton? If she betrays him in some way—"

"No," Dillon said. "Paxton's obsession is sick, but it's not going to turn to hate. Lucy could tell him she hates his guts, and he would understand and forgive her. I don't think anyone really understands how deep this goes for him. How important Lucy is to him and his mission. To him, Lucy is a hero. She killed Adam Scott. Thus, she can do or think no wrong. He doesn't blame her for marrying Sean; he thinks Sean manipulated her, that he'll hurt her, that he puts her in danger simply by the fact that he is a Rogan."

"And that's why he kidnapped Kane?"

"I've been thinking about that," Dillon said. "I think including Kane and Brad was part of his agreement with Hunt. He wants Sean, he gives Hunt the men who killed his family. But my guess there is that he didn't use *his* men for those jobs; he gave Hunt the money, but it's up to Hunt to follow through. Which is why Kane escaped, and Jack has been working with him to find Hunt. Hunt most likely escaped to Mexico—it's where he's most comfortable."

"No," Lucy said.

"You think he's elsewhere?"

Megan said, "Brad Donnelly overhead a conversation between Elise and Jimmy and Jimmy stated that he was still in Texas but would meet her in Mexico tomorrow."

Lucy said, "I think he's dead."

And she feared Sean was, too.

"Why?"

"Because I *do* know Jonathan, even better than you, Dillon. I may not have understood his obsession with me until now, but I know him, and there's no way he would let that man live, knowing what he did. Hunt's son was too much like the man who killed his daughter; he'd never let him walk away."

"Well. You might be right."

She was right. "But what does that mean for Sean?"

Dillon shook his head. "I don't know, Lucy. I don't know."

Chapter Forty-seven

After Paxton killed Hunt, he'd lost the desire to talk to Sean. It was like a switch, and he wasn't himself.

And not in a good way.

Sean began to wonder if Paxton had snapped. When he lost everything two and a half years ago—everything except his wealth—he broke. His obsession with Lucy and Lucy's resemblance to his dead daughter took over all reason.

Colton seemed to sense the change in Paxton and without commenting and waiting for permission, he escorted Sean out of the library.

His shackles rattled through the cavernous hall until they went outside.

"What's going on here, Colton? What *is* the plan? You must know what's going to happen next."

Colton didn't say anything.

"He's going to kill me, isn't he?"

Of course he was, but he wanted to destroy him first. How? By trying to turn Lucy against him? That couldn't happen, could it? She wouldn't believe whatever lies Paxton and Colton came up with, no matter what "proof" they had.

Would his son believe it?

What if the evidence was good enough for the cops? The FBI? What if he lost his house, his money, everything . . . and disappeared because he was dead, but no one knew? Everyone thought he was on the run because he was considered a fugitive?

Lucy would be left with nothing and a teenager to raise, broken, heartbroken, confused.

Sean felt ill. It might not matter that Lucy would never believe he could kill a cop or . . . do whatever Paxton had planned . . . if the world came crashing down, it would crush her.

What did Paxton hope to gain from it? Just . . . keeping him away from Lucy?

Colton remained silent. They walked past the limo and to the garage. Through a side door that was opened only by a code. Colton didn't even attempt to hide it from Sean—0217. Sean didn't know if he could use it, but it was always good to have as much information as possible.

February 17. Lucy's birthday.

Sean felt physically sick.

"You have to see that Paxton isn't sane. He's not going to get away with this, and you know it."

Colton led Sean down a wide hall, then turned and went down narrow stairs to a basement. It was cold down here, humid, musty. There was also a cage. An eight-by-eight-foot cage.

"No," Sean said.

Colton more than anyone—even Lucy—knew how much Sean hated confinement. He wouldn't say he was claustrophobic—small spaces didn't bother him, as long as he knew the way out. But being trapped terrified him.

And Colton knew it.

* * *

Sean had one semester left before graduation; Colton had graduated a week ago. It had taken him four and a half years because he took time off to take care of his ill little brother, and that experience had changed him. In both good ways and bad. But Sean had stuck with him because Colton was his best friend. More a brother to him than Duke, who acted like a dictator, or Kane, who fought other people's battles all over North America and had made it clear he didn't think Sean was capable of helping him, outside of a couple of isolated piloting gigs when Kane had no one else to call.

Sean and Colton lived together off-campus and it was Christmas break. Sean didn't want to go home—he had hardly spoken to Duke in three years. Only when absolutely necessary. He still hadn't forgiven him for sending him off to MIT, for not listening to him, not believing him, not trusting him.

Some things were more important than rules.

Sean and Colton had four weeks before the next semester started, and time plus genius-level IQs plus anger was a recipe for disaster.

But all their previous plans had worked perfectly, for the most part. They needed something to do, something to believe in.

A rumor had been going around campus for the last few months that one of the RAs, Brian Bean, was videotaping the showers in his dorm—both girls and boys. An investigation had been launched, but the campus police couldn't find any evidence. A few videos that had surfaced on the internet were untraceable, according to law enforcement.

But Sean and Colton weren't law enforcement, and nothing was foolproof. They'd been tracking Bean, and Colton cloned his hard drive to figure out how he had been recording when there was no evidence of cameras or wires in the community bathrooms. That's when they realized he was recording live—he didn't need wires if he went in between the floors whenever he felt like it. And not just the showers—they found recordings from the dorms as well.

Because the campus police had screwed up the initial investigation—and because Sean had no faith in the system after he'd been expelled for hacking, for doing the exact same thing as he was doing now—Sean and Colton wanted to destroy this bastard themselves. Justice came in all forms.

That's why they had to wait until winter break. First thing they did was break into his dorm room, hack into his computer, and destroy everything he had on the cloud. Sean suspected he'd hidden the files on his computer so they wouldn't be easy for law enforcement to find—or he hid them on another website. So he downloaded his history—history the jerk thought he'd erased—to analyze later, then he destroyed his hard drive.

But they couldn't be sure they had sent a clear enough message to the asshole, so they tracked Brian down to where he was visiting his parents in South Carolina.

At first, everything went perfectly. They waited until the family left one evening, then they broke into the rural home and found Brian's laptop. Destroyed it. They searched his room and found an extensive amount of pornography—some of it clearly underage. They grabbed it to burn. The guy was an asshole, and neither Sean nor Colton cared what happened to him.

It was Colton's idea to take one of the photos and leave it in the mother's drawer with a note.

Do you know that your son is a pervert?

Sean didn't know if that was a good idea, but he let Colton do it.

They were leaving when they saw lights coming down the road. They didn't know if the Bean family was already home—only an hour after they left—or if it was someone else. They'd parked down the street—smart, considering—but now their car was too far for an easy escape. They ran across a small field to a barn. They hadn't spent time to do recon because they didn't know how long Brian would be here.

But they should have. If they had checked things out first, they would never have entered the barn.

The structure was falling apart, not used for much of anything except storing junk. It reeked of rotting wood, animal feces, and stale, cold air.

The car turned down the drive. Sean and Colton watched from a crack in the door. They didn't want to wait in here longer than necessary—it really stunk—but as soon as the family went inside, they could cut across the lawn and head to the road. They weren't parked that far away, and it was dark, so minimized their chances of being seen.

Someone went up to the door, but it wasn't the Bean family. It was a delivery. The individual dropped two packages at the door and left.

Sean breathed easier.

"Let's go, C. We did what we came to do."

"I hate that he's going to get away with this," Colton said.

"What can we do? The police did shit because Bean was good enough to cover his tracks and the cops don't have anyone good in cybercrimes. We destroyed everything he saved. He'll think twice before doing it again, especially on campus."

"So we protect the dorm, what's to say he doesn't go after the girls in the gym? Maybe finds a way to get into the high school?"

"I don't know." Sean had hoped that fear would keep Bean in line.

"We have to do something, Sean."

He thought about it, came up with an idea. "He's going to have to get a new computer, but I can plant a virus. He records anyone in the dorm and I'll know. I'll monitor his cloud account. If he steps out of line once, I'll send an anonymous feed to the dean, the police, to whoever can do something about him." He had to do it anonymously. He didn't want to go through what he went through at Stanford, where doing the right thing had resulted in him being expelled.

Of course, he had made a big production out of exposing his pedophile professor. And knowing how the police handled a pervert like Brian Bean told Sean that maybe it was worth it.

"Can you do that?" Colton asked, surprised.

"Yes." Sean wasn't positive, but he would figure it out. He'd never encountered a computer problem that he couldn't solve. "Let's go, okay? I don't want to be here when . . ."

As Sean pushed on the barn door something scurried across his foot, startling him. He jumped to the right. The floor cracked, and suddenly he was falling . . .

He landed ten feet down into a root cellar of some sort, except that it was small. Dark. He brushed it aside and heard rodents running in the small space.

"Sean!"

"Step back or you'll fall, too."

"How far?"

"Ten, twelve feet."

"I can't see anything."

Neither could Sean. He stood up and groaned. He'd fallen on his wrist. He didn't think it was broken but it hurt. He shook it, but the pain only got worse.

"Go back to the car. Get the flashlight." Why hadn't he brought it with him in the first place?

Because if you were caught you didn't want the cops thinking you were a burglar.

Idiot.

"Okay. I'll be back, ten minutes tops."

"Drive back, I don't care if we're caught, we need the car to help pull me out. Be careful when you walk back in."

At first, the silence didn't bother Sean. He figured Colton would be ten minutes. His watch had a small light on it. Nine ten P.M. He hoped Brian and his family didn't come back because he had no idea what he would tell them. The truth? That Brian videotaped naked men and women in the shower at college? Like that would go over well. Breaking and entering . . . destroying private property . . . what else would the cops throw at him?

Sean didn't want to think about that.

He tried to feel around, see if there was a ladder. The room was small, maybe six feet by four feet.

A little bigger than a grave.

Where the hell was Colton?

He checked his watch. Nine twelve. Shit, it had only been two minutes? It felt like thirty . . . more.

Sean took a deep breath. On one wall were jars. They felt grimy, like someone had forgot they'd canned fruits and veggies and they'd been down here for years. There had to be a ladder here, didn't there? How did people come up and down to get the jars?

They don't. They forgot about them.

A mouse . . . no, larger than a mouse . . . ran across his foot. He kicked it and the sound it made when it hit the wall made him think larger than a rat.

He wasn't normally skittish about bugs and rodents, but he couldn't see them, and what if they had rabies?

Something crawled over his face and he shook his head back and forth. He was shaking; he couldn't control it.

Dammit, where are you, Colton?

He looked at his watch.

Nine thirteen.

No, his watch had to be broken. Three minutes? It felt like hours.

He looked up and saw nothing and for a second thought that the roof had caved in, that Colton wouldn't be able to find where he was buried. That he could be down here for hours . . . days. That he would die.

Don't be stupid. Colton will get help. If he can't get you out, he'll get help.

Every time Sean moved, he felt something else . . . a rodent, a bug, a cobweb. So he stood still and waited.

He couldn't stop shaking.

He'd never been so terrified.

It's just a hole! Colton is coming back!

But it wasn't just a hole. It was a grave. Why was it even here? Why didn't they board it up?

Stop, Sean! It's not a grave.

He reached up, hoping to feel the floor above him, but he couldn't. He was six foot one, and with his arm extended what? Seven feet? But he still couldn't feel a ceiling. Had he fallen farther than he thought?

He kept telling himself that Colton was coming back, that he was just in a root cellar, that there was nothing here that could hurt him . . . but he felt the walls closing in on him.

Nine sixteen.

Six minutes . . .

Something flew by his face and he screamed.

"Please, C. Don't do this."

Colton opened the cage.

"In."

"No."

It was just him and Colton. He had cuffs and shackles, but if he could incapacitate Colton then maybe he had a chance to get away. Hide. It was dark outside. He had to try.

He didn't want to be locked up again. Prison. The root cellar. Might as well be a well in the middle of nowhere. He didn't care, he couldn't do this!

Sean turned and with all his strength head-butted Colton as hard as he could. He ran up the stairs. He tripped over his shackles, struggled to get up. He half crawled up the stairs. If he could just make it to behind the garage . . .

He hadn't thought this through, he knew, but the panic was real. He could taste his own fear and mortality. He had to get away or he would be dead.

He was nearly to the top of the stairs when a blinding pain hit him in the back. He collapsed and half fell, half slid down the stairs.

Colton had shot him.

His body convulsed and he heard the zap as Colton held the Taser on him until the charge was spent.

He almost couldn't breathe.

His limbs twitched. He couldn't speak.

Colton dragged him by his feet into the cage. His head banged on the stairs and he saw stars. He didn't know if it was from the pain in his skull or being Tasered.

"D-d-don't," Sean squeaked out.

"It's over, Sean. *Over.* You think you are some sort of genius? You think only you know what's right and what's wrong? If your wife knew half of what we did, she would never forgive you. Yet you turned your back on *me.* On what we *were!*"

"C. Please."

Colton kicked him, pulled the barbs out of his back and Sean cried out, then bit the inside of his cheek. He tasted blood. Not just from the inside of his mouth, but his face had been cut on the stairs and blood dripped onto the stone floor.

"You lied to me. Infiltrated my group. You used me, betrayed me, used our friendship to clear your name. You walked away, not caring that everything we did was to make the fucking world *better*!"

"Not. The same." He cleared his throat. His body felt like it was on fire and he had little control of his tingling limbs. He tried to get up, but fell back down.

"The senator sees the world as I do. The innocent and the evil. We could have done *great things*!"

"What are you going to do?"

"No one will ever find you, but I promise—everyone who thinks they know you will see you for who you really are. A selfish bastard who cares for no one, cares for *nothing* but himself."

Colton leaned over him. "And if you think we won't get away with it? You're wrong. It's already in motion."

Sean heard Colton walk away, the cage close, the lock turn.

Colton walked up the stairs, turned off the light. Sean laid on the cold stone floor in the dark.

In a cage.

Trapped.

He heard a click above him, then speaker static followed by an odd sound. At first he didn't know what it was. Music? White noise?

No. The sound of rodents scratching on walls. Scurrying around. Faint, intermittent. Sean couldn't see anything in the windowless room, but felt as if animals surrounded him. He tried to tell himself it wasn't real, it was psychological warfare. But his fear grew with every passing minute.

Jonathan left his library while his men removed the body and cleaned the mess.

He shouldn't have killed Hunt. He hadn't planned to kill him until he'd finished setting the plan in motion. His daughter was a problem—a threat, truly, to Lucy—but Jonathan would deal with her accordingly.

No one would hurt Lucy again.

He sat in his small office off his master suite. He'd poured a double Scotch because sleep was always elusive, and a stiff drink before bed helped.

He hadn't done what he needed to do. He hadn't protected his people. He hadn't made it clear to Sean Rogan what he had planned.

But Jimmy Hunt was a problem, and problems needed to be solved.

It was after midnight when a knock on the door disturbed his contemplation.

"Come in."

Colton stepped in. A man who should have been his son.

Jonathan motioned to the bottle of Glenlivet. "Please."

Colton poured himself a single shot, drained it, put the glass down. "Sean attempted to escape. He baited me."

"And?"

"He's in the cage."

"No harm, no foul."

"I should never have reacted. You taught me better than that."

"Sean Rogan always gets under the skin. You are a much better man, and faltering in the face of betrayal? Understandable."

"Are you okay, sir? I spoke to Margery."

"We may not be able to stay under the radar, but we'll be okay. We need to collect Rogan's prints, hair, DNA, everything. Preserve it. Photos. You know what to do. Then tomorrow we'll head for Cape Verde."

"You may never be able to return."

Colton sounded worried, and Jonathan appreciated his loyalty. "I have already liquidated most of my assets. If the government comes after them, they won't find much. Eventually, we'll be able to come and go as we please. But Colton, I need you to listen to me: if anything happens, you and Sergio go to the safe house in Canada. You will have enough resources there for the rest of your lives."

"Don't talk that way. Please."

Jonathan rose, put his hands on Colton's shoulders. "Son, you have made me proud. I would never have been able to accomplish everything I have without you and Sergio by my side. If anything happens to you—my heart will be broken. If I know you're safe, I know you will continue my legacy."

"I'm not leaving without you."

"We'll cross that bridge when we come to it."

Chapter Forty-eight

Elise was angry.

She ditched the van quickly—she wasn't an idiot—and walked half a mile to where she'd stashed her backup car. She headed south; she had a passport under the name Elizabeth Hansen. She was young and cute and figured no one would give her shit.

But she didn't *want* to go to Mexico. She *wanted* to go back to Los Angeles. But now she couldn't. Now she had to go to Mexico and listen to her dad and his stupid mistress Portia go at it day and night because they were horny dweebs. And she didn't like Mexico. She liked California. Or Texas. Or Washington. Or anywhere else in the United States where there was fun and money and people to give both to her. Where people had the money to buy the drugs that her family brought in.

Used to bring in, she reminded herself.

She liked life a lot better when she could do anything she wanted.

How *dare* those cops come in and kill Donny. She'd liked him. He worshipped her. She remembered how Joseph had worshipped Nicole. Of course, Joseph was a lot smarter and meaner than Donny, but Elise would rather have a cute dumb guy do her bidding than a smart ugly guy.

One of her phones rang. It took her a second to fish it out—she had three burn phones. One she should probably toss because it was how Clara and Donny called her. That wasn't ringing; she threw it out the window.

It was the pink phone and she smiled. *Daddy!*

He wasn't going to be happy . . . but she didn't have to tell him everything. Yet.

"Hi, Daddy!" She sounded as cheerful as she could be.

"It's Travis."

"Oh."

Travis was okay. He'd been around a long time.

"I just texted you our location. This job has gone south real quick. Jimmy was supposed to meet us two hours ago."

"What happened? Where is he?"

"He went for a meeting with this guy named Colton and his partner, the moneybags. He didn't come back and I can't reach him on his phone."

"What about getting paid?"

"Don't know."

She looked at the text message. "Where's Montgomery?"

"Texas."

"No shit, how far from San Antonio?" She was nearly to Austin.

"Couple hours. Maybe three."

"See you in three—"

"Be careful here, this guy has fucking armed soldiers patrolling and I'm getting a real bad vibe."

"I'm always careful, *sugar.*"

She ended the call. She wasn't concerned about any of that. She would assess the situation and could play any part she needed. Seductive slut, or sweet innocent schoolgirl. She'd know exactly what to do when she met Mr. Moneybags himself.

She typed the address into her GPS. Two hours, thirty-one minutes.

She started cruising, then saw a sign for food. She was *starving*.

Everyone could just chill. She needed to eat, she needed to sleep, and then she'd decide whether to go rescue her dad . . . or maybe just drive down to Mexico, kill the bitch who was screwing her father, and relax by the pool until her daddy got there. She could just say she didn't know where Portia was, she wasn't here when she arrived, act all innocent and whatnot.

Her dad was usually good at getting out of his own messes.

Chapter Forty-nine

Kane and Jack waited until Dyson arrived at the safe house and then he and Ranger escorted Peter Blair to the border. Jack couldn't wait to get him into the system, and hopefully they'd lose him somewhere in a maximum security facility. He had no guilt that Kane had lied to Blair about letting him go. They had at least enough evidence for the feds to make a run at him, and if they failed to make the case, Kane would follow through on the whisper campaign to discredit him.

As soon as they left, Kane and Jack headed to Ebano. They didn't trust Blair, not 100 percent, but they had confirmed through another source that Portia Ortiz owned a club in the small tourist area. Ebano wasn't even a town—it was a community across the lake from Santiago. Hotels, resorts, restaurants, a few estates. She lived in a spread in the hills with a view of the lake. They couldn't easily get the property records, but assumed that Hunt owned it under a shell corp or a fake identity.

The Santiago area, southeast of Monterrey, was relatively safe compared to other areas of Mexico. They prided themselves on their tourist trade, so it benefited them to keep crime low through an active law enforcement presence. That presence might hinder them from grabbing Hunt when he arrived. Jack wanted to do this quick and efficiently.

They watched the house for an hour early that morning, before the sun came up. No movement, but that wasn't surprising. According to Kane's contact, Portia Ortiz worked at the club every night. She was well-liked and had grown the business over the last two years.

Interesting, Jack thought. Two years ago was when Hunt had been extradited to the U.S. He'd been located in Sayulita, close to Puerto Vallarta, living quite well while in hiding.

They didn't have the time to run a full background on Ortiz, but they learned enough—including the fact that she'd been a waitress in Sayulita up until two years ago and was currently thirty-one years of age. So Hunt gave her what? Money? Contacts? Had she moved here on her own . . . or had Hunt set her up? How loyal was she?

"I have an idea," Jack said. "What if we can gain her cooperation?"

"What incentive?"

"Hunt is more than twenty years her senior. What if she hooked up with him to get out of a crappy life? She's been on her own for two years, living well, enjoying her club and her freedom. Let's approach this differently."

"Or she could play along and shoot us in the back."

"I'll do the talking, you listen."

"Don't get dead."

"Not today."

They approached the property. There were no external cameras, but the house had a security system. If she called the police, they were screwed—though they could probably disappear faster than the cops could arrive. It was a risk, but between what they'd learned of her past and from their local contact, Jack thought this was the right approach.

It was early in the morning—six o'clock now, the sun just starting to creep up on the horizon. He left Kane in a closer hiding spot, hid his own weapon, and rang the bell.

Several minutes later, a sleepy female voice said through a speaker in the door, "It's the middle of the night! You think I'm stupid enough to open this door to a strange man?"

"Ms. Ortiz, my name is Jack Kincaid, and I have a proposition for you."

"I'm not interested."

"I'm friends with Raul Gomez."

Gomez was Kane's contact. He owned a resort and was one of the wealthiest people in town. Plus, his brother was a priest at the local church and between the two of them, they did what they could to keep the cartels out of the area.

"You have thirty seconds. I'm not opening the door. I have a gun."

"Yes, ma'am. Your friend Jimmy Hunt has claimed that this is his safe house. He hired a man by the name of Peter Blair to kidnap my partner and bring him here, and Jimmy is supposed to arrive later today. He broke out of prison, so we have every reason to believe he's telling the truth. Blair failed in his mission and is currently in the custody of U.S. Border Control and will be turned over to the proper authorities."

"What's all this to me?"

"The question to you is this: do you want this house and your club all to yourself, or do you want Jimmy Hunt to share in the fruits of your labor? Because we can take him off your hands the easy way or the hard way. Easy?

You help us, we don't care how you got this house or the club. Hard? We take him anyway when he arrives, and notify the authorities that his illegally gotten gains bought this place and your club, in an effort to hide his money from the U.S. government."

There was a long pause and for a moment Jack thought she might be calling the police. Then two locks clicked, and the door opened. Portia Ortiz was a stunningly beautiful woman.

She smiled. "I always like to do things the easy way. I have one request."

"Of course."

"You take Jimmy, you take his insane daughter, too."

Thirty minutes later, Kane and Jack were having coffee in Portia's kitchen. She put out fruit and pastries as well.

"You don't have to feed us," Jack said.

"Nonsense," Kane said. "I'm starving."

Portia laughed. "I don't work Sundays; it is my day to sleep. But this is more interesting."

"When was the last time you talked to Jimmy?"

"He sent me a message yesterday. After he escaped. I know he's still in Texas, said he had to be paid the rest of his money, then he would be down later today." She sat down and poured herself fresh-squeezed orange juice. "I do not know why Jimmy has not returned my message. He always does."

Jack had asked her to send him a message—something that wouldn't arouse his suspicion.

"Will this put you in a difficult situation?"

"No. Jimmy is a . . . what do you say, a *buffoon*. I would have left him, but he had his moments. And he was very generous." She smiled slightly. "So, he liked sex a lot, who doesn't? With sex came . . ." She waved her hands to indicate the house. A house that was spacious and well-appointed. "When he was arrested, he told me he'd bought this place, gave me the codes and banking information. I never expected him to get out of prison—I knew he had done many crimes. I helped myself to some of his money, bought my club—it is *my* club, not Jimmy's—and it is doing very well. He doesn't need to know that I don't need him, it's better this way."

Sly woman.

"I don't know why he doesn't respond. He said he would send a message when he was leaving. He is very particular about these things."

Kane asked, "Do you know who helped him escape? He had to have someone funding him, unless he had a stockpile of money that wasn't seized by the U.S. government."

"All his money is here, with me. And it is small compared to what he had before. But I don't need much."

"So you don't know who helped him?

"Oh, yes, of course I do. Jimmy, he likes to talk, but he can't tell his daughter anything. She has no, what do you say, *control*. He only has me. He says he loves me, but he said he loved me when he still had a wife. It's the way he is. Last year he was approached by someone who works for a very important man, a senator."

"A *United States* senator?" Jack said.

"Sí. He asked for a favor, Jimmy says yes, asks for a favor back. An advance, I believe. Money to help him get revenge." She looked at Kane. "You killed his son."

Kane tensed next to Jack. "I did," he said.

"Thank you. Tobias was evil and stupid. I was fearful. I made sure I was never alone with him, the way he looked at me . . ." She shivered. "He hurt a lot of people."

Jack went back to the senator comment. "Do you know the senator's name?"

"No, I'm sorry. Jimmy only called him the senator. But

his employee, the man who met with Jimmy in prison, his name is Colton. I never was told his last name."

"Colton Thayer?" Jack asked.

"I do not know. He only called him Colton. He said he was, umm, a geek. I wasn't quite sure what that meant, but I assume unflattering."

Jack turned to Kane. "This is confirmation that Paxton is behind this." Megan had told him of Lucy's theory, but they had no evidence. "But how in the hell is Colton Thayer working for him?"

"Colton was Sean's best friend for years," Kane said. "The question is, *why* would Colton work for Paxton against Sean?"

Jack didn't like what he was thinking. "Sean infiltrated Colton's hacker group. The FBI investigation when he went undercover in New York."

"Why the hell aren't both Thayer and Paxton in prison?"

"Paxton cut a deal, and Thayer—I don't know."

"We have to tell Rick," Kane said. "Even if he knows, we have to make sure he understands the seriousness of this situation. Friendships like Sean and Colton's are once in a lifetime—like falling in love. And when someone is betrayed, it can turn dark, real fast."

"Umm, Mr. Rogan? Mr. Kincaid?"

They turned to Portia.

"I have Colton's numbers. Would you like them?"

Chapter Fifty

Lucy was losing her patience.

The information Kane and Jack got from Hunt's mistress was invaluable, but it didn't tell them where Jonathan Paxton was right now. Rick Stockton was working on getting a warrant to trace Colton Thayer's cell phones—Portia had three numbers for him. Lucy wanted to bypass all the rules because she feared for Sean's life.

At the same time, she didn't want to break the rules in a criminal investigation where Thayer and Paxton might walk free on a technicality.

Lucy didn't want to believe everything Dillon had said last night, but after two hours of restless sleep, she woke knowing he was right. Jonathan had a twisted belief that she was his daughter—or *should* be his daughter. Jack reminded her that Jonathan had called her his daughter when she and Sean were missing in New York. He'd called her Monique to her face on more than one occasion. She'd cut him out of her life three years ago . . . what had that done to him? Did it twist him further? Allow him to create a fantasy world?

He was a brilliant man on many levels. Smart, shrewd, educated. He'd been a powerful senator and politician. He had men and women at his beck and call, available to do his bidding. To take the fall for his crimes. To kill for him, like Michael Thompson.

Did Colton hate Sean so much that he was willing to kill him? They had been best friends . . . was it a case where love turned to hate? Where respect turned to contempt?

Sean only told Lucy that his visit with Colton after the shit hit the fan in New York hadn't gone well.

"I betrayed him, Lucy. I lied to him. It was the only way to catch Paxton . . . but he had been my closest friend for so long. My only real friend after everything that happened at Stanford. And he'll never understand why."

Colton must have no idea that it was Sean who kept him out of prison. He pleaded with Rick Stockton not to send him away, and Rick agreed to probation.

She'd hoped that at some point, Sean could try again with Colton, but when she mentioned it Sean said it was impossible. So she dropped it, then they moved to San Antonio and never talked about it again.

A loud knock on the hotel door made her jump. She walked into the living area but Patrick was already answering the door, his gun in hand.

It was John Banner. He held up his badge to Patrick. "Are you Patrick Kincaid?"

"Yes."

"What the hell are you doing interfering with my investigation?"

"What investigation?"

Banner tried to step inside, but Patrick blocked him. "Can I come in?"

"No."

"You're obstructing justice."

"Arrest me."

"Are you all this way?"

"All who?"

"Fuck! You talked to one of my witnesses yesterday. You're interfering with my investigation."

"You closed the investigation. You arrested Sean and didn't follow up with the witness. That's on you."

"He came down to the station yesterday because *you* talked to him. He said he was afraid we'd tried to talk to him but couldn't find him on campus and he wanted to do the right thing. Did you pay him off?"

"You can go."

"I'm serious! Because all of the sudden there's another suspect? He *saw* someone coming from Hill's apartment?"

"He didn't see her leaving the apartment, but she passed him in the hall from the direction of the apartment."

"Did you coach him?"

Patrick started to close the door.

"Dammit, this is fucking a mess, Kincaid! I have a cop killer on the loose and the FBI arrested my witness!"

"The escape is not your case," Patrick said. "And Sean Rogan is not a cop killer. Your rhetoric is going to get him killed. You don't want the truth. You have a fucking theory you want to prove."

"I want justice."

"So do we."

Megan came out of her room, her hair damp, but she was dressed. "What is all this yelling?" She straightened when she saw Banner. "Detective."

Banner ignored her. "Do you realize that withholding information in a police investigation can get you tossed in prison?"

"I'm not withholding information. I told Ned that a detective may come and speak to him as they continue to investigate Mona Hill's murder. It's not my responsibility to do your job for you."

"Yet you think your friend is innocent."

"My partner. My brother-in-law. And he is. And the fact that you bought into this so quickly tells me either you're corrupt or an idiot."

Lucy stepped forward. "Patrick, stop."

"If you know where the escaped prisoners are, you have an obligation to notify authorities."

"I don't know where Sean is, and if I did, I would notify the authorities, but sure as hell not you because I don't trust you won't shoot first, ask questions later. Maybe you should read Kate Donovan's reports on this, because she's been copying in your office from the beginning."

Banner looked confused. Then he said, "Take my advice and back off."

"Good-bye." Patrick closed the door.

"What was that?" Megan said.

"He's a prick. And if he hasn't read Kate's reports that's on him."

Kate had been sending frequent reports as she confirmed facts. She confirmed that the phone found in Sean's cell was *not* used to change the transfer orders. She located the exact terminal where the transfer orders were changed, and had proven that Sheffield had used the terminal at the time the orders were changed. They had Erica Anderson's statement that she had been working for the Hunt family for the last three months but when she heard a cop was killed during the prison break, she wanted to come forward—but feared for her life and the life of her children. And Kate had sent Erica's statement to Houston that she planted the gun in Sean's plane. And yet here they were, still thinking that Sean was guilty.

Sheffield hadn't spoken since asking for his lawyer, but that wouldn't last long, and Anderson was already on record. All that information Kate had shared with every law enforcement agency investigating either Mona Hill's murder or the prison break. She wanted to make sure that the authorities knew that Sean was a victim, not a perpetrator.

All this was great news, but it still didn't help them find Sean.

"Where *is* Kate?" Lucy asked.

"Houston headquarters. She slipped out early this morning—she's calling now." Megan answered. "Kate, you're on speaker with me, Lucy, and Patrick."

"I might have found Paxton."

"Where?"

"Jack and Kane made friends with Hunt's mistress. She shared all her financial records with them. Including recent payments. He was paid $150,000 last summer, then $150,000 three weeks ago—the day after Elise Hunt was released from juvie. Portia said that Elise took all the second payment for what she called 'Operation Payback.' Hunt was supposed to collect the final payment yesterday after the escape, but no money has been wired."

"How does that help us find them?" Lucy asked.

"The money came from a shell corp. It took me and the two best people in the white-collar crime unit a couple of hours to trace it. It's the parent company of the shell corp that paid Michael Thompson."

"You connected Paxton to Thompson? On paper?"

"No, because I don't have a connection between these shell corps and Paxton, but we connected one of them to Colton Thayer and found property in the corporation's name in Montgomery, Texas."

"That's less than an hour away," Lucy said.

"Rick thinks it's actionable, we're putting together an FBI SWAT and hostage rescue team right now. We're not informing Houston PD. They have been riding our ass about Sheffield, and we're not budging. Rick and I both think someone will get trigger-happy. They are looking for two escaped convicts. We know Sean's innocent but it still looks bad right now."

"What about the tape from the bus?" Lucy asked. Someone had shot out the cameras on the bus, but techs were working on salvaging the tapes.

"We're working on it. I don't want to get your hopes up, not until I know whether we have the potential to retrieve the data or not. It's seriously damaged. I'm going to go back and take another run at Sheffield, he might know more than he's said."

"I need to be part of the raid," Lucy said.

"No."

"If Jonathan Paxton is there, I'm the only one who can talk to him. You heard Dillon last night. Jonathan thinks of me as his daughter. He framed Sean because he thinks Sean is bad for me. Everything he did, he did because of *me*. I don't want anyone else to die. There's been too much bloodshed, both the guilty and the innocent."

"Don't let them know I told you that they're staging at headquarters right now and ETA to leave is twenty-two minutes."

Patrick said, "Go, Lucy." He looked at Megan.

"I got her," Megan said and followed Lucy out.

It was Rick Stockton who gave the okay for Lucy to join the team. Her phone rang as soon as they started toward Montgomery.

"Kincaid," she answered.

"It's Stockton. Don't make me regret this. Not only is your job on the line, but mine as well."

She swallowed heavily. "I—I truly appreciate this."

"I sensed you think that I believed Sean was guilty. I never did. Sean drives me crazy sometimes, but he's one of the best men I know, and I am destroyed that he's gone through this. I helped negotiate the pleas for Paxton and Thayer to keep them out of prison. Paxton because he would have really screwed the FBI and a multitude of cases, it would have been a fucking nightmare with all the legalities, lawsuits from families of the sex offenders, and more. And Thayer, because of Sean. He pleaded with me to find a way to give him probation or time served. I know that Sean felt guilty for infiltrating Thayer's organization, his past friendship, everything they'd been through together—all that played into it. I shouldn't have done it, I was wrong. I might have lost Sean's respect and friendship, but Thayer should have gone to prison. I made a mistake."

"No, Rick, you did the right thing. You were between a rock and a hard place with Paxton because of who he was and what he'd done . . . and Thayer did the wrong thing for the right reason. They both could have started fresh, done something good with their lives; instead, Paxton used Thayer to fulfill his vendetta against Sean."

"I talked to Dillon and while I know you and your brother believe that Paxton won't harm you, don't go in thinking you're bulletproof. He's working with Jimmy Hunt, which tells me he's a changed man. The Jonathan Paxton I knew would have killed Hunt before he worked with him."

"Or," Lucy said, "used him before he killed him."

After ending the call with Rick, Lucy spent the rest of the drive convincing the lead agent, SSA Steven Pierce, to let her go in alone.

The only reason he finally—reluctantly—agreed was because he didn't want bodies to drop. No one in the FBI wanted another Waco or Ruby Ridge. They wanted a peaceful resolution without an armed standoff, especially when they didn't know how many hostiles or hostages were on site.

And thank God they considered Sean a hostage, not a hostile. That was because of Rick, Lucy was positive, because Sean's name hadn't been cleared by Houston PD.

"He's going to know we're out here," Pierce said.

"Yes. I'm going to tell him, but he'll know as soon as he sees me. I'm going to explain to him that the only way this ends is with him surrendering."

"You think that will work?"

"It's the only way it'll work. If we storm in, we put Sean in jeopardy."

"You need to be wired and wear a vest."

"Agreed."

"If I think it's going south, we're coming in hot."

"I understand." She hoped it didn't come to that. "I'm going to try to get Jonathan to tell me where Sean is— you might be able to rescue him while I keep Jonathan occupied."

"We're working on disabling the cameras, but if they have someone monitoring the feeds they're going to notice a change, even if we loop it. When we get them down, we'll move into a closer position."

Lucy took a deep breath. This was it. She couldn't screw up.

Jonathan Paxton watched as Elise ate a full brunch as if she'd missed a week of meals.

He didn't want to kill her. When she showed up early this morning, Colton wanted to turn her away, but Jonathan didn't trust her. She hated Lucy; he wanted to know why.

Sadly, if she was a threat to Lucy, she would have to die. But he couldn't help but see her as a young girl, raised by brutes, abused, unschooled in proper behavior.

He wasn't ignorant of her crimes. He'd read her files—all of them. He'd read Lucy's testimony against her. But he wondered if Lucy herself was a tad biased against Elise because of who her family was. That, perhaps, Elise was a victim who only did what she had to do to survive.

Lucy, of all people, should understand that.

"Wow, Senator, that was delicious," she said.

"I'm glad you enjoyed it." He sipped his coffee. He'd eaten long ago.

"So, my dad."

"He left for Mexico last night."

"Really? When? Because when Travis called me he said he was supposed to bring them."

"Late." He'd found out about Travis's call to Elise after the fact. The men loyal to Hunt were no longer a problem. "If I recall, your father instructed you to meet him there."

"Yeah, well, I don't do everything he says. And I don't like his girlfriend."

"You had an unusual childhood."

"You're telling me. My aunt Margaret was crazy. She liked me, though I don't know why, considering her sister screwed my dad and got me out of it. But she was like, you're the daughter I never had, blah blah. And my mom was just . . . a wacko. I don't think there was a day she wasn't high."

"You've done some bad things."

She shrugged. "You do what you need to do, right?" She picked at crumbs on her plate and looked at him. "I should probably go now. If my dad isn't here, I'll catch up with him across the border."

"You can stay for a while if you like."

She snorted. "Not. I mean, you're nice and all, and this place is fucking *amazing*, but I should probably disappear for a while."

"Did you do something for which you need to disappear?"

"Sort of. Sometimes I really hate it when my dad's right."

"Dads usually know what's best."

"Not always. But this time, I should have listened to him. I wonder if I'll ever figure out when his advice is bad or on target."

Jimmy Hunt wouldn't be giving anyone any advice again.

"Your father's plans for the Rogans. Did something happen?"

"Well, I know they got Kane. He killed my brother. I miss Toby. I kind of screwed up with Agent Donnelly. He killed my sister. I liked her, she was smart. That's kinda why I have to disappear for a while."

"They saw you."

"Well, yeah. But I always have a backup plan."

"Smart. Your father wasn't happy when I took Sean off his target list."

"I don't care. Dad said you wanted to take care of him yourself, fine by me. He didn't kill anyone I care about, and he's really smart. Totally fooled my sister and everyone. I kinda think that's cool."

"And Lucy Kincaid. You know she's off-limits."

"Yeah, of course. But why?" she asked bluntly.

He admired that directness. "I have history."

"You screwing her?"

He bristled, forced himself to remain calm at the disgusting image Elise put in his head. "No. I'd like to know why you don't like her."

"She can read my mind. It freaks me out."

"She reads your mind?"

"Yeah. Like a psychic. She knows exactly what I'm

thinking. And, like, how I think. She got me all twisted up when she interviewed me and I didn't know what I was saying. Because she, like, had it all down already." She frowned. "I'm not making any sense."

"I think I understand you."

He remembered her conversation with her father. Would she go after Lucy when she realized her father was dead? Could he risk it?

Elise Hunt wasn't a good kid, but she was practically a child. He didn't want to kill her.

"If you'd like to stay, you can. Even just for tonight." That would give him some time to ponder the situation. "I might have a job for you."

"Really?" she perked up. Then she shook her head. "I appreciate it and all, but I need to go."

"Of course." He didn't have much time to make his decision.

"But can I have a favor?"

"What do you need?"

"I don't know how hot my car is, and I'm really low on cash. When I was low on cash before my brother told me to just sell my body, but I don't really want to do that anymore if I don't have to."

Jonathan saw red. "You do not have to ever sell your body."

"I don't need a lot. My dad got paid, he'll take care of me once I get there."

Colton walked into the doorway, worried. He motioned for Jonathan.

"Excuse me," he said to Elise. "I'll see what I can do about a vehicle and spending money."

He left the room with Colton. Colton said quietly, "Lucy Kincaid is at the main gate."

"Alone?"

"I don't see anyone, but I told Team Alpha to broaden the perimeter and check for mercenaries. If she came in with RCK she might be a diversion."

"No. She came with the FBI."

"How do you know?"

He knew because he knew Lucy. "I need you to leave. You know how to go. You have been the son I never had, I do not want you hurt by what's about to happen."

"I'm not leaving you, Jonathan. We can get out of this."

"There's a chance they are bluffing, a good chance. I will know when I talk to her. But I'm not going to risk you."

"What about her?" he nodded toward the dining room.

"Give her a car and a thousand dollars. If she can elude the FBI, she'll make it to Mexico. If not, it's not my problem."

The gate opened ten minutes after she stood there, making sure the camera could see her. Lucy walked in. No one was around. As soon as she stepped through, the gate closed, the *click* of an electronic lock sealing her in.

She wasn't truly trapped. This was a vast estate and there were ways to get out—the rear boundary was trees and a seasonal creek—and the fencing was scalable in places.

"I'm through the gate," she said. "I don't see anyone, but I feel someone watching. Okay, now I see him, an armed man to my right standing between two trees. He's not making a move toward me."

She continued walking down a long gravel drive. The house came into view, a beautiful estate, far too big for one person. Even her entire family—parents and six brothers and sisters—would find the house spacious.

It took her ten minutes to reach the porch, and she didn't see anyone else until she started up the stairs and spotted two men, one on each side of the porch, standing sentry. They ignored her.

An older woman, impeccably dressed, opened the door before Lucy knocked. "The senator is expecting you," she said.

Lucy entered; the woman closed the door behind her.

She looked around her surroundings. The entry was large, with a sweeping staircase. A grand room to the left seemed to be a sitting room with one wall of bookshelves; the room to the right an even grander living room, everything decorated in traditional American. It was a comfortable house, even with the vast spaces.

But she stared at the fireplace in the living room.

And the painting above it.

She froze.

That's me.

"The senator lost his daughter thirty years ago," the housekeeper said. "She was lovely."

Yes, it was Monique, but it was also Lucy. Lucy had seen pictures of Monique, but not this one—she wondered if Jonathan had commissioned it based on both her and Monique's photos. Monique died when she was seventeen, this was Monique . . . older. It was the eyes . . . Monique's eyes were more catlike and a lighter brown than Lucy's. They had almost identical wavy long black hair and the same general build, similar cheekbones, and proportions, and Monique's paler skin was reflected in the painting. But Lucy's eyes were dark brown and rounder, and those were the eyes that stared back at her.

That was the moment Lucy realized the depth of Jonathan Paxton's obsession with her.

"Agent Kincaid," the woman said. "This way, please."

Lucy followed the woman past the grand staircase and to the left. The hall was wide; to the left were windows that looked out on a courtyard. At the end of the hall, double doors led to a library.

It was one of the most beautiful rooms she had ever seen.

And standing there in the middle of the room, in front of a large wood desk, was the former senator.

"Lucy," he said. "I should be surprised, but I'm not. You are, truly, one of the most intelligent, insightful people I've ever met."

"I came for Sean."

"Please sit," he said, motioning to one of the couches that sat, face to face, in front of a two-story window. "I'd like to talk."

She weighed her options: be forceful and demanding or listen and be ready to act.

Dillon had always told her that she could learn more about a psychopath by being observant.

Watching, listening, sensing his physical response. Tension, relaxation. Sociopaths are liars by nature but everyone—even the best sociopath—has a tell. Mostly, listen. They want to be understood, accepted, revered.

And for Jonathan Paxton, he wanted her love.

She sat on the couch that faced the door. There was another door, smaller, almost hidden, embedded between two built-in bookshelves. She could see that from here as well. Plus she had a line of sight outside the windows. She saw no one.

But someone was watching. Another bodyguard? Colton Thayer?

She sat. She was armed; no one had searched her. She would have given up her gun if they had. But Jonathan must know she was armed. And he also must know that she didn't come alone. Yet he was calm, almost at peace.

A sliver of fear worked its way up her spine.

Is Sean already dead?

She almost pulled her gun and demanded to see her husband. But she didn't. She sat quietly, waiting for Jonathan to talk.

To listen. To assess. To find the truth.

"I have missed you, Lucy," he said. "I hate how we left things."

"Jonathan," she said, using his first name for the first time. She'd always called him senator, out of respect and position. But they were peers now. "I admired you, believed in you. You used me and betrayed my trust. That is why I walked away."

"I never wanted to hurt you, Lucy. It pains me that I did."

"I believe you. What is it called, the law of unintended consequences? Yet, I can't imagine that you could think that I would accept murder. You hid that from me because you knew I wouldn't participate; that I would in fact turn you in."

"Would you have?"

"Yes."

"The system is broken. You and I both know that."

"No. The system is imperfect, not broken."

He leaned back on the couch, as if they were having a philosophical discussion over a glass of wine, and there wasn't an imprisoned man somewhere in this compound, or an FBI SWAT team surrounding the place.

He didn't live in reality.

"Shouldn't we do everything in our power to fix what's *imperfect*?"

"At what cost?"

"What is the cost of a rapist going free versus his death? Should other women suffer a horrific fate because the system released a predator early?"

"When you were a prosecutor, you lobbied for tougher penalties for sex offenders. You won many battles. That's where our focus needs to be. But deciding the law is wrong—and it might be—and then creating your own laws and executing them—where does it end?"

"In justice."

"No. It's not justice. It's vengeance. It's a slippery slope to anarchy."

"An eye for an eye."

"And you are destroying your own soldiers. I talked to Michael Thompson. He didn't betray you—he's a true believer. He is so filled with pain over the loss of his daughter that he is but a shell of a man. A steel shell, fighting your battles."

"They are his battles."

"He should have gotten help. He's still suffering, every day. He lost the most precious thing in the world to him, his daughter, to an evil predator who should have been locked up. Yes, the system fails. I hate that it does. But *you* destroyed Michael's soul."

"Had someone killed the evil that raped and murdered little Sarah when he first committed his heinous acts, she would still be alive. She would be graduating from high school this year."

This was where Jonathan could sway her. The old adage, if you could go back in time and kill baby Hitler, would you? Who said no?

It wasn't an argument she could win with him so she said, "I am working within the system to change it."

"A noble, if imperfect, calling."

"I take pleasure in putting bad guys behind bars. Criminals like Jimmy Hunt. While I wasn't a part of his investigation, I helped take down his criminal network and I'm damn proud of that."

He didn't say anything.

"You worked with Hunt for the last year to orchestrate

this plan, and I don't understand why. You, of all people, working with someone like Jimmy Hunt."

"I would consider the relationship akin to, say, a criminal informant."

"Who has his own twisted way of looking at the world. And you helped him escape from prison."

"Did I?"

"Don't lie to me, Jonathan. Do you remember Kate Donovan?"

"Of course. She married your brother, didn't she?"

"She's traced your shell corporations. She's brilliant, and more, she's determined. So we can prove that—financially—you gave $300,000 in two installments to Jimmy Hunt. We've traced the money that Michael Thompson was paid. We know, for example, that you've created a trust for his other daughter and paid into it every year that he has been working for you. We know that Colton Thayer works for you. We know that he met with Jimmy Hunt at Victorville prison. We're getting the surveillance logs from Houston for the visitors that Michael Thompson had—we have the names, and one name is, not surprisingly, fake. My guess? It's Colton. It's only a matter of time and persistence before I find the truth. And I will."

She was bluffing on the Thompson surveillance. Houston didn't have video surveillance from a year ago. Victorville did and Megan had already requested it. Colton made one big mistake—he used the same false ID both times, but she didn't say that.

Wisely, Jonathan didn't speak.

She said, "Why, Jonathan? Even though we had differences, I never thought you'd hurt me."

"I would never hurt you. Lucy, please don't think that Sean's crimes had anything to do with you."

"Are you really going to play that game? Sean didn't kill Mona Hill; we now have evidence. A witness who saw Elise Hunt. The woman who planted the gun in Sean's plane confessed. Sean didn't set up the escape; we have evidence that it came from a corrections officer in Beaumont. Kate proved the phone in Sean's cell was a plant, that it wasn't used to hack into the system. Sean didn't kill the guard in the bus; we will have the evidence because the best people in the FBI are working on retrieving the corrupted digital files. Everything on that bus was recorded. So I ask you, Jonathan, why did you want to punish *me*?"

"Sean does not deserve you."

"Shouldn't I be the judge of that?"

"Sometimes, our children are blind to the truth."

"I am *not* your child."

He stared at her. There was pain and heartbreak and more in his eyes. She shielded her empathy for him. She'd always empathized with Jonathan because he lost his daughter. Because he understood things about her that she had only been figuring out when she was in college. She missed her past relationship with the senator she admired so much . . . but he was gone. Had it all been a lie?

"You will be better off without him. I know it'll hurt for a while, but you're strong, Lucy. You're a survivor."

Her fear grew exponentially. "Where is Sean? Jonathan! What did you do to my husband?"

Lucy heard laughter. She had been so focused on Jonathan that she hadn't heard the door open; neither had he.

She turned and couldn't have been more surprised to see Elise Hunt walk in. She had a gun and she aimed it right at Lucy.

Chapter Fifty-one

"Hello!" Elise said with false cheerfulness. Or maybe it was real. Lucy wasn't sure.

Jonathan said, "This is a private conversation, Ms. Hunt."

Didn't he see the gun in her hand?

Why wasn't he surprised to see Elise?

Lucy was missing something.

"First, this is just so *rich* to have you both here. I gotta tell you, Lucy, he really, really, *really* hates Sean. Maybe even more than my daddy and my daddy really hated Sean, too. Sometimes, I think my daddy hated Sean more for stealing our money than he hated Kane for killing my brother."

"Put the gun down, Elise, and we can have a conversation," Lucy said. She spoke distinctly, hoping the FBI who were listening to this conversation would realize that they were in a volatile situation. Elise was not someone who could be reasoned with.

"Right . . . put it down. Sure." She rolled her eyes. "I hate you," she said to Lucy.

Then she turned to Jonathan. "But I hate you more. You killed my daddy. You know how I know? Because it's all on tape. I knew something was wrong when I got here, but couldn't figure it out. Maybe because you were being all nice to me. Maybe because you kept asking me what I thought of *her*." She waved her gun toward Lucy. "And then about your arrangement with Daddy, and I remembered my conversation yesterday. And how he promised to let me kill her once we got everything settled down. Then I saw all the cameras and the security and your guy seemed . . . just *off*. Like he couldn't quite look at me. I thought he might kill me, but he didn't seem to have it in him. He seemed more . . . sad. So I started looking around and found the security room. You actually have a camera in here." She looked around and then grinned. "There, right? I know from the angle because I saw you stab my daddy in the stomach, you fucking prick. Why? Didn't want to pay him what you owed him?"

"What did you do to Colton, Ms. Hunt?"

Jonathan sounded so calm, didn't he see that Elise was extremely volatile?

"'What did you do to Colton, Ms. Hunt?'" she mimicked. "*I* didn't do anything. *You're* the one who told him to give me the car."

"What does that mean, Elise?" Lucy asked.

"You can read my mind," Elise said. "You tell me."

Lucy didn't have control of this situation, and Elise was angry and . . . lost. She didn't know what to do, Lucy realized. She had depended her entire life on first Tobias then Jimmy telling her what to do. She certainly played her own games—like torturing Brad when she was supposed to kill him—but she always went back to her family.

And now she had no one.

"I think you left Colton unconscious in the garage," Lucy said. She hadn't shot him because Jonathan had too many people around. They would have heard, alerted him.

"See? You *can* read my mind. Fuck, how the hell do you do that?"

"Educated guess."

"No, you did it in court. And when we were talking. You, like, *know* me and, like, don't and it freaks me the fuck out."

"Elise, I know Jonathan hired you to frame Sean for murder. Why Mona Hill?"

"You know why."

"Because she left you behind."

"She abandoned me when I needed her the most. And you know why? Because your husband told her to leave. He *told* her to leave me. And why is that? Because he *blackmailed her*. Prick. Then I get arrested and that sucked. It totally screwed with our plans."

Was that enough? Did the FBI believe based on what Elise said that *she* had been the one to kill Mona, not Sean?

It won't matter if Sean is dead!

Elise said to Jonathan, "You owed my dad a quarter of a million. You were going to give me a fucking *thousand*? Nope. I want the money we were promised. Then I'll get out of your hair."

"All right. I will have Colton transfer it to you."

"Really? Transfer it? You're a fucking *joke*. Like I would *trust you* to *transfer* me the money. Like, tonight? Next week? Never? I'm not an idiot. What do you have in your safe? I know a guy like you will have money in your safe."

She waved the gun around.

Jonathan rose and headed over to a picture embedded in one of the bookshelves.

"Stop," Elise said.

He stopped.

"Lucy, get up."

Lucy rose.

"Together," Elise said, "go over and open the safe. I need to keep you both in my sight."

Elise had a look in her eye.

Lucy followed Jonathan to the safe. "Was this worth it, Jonathan? Was setting Sean up worth all this?"

He looked at her. "Yes. I only regret that I couldn't prove to you that he's no better than any of them." He waved his hand toward Elise.

Elise laughed. "That's funny. Open the safe, Mr. Senator."

Lucy had to call in the FBI. They should be close, if they'd been listening.

Of course they were listening.

She gave the code phrase.

"Jonathan, I love my husband. I will never forgive you."

How long was it going to take? Where were they? How many of Jonathan's men would attempt to stop them?

Jonathan put his finger on the safe and it clicked.

"Back off," Elise said. "How do I know you don't have a gun in there or something?"

She kept her gun aimed at them and walked to the safe. Looked inside. "Wow, fabulous. Good-bye, Lucy."

She pulled the trigger.

The bullet hit Lucy in her chest, pushing her to the ground and knocking the wind out of her. If she hadn't had her vest on, she would have been in serious trouble.

"No!" Jonathan screamed and rushed Elise.

She fired twice, hitting Jonathan both times.

Lucy struggled to pull her gun from her rear holster. She watched as Jonathan staggered backward, his chest red. She aimed at Elise and fired three times in rapid succession. The third bullet hit her in the face.

Elise fell to the floor, dead.

Lucy crawled over to Elise, pushed her gun away though she was clearly dead, then crawled over to Jonathan as she fought to catch her breath.

"Jonathan," she breathed awkwardly. "Stay with me. Oh God, dammit! Where is everybody?"

She put her hands on his chest, trying to stop the blood. His eyes were wide.

"Lucy."

"Where's Sean? Dammit, don't die! Where's Sean? Please, Jonathan—please tell me. I love him so much. Tell me what you did to him."

"You. Don't need him."

His eyes closed.

"Don't you die! Don't you dare die!" She shook him. "Tell me where Sean is!"

"Monique," he whispered. Blood dripped from his mouth. "I love you, Monique. Forgive me."

"No!" she screamed.

She hadn't heard SWAT burst into the house, but they now came through the library doors. Steven Pierce led the team.

"Kincaid! Are you shot?"

"He wouldn't tell me. Dammit! Jonathan!"

One of the cops checked his pulse then shook his head. Lucy jumped up.

"Kincaid, you're bleeding."

"It's his. She shot me in the vest."

It hurt and it would bruise, but it didn't hurt a fraction as much as her heart right now. "We have to find Sean."

Though the radio, Pierce ordered his team to search the grounds for additional hostiles and one hostage.

"We got most of his team, if not all of them. No one engaged us. They put down their weapons as soon as we approached. One unconscious suspect in the garage. We think she hit him with a shovel. One unconscious woman in the kitchen. Ambulance is on their way. Do you need a medic?"

"No. Let me search the house."

"With me," Pierce said.

They started downstairs and were halfway down when Pierce got a call on the radio. "Sir, I found something, come to the gatehouse at the front of the garage stat."

Lucy followed Pierce out and they walked briskly across the courtyard to the gatehouse, right outside the interior gates.

It was a security room. Cameras were everywhere, inside and out, rotating images on four screens. "I don't know how this works, they rotate, but this one"—he pointed to one—"will show what you need to see."

The next thirty seconds nearly killed Lucy as she waited, staring at the screen, as it rotated through five second shots of multiple places on the property.

Then, there was Sean.

He was chained in a prison. An actual cage, somewhere on the property.

Pierce relayed this discovery to his team. No one had found it yet.

"Where's Colton Thayer?" Lucy asked.

"Detained in the garage, we have a man on him," Pierce said.

Lucy went out; Pierce followed. He didn't try to stop her. "We'll find him—there are only so many places he can be."

She went to the garage. Colton was leaning against the wall, eyes closed, blood caked on his head.

He looked at her. "The senator."

"Elise Hunt killed him. Where is Sean?"

He didn't say anything.

"You were his best friend. You did this to him? Locked him in a cage? Framed him for murder? Why?"

"Jonathan loved you, Lucy. He knew you'd be better off without Sean. We all would have been better off without Sean in our lives."

"Revenge. Petty revenge. Hurt feelings. And once you were closer to him than his own brothers. You make me sick."

"I don't know why you love him. Jonathan saw Sean as I did. Selfish and disloyal. Jonathan was a great man. I can't believe he's gone. He's . . ." Colton sighed, put his head down on his knees. Then he said, "There's a basement under the guesthouse. The code on the door is oh-two-one-seven."

Lucy turned, then looked back. "Oh-two-one-seven?"

"Your birthday. Jonathan used it for everything."

She forced that thought out of her mind and followed Pierce across the courtyard and behind the garage to the guesthouse.

She let Pierce go first, though it almost killed her to wait. "Clear," he said.

She ran down the stairs. The basement was dark, a single bulb lighting the narrow hall outside the cage. Sean's ankles were shackled, his hands cuffed, and he was still dressed in the orange prison jumpsuit—it was bloody and filthy. His face was bruised and he was pale. Tears ran down his face when he saw her.

"Lucy?"

"We'll get you out of there."

There was a keypad on the wall. Pierce typed in the code; it worked.

The cage clicked open.

Lucy ran in and hugged him while Pierce looked for a key to get him out of the chains.

She kissed him, held him, started crying.

"I can't believe you're here," he said, holding her.

She had no words. Nothing. "I love you. I love you." It was all she could say, over and over.

Sean broke down sobbing and held her tight.

Chapter Fifty-two

The Houston police had Sean handcuffed to a hospital bed until they were satisfied with the evidence the FBI had retrieved at Jonathan Paxton's estate and the FBI recording from Lucy's wire that Elise admitted she'd killed Mona Hill. They tried to stomp their feet and demand an investigation into the other claims Elise made about Sean letting Mona escape and blackmailing her, but Steven Pierce got them to stand down. Lucy greatly appreciated his efforts.

Kate finally convinced Sheffield to tell the truth about the shooting in the van, so Sean was cleared of escaping from custody and killing a cop. That, coupled with Erica Anderson's testimony, fully cleared him.

On Monday morning, Nate drove Jesse to see Sean in the hospital. Sean hadn't wanted Jesse to see him hurt, but Lucy told Sean that they both needed each other.

She was right.

That night, when Sean was released from the hospital, Patrick and Nate drove everyone back to San Antonio, except for Kate, who stayed in Houston to help wrap up the reports with Houston PD and the FBI. There was a lot to do and Kate would be there all week making sure that Sean was completely cleared by all law enforcement authorities—as well as making sure that the media reported on it so a private citizen didn't see him and pull a gun, thinking Sean was still a wanted fugitive.

When they arrived home that night, Jack and Kane were already at the house along with Siobhan. They'd set up a large buffet of food for the group, but Sean said he was tired and wanted to sleep.

"What can I get for you?" Lucy asked him quietly as she helped him up the stairs.

"Nothing. I want to shower. Sleep. Just—go talk to Jack and everyone. Tell them I'm fine."

"You're not fine."

He kissed her. "I will be."

"Do you need help?"

He shook his head. She wanted to help him . . . but maybe he just needed space.

Bandit followed him into their bedroom and Sean closed the door.

Lucy was worried about Sean, but maybe he was right—a shower and sleeping in his own bed was what he needed. He was home safe, and that's what mattered.

She went back downstairs. Siobhan hugged her. "You need food."

"I will. In a minute." She watched as Nate, Patrick, and Jesse all dished up food. They were worried about Sean, too, but now that they were all home the pressure was off.

She sank onto the living room couch and sighed. It had been the worst three days of her life.

Jack sat down next to her. "Hey."

"Hey," she said.

"It's going to be okay."

"I know." She looked up the stairs. "He's safe, he's alive, but I'm worried about him."

"He has you, Lucy. He needs some time to process all of this. I can stay as long as you need me."

She took her brother's hand and squeezed it. "You and Megan and Patrick—everyone rallied for Sean. I—" Tears threatened and she didn't want to cry again. She didn't think she'd ever get the sight of Sean in so much pain out of her mind. In a cage. Sobbing, bloodied, nearly broken.

"Family, Lucy. We'll always be here."

Patrick came over and handed Lucy a plate of food. "Eat, or else."

"Yes, sir," she said and smiled. He sat across from her with his own food. "How long can you stay?"

"As long as you want," Patrick said. "But you and Sean might not want a full house."

Jack waved his hand. "This place is huge. There's an apartment over the garage, that's mine and Megan's right now. Kane and Siobhan always take the pool house. Nate practically lives in the downstairs guest room.

"We have another bedroom upstairs," Lucy said. "It's all yours."

Family, Jack had said. And really, that was all anyone needed.

On Tuesday morning, Lucy slipped out while Sean was still sleeping and went to her office.

Rachel, her boss, had insisted.

Nate was also there. Before she went in, she asked, "What happened?"

"Suspended without pay for two weeks. I knew that already, but I had to brief the team on my active cases. I'm fine with it. Honestly, it could have been worse."

"What did you do? You weren't suspended for helping me, were you?"

"No. I disobeyed orders and worked a case after being suspended. The drug case. Seriously, I could have had to go in front of OPR. I could have lost my job. I might the next time."

Lucy was stricken. She knew that was a possibility . . . but she didn't want to think about it. "Nate, I don't know what to say."

"Lucy, it's okay. Aggie and I saved Brad's life, I'd do it all again. In fact, if I lost this job, I'd be okay."

"As long as you're okay," she said, hoping that he wasn't lying to her.

"I am. But what happened to Sean—how everyone here was slapped down if they wanted to help you, I'm *not* okay with that. We have to be there for each other. We're supposed to be a team."

"You are, Nate. I would never have gotten through this without you."

"Something good came out of it."

"What? I can't be happy about all the bloodshed. It didn't have to end that way."

"No, it didn't, but it did and we'll get through it. We saved Brad. He's being released from the hospital tomorrow."

"Good. I'll go over to see him. Is he really okay?"

"I don't know—he has a long road ahead of him. Physical therapy. Plastic surgery. But he's a tough guy. I'll join you when you visit him. Aggie will, too."

"Aggie?"

"That's the good thing that happened. I asked Aggie to go out with me."

She blinked. "Like on a date? You never talk about dating anyone."

He shrugged. "Never found anyone I was interested in enough to share with my friends. She's smart. She's not intimidated by me, she's willing to stand up for what she wants. I like that. She's not perfect—she needs some training."

Lucy started to get angry. *"Training?"*

Nate laughed. "You should see your face. Tactical

training. She's good at the gun range, but she made a tactical error at the house and put herself in the line of fire. Fortunately, she's a quick study and I'll have her up to speed in no time. It'll be fun."

Lucy was embarrassed. "I can't believe I thought anything else."

"She got suspended, too. One week, but with pay—Brad vetoed Salter on that one. We're going to visit her family in Dallas. Flying out tonight. I'm just going to stop by and see Sean again first, make sure he doesn't need anything."

"You're already visiting her family? That was fast."

"Is it?"

"I'm really happy. I like Aggie a lot."

Rachel opened her door. "Lucy."

"It'll be okay," he said.

Lucy walked into Rachel's office and closed the door behind her. "You've already talked to Nate, I see."

"Yes, ma'am."

"Two weeks, unpaid leave. A mark in your file. And OPR wants to interview you."

Her heart sank.

"Sit."

She did.

"I understand that this was an unusual and difficult situation. On the one hand, Houston FBI wrote up an accommodation and I heard the recording. There is nothing wrong with what happened at Paxton's. Except for the fact that you weren't supposed to be there in the first place. If anything had gone wrong—this would be a far more serious conversation.

"The problem is your investigation into Mona Hill's murder. Your brother as well, but he's not an FBI agent, and I have no authority over him. Houston PD is livid. They feel we kept information from them, and that you and your brother interfered with their investigation. You're going to have to answer to OPR on that. This will be your third time in three years in front of them. I think you need to be prepared for the worst."

"Honestly, ma'am, I've already faced the worst."

Rachel rubbed her eyes. "I know. For what it's worth, you don't have to be in D.C. until Friday. They've asked for all your records. Abigail has been talking to some people who have verbally praised your work and asked for a written letter, without saying why. We already have glowing letters from several local law enforcement and she expects more. The head of SAPD SWAT during the hostage situation last year is sending one, and of course the DEA has sent multiple letters over the last two years, every time you've helped. I don't know if the positive commentary is going to sway them, but I hope it does."

"Thank you," Lucy said, surprised.

"This wasn't an easy decision for me, to be honest. Losing both you and Nate for the next two weeks is going to be hard. But . . . take the time to heal. I know these last few days have been hell."

Sean half listened to Kane and Jack tell their tale of Mexico. It sounded interesting, but he was still having a difficult time coming to terms with everything that had happened. He still felt like he was trapped. Even though he was here, at home, with his family and his dog, he felt like he was suffocating. Or in limbo. Definitely not himself.

"Sean," Kane said.

"Hmm?"

"Talk."

"Nothing."

"It's not nothing. You hurting?"

"No." General soreness, cracked ribs, and he still had some bruises that smarted, but he wasn't in pain.

Jack walked out of the sunroom, leaving Sean with his brother. Sean still didn't want to talk about everything that had happened. He stared out the window at the pool. Someone had turned on the waterfall, but Sean really wasn't focused on anything. Bandit was at his feet; his dog hadn't left his side since he came home.

Kane stared at him. "What did he say that has you so twisted inside?"

How did Kane know?

"It's called psychological warfare, Sean."

"It goes back to my deepest fear. That I don't deserve Lucy. That she would be happier—safer—with someone else."

"Oh for shit's sake."

Kane would never understand. And Sean wasn't quite ready to talk about the sound of rodents, the fear of being trapped, helpless.

"Do you think that I *deserve* Siobhan? I can tell you flat-out that I know she'd be safer without me in her life. Does that make me selfish? Maybe it does. Because I pushed her away time and time again because I was worried that I'd get her killed. But dammit, I know she's happy with me. Safety. That's just bullshit. Who the fuck is ever truly safe? We either live big or die small. I see how Lucy looks at you and I know that she loves you. And that is all that fucking matters. She loves you, she's happiest when she's with you, end of story."

"Colton hated me so much that he helped Paxton set this all up. He really hated me. I've never felt it so strongly . . . and it was my fault. I hurt him, and I knew I would hurt him, and I did it anyway. To save my own ass, to save my relationship with Lucy."

"Sean, I've done things I wish I'd done differently. But you can't live in the past with constant regrets. You learn from your mistakes and move on. Colton was no saint, either."

Sean heard Lucy come in through the garage, heard Jack tell her that he was in the sun room. She walked in and Kane stood up. "Talk to your husband," he said and left.

Lucy sat next to him on the couch and kissed him. "What's wrong?"

He didn't want to talk about it. "What happened at work?"

"Two weeks unpaid vacation," she said, trying to make light of it. "And we get to visit Patrick and Dillon and everyone in D.C. this weekend."

"OPR?"

"It'll be fine."

"What if it's not?"

"Then it's not."

"How can you be okay with this? You didn't do anything wrong."

"I'm okay. Nate's okay. But you're not. Talk to me."

He didn't say anything for a long minute. He just held her, the woman he had loved from the day they met. "Mona Hill's murder and the jailbreak and killing the guard wasn't enough. Paxton didn't know if all that would destroy me or make you think that I was bad for you. They had another plan. Colton was going to frame me for a major cyber breach—then confess that he helped me with the crime. And the crime was something he and I had talked about in college. Something we had wanted to do . . . and he had a record of our planning. He was willing to lie because Paxton asked him to . . . and because Colton hated me so much he wanted to hurt me. And this was how to hurt me. To destroy me in your eyes."

His voice cracked. He couldn't bear to think about what might have happened if he didn't have family and friends. If Paxton had killed him first, set him up later. If Lucy believed the lies . . . the frame . . . because it was so well done.

"I will always believe you, Sean. *Always*. Paxton was obsessed with me—I didn't believe Dillon when he said it, then I saw the portrait of me on his wall. It hit me. You are not to blame. For any of this."

"I don't know what to think anymore."

"It hurts because you and Colton were so close for so long."

"He saved me, Lucy, after I was expelled from Stanford. For four years we were inseparable. And now, he wanted to hurt me. It's my fault."

"It's *Colton's* fault. He couldn't get beyond what happened in New York. Remember, everything then was his idea, and if you weren't there he would have died. You saved his life—he should have forgiven you for lying to him."

"He'll never see it that way."

"That's on him. Sean—none of us are perfect. But no one—not Colton, not Paxton—can come between us. I will always love you."

He pulled her close and closed his eyes.

"I want so much to go back to the way things were last week. Before this. I don't know."

"Don't know what, Sean? Talk to me."

He didn't know if he could. "I guess I need time. I need . . . peace."

"Anything you need, I'm here."

He held her tight. He needed Lucy so much, but feared he was broken.

"Hey," she said, making him look at her. "I mean it. We're going to get through this together."

He stared at her and saw the truth in her eyes. He slowly began to believe it. With Lucy, he could do anything. His heart was still heavy, but he felt it get just a little bit lighter.

He kissed her. Held her lips to his for a long minute. Live big, Kane had said.

All Sean wanted, right now, was his family.

"I love you, Lucy Kincaid Rogan."

Acknowledgments

Dear Reader,

I have always wanted to be a writer, but it was a distant dream, interrupted by life—raising a family and working full-time, I figured I didn't have the time to write. After my son was born in 2001, I had an epiphany: If I wanted to write, I needed to make the time. I gave up television for three years (my friends and family know I love TV!) and I wrote every night after the kids went to bed. I finished five books in two years, selling my fifth book, *The Prey*, which was published in January 2006.

Most of my research for my early books came from reading. My research shelf overflowed with books on criminal psychology, forensics, police procedures, and true crime. I knew a few people who could help me with some of the details I couldn't find in books, but mostly I made stuff up. And sometimes I got things wrong. There's a phrase I heard that resonates with me: "You don't know what you don't know." I try to keep that in mind when I write so I can research points where I might not even realize I got it wrong. If it's plot-critical, I want it to be right.

Another hurdle in research is making sure that it doesn't show. I only want enough information on the page to make the story work without halting the pace to explain too many details. There's nothing that irritates me more than when I'm reading a thriller and the story just stops to explain a minute forensic detail for five pages. Sometimes I want to share all the fascinating things I've learned when I toured the morgue or interviewed a pilot or participated in SWAT training, and I have to rein myself in and remember to only put enough on the page to keep the story believable. I work on it in each and every book, to make sure I keep that balance. Sometimes I fail, but I think mostly I succeed. And sometimes, I rely on my readers' willing suspension of disbelief.

I have been so blessed over the nearly fifteen years I've been published to have cultivated an extensive group of experts who help me learn what I don't know. Doctors, nurses, cops, FBI agents, a SWAT commander, lawyers, firefighters, accountants, and more. Sometimes I intentionally strain plausibility in order to serve the story—but because of the selfless help of others, I'm able to get things mostly right, which hopefully makes your reading experience that much more enjoyable.

I've acknowledged author Robin Burcell, a retired police officer and forensic artist, several times in the past. Robin is one of the most selfless writers I know and always willing to help her fellow writers with details. One of the best things about having a former cop as a writer is that Robin understands that you can't put in every detail about investigating a crime. She understands how we need to focus on the core story and details complement that story. In *Cold as Ice,* Robin went above and beyond in helping me get my opening right—or at least believable. When Sean is arrested, I needed to make sure that those details were accurate. That they could arrest him, how they would arrest the husband of a law enforcement officer, what courtesies might be extended. We exchanged more than a dozen emails going over this one chapter, and I am forever grateful. If I tweaked a detail to serve the story, that's on me.

Another person who went above and beyond in helping with this book was Mark Pryor, a prosecutor from Texas, who explained warrants and interviews and probable cause and a whole host of legal issues. I'll admit, sometimes the legal issues trip me up because I'm not a lawyer and common sense can only take you so far. If I got anything wrong here—that's totally on me.

Thank you, Robin and Mark! This book is better because of your help.

Many people make my books shine. First and foremost, my editor, Kelley Ragland. A great editor is worth her weight in gold, and Kelley is priceless. She knows my strengths and weaknesses and helps me maximize what I do best and fix what I do wrong. She asks smart questions and makes sure the story is well-paced, the characters true, and the ending satisfying. I would not be a bestselling writer without a great editor behind me. Thank you, thank you, thank you!

Supporting Kelley are many people who make everything in the publishing process work. Joseph Brosnan, in marketing, does more than "market."

He manages the terrific blog Criminal Element, he and his team provide me fabulous graphics for social media, he has great ideas, and he always has a smile on his face. Who cares that he's a Yankees fan? (Hahaha.) Madeline Houpt, Kelley's right hand, is invaluable day-to-day in juggling me and so many other authors. The art department is amazing—*Cold as Ice* is one of my favorite Lucy Kincaid covers. And a special shout-out to Macmillan Audio for all their hard work on the Lucy audiobooks!

Last but never least, my agent, Dan Conaway, has stuck with me, a neurotic and prolific author, for ten years now. Ten years . . . longer than many marriages! Ha. Thank you, Dan, for keeping me sane and focused and managing my business with professionalism and a touch of humor. And thank you for bringing in Lauren Carsley as your right hand to stay on top of everything. Lauren, you rock.

I have been blessed to have a family who is super supportive of my writing. My mom, who gets the first copy of each of my books and reads it in one day. My husband, Dan, who gives me the space to create and never thinks twice when I ask him odd questions like, "Where can I steal C-4? Or is there a better way to blow something up?" My kids, all five of them, have been used as sounding boards for years, and take it in stride. I am lucky to have you all.

To my readers, who love Lucy and Sean as much as I do: THANK YOU. Seventeen books, six novellas, and one short story later . . . thank you for reading and keeping Lucy strong. Without you, there would be no stories. I am forever grateful that you've helped me do what I love best: write.

Happy Reading,
Allison

Don't miss the Lucy Kincaid e-novella

A DEEPER FEAR
By Allison Brennan

Coming in January 2021!